KAREN HAWKINS

The Prince Who Loved Me

Pocket Books

New York   London   Toronto   Sydney   New Delhi

Pocket Books
A Division of Simon & Schuster, Inc.
1230 Avenue of the Americas
New York, NY 10020

First Pocket Books paperback edition October 2014

POCKET and colophon are registered trademarks of Simon & Schuster, Inc.

For information about special discounts for bulk purchases, please contact Simon & Schuster Special Sales at 1-866-506-1949 or business@simonandschuster.com.

The Simon & Schuster Speakers Bureau can bring authors to your live event. For more information or to book an event contact the Simon & Schuster Speakers Bureau at 1-866-248-3049 or visit our website at www.simonspeakers.com.

Interior design by Yvonne Chan
Cover design by Alan Ayers
Cover illustration by Jon Paul

Manufactured in the United States of America

10 9 8 7 6 5 4 3 2 1

ISBN 978-1-4516-8524-4
ISBN 978-1-4516-8526-8 (ebook)

To my beloved husband HOT COP,
for cheering me on every day,
making me smile when I'm not,
bringing me coffee when I'm dragging,
and especially for rarely getting grumpy
when I ask him for the fortieth time
to spell something that "doesn't look right."
You are the best writer's husband ever.

Dear Reader,

In *The Prince Who Loved Me*, our heroine is reading a fictional book written by an equally fictional authoress of the Regency era, Miss Mary Edgeworth. My fictional authoress was inspired by a real authoress during this time, Maria Edgeworth. The real Miss Edgeworth wrote both children's books and adult novels, but with a far higher purpose in mind than my fictional author. Miss Edgeworth often explored such lofty topics as land management practices, anti-Semitism, and morality. Like the heroine of this book, Bronwyn Murdoch, Maria lived with her father, who was an inventor as well as a writer, and helped raised her stepsisters and stepbrothers.

You might also be interested in knowing that Bronwyn's father is loosely based upon William Murdoch, a Scottish inventor and engineer. Murdoch has been credited with a wide number of important inventions, from steam engines to gas lighting.

More information about both of these interesting people from history can be found on my website. Just visit Hawkins Manor and enter the Oxenburg Library.

Enjoy!
Karen

Chapter 1

Gentle reader, our innocent heroine, golden-haired Lucinda Wellville, is in grave danger. Unbeknownst to her, evil Sir Mordred has slipped into her bedchamber whilst she was dancing at her uncle's ball, and is even now hidden behind the silk bed curtains, a knife clutched in his gnarled hand. . . .

—The Black Duke *by Miss Mary Edgeworth*

Sitting under the shade of her favorite tree, the scent of damp grass and leaves tickling her nose, Bronwyn Murdoch turned the crisp vellum page and tried not to grimace. Somewhere around chapter seven she had started wondering if Lucinda, the annoyingly incompetent heroine of *The Black Duke*, truly deserved to live. The chit was forever whining about her life, while refusing to *do* anything about it. "I daresay once Sir Mordred flashes his villainous knife, you'll scream and run away. Although knowing you, you'll trip on your skirts on your way out the door and someone will have to rescue you."

Bronwyn looked over her spectacles at her audience, two huge deerhounds she'd had since they were pups. "Shall I read aloud for a bit?"

Walter, his large head in her lap, opened one sleepy eye and wagged his tail, while Scott yawned so widely she could see all of his teeth.

"I'll take that as a yea." She settled against the huge tree trunk, the thick grass a soft cushion beneath her. *"Lucinda reached the sanctuary of her bedchamber and closed the door, leaning upon it, grateful for the peaceful silence that awaited her. All evening long, she'd been paraded by her uncle before a horde of determined suitors who'd watched her like a set of hungry wolves eyeing a particularly plump duckling."*

Bronwyn looked down at Walter. "I would be quite upset if someone eyed me like a plump duckling."

He blinked sleepily but looked as if he agreed.

"I'm glad Papa has no wish to marry me off," she told the sleepy dogs. Bronwyn's stepmother had been another story. The youngest daughter of an earl and far more concerned with societal advancement than either Bronwyn or her father, Mama had attempted far too hard to procure an advantageous match for Bronwyn during her disastrous first season, one marred by Bronwyn's inexperience with society and her natural tendency toward solitude. After the debacle, Bronwyn had refused to repeat the performance, which had caused Mama to go into a rant until Father had stepped in and demanded the topic be dropped. A solitary man himself, he understood Bronwyn's distress all too well.

Bronwyn couldn't help but be glad; one season had been enough, thank you very much. Fortunately, as the years passed, Mama's attention had thankfully shifted to Bronwyn's stepsister Sorcha, who would be making her debut in London next season. Sorcha liked balls and dressing up and couldn't wait to be presented on the marriage mart.

"But not me." Bronwyn kicked off her slippers and curled her toes in the thick, cool grass before sinking back into the exciting pages of her book. "*Lucinda pressed her hands to her beating heart and hung her head, her composure slowly returning. Some of the suitors had been handsome, some wealthy, and some charming, but none had made her feel the way Roland did, he of the steely blue eyes and glinting smile.*"

Bronwyn snorted. "You already had the chance to run off with him, you spineless fool, but instead you wept like a broken cup, sniffling about how you'd miss your sisters too much to leave. You don't *deserve* Roland."

Roland was brave and romantic, and his speech imploring Lucinda to flee with him had filled Bronwyn's eyes with tears. "I wish I knew a Roland."

During her unpleasant season, she'd come to realize that the world was woefully short of Rolands. That suspicion had been confirmed as the days after her season had ticked by into pleasant weeks, and then busy and blurry years. Now, at the ripe old age of twenty-four, Bronwyn was firmly on the shelf. But as long as that shelf held plenty of books, her beloved family, and her lovely dogs, she was quite content.

She turned the page and continued to read. "*Behind Lucinda, the curtains stirred as a hand holding a knife appeared. With a harsh cry, Sir Mordred leapt from behind the curtains and plunged the knife toward Lucinda.*" Bronwyn gulped. *"Time froze. The youthful innocent stared in horror as the knife seemed to slowly arc toward her pure, untouched heart! And in that second, balanced so precariously between life and death, she thought of the one man who held that very heart, though he might not know it—brave Roland."*

"Thinking of him is the least you can do, you spalpeen ninny," Bronwyn told Lucinda. "Especially when one considers how you left him at the altar at the end of chapter eighteen."

Walter sighed gustily.

"I know. She's a fool." Bronwyn shook her head. *"'Oh, Roland,' Lucinda whispered, remembering how he'd claimed her innocent lips with his in the tenderest of caresses. 'Oh, Roland!'"*

"Ha! You're four chapters too late, woman." Bronwyn turned the page. *"Unable to watch the knife enter her tender skin, Lucinda closed her eyes tightly as—* Oh!" Bronwyn lowered the book as Scott looked at her with concern. "Why would you close your eyes? You should fight, not just stand there like a— Argh! If I wasn't certain Roland was about to arrive, I'd stop reading right here." Sighing, she returned to the book. *"Lucinda closed her eyes tightly just as the door burst open. Roland, handsome and stalwart Roland, had come!"* Bronwyn nodded with satisfaction. "Of course he did. He always does, whether Lucinda deserves him or not."

Scott barked in agreement and Bronwyn rubbed his ear.

"Without hesitation, the brave young lord lifted his sword and struck the knife from the evil hand. Not to be denied, Mordred drew his own sword and, with a hideous cry, at-

tacked, raining blows upon the younger man. Roland met the onslaught stroke for stroke, sparks flashing as metal chinked metal. Furious blades struck again and again, but Lord Mordred was no match for Roland.

"*Blow by blow, Roland fought back his foe until the sword was struck from Mordred's hand. Red-faced and furious, the evil lord broke free. Seeing the fury in Roland's fine eyes, Mordred knew his life was in danger. With a final, evil glare at Lucinda, the craven lord ran from the room, his desperate footsteps echoing in the marble-floored hallway. Instantly, Lucinda fell to the floor in a swoon—*" Bronwyn groaned. "Not *again!*"

Walter sneezed, looking bored.

"I know. That's exactly what I think." Bronwyn smoothed the page. "*—Lucinda fell to the floor in a swoon as pale as death. Roland gave a mad cry as he rushed to her side. Seeing her pulse beating rapidly under her fair skin, he lifted her in his strong arms and placed a tender kiss upon her soft lips.*"

Suddenly she couldn't read fast enough. "*Love called. Beckoned from her slumber, Lucinda sighed awake. Her eyes fluttered open and she gave a glad cry upon seeing her beloved Roland. Smiling, he held her to his broad chest and proclaimed his love.*"

Bronwyn hugged the book and sighed deeply. "*Love called.* I wish I knew what love calling sounds like."

Walter licked her elbow.

She smiled at him. "Roland is wondrous, isn't he? But Lucinda should have helped him! If I'd been there, I'd have whacked Mordred over the head with a candlestick, or used a curtain tassel to trip him, or stuffed a pillow over his knife blade, or—oh, a thousand things! But Lucinda just stood there like a lump, and then she *fainted*." Bronwyn flicked the book with impatient fingers. "I don't know why Roland even *wants* to kiss her. I'd be far more likely to smack her—though Roland would never do such a thing, for he's far too noble."

What would it be like to be kissed? *Really* kissed. And by a man like Roland. "Therein lies the rub, eh?" she told the book that now rested in her lap. If she just wanted to be kissed, there was the butcher's son, and Lord Durning's nephew, who was often drunk in front of the baker's shop, and several others. But finding a man, a *real* man, one who liked a good book as well as a game of chess, who could discuss favorite authors and current events, exciting new inventions, and—oh, so many things—that was the truly difficult part. During her London Season the men she'd met had been interested only in current gossip, horses, gambling, and the latest fashion. None of them had possessed even a rudimentary interest in books or history or any of the things she lo—

Walter and Scott bounded to their feet, staring into the forest, heads lowered, teeth bared.

Bronwyn scrambled up, her book left open in the grass near her abandoned slippers. Her heart thudding, she peered over their heads.

A faint rustle shook a bush.

The deerhounds growled louder, Scott creeping forward as if ready to charge.

A shrub to her side rustled loudly and she whirled to face the new danger, hands fisted. A furry flash of white and pink burst from the shrubs, and a small dog bounded out, took one look at Bronwyn, and, with a wag of its tail, threw itself into her arms.

She gaped at the animal as, tail still wagging, it growled fiercely down at the bewildered deerhounds. It was the tiniest dog she'd ever seen, and the most ridiculous. Its long hair fanned over oddly up-pointed ears, until it appeared to be wearing a large, butterfly-shaped hat that framed its dark eyes and pointy muzzle. That very muzzle was now parted in a grimacing snarl at Scott and Walter.

"Stop that," Bronwyn admonished, trying not to giggle as the little intruder licked her face. A huge pink bedraggled bow hung about its neck.

Scott came to sniff at the dog.

The little dog instantly snarled, and Bronwyn tapped a finger on its head. "I said, stop that."

The dog gave a last bark at Walter and Scott, who were plainly confused by the tiny warrior, and then settled into Bronwyn's arms with an air of finality.

Bronwyn smothered a laugh as she bent to kiss the dog's head. "Be nice, little one."

The dog wagged its tail and licked her ear, knocking her spectacles to one side. She straightened them as Scott cautiously approached once again and sniffed the little dog's foot. The tiny dog bent down to sniff back and their noses touched, both of their tails wagging cautiously.

"Aye, that's more like it."

"Hello." A deep voice, rich and smoky, filled the small clearing.

Bronwyn and the dogs turned toward the sound. There, on the far edge of the clearing, stood a man Bronwyn had only seen in her imagination. A man far handsomer than any she'd ever met. A man who must—simply *must*—love poetry and kindness and long kisses.

"*Roland*," she whispered.

Chapter 2

What was it about Roland? Lucinda wondered as she watched the gentleman pass by during the dance. What made Roland superior to all other men? Was it his sense of honor, his innate kindness, the strength of his arms, or something as simple as the strong line of his jaw? She didn't know. All she knew was that in her world, there was Roland . . . or there was nothing.

— The Black Duke by Miss Mary Edgeworth

She couldn't look away. Strange men—especially tall, handsome ones who looked like the heroes of novels—never came to Dingwall.

Never. Ever.

And in her mind's eye, Roland had been *exactly* such a man as this—tall, dark, foreboding even, with a strong jaw that bespoke a character worth knowing, and intelligence agleam in his eyes. As if to reaffirm her imagination, the sun broke through the trees to limn his broad shoulders with gold. *By Zeus, what did one say to a god walking among mortals?*

"What are you doing here?" she asked, wincing inwardly at the abruptness of her tone.

He smiled. "I am looking back at you."

He was indeed examining her just as thoroughly as she'd been examining him, though his gaze lingered in places hers had never dared.

Face heated, she asked, "Who are you? Why are you here?"

The stranger's smile widened into a grin, his teeth flashing white. His bold jaw, forged of raw masculinity and shadowed by the lack of a shave, indicated a determined character, confirmed by the nose of a caesar. High cheekbones slanted beneath eyes that held the hint of an exotic flare, and his skin was the golden hue of someone who'd spent many hours outdoors.

And now this paragon was walking toward her, oblivious to the growls from her deerhounds. Her gaze couldn't help but follow the line of his broad shoulders as they converged with his muscled chest before tapering down to a narrow waist. He moved gracefully, but with a raw power, rather like a boxer she'd once seen at a fair.

Unsure what she should do—run or stay and slake her burning curiosity—Bronwyn held the little white dog closer as the man reached the edge of the clearing and then parted the shrubs and stepped onto the thick grass.

Walter and Scott moved to stand before her, their teeth in white-fanged snarls.

The man eyed the dogs. "Your horses, they growl." His voice was as silken as thickly napped velvet, and with an accent she didn't recognize.

"They're dogs," she said. "*My* dogs. I'm sorry if they frighten you."

Amusement warmed his gaze. "They do not frighten me, little one. It is their health I fear for, not mine."

She stiffened and moved closer to her dogs. "What does *that* mean?"

He merely smiled, a lazy, I-never-hurry sort of smile. There was something of the rebel about this man, something that whispered of forbidden kisses and broken rules. He nodded at the dogs. "Make them sit. I do not wish to fight my way to you."

"*Fight*—?" She finally noticed the large hunting knife at his belt. "No! Don't come any closer!"

He looked surprised. "But I must come to you." His gaze flickered over her, and her body warmed as if he'd used his hands. "You have what belongs to me."

Her heart gave an odd leap. "What . . . belongs to you?"

"*Da.*" He nodded to her arms, and she followed his gaze to the little white dog cozily resting there. "She is mine. She was chasing the . . . how you say, *krolik*?"

Bronwyn blinked.

"The *krolik*. They run through the fields and live in little holes in the ground."

"Foxes?"

"*Nyet.* Those, I know. The other animals." When she didn't reply, he sighed, frustration on his face. "They have—what you say—hop, hop. And they have the—" He put his hand behind his head and made a "V," then wiggled his fingers.

"Ah! You mean hares."

"Hares, *da*. Papillon likes to chase them." He looked approvingly at the dog. "She may have short legs and look like a mop, but Papillon is very quick."

Bronwyn had to fight for her breath. The softening of the bold lines of his face as he regarded his dog had the power to melt bones. *Of the hundreds of men I met during my season in London, none of them affected me like this.* "You . . . you have an odd accent."

His gaze moved back to her. "I am from Oxenburg. It is a country far away from here."

Her face heated. "I'm sorry. I'm very bad about saying the first thing I think."

"That is honest, which is good, *nyet*?"

"Not always." Certainly not in London, during one's first season, and definitely not when one was dancing—or trying to dance, and wretchedly at that—with an earl's son who was tipsy and smelled of onion. Bronwyn had been a wee bit too honest with him and he'd left her on the dance floor, abandoned and humiliated. Worse, to Mama's chagrin and Bronwyn's irritation, he'd then mocked her every time their paths had crossed afterward, and had spread some entirely untruthful rumors, too.

Mama had been furious with the earl's son, though she felt Bronwyn was partly to blame for her thoughtless comments. Papa had said it wasn't her fault, for Ackinnoull Manor was tucked away far from the dances, dinner parties, and such that might have allowed her to develop a level of control over her unruly tongue. In addition, her mother's death when Bronwyn had been quite young had made their lives even less social than they might have been. Until her father had remarried, Bronwyn had been left alone with her books and dogs while Papa sank into his work, creating his wonderful inventions.

To be honest, she was glad for that earl's son, whose name she could no longer remember. His ill behavior had solidified her decision to end her season and never return to London. Even her stepmama now agreed that Bronwyn wasn't made for London society, nor it her.

They were all happier for that decision, too. Besides, Papa needed Bronwyn's help with his inventions; she was the only one who knew how to file the valuable patents.

"You do not answer, little one."

Bronwyn realized the stranger had said something while she'd been lost in her thoughts. "I'm sorry. I was thinking."

"And you cannot listen while you're thinking." He nodded thoughtfully. "I cannot listen and read at the same time, which has given my family much cause for complaint."

"You like to read?"

He looked surprised. "Who doesn't?"

Perhaps he is Roland, after all. But no, that was a dangerous way to think. Roland only existed between the pages of books, not in Dingwall. The small dog reached up to lick her chin. "Papillon is an unusual name for a dog."

"*Da*. Her name is French for 'butterfly.' She is a good hunting dog."

"While wearing a pink bow?"

His lips twitched. "The hares did not seem to notice as they scampered away from her."

It was difficult to imagine that this tiny, bepuffed dog belonged to this huge, broad-chested man who could easily hold the animal in one hand. The contrast made her smile, and feel a bit breathless, too.

Bronwyn sighed. *This is exactly how Roland would look if he dressed like a huntsman.* The beauty of novels was that one never grew tired of the heroes, because as soon as one closed the book and mourned the loss of the characters—for such was the way of good books—one could open another and fall in love all over again. Thus, one was forever being swept off one's feet. Bronwyn rather liked that.

She wondered what the stranger would look like in a cravat and fitted coat, like Roland wore. This man's black coat was shapeless and shiny from wear at the elbows. His broad belt was worn, as was the sheath for his hunting knife. Now that he was closer, she could see a quiver of arrows behind his shoulder, the red and black fletching belonging to Selvach, the gamekeeper at Tulloch Castle. *Ah. So my Roland is a huntsman, which explains a lot.*

A grand old family, the Davidsons, owned Tulloch Castle but rarely inhabited it, preferring to reside in the city. Indeed, Sir Henry hadn't been to visit his Highland holding in over ten years, which had left Selvach and the other servants to run the castle and grounds as they saw fit. Whenever game threatened to overrun castle lands, Selvach hired men from the surrounding boroughs to thin the herds and flocks, which explained why Bronwyn hadn't recognized this man.

But of all the huntsmen Selvach had employed over the years, she'd never seen one so pleasantly formed. Her gaze drifted over his obviously muscled chest and lower, down to the man's breeches, which were tucked into scuffed riding boots. *His legs are so muscular. I've never seen anyone with such thighs—*

"Do I have mud on my breeches, that you stare so?"

Her face heated and she nervously adjusted her spectacles. "Your clothes and the arrows—I see you're a huntsman."

Humor glinted anew in his eyes. "I am always on the hunt."

Bronwyn's mouth went dry. *He's flirting with me!* Never in all her years had that happened. Usually whomever she was speaking with would have stomped off, irritated at the way she blurted out pronouncements, or simply been bored because she hadn't spoken at all. Her most interesting thoughts always seemed locked in her mind.

"What are you thinking about now, little one? Me?"

"No."

The huntsman looked astonished, then broke into a deep laugh as he stepped forward.

The deerhounds stiffened, lowering their heads as they growled.

"Walter, Scott, down," she commanded.

The man looked curious. "Walter and Scott. For the poet, eh?"

"You know of Sir Walter Scott?"

"I like his poetry very well. Your mistress must allow you use of the library."

Mistress? He thinks I'm a servant. She supposed she looked like one, for she'd donned her most worn gown in preparation for helping with the wash later. Plus, in her hurry to dive into her book, she'd merely scrubbed her face and pinned her hair into a hurried bun that was already falling down, if the tendrils that had fallen at the sides of her face were an indication.

The huntsman moved closer, and Walter leapt forward to stand between him and Bronwyn. A flash of annoyance crossed the man's face. "Tell your horse to stop growling."

"He is protecting me, as is his job."

The man looked positively amazed. "I would never harm a woman, little Roza."

"Roza? Do you mean . . . the flower, a rose?"

The man's fine mouth curved in a smile. "Yes. You are a *roza*, with your pink cheeks and"—his gaze swept her from head to toe with obvious approval—"and the rest of you. *Bozhy moj*, you are a beauty."

Never in all of her twenty-four years had anyone called Bronwyn a beauty. Pretty, yes. Attractive, several times. But never, ever "a beauty." Bronwyn had always thought she'd enjoy hearing it, as she'd often read in the pages of her novels, but enjoyment was the last thing she felt. She didn't know what to say or where to look. Worse, she had to swallow the impulse to deny the truth of the words. *Which is silly. I look like Mother, and everyone said she was a very pretty woman.*

But somehow, among the dancing lessons (which she'd detested) and the French lessons (which she'd avoided by pretending to be ill) and the endless watercolor instructions (useless, when one had no talent for it), no one had ever taught her how to receive a compliment.

Was a mere "thank you" enough, or would it make her sound conceited, as if she expected such praise? "No one has ever called me beautiful," she blurted out.

"The men of your country are blind, then."

She didn't believe it for an instant, but it was tempting to pretend for a moment that it was true. That society was wrong for favoring reed thinness instead of her plumper form. And that blond hair, which was the current fancy, was pallid beside her rich brown hair. That oh-so-desired white-as-cream skin was boring and bland beside her own tanned and freckled face. So, so tempting—

"I have made you tongue-tied."

"No, I was trying to decide how to answer your compliment. It seems conceited to accept it and silly to refuse it, but I think—" She dipped a short curtsy. "Thank you for the compliment. It was very kind of you." She bent down and placed Papillon on the ground. "Goodbye, little dog. Sadly, it's time for you to go."

The stranger snapped his fingers. "Come, Papillon."

The dog took a few steps forward, but then stopped and looked back at Bronwyn. Bronwyn shook her head. "I'm not going with you."

The stranger snapped his fingers again, this time more sharply. "Come."

The dog looked between Bronwyn and the stranger and then sat down.

The man gave a muffled curse and strode forward to

scoop up the dog, who tried to lick his face. "Stop that, mongrel! You have caused enough trouble."

Papillon's tail couldn't have wagged faster. With a reluctant smile, the man rubbed the dog's head. "Thank you for capturing her. I hope she didn't disturb you." The huntsman's gaze flickered between Bronwyn's discarded shoes and her book. "She interrupted your reading, *nyet*? It's a good day for reading."

Bronwyn glanced up at the sun shining through the leaves. "It was, but I must return home. I've chores to do."

He placed the dog at his feet, where it stood expectantly. "Where do you work, little one? Who is your mistress?"

She supposed she could tell him she wasn't a servant, but something held her back. A whisper of warning that perhaps it would be better if he didn't know anything more than necessary. "Where I work is none of your concern."

"You will tell me." The stranger gave her a quizzical smile that sent an odd shiver through her. "I will know."

She lifted her chin. "You don't need to know anything."

"Ah, but I do." He walked toward her, ignoring the growls of her deerhounds.

Papillon followed, prancing along, her ribbon dragging behind. As she came abreast of Walter they sniffed one another, tails suddenly wagging. Scott cautiously approached the stranger and sniffed at one of the huntsman's boots.

Bronwyn took a step back but found her feet unwilling to move any farther away. He was just so *tempting*.

The huntsman stood directly before her, a wolfish sparkle in his eyes. "This is much better. We can talk more easily now."

Bronwyn craned her neck to look up into his face. An intriguing scar split one eyebrow. Now that she saw him more closely, she realized his eyes were the most beautiful dark green, his lashes long and thick, shadowing his expression in a mysterious, sensual way.

She could easily drown in such eyes.

"What is your name? The least you can do is tell me that."

She shouldn't even be talking to this stranger, alone in the woods like this. Her stepmother would screech in distress at the mere thought.

He shrugged. "Then I will tell you mine. Perhaps then you will feel free to share yours." He bowed. "I am Alexsey Vitaly Grigori Romanovin."

"Romanovinin?"

He chuckled, the sound deep in his chest. "Just call me Alexsey. I prefer it."

"It's not proper to call someone by his given name unless you know him very, very well."

"Ah, but soon we will know each other very well. Of this I am certain."

That simple sentence made her beam with an odd happiness and she said in a flustered voice, "You seem very certain, Mr. Romanovin."

"*Nyet.* Alexsey." He spoke gently, but there was no

doubt he expected her to do as he said. He stooped and picked up her book. "What have you been rea—?"

"No!" She held out her hand. "Please return that."

"Soon. Ah, *The Black Duke* by Miss Mary Edgeworth." His gaze shifted back to her. "I've never heard of this author."

"She's very popular, but only recently."

"Hmm." He opened the book and flipped through the pages.

Her chest grew tight. Mama teased her constantly for reading "nonsense," but Bronwyn loved her books. They let her soar to places far away, to adventures she could only dream of, and to meet people who'd never find her in her tiny corner of the world.

She reached for the book, her fingers just grazing one corner.

"Tsk, tsk. So determined." Alexsey held it well over her head, a thoughtful look on his face. "What do you read that you must hide it?"

"I'm not hiding anything. It's not nice to take someone's book."

He gave a lazy chuckle. "Do not look so angry, little Roza. I will give it back after I see what you find so fascinating." He read a few lines to himself, and then lifted his gaze to hers. "Perhaps I should read a few pages aloud, so that we may share th—"

She lunged for the book, her spectacles bouncing on her nose.

"*Nyet.*" He easily moved the book out of her reach again. He turned a page and then another, finally coming to a stop. "Ah, here. I will read. You will listen."

He plunged into the story, his deep voice caressing the words. "*Love warmed his eyes from blue to gray. 'It is you I love,' Roland declared.*

"*Lucinda threw up her hands. 'You are mistaken, sir. You don't know me as you think, for I love no one.'*" Alexsey made a face. "I do not like that name, Lucinda."

"Neither do I." On that, they were in agreement. "She's a very weak character," Bronwyn confided. "She's forever fainting."

"Fainting?"

Bronwyn threw a hand over her forehead and tossed back her head, closing her eyes in a pretend swoon.

Alexsey chuckled. "You are a good actress, but I would find this a most annoying trait. Characters of such weak heart make for a poor story."

Indeed—Lucinda's weakness had been plaguey since the first page.

"Let us hope this Roland finds another woman to love, one not given to such silliness." Alexsey returned to the book. "*'Ha!' Roland cried. 'You cannot mean it. I will prove your feelings, for I can see them in your eyes.'*

"*Lucinda placed a gentle hand upon his cheek. 'I don't deserve your love. I've doubted you and more—'*

"*Stilling her anguish, Roland placed his lips upon fair Lucinda's and kissed her with a chaste passion—*"

"Pah!" Alexsey frowned.

Bronwyn had fallen into the story as his seductive voice rolled over the words, adding a depth that had her leaning forward in breathless hope. "Don't stop!"

But he snapped the book closed, his huge hand almost engulfing it. "I cannot continue. It is not a real kiss."

Her fists balled on her hips. "That is a perfectly good kiss."

"*Nyet.*" He reached down, uncurled one of her fists, and placed the book in it. "There is no such thing as 'chaste passion.' If chaste is here." He held his hand far to one side. "Then passion is here." He held his other hand to the other side, as far away as he could. "When they come together—" He clapped his hands so loudly, it sounded like a thunderclap.

The three dogs looked up in surprise.

Bronwyn's fingers tightened on the book. "*I* think it's a perfectly good kiss." She'd reread it a dozen times; it *was* perfect, and she knew it.

There was a slight silence. "You've never been kissed."

"I—I—I—" Her face burned so hotly, she wondered her hair didn't catch afire. "Of course I've been kissed! Dozens of times. Now if you'll excuse me, I must go. Good day, sir." How *dare* he insult Roland's most romantic moment?

"You are angry I have ruined your story. I am sorry, but the truth is the truth." He took a step forward, his warm hand closing gently over her elbow.

A flash of tingling heat raced through her. She could easily have broken free had she wished, but there was something about the warmth of his skin on hers, something delicious and shiver-inducing.

Alexsey smiled, his firm lips drawing her gaze as he said in his whiskey-silk voice, "You need a kiss, a taste of true passion. Just enough so you will know why there is no such thing as chaste passion."

She blinked at him, unable to form a single thought.

His large, warm hand cupped her chin and tilted her face toward his. "I do this so you will know the difference between 'chaste' and 'passion.' All women should know that."

Then he captured her lips with his—and in that second, Bronwyn went from unkissed to kissed.

Chapter 3

And with that kiss, her soul was set free. . . .
       —The Black Duke *by Miss Mary Edgeworth*

Bronwyn couldn't move, aware only of the firmness of the huntsman's lips upon hers and the way her heart thudded as if in welcome.

He slid his hand from her cheek to her neck and then tugged her forward until her chest pressed to his. Her book dropped from her nerveless fingers as she grasped his coat to steady herself.

His mouth moved over hers, nipping softly, teasing, sending wave after wave of heated shivers through her. Her knees quivered and began to fold, but his arm slid around her waist.

Without breaking the kiss, he lifted her to him, his body large and firm against her curves.

No man had ever held her in such an intimate way; it was shocking—and surprisingly exciting. She slipped her arms about his neck, and he slid his tongue over her bottom lip.

Her lips parted in surprise and instantly, his warm tongue slipped between them and stroked the tip of her tongue. A jolt of pure heat rippled through her, her nipples tightening in wanton reaction. She gasped and pulled back.

With a reluctant sigh, he set her back on her feet. "I would like to kiss you more, little Roza, but I do not wish to overwhelm you." His eyes twinkled devilishly. "Not yet, anyway."

She stared up at him, her fingers pressed to the corner of her swollen mouth. Her heart seemed unable to stop skipping in pure excitement, while her skin prickled with a deliciously heated yearning—a yearning for more kisses, more caresses, more *everything*. For one splendid moment, she'd lived a page from one of her beloved books, and she wanted more.

He brushed his thumb over her mouth, sending new sensation rippling through her. "You see? 'Chaste' and 'passion' do not belong in the same sentence. And a woman with such tempting, plump lips must know the difference."

So true. *A real* kiss was *far* more thrilling than the book's weak description.

She suddenly realized that she was still gripping Alexsey's coat with one hand and staring up at him in speechless wonder. *I must look as silly as Lucinda.* Flushing, she forced her clenched fingers to release his coat and, stiffening her weakened knees, she stepped back. "That—that was interesting." Her voice, quavery and husky, sounded as shaken as she felt.

Alexsey had been celebrating the unexpectedly passionate kiss, but at this, he lost his smile. Naturally he didn't expect accolades, for it had been brief and gentle, but to call such a wondrous kiss merely "interesting"? "I do not accept that."

The girl blinked up at him, her spectacles making her brown eyes seem even larger, looking every bit the lush flower he'd named her. "Accept what?"

"'Interesting' is what you call porridge when you do not wish to insult the maker."

Her lips quirked, amusement warming her expression, and his outrage softened. There was something fascinating about her, something that had caught him when she'd curtly demanded to know who he was. No one, especially women, spoke to him in such a way, and he found her a welcome diversion after what had begun as a rather boring day.

He liked women. All women. And this one seemed more interesting than usual. She was small and round, like a flower in full bloom, with thick, shiny brown tresses, her skin dusted with dainty freckles, her moods flashing through her eyes and tripping off her tongue.

But her strongest and most sensual feature was her mouth, so plump and ripe for kisses.

Oh, how he'd loved kissing that mouth.

Very little—and very few women—had the power to intrigue him, but somehow, with just one kiss, this bespectacled little maid had managed to do just that.

He took her hand and uncurled her fingers, smoothing his thumb over the ink stains. *Wherever she works, she obviously keeps the accounts. They must trust her.* He smiled. "Ah, Roza, I know one thing and one thing only—that our lips were made for one another."

Her gaze flickered to his mouth, and then—her color high—she tugged her hand free. "No."

Alexsey's smile slipped. "No?"

"It was just a kiss—nothing more."

Her no-nonsense tone made him want to kiss the sensible thoughts right out of her head. She was so appealing in her grass-stained gown and bare toes. A flower hung from her hair, which was half fallen from its binding and hung about her face. Fresh-faced and stubbornly independent, she was a welcome change from his last mistress, an overly perfumed and powdered Italian opera singer who delighted in expensive presents and unending drama. No tight-laced woman of quality would be caught dead reading a novel on the forest floor, surrounded by dogs the size of horses, either. Despite her respectable air, this maid had returned his kiss with the wild passion of a Romany, clinging to him with both hands, her eagerness stirring his passion more than any skilled seductress.

He traced a finger down her cheek. "Do you often come to this place to read?"

"Sometimes."

Such caution. You didn't display any when you were kissing me. "And to kiss strangers?" he teased, unable to resist.

Her plump lips thinned. "Mr. Romanovin, as you must know by now, I don't normally kiss strangers, or anyone else. It's not proper."

"We are far beyond proper, little Roza. And call me Alexsey."

Delicious color again flooded her face, but she didn't relent. "It's better if I call you Mr. Romanovin."

Her voice lilted in an intriguing way, lifting his name and softening the ending. Alexsey liked a Scottish accent very well indeed. "You are very formal for someone not wearing any shoes."

She adjusted her skirt so that her toes were hidden from view. "I didn't expect to meet anyone here."

"Nor did I. In fact, I came for some peace and quiet. They are readying Tulloch Castle for the arrival of Sir Henry and his guests, and it is very noisy."

Her gaze jerked to his. "Sir Henry is returning? With his nephews?"

"Sir Henry and one nephew, aye."

"And more?"

"I believe he brings twenty to thirty additional guests. Many rooms are being prepared."

"That's odd; Mrs. Durnoch didn't mention it when I spoke to her a week ago."

"Who?"

"The housekeeper at Tulloch."

"Perhaps she did not know. This gathering, it is not long in the planning, I think."

"Ah. That would explain it. I'm—" Her gaze flickered over him, and then away. "It's getting late; I should return home."

"Nonsense. It is early still." He leaned a shoulder against the tree and crossed his arms over his chest. He wasn't ready to leave this ink-stained charmer of dogs. "Besides, we have much to talk about. Such as whether we should attempt another kiss."

"That would be a very bad idea. No one has introduced us—I don't even know you."

He spread his hands wide. "I am here, ready to become known. All you have to do is stay."

Bronwyn bit her lip. He made it sound so easy. All she had to do was stay, and this magical moment, in which a handsome man found her too fascinating to maintain a sense of propriety, would last.

But she'd already allowed him to kiss her. What other liberties might she be cajoled into permitting? The thought both thrilled and terrified her.

He pushed away from the tree. "Are you not even a little curious whether a kiss would be as good the second time? Perhaps the first was an aberration, an odd happenstance."

She fought a smile at his hopeful expression. "Curiosity killed the cat."

"You are no cat. You are a thinking woman. I can see it in your eyes." His smile turned devilish. "Now, if you'll just think about our kiss, and how we should try again . . ."

Och, how she longed to, but her good sense clamored against it. Reluctantly, she stepped away to retrieve her book from the grass. "The kiss was lovely. You were quite . . . skilled."

His eyes glinted warmly. "So I've been told, many times."

Wait. *Many* times? Did he just walk about looking for women, then ply them with charm until they agreed to kiss him? Was that the sort of man he was? *Of course it was*, her good sense whispered. *That's reality versus Roland*. Aware of a deep and bitter flicker of disappointment, she shoved the book under her arm, then collected her shoes. "Good day. I have chores to do."

Alexsey's smile faded. "Don't go. You cannot—"

"Come, Scott, Walter." She stuffed her shoes in her pocket and headed toward a path on the other side of the clearing, walking as fast as she dared. "Good-bye," she called over her shoulder.

Frowning, Alexsey watched as she disappeared into the woods, her dogs following after.

Papillon whined and looked up at Alexsey. "I am disappointed, too." He wondered if he should follow her. Women didn't usually dash away after he'd expressed an interest in their company. In fact, most of them threw themselves at his head in a rather annoying fashion. But not Roza.

Of course, she didn't know he was a prince, a fact he'd purposely avoided mentioning, since he hadn't wished to turn her head in his direction using anything other than kisses. But now . . . perhaps he should have mentioned it. Would it have helped his cause?

Somehow, he doubted it.

He stifled an impatient sigh and made his way to where his horse was tied beside the path, wishing he'd spent less time talking and more time kissing that tempting mouth. Such lovely, full hips and breasts—he could still feel them pressed against him. Everything about her was lush and rich and made him think of satisfied, heated nights beside a roaring fire.

She might well be the perfect woman for a few weeks' tryst—passionate, promising, amusing, and unfettered by the societal rules of a woman of noble breeding. Plus, she wouldn't tempt his Tata Natasha into a tizzy of hope for matrimony.

For such were Tata's ways. His grandmother, the Grand Duchess Natasha Nikolaevna, might think he was unaware of her reason for wishing him to accompany her to Scotland to attend Sir Henry Davidson's out-of-the-way house party, but Alexsey knew all too well. Though she might think otherwise, he wasn't about to let her dictate his selection of a wife.

This is your fault, Wulf, Alexsey informed his absent younger brother. Last year, Father had convinced Tata Natasha to escort Prince Wulfinski to Scotland, where, against his grandmother's wishes, Wulf had met and married the woman of his dreams. Though Tata Natasha had vehemently opposed the match in the beginning, that didn't stop her from taking credit for it—especially once the entire family fell in love with Wulf's new bride, Lily.

Sadly for Alexsey and his other two bachelor brothers, that unexpected success had gone to Tata's head. And now her sights were set on them.

Alexsey mounted the horse and then turned it onto the path leading to the moors, Papillon trotting behind. He would eventually have to marry, of course. Even though his parents had blessed Oxenburg with four healthy princes, they were all expected to secure the family line with legitimate heirs. But he saw no need to rush things, especially when there were so many lovely and eager women to enjoy.

Besides, he had things to accomplish, things that were growing increasingly urgent. His mother's people, the Romany, needed him. At one time, Tata Natasha's husband—Dyet Nikki—had been the *savyet lidir*, his position noted by a heavy gold *kaltso*, a large ruby ring he'd worn on his left hand that sparkled whenever he moved his hand. As the *savyet lidir*, he'd overseen the council that ruled the Romany; decided their route for the summer months; served as the spokesman for the people during troubles; officiated over weddings, funerals, and trials; and a dozen other important duties. He'd been king, counselor, priest, and father to his people, and under him the Romany had prospered.

Alexsey had idolized his grandfather and had been closer to the old man than any of his brothers. As Alexsey spent time with his grandparents, sharing their colorful caravan with the Romany, he grew to love the people. Everyone assumed that he would follow in his grandfather's large footsteps and one day wear the *kaltso*, but when he was only twelve, an unfortunate hunting accident had taken his grandfather away, and the *kaltso* was left in older, more experienced hands.

Alexsey looked down at his bare hand, impatience curling his fingers into a fist. *When I return to Oxenburg, I will address this, for the time has come. But I can do nothing now.* He uncurled his fingers and stretched them, though his chest remained tight. *I need a distraction. I shall find this maid whose kisses are like fire, and we will enjoy more time together. Someone at the castle will know her and I will find her through them. That should make the weeks pass quickly.*

With a satisfied nod, Alexsey lifted his face to the fall sun. All he had to do was avoid Tata Natasha's scheme to throw every eligible well-born maiden in Scotland into his path. Though he was immune to her efforts, her determination could be annoying. Fortunately, he had much that would keep him from the castle.

Papillon's oddly muffled *grrrr* drew his attention, and Alexsey looked down to see the dog trotting beside his horse, a slipper in her mouth.

Remembering the girl's bare feet, Alexsey pulled his horse to a halt and swung down. "So she dropped one of her shoes, did she?"

He took the slipper from Papillon, noting that it was well worn but of good quality, perhaps passed on by a generous mistress. The toes were scuffed and the heel worn down, but it showed perfectly the outline of the wearer's foot. Each of her toes had made a pocket in the thin leather, and he could almost trace her foot. "Perhaps I shall order her a new pair of shoes. That would be generous and might make an impression. What do you think, Papillon?"

Papillon sat on her haunches and cocked her head to one side.

"*Da*," he agreed reluctantly. "It is probably too much. She might feel she owes me something, which is not what I want."

As he went to tuck the shoe into his pocket, something fell from the toe—a small roll of paper that had been pressed into the front to make it fit better. "So even this little shoe is too large. Roza has a dainty foot, *nyet*?"

Papillon yawned.

Alexsey laughed and untangled the wad of paper.

It was a piece of a letter written to a firm in London; something about a patent. *Intriguing. This must be her handwriting, for it is like her—slanted against the normal way of doing things.* He folded the paper into a neat square and tucked it and the shoe into his pocket. "I will find her again and then, there will be more kisses."

Whistling a merry tune, he returned to his horse, Papillon bounding behind him.

Chapter 4

Lucinda had no family, no gentle mother to teach her the ways of a woman, no strong father to protect her from the wiles of men. She was utterly and completely alone. More alone than any woman, man, or child should be.
—The Black Duke *by Miss Mary Edgeworth*

Something hit the side of Bronwyn's book and then fell into her lap.

She moved her book and looked down. Someone had thrown a roll.

Faking a scowl, Bronwyn peered over the rim of her spectacles to find Sorcha and Mairi across the breakfast table, the picture of innocence. One of them was reading, while the other poured herself more tea.

The decidedly virtuous looks on her stepsisters' faces would have aroused her suspicion on the best of days.

Bronwyn marked her place with a playing card and closed her book. "I suppose you two hoydens think that was funny."

Mairi giggled and then tried to turn it into a cough, but failed miserably.

Sorcha gave her sister a half-exasperated look.

Bronwyn had to grin. "I thought as much."

Mairi hurried to say, "It wasn't me! Sorcha did it."

"Tattletale!" Sorcha couldn't contain a gleam of humor.

"Well, you did." Mairi chuckled. "And it hit perfectly, right on the corner and then *bop*, straight into your lap!"

Bronwyn smiled. She loved them dearly. They were both lovely, with blond hair, blue eyes, and graceful figures. They were also the perfect height to wear the current fashions with ease. All things she was not.

Still, they shared the important things. She smiled as her gaze fell on Sorcha's novel. Mairi had just finished the book the day before and had handed it to Sorcha on entering the room. Despite their mama's best efforts, they were both enthusiastic readers.

Bronwyn could still remember the day they'd arrived and how agonizingly nervous she'd been to meet her new mama and sisters. Papa had courted Lady Malvinea for only a few weeks before marrying the younger widow and bringing her and her daughters to Ackinnoull.

Bronwyn shouldn't have been surprised; she'd known her father had been lonely in the years following her mother's death. Still, during that time they'd settled into a comfortable pattern. She'd had free rein to run the house and to live as she wished, providing Papa wasn't disrupted from working on his inventions. Her life had given her plenty of time for her books and dogs and roaming the vast woods that surrounded Ackinnoull, and she'd been happy.

All had been well until a new vicar and his wife had arrived. The vicar's wife hadn't been happy with Bronwyn's unmarried state and lone forays into the countryside. Her disapproval had turned into true dislike when Bronwyn had ignored the woman's cow-handed attempt at matchmaking Bronwyn with that lady's lack-witted brother. After that, the vicar's wife had made it her business to criticize Bronwyn every chance she got.

Bronwyn ignored the woman's venomous comments, but Papa wasn't so immune. The day after her sixteenth birthday, Bronwyn had returned from a long walk to find the vicar and his wife leaving Ackinnoull. Papa wouldn't say why they'd come, but the effects had been immediate.

After that day, Papa had seemed to see her differently, asking her silly questions: if she didn't want to wear prettier gowns, if she missed attending assemblies and balls, and, strangest of all, if she ever thought of marrying. She hadn't, for there were no eligible men about, and she was far too busy assisting Papa and reading every book she could find. Yet somehow, saying so hadn't calmed whatever fears her father now had.

Not long after that, Papa left for Edinburgh, and when he returned, he announced his marriage to Lady Malvinea.

Though he never admitted it, Bronwyn knew he'd married for her sake, to give her a mother who would help her develop more genteel habits. The thought that he might be disappointed in her weighed heavily and had stiffened her resolve to please her new mother, whatever effort that might take.

When Lady Malvinea and her daughters had arrived at Ackinnoull in a carriage followed by two wagons piled with furnishings and clothes, Bronwyn had been torn between apprehension and hope. The thought of having a new mother was awkward—but sisters? She had never wanted anything more.

Within a very short time, ten-year-old Sorcha, eight-year-old Mairi, and sixteen-year-old Bronwyn had formed a deep bond. The younger girls admired Bronwyn's independence, something they'd never been allowed. For Bronwyn, having two little sisters who shared her sense of humor and her love of reading was a dream come true.

Sadly, things hadn't proceeded as smoothly with her new mother; she and Lady Malvinea had clashed from almost the first moment. Bronwyn had thought of herself as already grown, while Lady Malvinea felt a decided need to mold her into something more pliable.

To be fair, Bronwyn was far too used to going her own way, and she'd had to fight the urge to argue about every "improvement" Lady Malvinea wished to make to Bronwyn, Papa, and the house. Sometimes Bronwyn's struggle to contain herself was far more visible than it should have been, but she'd been as conciliatory as possible.

Unfortunately, her stepmama had been unable to return the favor. Lady Malvinea, driven by a need for constant affirmation by members of "high society," believed she knew best, and no amount of argument or common sense would ever convince her otherwise.

It might have helped if Papa had stepped in to smooth things over between his daughter and his new wife, but he'd spent years avoiding unpleasant reality and saw no reason to change that now. The more Bronwyn resisted her stepmother's attempts to "civilize" her, the more Papa stayed in his workshop, until they only saw him for dinners, and even then only on occasion.

It took time, but eventually Bronwyn realized that for all Lady Malvinea's flaws, she truly wished for Bronwyn to be happy and successful. The problem was that to Lady Malvinea, that meant a successful marriage to a man of title, birth, and property.

But Bronwyn couldn't be something she wasn't, and her explanations merely irritated Mama. She and her stepmother might have continued their struggle except for one thing—Sorcha.

At eighteen now, Sorcha was tall and graceful, and possessed the sort of rare beauty that had caused the meteoric rise of Elizabeth and Maria Gunning, young ladies of Irish decent who'd achieved legendary social success many years before. Mama often spoke about them with awe.

Sorcha loved balls, flirtations, and the latest fashions. She was her mother's daughter in every way, except for her love of reading and her strong sense of humor. Bronwyn might wish her sister didn't see marriage as her one and only path to happiness, but Sorcha was adamant. And with her looks and natural charm, it wasn't difficult to imagine her finding a worthy, titled husband who would treasure her for the rest of her life.

Bronwyn's only fear for Sorcha's plan was Mama. Although she wished for the best for her daughters, Mama was often blinded to a person's true nature if they possessed both wealth and a title. Bronwyn had witnessed it time and again, and she had no desire to see Sorcha unhappily wed. So, hoping to protect her stepsister from any sort of disastrous consequence, Bronwyn had become involved in her stepmama's search for a mate for Sorcha. A fortunate side effect of this involvement was that Bronwyn and Mama now found themselves on much more charitable footing.

Together, they'd exhaustively searched out events for Sorcha to attend so she could gain some polish before her presentation to society, had honed the household budget so that funds could be found to buy the silks and satins so necessary for a proper wardrobe, enlisted their housekeeper's help in saving the trim from some older gowns for reuse, and—oh, the million little things that would make Sorcha's debut a success. And all too soon, Mairi would be old enough for the same. Though she was not quite as pretty as her sister, her liveliness promised to make her equally sought after.

Bronwyn set the roll on her plate. "I assume there's a reason you're launching rolls at me?"

"Oh yes!" Sorcha set down her teacup, an eager expression on her face. "I heard the most wonderful news, and I wanted to tell you before Mama came down."

"She tried to get your attention three times," Mairi said, buttering her toast. "You didn't even blink."

"Your ploy worked; I'm now listening." She tore open the roll and reached for the butter. "What wondrous news are you so anxious to share? Is there a new hat in Mrs. MacLeith's window in Inverness? Or a new pair of shoes on—"

"Sir Henry is opening Tulloch Castle!"

Bronwyn stopped buttering her roll, a vision of deep green eyes flickering through her mind and causing her heart to race. "Och. Yes."

"And he's bringing dozens of guests!" Mairi added excitedly.

"*Dozens*, Bronwyn. *Eligible* guests." Sorcha couldn't have looked happier.

Mairi leaned forward. "Sorcha means eligible *men*."

"How lovely. We shall have something to look forward to." Bronwyn took a bite of her roll and then reopened her book. Since meeting the huntsman in the woods, she'd done her best to not think about those confusing moments, for they had bothered her. Had she been too brash? Too forward? Those thoughts had pinched, but the ones that had really tormented her . . . Should she have stayed for more kisses? And if she had, what might have happened then? It was the last thought that had kept her awake far too often since that day.

"Bronwyn?" Mairi's smile had faded. "Don't you think that's exciting news?"

"Oh yes. Quite." She traced a finger down the page to find the last line she'd read; she couldn't seem to concentrate on the words.

"Wait a moment," Sorcha said. "You're not at all surprised. You knew about this!"

"How could she?" Mairi asked. "*We* didn't know until this morning. Mama only found out because Cook spoke to the housekeeper at Tulloch Castle."

Sorcha nodded. "Mama said Mrs. Durnoch didn't know Sir Henry and his party were coming until she received a letter a little over a week ago. So how did *you* know?"

Bronwyn put her book on the table. "I was going to tell you this, but I forgot." It had been a waste of time trying to forget the stranger in the woods; dreams and thoughts were far more unmanageable than she'd realized.

"What did you forget?" Mairi asked.

"A few days ago—three or four—I ran into a huntsman in the woods, one of Selvach's. The man mentioned Sir Henry and his party might arrive soon."

"And you didn't mention it to *us*?" Sorcha demanded.

"I wasn't sure he was telling the truth." At Sorcha's quizzical look, she added, "I'd never seen the man before, and after I'd thought about it, it seemed farfetched. Sir Henry *never* visits Tulloch." Plus, the more Bronwyn had thought about her meeting with the huntsman, the more it had all seemed like a very vivid, but impossible, dream.

"I was shocked to hear the castle's being opened, too," Sorcha said. "Perhaps Sir Henry is planning on gathering his family and friends at Tulloch for a few weeks before heading to Inverness for the Northern Meeting?"

The Northern Meeting was the grandest social event

in Scottish society. Started in 1788 by a group of gentlemen as a way to enliven Scottish society, which had been demoralized by the sanctions following the Jacobean uprising, the meeting was aided liberally by the Duchess of Sutherland, who had added activities and balls for the ladies to attend. Held without fail every year in Inverness during the month of October, the meeting was a roaring success from the beginning, and had grown to include elaborate balls and fancy dinners, punctuated by bagpipe competitions and military drums. It was the highlight of the Scottish season, and Sorcha was to be presented there for her debut.

Sorcha continued, "Whatever Sir Henry's reasons are, Mama is certain he'll be holding at least one dinner, and perhaps even a ball!"

"We can't wait!" Mairi gave a little hop in her seat.

"Yes." Sorcha smiled. "But Bronwyn, why didn't you tell us about this huntsman? You could have at least mentioned him."

"Oh!" Mairi's eyes widened and she leaned forward. "Was he *handsome*?"

Bronwyn had relived those moments in the forest so many times, had imagined going beyond them, and had seen the huntsman's face in her dreams so often that she was certain she could draw it from memory. "I don't recall."

"You don't remember *anything* about him?" Sorcha didn't look as if she believed a word.

"He . . . he was . . . tall." Bronwyn quickly took a bite of her roll to keep from having to answer any more questions.

Sharing those moments, even talking about them to her sisters, seemed . . . intrusive. As if she'd lose something precious—which was silly. *It's just a memory, but it's my memory.*

When her sisters continued to watch her, she forced a shrug. "He had dark hair and wore a shabby jacket. That's all I remember. I was going to tell you what he said about Sir Henry's arrival, but only after I visited Mrs. Durnoch at Tulloch to confirm the story."

Sorcha's delicate brows rose. "Why didn't you see Mrs. Durnoch at once and verify the man's information?"

"That's what I would have done," Mairi added.

"I didn't have time, with the extra work I've had to do for Papa's newest patent request." But there was another reason she'd hesitated in visiting Tulloch Castle. A much bigger reason . . . one well over six feet tall.

She'd never met a man who'd made her feel so exposed. And excited. And alive. Had those moments mattered to him at all? And why did she care?

She shifted impatiently in her chair. It was silly to keep thinking about a one-time event. Yet late at night, her imagination took over and she not only remembered the kisses, but elaborated on them as if she were writing one of Miss Edgeworth's books.

Just thinking about those kisses sent a warm shiver through her, and made her acutely aware of an odd sense of loss, of missed opportunity, of . . . loneliness. *How silly is that?* She hadn't felt lonely since her sisters had come to live with her.

She pushed the odd thought out of her mind and smiled brightly. "Now that Sir Henry's arrived, I hope there are several dinners *and* a ball. If not two."

Mairi sighed blissfully. "I would love *two* balls and *four* dinners. Oh, and perhaps a carriage outing to the loch, or a picnic in—"

Lady Malvinea sailed into the room, waving a letter in the air, her fashionable green gown rustling with each step. "Look what just came!" Though her burnished blond hair owed its color to artistry rather than nature, and her figure had settled into a thicker cast over the years, and she claimed that her eyes were puffy some mornings, Mama was still a handsome woman.

She beamed at her three daughters now, though Bronwyn saw a determined glint behind the excitement. "All my lovely daughters in the same room, and here I am, bursting with good news!"

Mairi scooted forward, an eager expression on her face. "Is it about Sir Henry? Is he having a dinner for—"

"Mairi, please. All in good time." Mama took a chair at the table with her daughters. "A lady *never* rushes."

Mairi slid back in her seat and clasped her hands before her, though a hint of stubbornness marred her subdued expression.

"There," Mama said approvingly. "What a pretty picture! Such—" Her gaze found Bronwyn's gown. "Bronwyn?"

Bronwyn lifted her gaze to her stepmother's. "Yes?"

"I thought you threw out that gown."

"This one? No, I threw out the gray one." Actually, she hadn't thrown that out, either, but had designated it as a to-only-be-worn-out-of-doors gown. When she remembered.

"But we spoke about *that* gown, the green one. Not the gray one."

"Did we?" Bronwyn tried to look confused but was fairly certain she was failing.

"Yes. We spoke about how it was out-of-date, and needed to be resewn in a dozen places, and did very little to flatter your figure, and—"

Bronwyn had to laugh, though it made Mama's mouth tighten. "This gown needs some repair, I'll agree, but only where the pocket snagged on a door handle. It served well enough for the chores I've done this morning." When Mama's pained expression didn't lighten, Bronwyn hid a sigh and threw up a hand. "I promise not to wear it in front of guests. Ever."

Mama opened her mouth to argue, but Sorcha was faster. "Tell us about this invitation. Will we need new gowns? Or will the ones we ordered last month do?"

"I'm so glad we ordered those extra gowns for your coming out, although it's a pity we've none for Bronwyn." Mama *tsk*ed at her stepdaughter. "I do wish you had allowed me to order you some gowns when we had the chance."

Bronwyn could have pointed out, as she had at the time, that the budget didn't allow for them all to order new gowns at the same time, but she refrained. "I have three excellent gowns for visiting, and I rarely wear them now."

"Visiting gowns, yes, but no ball gowns. I'll have to give you one of my older gowns and have it altered to fit now we've been invited to Sir Henry's opening ball—"

"A ball?" Mairi broke in, her eyes wide with excitement. "Sir Henry is having a *ball*!"

Sorcha clapped her hands together. "And he invited *us*!"

"Indeed he did!" Mama gave an excited laugh as she waved the paper once again. "My dears, you will never believe this, but Sir Henry has brought more than *thirty* guests with him to Tulloch Castle, all men and women of breeding and gentility. Our sleepy little hamlet has never seen the like!"

Mairi gave another hop in her chair.

Mama fairly beamed. "Sir Henry is scheduling all sorts of events, beginning with an opening ball. And yes, he invited *all* of us, as is only right, since your papa has been his nearest neighbor for years." A flicker of displeasure darkened her eyes. "Of course, Papa is already saying he cannot go, for he's too busy with some project or another, but that's quite all right. Bronwyn and I will chaperone the two of you."

"So I may go, too?" Mairi asked in a breathless tone.

Mama's face softened. "You may. Papa and I have already spoken about it, and we believe it will serve as good training for when you're to be presented. But if I see any hoydenish behavior, it will be the *last* time you enjoy company until you're eighteen. Do I make myself clear?"

Mairi nodded emphatically. "Yes, Mama."

"It is quite unusual for a girl of sixteen to attend such a grand event, but Papa pointed out that it's a country ball and not a formal one, so it will be quite all right for you to attend this one time."

"I shall behave myself, I promise." Mairi's voice was fervent.

"Why is Bronwyn to chaperone?" Sorcha looked displeased. "She's too young to chaperone."

"Nonsense. She's twenty-four, and the perfect age to watch over her younger sisters." Mama took a sip of her tea. "Besides, it will take both of us to keep an eye on you two. I daresay your dance cards will be filled before we're even there five minutes."

"I'm always glad to chaperone," Bronwyn added. "Relieved, in fact. I dislike talking to people I've nothing in common with, and if I sit with the other chaperones I can speak with Miss MacTavish, who has been making the loveliest jellies for her father. She's promised me the recipe every time we meet, but keeps forgetting to bring it by."

Sorcha was already shaking her head. "Miss MacTavish is forty if she's a day. You're too young to sit with the chaperones."

"Sorcha's right. Besides," Mairi added, "how do you know you've nothing in common with someone until you talk to them?"

"Because I dislike talking to gaggles of strangers. And don't say I'll miss the dancing, for I won't at all. Remember our lessons?"

Mama had insisted on those lessons, no matter how Bronwyn begged to be excused. Fortunately, after several painful sessions, their dancing master had agreed that Bronwyn was a lost cause. She could never keep time, which made dancing impossible.

Bronwyn chuckled. "Poor Monsieur Beaumont was tearing out his hair in frustration with me. It wouldn't be fair to the men of Sir Henry's party to be subjected to both of my left feet at the same time."

"Dance Master Monsieur Beaumont wasn't a patient man." Mairi sent her sister a sly look. "He was quite fond of you, though, Sorcha."

Sorcha flushed. Monsieur Beaumont was one of a long list of tutors who'd been dismissed after falling wildly in love with her, something that had happened quite frequently since she'd turned fourteen.

Mama sent Mairi a quelling look. "Say what you will about Monsieur Beaumont, he was a highly sought-after dance master. One of the best."

"But a wretched poet." Encouraged by Sorcha's flushed cheeks, Mairi added, "Bronwyn, do you remember the poem he wrote for Sorcha?"

Bronwyn had to grin. "It started with—what was that line? Oh yes, 'Fair maid who doth stand in the night's window—'"

"'—and chase the sun with her stare of beauty,'" Mairi finished, laughing. "'Her stare of beauty'! What on earth is that?"

Sorcha's face flamed. "I wish you would forget that wretched poem, for I have."

"How can I forget your stare of beauty? And what else did he say? Oh yes, he said your white shoulders were 'mountains of granite and silk—'"

"Mairi, that's enough," Mama said firmly. "Or perhaps you've already decided not to attend Sir Henry's ball and would prefer to stay at home with your papa?"

Mairi's smile disappeared. "No, no! I was only teasing."

"That's too bad." Bronwyn pursed her lips. "I believe Papa plans on perusing a treatise on gas lighting this week. I'm sure he would be glad to read it aloud, should you be bored."

Mairi shuddered. "I'd rather eat raw eggs than listen to Papa read another one of his papers. Mama, I'm very, *very* sorry for teasing Sorcha."

Satisfied by her daughter's chastised expression, Mama nodded. "Good, for I've something more to tell you, some *truly* exciting news this time."

Sorcha's eyes widened. "There's more?"

"*Much* more," Mama said with an air of suppressed excitement. "I was able to discover that one of Sir Henry's nephews, Viscount Strathmoor, is joining the group, and"—she looked around the table, a sparkle in her blue eyes—"there's also a prince!"

Sorcha gasped. "A *real* prince?"

"Of course! And one with an income of thirty thousand pounds a year! Mrs. Durnoch overheard one of the ladies in Sir Henry's party telling another all about him."

"Thirty thousand pounds," Sorcha said in an awed tone. "I can't even imagine."

Neither could Bronwyn. She knew to a penny what it cost to run Ackinnoull, and annually it was far, far less than the prince's daily income.

Mama smiled with satisfaction at their astounded faces. "I'd think a prince with an annual income of thirty thousand pounds must be in want of a princess, don't you?"

"I would think so," Mairi agreed. "One person couldn't spend that much in a year, not by himself, anyway."

"My thoughts, exactly." Mama reached over and placed her hands over Sorcha's. "And I don't know why he shouldn't choose you!"

Sorcha flushed and pulled her hand free, sending an apologetic look at Bronwyn. "Or Bronwyn."

"Lud, no." Bronwyn plucked another roll from the bowl and then reached for the butter. "I can't imagine anything worse than having to constantly be on display like a museum exhibit, having to curtsy all day, forced to smile when you really feel like settling in with a good book—no, thank you." She buttered her roll. "I'd rather own a subscription library than be a princess."

"You can't mean that," Mairi said.

"I do mean it. All of those people wishing to gain your attention— Just think of all the articles we've read, where poor Princess Charlotte's carriage was mobbed. Madness." She wrinkled her nose.

"I like people," Mairi said stoutly. "And it wouldn't bother me to curtsy all day."

"I hadn't considered it," Sorcha said thoughtfully, "but I could see where that might become onerous."

"Nonsense," Mama said. "You'd enjoy being a princess, my dear. It's what you've been raised for."

"I wasn't raised to be a princess," Sorcha protested.

"You were raised to be a wife to a powerful, well-bred man, which includes princes." She beamed at Sorcha. "I hear Oxenburg is lovely, too."

"*Oxenburg?*"

Everyone looked at Bronwyn, and she realized she'd said the word much louder than necessary. "I . . . I read about Oxenburg somewhere recently. The name seems familiar." *So the huntsman must be one of the prince's servants, and not employed by Selvach, after all. That explains many things, such as the fluffy dog. I daresay he was watching it for the prince.* A smile tickled her lips. No doubt the man was as small and poofed as his pet.

Unaware of the unattractive image Bronwyn had of the prince, Mairi sighed dreamily. "I think marrying a prince would be the best of all things. Coaches and eight, diamond tiaras, new gowns every day of the week, jeweled slippers, people to bring you whatever you want, whenever you want it—how could you hate being a princess?"

Bronwyn poured herself some tea. "Perhaps I'm too particular for my own good. If you don't mind, I'll leave all princes to you and Sorcha."

Sorcha shook her head. "But Bronwyn, just think of all the books a princess might have." She waved her hands. "*Rooms* of books."

"That *might* make it worthwhile." Bronwyn pretended to consider it. "But then again, I could also get a subscription to the library in Inverness and have access to *their* rooms of books, without having to stand in receiving lines until my feet and back ache."

"Nonsense," Mama said briskly. "Being a princess

would be lovely, and I won't hear anything otherwise. Sorcha, which gown will you wear? We've only five days until the ball and we've much to get ready between now and then."

Instantly, Sorcha, Mairi, and Mama began to discuss gowns, shoes, hair ribbons, and other absorbing items. Bronwyn listened for a short while, then found her book and tried to read.

But somehow, her mind kept wandering to the huntsman from Oxenburg. Was the country as beautiful as the man? And why, oh why, was she still thinking about him, wondering about him, *dreaming* about him? Fortunately for her, there was very little chance she'd ever see him again. And yet . . . she wondered where he was now, and if he thought about that moment in the forest at all. For she did, far more than she wanted.

But all first kisses were like that, weren't they? she told herself, trying to reduce the memory into something that wouldn't disturb her sleep or her imagination quite so much. But her task was hopeless. The huntsman had possessed an unearthly skill that even her novice lips had recognized. *Blast it, why couldn't he have been horrible at kissing? I might have stood a chance then.* But she'd had no such luck.

With a resigned sigh, she forced her mind to the pages of her book and to the adventures of Roland, whose words now echoed in her mind with a distinct accent and a smoky-smooth tone.

Chapter 5

Roland remembered the first time he'd laid eyes upon Lu-cinda, and how he'd been instantly taken by the innocence that shone from her face like a beacon on a misty shore.

What more could a man wish of a maid than purity of mind and heart?

—The Black Duke *by Miss Mary Edgeworth*

Alexsey Vitaly Grigori Romanovin, Royal Prince Men-shivkov of Oxenburg, and honored guest of Sir Henry Davidson, was bored. Here he was, a man of action forced by his position to don silks and stand in a ball-room filled with preening peahens.

Alexsey bit back a growl as he surveyed the women before him. There were redheads, brunettes, and blondes. Tall ones, short ones, and middling ones. There were plump ones, thin ones, and curved ones. Some were quite attractive, some were not, and at least three of them were beautiful. But what none of them was, was *interesting*.

"Well?" Tata Natasha asked from where she stood at his elbow, her voice impatient. "Which do you wish to meet?"

Alexsey's gaze swept the room again, lingering on this woman, then that, searching their faces for something . . . intriguing. Finally, he shrugged. "None of them."

"Pah!" Tata Natasha pinned him with a black gaze, disapproval an almost tangible cloak on her small shoulders. "There are more than fifty well-born, beautiful women here tonight. Sir Henry assured me they were all gently raised and are well suited as potential brides. You have your pick, *durahk*. So pick!"

"Your concern for my happiness overwhelms me," he said in a dry tone.

"You will be happy once you are married. Talk to one. Ask her to dance. You won't know if you'll enjoy her company until you speak with her." When he didn't answer, she added, "Sir Henry promised that *all* the women here possess a proper, genteel education, and are well bred—"

"So you've said ten times now. Please stop your infernal matchmaking. I escorted you to Tulloch Castle because you asked me to; I did not come to find a wife."

Her eyes narrowed. "What if one finds you? What then?"

For some reason, an instant image of the fresh-faced brunette he'd met in the forest a week ago flashed through his mind. Which was a pity, for no amount of questioning had yielded her name. Though it was obvious the servants knew who she was, none of them had admitted to knowing her. It had been maddening.

Realizing his grandmother was still watching him, he gestured to the refreshment table. "Shall I procure you a glass of orgeat?"

Her expression soured. "You won't talk about marriage."

"*Nyet*. Not here. And not to you."

"The day will come when you can no longer avoid the subject. You are a prince, and a prince must wed."

"True, but that day is not today." When that day did come, Alexsey could only hope he'd have his father's good fortune in finding a mate. With just one glance at a lovely Gypsy maid, his father had fallen deeply, madly in love. The laws of Oxenburg hadn't allowed marriage between the member of the royal family and a commoner, but that hadn't stopped Alexsey's father. Ignoring the outraged gasps and furious warnings of his advisors, he'd issued a decree allowing members of the royal family to marry anyone they wished, and then proceeded to parade his lady love before the people of his country. His plan had worked; the people of Oxenburg had fallen just as wildly in love with his beautiful, charming bride-to-be as he had. They'd welcomed the new queen with celebrations of such enthusiasm that his advisors were silenced, and the laws of Oxenburg changed forever.

One might assume that such a change would mean that the king's sons could follow their hearts on the path to true love. One might also assume that the Grand Duchess Nikolaevna, the mother of the Gypsy-turned-queen, would encourage her grandsons to marry for love as her daughter had done.

But no.

No one was more critical of bloodlines than his Tata Natasha. A tiny woman with a fierce pride, she was more conscious of her new title, and those of others, than anyone born to the velvet. Worse, she acted more queenly than any born-to-the-throne queen Alexsey had ever met. And he'd met them all.

Tata Natasha pinched his arm.

He flicked a glance her way. "Stop that."

"You were not listening. I was pointing out the beauties in this crowd and you were staring at the opposite wall as if you were in hell."

"Is there whiskey in this hell? If so, I'd gladly— Tata, stop that. Pinching my arm will not encourage me to listen. In fact, it has quite the opposite effect."

"You are fortunate to be here. Otherwise, you would still be in Oxenburg with that—"

"Don't!" Alexsey scowled. "It's always the same with you: you spend too much time trying to order my life, and I need no such help. I know what I want." *And at the moment what I want is a few hours under a tree with a certain bespectacled, round-cheeked housemaid.* He'd visited her reading spot every day but she'd never reappeared; she had disappeared like the morning mist. He could find another woman, he supposed, but he doubted he would find one as tempting.

Tata Natasha clicked her tongue, a contrite look in her gaze. "Come, Alexsey. Do not look so troubled."

He didn't trust her for one moment, and just lifted a brow in her direction.

She scowled. "You have an affinity for the most

unsuitable women. Why will you never select a woman
of noble birth?"

"I enjoy women who challenge me, who do not
whine when they get damp or must sit in the dirt."

"And that is why you like the Romany women so
much? Because they do not 'whine'?"

"They are very independent and have such spirit."
He twinkled down at her. "The truth is, I wish to find
a woman like you, Tata Natasha. One who always surprises and never takes no for an answer."

Her expression softened, and she said grudgingly,
"There are not many women like me, even among my
people."

"There are more there than here." He nodded toward
the ballroom. "Beside you, these women are colorless."

"You are too particular in your tastes." Her wrinkled
fingers touched the heavy gold rope necklace that hung
about her neck, one of many. With a practiced twist, she
pulled it free. There, swinging from it like a heavy pen-
dulum, was his grandfather's *kaltso*, heavy with gold,
the ruby flashing a deep red.

Alexsey's hands curled into fists. "The *kaltso* should
be mine."

"You will get it when you've earned it." Her voice
cracked sharply. "You've romanticized our people,
Alexsey. I sometimes think that will keep you from being a good *voivode*."

"Try me, old woman. Dyet wished it; you know he
did."

"You know as well as I do that your grandfather
would wish you to prove yourself." She clutched the

ring, her fingers caging it as if it were alive. "I will recommend you to the council only when you've proven you're mature of mind, settled in your ways, and capable of leading a people of vast complexity."

"I know the Romany, Tata Natasha. I've stayed in their tents, shared their food—"

"Yes, yes. And slept with their women." She sent him a sour look. "A great many of them, from what I've heard."

"Nonsense. You exaggerate, though I admit they are appealing. They are unfettered, free, and passionate."

"If you wish to be their leader, you cannot sweep through the women like a scythe through grass."

"Give me the *kaltso* and I'll never sleep with another."

She fingered the ruby ring, her dark gaze searching his face.

He didn't flinch.

After a moment, she snorted. "I don't believe you." She tucked the ring away.

Alexsey's jaw tightened. "You know I am what's best for our people. Other than you, no one in our family understands the Romany the way I do."

"And what would you do if you became the *voivode*?"

"I'd build permanent camps."

"The Romany would never stay in one place."

"I don't expect them to. They leave every spring and come back each fall. I would never change that, but I'd give them permanent camps on the river in Oxenburg— snug, safe wooden structures where they could live through the winter. It would keep them warm, dispel the damp that is so harmful to the old, and let them repair their caravans and tents for their spring journey.

During the winters I'd provide schools for the young, and bring a doctor to consult with their healers."

"You think a doctor could teach something to a Romany healer? Ha!"

"They could learn from one another if someone but gave them the chance," he said quietly.

She didn't look convinced. "You would never get them to agree to such changes. They are people of the wind and have no wish to be walled in."

"I could if I were the named *voivode*, as Grandfather was."

Her expression softened. "Your Dyet Nikki was an exceptional *lidir*."

"I would never presume to say I could do as good of a job as he. He had much more knowledge of the people, how to pull them together, despite their independent spirit—but I would try, Tata. And I wouldn't stop trying until I had improved their lives."

"Improve? You judge—"

"I do not judge, but neither do I pretend all is well when it's not. I am a realist, not a romantic as you seem to think. I love the Romany, true, but I know their shortcomings. I am not blind to their flaws. They can be far too quickly swayed by gold."

"Perhaps you see them clearly enough," she admitted, her tone grudging. "But it does not change my mind. For now, the *kaltso* stays with me, around my neck, where your grandfather placed it."

"*Bozhy moj*, what must I do?"

She clutched his arm and leaned forward. "Marry a woman of good breeding, someone who will settle those restless ways of yours, and have sons to carry our family name."

"How do you know I'll have sons? You only had a daughter."

She sniffed. "Aye, but she has produced four fine strapping sons. She has good, strong blood, she does. *My* blood."

Despite his vexation, he had to grin. "You take credit for far too much, Tata Natasha."

A twinkle lit her black eyes. "Perhaps." She patted his arm and released him. "You must let me help you, Alexsey. Last year you were this close"—she held up her finger and thumb, with almost no space between them—"to making a *proskchek* a member of our family."

He stiffened. "I can't believe you'd use such a word."

Tata waved a hand. "I say what I see."

"You know nothing. I spent a lovely few weeks in the company of a nubile young dancer—"

"A *proskchek*."

"I never planned to make her a member of our family, and you know it. I had tired of her long before you even knew of her existence."

"Humph. I heard you were mad for her."

"I have never been mad for any woman."

Natasha's gaze sharpened, a look of true curiosity crossing her face. "*Nyet?*"

"I think I am not cut of the same cloth as Father, who fell deeply in love at one glance." He shrugged. "I do not have that capacity."

"Which is fortunate for all of us, considering the low company you keep," she muttered.

Alexsey raised a brow. "Stop consigning me to the devil for being a man." He smiled at her. "If I could find a woman with your spirit, I would marry her today."

"Pah! Don't try to charm me. I am immune to compliments."

He laughed and bent to kiss her cheek. "Then I won't say another word. In fact— Ah! I see someone I've been waiting to speak with. If you will excuse me, Tata."

"Who is it?" She stood on her tiptoes. "Is she lovely? Tell me who she is and I'll ask Sir Henry to introduce you."

"*Nyet.* I have been waiting for Viscount Strathmoor. Though he is of good birth, even you would not wish me to marry him, for he is very short and has the devil of a temper. Now excuse me. And no more matchmaking, please. It is wearing." He kissed her hand and then left, ignoring her frown as he made his way across the room to Strath.

Alexsey had known the viscount for more than ten years. Strath's sharp wit always made him laugh, and if there was one thing he could use right now, it was a laugh.

Aware he was being surveyed from head to foot by every woman present as he crossed the room, Alexsey eyed them all back. They stared, measured, and—sadly for them—hoped. There were several beauties among them, but none possessed anything that tantalized him. His Roza would outshine them all.

He'd liked that she was innocent and exotic at the same time, curved and welcoming. A man could sink into bed with such a woman and not rise for a week.

He suspected she possessed the same innate natural passion as the Romany. Perhaps it was that which had drawn him to the beauty in the woods?

"I cannot believe it." Strathmoor stood before Alexsey, a glass in each hand. "All these beauties parading by, and you're making no effort to speak to a one. Are you ill, brother?"

Alexsey gladly accepted the proffered glass from his friend. Small and quick like a sparrow, Strath made up for his lack of height with his humorous outlook and generous spirit. Alexsey took a sip of the drink he'd been handed. "What ambrosia is this?"

"Good Scottish whiskey—a rich peaty one that you'll like. It's better than the sweet stuff my uncle favors." Strath shuddered. "Pale and weak. I'd rather drink water."

Alexsey took another drink. "Excellent." Strath was a fine fellow. They had come to know one another when the viscount had visited the Italian court during his Grand Tour while Alexsey was the emissary from Oxenburg. The position was a lightweight training mission, and with no real duties he'd been bored out of his mind until Strath, with his ready laugh and his thirst for adventure, had arrived.

Strath and Alexsey had spent three glorious months drinking and carousing, enjoying the lazy Italian sun and beautiful women. Since then, they'd maintained a sporadic correspondence and visited one another every year or so.

"I'm glad you're here," Alexsey said, taking an appreciative sip.

"You should be. I came only because my uncle mentioned a few weeks ago that you and your grandmother were joining him here. The second I found out, I closed up my town house, packed my bags, and voilà, here I am."

"I assume you were alone in that town house, or nothing could have pried you away."

Strath sighed woefully. "It's true I am between mistresses."

"As am I." Alexsey swirled the amber liquid in his glass. "This whiskey is excellent; I need some of this for my private stock. Is that possible?"

"Of course. Tell me how much you want, and I'll have it delivered before you leave."

"You are a good friend."

Strath lifted his glass. "As are you. I hope you didn't mind my assumption that you needed a drink, but I saw you talking to your grandmother, and you looked as if you'd like to throttle her."

"Indeed. She is determined that I wed—and soon."

"But now you have escaped and you are here, a drink in your hand, surrounded by a bevy of lovelies and no wedding in sight. I call that perfection."

Alexsey shrugged.

Strath sighed. "Let me guess: you are still pining for your forest maiden."

"I'm not pining, but I've yet to see any woman who would match her." He sent a sour look at Strath. "I'd hoped you might know some of the local households who might possess such a maid, but you were next to useless."

"I can count on one hand the number of times I've been this far north. We should have asked my uncle for his help in identifying your mysterious beauty. Uncle Henry was quite the rakehell in his day and I'm sure he would have understood your impatience to find her."

"Of course he was a rakehell; he wouldn't know my grandmother, otherwise." Alexsey looked over his glass to where Sir Henry was now talking to Tata Natasha. *Plotting, more like.* Sir Henry was tall, with broad shoulders and a head of distinguished white hair. He carried a bit of a paunch from years of good living, but it was easy to see that at one time, he must have been an impressive specimen.

There was something about the way the man looked at Tata Natasha, almost as if . . . *Hmmm.* "I believe there's a history between my grandmother and your uncle."

Strath's gaze followed Alexsey's. "It's possible; they are close in age."

"I doubt Tata Natasha cares for age. Over the years, she's become far more concerned with pedigree."

"Yet she was once a Gypsy, true?"

"She still is. And, as she's quick to point out, she is the queen of the Gypsies. If you ever wish to see Tata Natasha angry—and you don't—then suggest otherwise."

A lady danced by, peeking over her partner's shoulder at them. Strath wagged his eyebrows at her. She was a rather faded-looking woman with pale skin and watery blue eyes, her red hair the only colorful thing about her. "That's Miss MacGregor," Strath confided in a low voice. "The things she can do with that mouth . . .

Lovely! I would dance with her, but I fear she might fall desperately in love with me. Women meet me and instantly offer their hearts. It's a burden I bear."

"How difficult for you," Alexsey said drily. "I prefer it when there are no hearts involved, only willing bodies."

Strath chuckled. "According to what your grandmother has told my uncle, that is the Romany way."

"My grandmother also thinks her potions can turn princes into frogs."

Strath's smile faded. "Frogs? Are you teasing?"

"Sadly, no." Alexsey swirled the remaining scotch in his glass. "Your Miss MacGregor has left her partner and is now trying to make her way through the crowd toward us."

Strath brightened as he put down his glass and smoothed his coat. "Is she, indeed? I must answer the call, then. If you'll excuse me?"

"Of course. After I finish tasting your whiskey, I believe I will retire to my room."

Strath blinked. "But . . . you're the guest of honor! My uncle will not be happy if you retire too soon."

Alexsey hid a grimace. There were times when being a prince was onerous. The second people knew it, they instantly assumed certain things. If they were parents of an eligible maiden, they assumed he possessed a wealth that few princes could. If they happened to be eligible young women, they assumed a romantic bent to his character usually involving white horses and flowing red capes, neither of which he possessed. And if they were hosts or hostesses, they believed he not only enjoyed being their guest of honor, but would be offended if they did not make him so. "I dislike being a guest of honor."

"But sadly, you're a prince, and as a prince . . ." Strath shrugged.

"I will stay until midnight but no more. I was up with the birds this morning. I visited the place I met my maid, thinking perhaps she would be there at an earlier hour."

"I take it she was not. She seems oddly determined not to be found. As much as it may hurt you to hear this, I can't help but think perhaps you should find someone else to amuse you. But who?" As he spoke, Strath rose on his tiptoes, looking over the crowd to check Miss MacGregor's progress.

"None of these women interests me."

"Then you have not looked hard enough. All women are beautiful, you know." He frowned. "Blast it, Miss MacGregor has been waylaid by Lord Dunn. I shall have to wait for her to break free."

"She will arrive anon. And I must disagree with your belief that all women are beautiful." Alexsey looked about the ballroom. "What about her?" He nodded toward a small, rather wispy-looking female with mousy brown hair and a receding chin.

Strath eyed her for a moment, and then said, "Her skin is like cream. She would glow by candlelight. Her figure is lovely, too. Lying down, you'd never notice she's a bit short. Spread across a coverlet, her hair about her, candlelight caressing her creamy skin—you would not be able to keep your hands to yourself."

"Hmm." He inclined his head toward another woman, a rail-thin blonde with an overly large nose. "And her?"

"That hair, unbound, would reach her waist. I'd wager my last groat it's soft as silk and would brush over your bare skin until you were eager for her touch. And note, too, her mouth. It's wide, passionate, and as warm as—" Strath sighed. "You can see her beauty now, eh?"

"Indeed. An intriguing way to view the world, my friend."

"Sadly, I am not a handsome man. I'm neither tall nor dashing. My title is negligible and I have no fortune to speak of. So how can I expect perfection when I have so little to offer myself?"

"What of the truly beautiful women? The one society deems to be diamonds of the first water?"

"I avoid them like the plague. All they'll do is use me as a partner for an empty dance, and when the dance is over, ask me to introduce them to my friend, the prince."

Alexsey cocked an eyebrow. "That has happened?"

"Five times this evening alone. And if you weren't here, they'd ask for an introduction to Loudoun or Portman. They're both earls and spend more per month on their hunting horses than I have for all of my expenses for the entire year."

"Not all beautiful women are as shallow as you think."

Strath sent him an amused glance. "So they would have you think; I am allowed to view them in their more natural state. Most, if not all, beautiful women are spoiled, and think they deserve the best life has to offer without making any effort to win it. Give me a woman who is grateful for a smile, someone like—" He glanced about the room. "There, by the door. I'm not talking about the goddess in blue; that's her sister, who is quite vain—you can see it in the way she holds her head. I'm talking about the one in pink who—"

"Wait!" Alexsey started. "That is her!"

Strath stared. "But . . . that's not a housemaid at all. That's Miss Bronwyn Murdoch, a member of the local gentry."

"Nye za shta!" He scowled. That would make a flirtation far more difficult. Still, it was very good he'd finally found her. "Bronwyn." He rolled the name over his tongue. "That suits her." He put his glass on a nearby table. "Come. We must go to her."

"But Miss MacGregor is—" Strath sighed. "Never mind. I'll find her afterward. First, I must meet this woman. I— Hold, Alexsey. Wait for me, damn you."

Alexsey didn't slow down, his gaze locked on Roza.

Strath caught up and followed him through the crowded floor. "I can introduce you; I met the Murdochs in the receiving line."

"They are a well-to-do family?"

"Not financially, but very much so by birth. Mr. Murdoch's a rather eccentric inventor. My uncle implied that Miss Murdoch helps her father with his patents."

Thus the ink-stained fingers and the letter wadded in the toe of the slipper. "And the others?"

"Her stepmother and stepsisters. The stepmother is Lady Malvinea, the daughter of an earl. That's all I really know of the family. I wish I'd listened more closely when my uncle was telling me about them; you know what a gossip he is."

It was a pity his Roza was a woman of good family, for it meant she was as trussed up by society as he. Perhaps more. As a prince, his behaviors were indulged. Society, never fair in its treatment of the gentler sex, wouldn't be so generous regarding the actions of a female of good birth, and even less so regarding those of a female of good birth but no income. *That lack of income explained her worn clothing, too. We will have to be very careful, Roza.*

As he drew closer, he saw that the gown she wore now, while of better quality than the one she'd worn in the woods, was unfashionable and of a brownish pink color that did little to complement her warm skin and brown hair. "She does not dress as well as her sisters."

Strath shrugged. "Miss Murdoch is on the shelf and is here tonight as chaperone."

"What does this mean—on the shelf?"

"She must be—oh, I don't know, twenty-five or so." Strath nodded to a man who waved as they passed in the crowd. "She has passed the marriageable stage of life."

Which made her even more perfect for a passionate affair. Things were looking up. A woman who was no longer considered of marriageable age would be much freer of the strictures of polite society, and less under the watchful eye of a concerned parent than a maiden of tender age. *Perhaps her genteel birth will not be such a burden, after all.*

Strath continued, "She seemed quite shy when we

were introduced. She only said two words, and from what I could see, that's all she's said to anyone."

Because she's bored. I can see it in her expression. "That is all?"

"Yes. To be honest, I didn't pay much attention to her. To any of them, really. I like women of more vivacious wit."

If there was one thing Bronwyn Murdoch possessed, it was vivacious wit. She just didn't bother to flaunt it at a boring ball. Strathmoor didn't appreciate Roza because he'd never looked into her eyes when she talked about books, nor heard that funny gurgle she made when she tried to hide a laugh, nor felt the warmth of her lips when kissed. The man didn't know how her brown eyes sparkled when she smiled, or how her mouth pursed when she was mad, as if she were unconsciously begging for a kiss.

As he drew closer, Alexsey eyed her with renewed relish. Her long brown hair was pinned up, but the unruly tresses were already fighting for their freedom, a few tendrils curling about her delicate neck. The regrettable gown did little for her lush figure. And she was outshone not only because of her dowdy gown, but because she lacked the sparkling jewels of the other women here.

Once she is mine, I will buy her jewels. He imagined her naked and aglow before the flame of a candle, rubies sparkling against her warm skin. *She deserves rubies, to reflect the passion I've seen in her eyes. Yes. Definitely rubies.*

"Oh, it's the prince!" a woman exclaimed as he and Strath tried to navigate past a final knot of guests.

Like a wind rippling through a field of wheat, word of their approach arrived before they reached their goal. Alexsey saw the instant Bronwyn's sisters realized who was coming to meet them. They smoothed their blond curls and wafted their fans, standing at attention in a way that pressed their bosoms into the bodices of their gowns, like preening peacocks on the strut.

The older woman with them—the stepmother, according to Strath—did much the same, her smile so wide, it appeared more a fixed grimace.

Roza didn't even look his way. She was gazing as if searching for someone among the chaperones, an assortment of hopeful-looking mothers and older spinsters.

Of course she isn't paying attention. What does she care for princes?

Smiling, he stopped with Strath in front of the group of women.

Bronwyn, still squinting toward the chaperones, lifted up on her toes and wondered where Miss Mac-Tavish might be. *I hope she'll remember to bring the recipe; I wrote her yesterday and reminded her.*

Sadly, the older woman was nowhere in sight. Bronwyn sighed. They'd been here less than an hour, but it already felt like days. And it was getting more and more crowded. Twice now, people had plowed into her without apologizing, even though one had spilled his beverage on her sleeve—

"Good evening."

Bronwyn turned to find Sir Henry's nephew, Viscount Strathmoor, bowing to Lady Malvinea. Yet as he did so, he slanted her a quick look, curiosity plain on his face. Bronwyn hid a surprised frown. *He barely looked at me when we were introduced earlier.*

His gaze turned politely to Mama. "Lady Malvinea. Allow me to introduce you and your lovely daughters to our guest of honor, His Highness, Prince Menshivkov."

Oh, good, Sorcha will be so pleased. Bronwyn's gaze moved past Sir Henry's nephew to rest on . . . the prince?

No.

The breath left her body in a flat second.

It can't be.

But it was.

As Lady Malvinea, Sorcha, and Mairi curtsied, Bronwyn's world froze.

My huntsman is the prince.

Chapter 6

Gentle reader, to say that Roland knew the depth of his love for Lucinda with his first glance would be akin to saying that one can know the depth of the ocean at a glance. It takes time, and a very long knotted rope, to work that particular measurement.

—The Black Duke *by Miss Mary Edgeworth*

Alexsey bowed to the group, his gaze locked upon Bronwyn. "Pleased to meet you."

Bronwyn didn't know where to look or what to say. All she could do was gaze into his green eyes, her mind whirling in disbelief.

How could this be? He'd been dressed so simply and had been carrying the gamekeeper's quiver and arrows and— *Good God, why didn't he* tell *me? He must have been laughing at me the entire time.* Her cheeks burned at the thought.

Unaware of her turmoil, her stepmother and stepsisters greeted the man with the greatest enthusiasm. "Your Highness!"

"Most pleased!" Sorcha, flushed with pleasure, dipped a curtsy.

Mairi followed suit. "Such an honor!"

He bowed absently to them, his gaze never leaving Bronwyn, possessive and hot. She felt every bit as exposed as she had in the forest—and more. Her heart thudded sickly against her chest and she felt as if she were caught in a horrible dream.

He looked so different in formal dress; lordly, prouder, and far less approachable. His perfectly cut coat fit across his broad shoulders and then tapered down to his narrow waist. His close-fitting knit breeches molded to his muscular legs and made her fight to breathe. *Now he truly does look like Roland.* "You are no huntsman."

Lady Malvinea's startled gaze flew to Bronwyn. "Bronwyn!"

Sorcha's eyes widened.

Mairi gaped as she looked at the prince from head to toe. "*This* is your huntsman?"

Oh dear. I shouldn't have said that aloud.

Alexsey took Bronwyn's hand, his green eyes twinkling as he bowed. "I am indeed a huntsman. Since our meeting, I've done nothing but hunt"—he flashed a wolfish grin—"for you."

She opened her mouth, but not a single word came out. This was not good. Not good at all. He was the prince, the very man Mama wished for Sorcha. And yet here he was, holding her hand.

He traced a circle over the back of her hand with his warm thumb, and she had an instant memory of his hands on her waist and hips, of his firm, warm mouth upon hers. Heat flooded her and her face burned yet again.

"Do not blush, little one."

Mama, who had been staring at them with her mouth agape, stiffened. "Little one?"

Strathmoor leaned forward to say something under his breath to the prince, who looked irritated. "Ah. I did not know." He inclined his head toward Mama. "'Little one' is what I call your daughter, but I have been informed that's not a polite form of address."

"Oh. I—I'm sure you didn't mean to be forward." Mama couldn't have looked more irritated. "That's . . . I'm certain there's . . . I just don't . . ." She subsided into red-faced silence, her eyes blazing.

The prince turned back to Bronwyn. "I am glad to have finally found you." His hand tightened over hers, warm and powerful.

"Oh. Yes. That's very nice." Bronwyn tugged her hand free. "Thank you, Al—Your Highness. You are too kind."

Alexsey's eyes warmed, and he moved closer.

A shiver traveled through Bronwyn, warming her skin and making her nipples peak. The reaction was so quick, so raw, that she had to fight to breathe.

Mama's brittle laugh cut into the moment and jarred Bronwyn back to her senses. "My goodness, I scarcely know what to say! How do you two know one another?"

Bronwyn shook her head. "We don't know one another. Not really."

"But we do," Alexsey said, his smile fading. "Lady Malvinea, I had the privilege of meeting your step-daughter several days ago. My grandmother's dog disappeared during a hunt and your stepdaughter, who was reading a book in the woods, found her."

"In the woods? Alone?" Mama cut a shocked, reproving glance Bronwyn's way.

"Actually, no," the prince said, looking regretful. "She had two large horse-dogs guarding her. She was quite safe."

Mama said in a stiff tone, "I didn't mean to suggest she wasn't; I'm sure you were a perfect gentleman. I'm just surprised Bronwyn never mentioned this meeting."

Bronwyn shook her head. "I didn't think it was important. He had some of Selvach's arrows and was wearing common clothing—he didn't look a bit like a prince."

Mairi leaned closer to Bronwyn and said under her breath, "How could you forget what he looked like? He's *perfect*!"

Alexsey laughed, the deep, rich sound sending familiar tremors through Bronwyn. "Miss Mairi, I am many things, but perfect is not one of them."

"I'll vouch for that," Strathmoor offered, looking amused.

Mama wasn't finished. "Bronwyn, you obviously told your sisters about this meeting in the woods, but you said not one word to me."

"I told them I'd met a huntsman, because that's what I thought he was."

"And she only told us because we made her." Mairi bit her lip when her mother's gaze flashed her way.

"I can see I've caused an uproar, and it was not my

intention." Alexsey tried to hide his impatience. "Roza did not know my title because I did not tell her."

"Roza?" Miss Sorcha frowned.

Bronwyn said, "I refused to tell him my name, so he called me Roza and—"

"But—" Lady Malvinea began.

"Pardon me." Alexsey bowed. "I will dance with your stepdaughter."

"Oh no!" Bronwyn moved back until she was slightly behind Miss Sorcha. "I don't dance."

"Bronwyn doesn't dance, and Mairi's too young." Lady Malvinea's back was ramrod straight, like a soldier preparing for battle.

Alexsey had to give the lady credit. Her words and expression were pleasantly polite, but her posture and the line of her jaw showed a determination that gave one pause. He knew many statesmen who would pay money to be able to use just such skills.

"Mama!" Miss Mairi hissed, her face red. "You said I could dance this evening!"

Lady Malvinea's smile didn't slip. "Not with the prince." She slipped an arm about Sorcha and edged her forward. "But Sorcha dances divinely."

Alexsey bowed. "I look forward to dancing with both of your daughters."

"Excellent! Sorcha will—"

"—dance with me *after* I have danced with Miss Murdoch." He captured Bronwyn's hand, tugging her forward.

She tugged back. "No, no. I'm only here to chaperone—"

"We will dance." Alexsey tightened his hold. He'd waited many long days to find this woman, and he'd be damned if he'd let her out of his sight. "I will not accept a no."

"But I—"

"Bronwyn!"

Everyone looked toward Lady Malvinea.

Her fan quivered, but she managed a credible smile. "Bronwyn, the prince has been most polite in his offer. You will dance with him. I'm sure someone will claim Sorcha's hand." Lady Malvinea looked directly at Alexsey. "Sorcha is in much demand. She may not be here when you return and you will have to wait for your dance."

"Strath!" Alexsey said over his shoulder.

The viscount, who'd been watching them as if he were at the theater enjoying a show, started with surprise. "Yes?"

"Dance with Miss Sorcha."

"But—"

"I will claim her hand at the next music."

"But—" Strath caught Alexsey's firm gaze and sighed. "Of course I'll dance with the lovely Miss Sorcha. It will be my pleasure." He bowed and held out his arm. "Miss Sorcha, shall we do as we've been royally commanded?"

Miss Sorcha looked as if she'd swallowed a bee, but after an awkward second, she gave a jerky nod and a fluttery, pained smile. "Of course." She placed her hand upon Strath's arm. Without looking at one another, the two joined the dancers upon the floor.

"There," Alexsey said with satisfaction. Refusing to look at anyone else, he placed Roza's hand upon his arm, and led her onto the dance floor.

Finally, he had her where she belonged: within the circle of his arms.

Chapter 7

There was something tantalizing about the way Lucinda's lashes trembled upon her cheeks, as if she were the smallest, most innocent dove. As Roland watched her, his heart swelled, and the urge to protect her filled his soul.

—The Black Duke *by Miss Mary Edgeworth*

No woman had ever danced with less grace. Still, though Alexsey feared his toes would be permanently bruised, he couldn't stop his wide grin. He was dancing with his Roza.

He looked down at her and wondered what she was thinking. She seemed lost in her thoughts, her brow knit, her gaze on her feet. Of the many ways women reacted to dancing with him, he'd never met with such silence.

Alexsey bit back an "oof" when her small, slippered foot came down on his boot again. Perhaps because her stepsisters and stepmother were so much taller than she, Roza seemed shorter than he remembered, more delicate in some ways. But her skin was just as sun-kissed, her brown hair gleaming with russet lights that glowed in the candelabra light.

But gone was her openly curious expression, and in its place a polite-society façade, the sort worn by someone uncomfortable in public. *Are you shy, little one? I did not see it before, but now I think it's possible.*

He noted how stiffly she held her chin in the air, her lashes low, almost resting on her cheeks. He wondered if she found the silence unnerving, and if that was why she refused to look at him. Then he realized the truth: she was struggling to keep up with the dance steps, her lips silently moving as she counted out the time.

Her attention on her steps didn't seem to help, for her dancing was worse than atrocious. She missed steps, had twice moved in the wrong direction, refused to allow him to lead, and had stepped on his left foot six times already.

Fortunately, while her eyes were turned downward, he had the opportunity to admire her at his leisure. How had he missed noticing how thick her lashes were? And how her small nose gave her a piquant look? He wanted to kiss that nose, along with other parts of her. He adroitly guided them out of the path of another couple.

Her hand tightened over his, and to his amusement, he realized she was once again trying to lead, a habit he attempted to squelch by refusing to follow.

Thwarted, Bronwyn flashed her gaze up to his. "I told you I don't like to dance."

"So you did. What you did not tell me is that you *couldn't* dance."

She flushed. "You should have danced with Sorcha. She's very good at it."

He glanced at Strath, Bronwyn's gaze following. The viscount and Sorcha were exceptional dancers, moving smoothly and without error, seeming to float as they swept about the floor. With her gown of white crepe sewn with tiny pearls, long white ribands floating about her, Sorcha looked as if she belonged in a fairy tale.

But though the couple danced divinely, their conversation seemed to be of a less perfect turn. It was obvious they'd exchanged harsh words. Strath looked as if for a penny he'd willingly strangle Sorcha, while she appeared ready to return the favor for free.

Alexsey looked down at Bronwyn. "I prefer to dance with you, wretched though you are at it."

"Why that's— How rude!"

"It is the truth. I would not patronize you with less."

She lifted a brow. "You truly are a prince charming."

"Was that . . . what is the word? Ah yes—you are sarcasm."

"The word is 'sarcastic.' And yes, I am." She frowned up at him. "Pardon me, Alexs—Your Hi—good God, I don't even know what to call you. This whole thing is confusing and awkward. I can't seem to accept that you are a prince. A *real* prince."

"If it bothers you, then tonight, I will be a huntsman once again." His expression warmed. "I love hunting, especially for you."

She narrowed her gaze. "I have the feeling you mean something else when you say 'hunting.'"

He laughed. "I might. Come, Roza. Do not become so disturbed over things neither of us can change. Besides, we are just dancing."

"If you think balls are held merely for dancing, then you're very naïve."

"Oh, I know that balls are for matchmaking. But I do not pay attention to such nonsense, and neither should you."

She eyed him with curiosity. "You're not looking for a wife?"

"I cannot think of anything I want less. I came to Scotland to escort my grandmother, who is older and far more frail than she will admit. Other than that, I had no purpose, and I certainly have no desire to marry. Not yet, anyway."

"Neither do I." She nodded thoughtfully and relaxed a little, her steps not quite so stiff as they turned to the music. After a moment, she peeped up at him through her lashes and said in a confidential tone, "Had I realized you were a prince when we met in the woods, I wouldn't have spoken to you at all, much less—" She glanced around, and then lowered her voice. "You know."

"Kiss—OW!" He stopped and another couple almost collided with them. "You stepped on my foot on purpose!"

"Did I? I'm sorry."

He could tell she damned well wasn't sorry at all. He firmly danced her to the side of the floor, keeping a cautious eye on her feet.

Once they were out of the main press, he slowed to a more comfortable tempo. They were now completely out of step with the music, but more in pace with her abilities. "There. Now you can stop pretending you can dance."

"I warned you."

"My ears did not work; I was too happy to have finally found you. Now, though, I regret not listening." He shook his head in mock despair. "The tops of my shoes will never be the same."

Her lips quirked into an irrepressible grin.

"So you have no shame for ruining my shoes, *nyet*? If it weren't so difficult to replace shoes here in the middle of nowhere, I would let you stomp on the tops of all of them, but such is not the case. If they are ruined, I must go without."

"A barefoot prince? That sounds like a bad Italian opera."

He chuckled. "So it does. And it will sound even more like one if you mar my shoes until I cannot wear them, for then I will have to punish you."

Bronwyn wasn't sure what it was, the golden glow from the hundreds of candles that lit the ballroom, the musical swirl of the orchestra, or the fact that she was dancing with a real, straight-out-of-a-fairy-tale prince, one so handsome that everyone was staring at her with obvious jealousy, but she felt light-headed, as if she'd had too much champagne. It caused her to look up at the prince through her lashes and say in a completely un-Bronwyn-like way, "Oh? And how will you 'punish' me?"

His eyes sparkled. "I would spank you." He bent until his lips were near her ear. "But in a *very* pleasurable way."

Bronwyn's heart leapt at the low-spoken threat. *I can't believe he's saying such things to me. Even more, I can't believe I'm letting him.* But some part of her, a part she'd never known even existed, thrilled at the naughtiness of it. For one mad moment, she *wanted* him to do something "pleasurable." In fact, she could think of several pleasurable things she would like from him right now—

I must stop this. Such thinking will only lead me down a very dangerous path. She knew there would be a price to pay, for actions always followed thoughts. She pulled back a little and forced herself to appear disinterested. "I suppose all princes are flirtatious."

"I can only speak for myself, but I am not usually so, *nyet.* Tonight I am flirtatious with you, and no one else."

He said the words as if conferring a great gift upon her. "I suppose I should be honored. For tonight, anyway." Oddly enough, she *was* honored . . . a little. And flustered . . . and still breathlessly happy, which worried her.

His smile warmed her. "I only know this, Roza: I am glad to find you, and I wish to kiss you more. But this time, I think it will be a different kiss from the ones we shared in the woods."

There are different types of kisses? Her chest tightened and her skin prickled in anticipation. "Oh?"

Alexsey laughed softly, soaking in the mixture of excitement and wonder that shone in her expression. *She is so lovely, so open, every emotion clear in her eyes.* The obvious excitement in her eyes spurred his own. "Our first kisses were gentle, new." Alexsey bent closer, the scent of her hair engulfing him in lilac and sunshine. "This time, I will kiss you without mercy. I will kiss you over and over and over, until you beg for more than mere kisses."

Her eyes widened and her lips parted, pure, naked desire in her dark eyes.

His body tightened instantly, his heart thrumming in an odd sort of recognition, as if his body, primed by her nearness, recognized hers.

Wanted hers.

Needed hers.

But as quickly as desire had flashed across her face, her lashes dropped and she banished every vestige of longing. With a faint look of regret, her jaw firmed and her face set with a new determination.

As he watched the play of emotion, disappointment settled on his shoulders. *So quick to deny your own desires. Why is that?* She was as prickly as the flower he'd named her after. He wondered why he found her so appealing, what trait of hers pulled him closer. But one glance at the plump curve of her lips and the apple-round silk of her cheek, and he only knew that he wanted to taste this lush maiden and stir her sensuality awake. Just a single touch would free it; he could see it in her eyes.

His gaze swept over her to where her bosom filled her gown in a delightful manner. He'd wager his favorite summer palace that her breasts would fill his hands like ripe fruit, soft and succulent.

His mouth watered and he wished they were alone, where he could explore such intriguing possibilities. She'd looked different when they'd been in the secluded woods—had *been* different, softer and more approachable. Her hair had been loose and her gown muddied, and—after he'd kissed her—she'd had a dreamy expression on her face. Now she was primped and starched, her expression as cautious as her clothing. *Ballrooms do not become you, Bronwyn.*

It would take some effort to loosen the bindings she'd wrapped about herself. "Tell me what sort of kisses you like best: slow ones that make your skin heat, or quick, urgent ones that make you ache for more, or—"

"Stop." She glanced around as if to make certain no one could hear, her cheeks flushed an attractive pink. "This conversation is not acceptable for a lady, and you know it."

"I do not like this word, 'acceptable.'" He wasn't overly fond of "lady," either, now that he thought about it.

"Well, I *do* like that word. And if you don't stop teasing me in such a way, I'll ask to be returned to my family."

He sighed. "So prim. This I do not like."

Her gaze darkened. "I'm not fond of it, myself, but it's how things must be."

"Why?"

She blinked. "Why? Surely you can imagine the horrible complications that could occur if we continue to—" She glanced over one shoulder and then the other, before she bent closer and whispered, "Push the boundaries of acceptable behavior."

He had to laugh. "I don't think you need to whisper that."

"Perhaps not, but we would both do well to behave with more propriety. You may not have a care about your reputation, but I care about mine. If I were to cause a scandal, my sisters could be harmed by it."

Alexsey found himself looking over Bronwyn's head to where Tata Natasha stood with Sir Henry. They were no longer deep in conversation. Instead, she was watching him dance with Bronwyn, a frown on her face. The heavy gold necklace that held the *kaltso* glimmered in the candlelight.

He returned his gaze to Bronwyn. "Sadly, there are people who will judge one based upon a reputation."

"It is unfair, but it is the way of the world. Therefore, it is better for us to put our past nonsense behind us, and remain acquaintances."

"What does that mean?"

"There will be no more kisses."

"*Nyet.*"

She frowned. "I didn't ask. I'm telling you."

"I agree we should be more circumspect when in public. But in private? That is an entirely different matter."

"Someone might catch us."

"No one caught us in the woods," he pointed out. "We must find more time in the woods."

"We were merely lucky. The next time, we wouldn't be."

"Then we would set a watch of some sort, bribe the servants to—"

"*Nyet.* No. Not in a million years."

Alexsey wasn't used to such direct speaking, and he

sure as hell wasn't used to being told *nyet* in such a bald way. He, a prince of Oxenburg, a huntsman without compare, the future *savyet lidir* of the Romany (or so he'd be once Tata Natasha was through trying to make a point), was being put in his place by a Scottish lass who enjoyed books more than his kisses. "You are making this most difficult."

"I'm making this simple."

Irritated, he snapped out, "Is this a trick, a way to make me want you more?"

She quirked an eyebrow in such an adorably threatening way that it made him yearn to kiss a smile back onto her plump lips.

He shook his head ruefully. "I will take that as a no. Ah, Roza. Why could you not have been a housemaid as I'd thought?"

"Why couldn't you have been a huntsman as *I* thought?" she returned, regret heavy in her tone. "You and I are from two different worlds."

"Nonsense. We have much in common. We both like books, dogs, poems, Sir Walter Scott, dogs—I could go on."

"You listed dogs twice."

"It does not matter; I still made my point."

"No, you haven't. That's everything you know about me, a paltry four things. It's not enough. Besides, whether we have something in common doesn't change one very major item—you're a prince. Everything you do is monitored, watched, scrutinized." She glanced around them. "People are watching us even now."

"I ignore them."

She looked unimpressed. "And that keeps them from gossiping?"

Well, no. Nothing stopped that. But admitting that wouldn't help his cause, so he shrugged. "People always talk."

"Not about me. If we pursued those kisses, someone would see us and then there would be a scandal." Her clear gaze met his. "A scandal my sisters and I would have to live with after you left."

A scandal would also make Tata Natasha hold even more tightly to his *kaltso*. He scowled. He'd thought Bronwyn's pragmatic streak charming until now. Now it irritated him, because he had to admit she was right.

As he met her gaze, he caught a hint of genuine regret in her eyes. He tightened his grip on her hands, pulling her closer. "I will not give up on us."

"I will." Her smile trembled only the faintest bit. "Now, let's talk about the weather like everyone else must be doing. That will be much safer."

But he didn't want safe. There was something about her that made him even more restless. A flicker of lust that grew stronger as the minutes passed. She was part wide-eyed wood nymph, part awkward society miss, and—he was beginning to realize—part testy library elf. "I will not waste precious time talking about the weather when we've so little time togeth—"

"Your Highness!" Lady Malvinea's voice cut through the music.

Bronwyn instantly stepped away from him. Alexsey's hands curled into fists.

Bronwyn's stepmother smiled, Miss Sorcha peering from behind, looking both embarrassed and excited. Alexsey bit back a curse, but inclined his head as was polite. "Lady Malvinea. Miss Sorcha."

Lady Malvinea favored him with a cringe-inducing smile. "Your Highness, I trust you can still walk after dancing with Bronwyn."

"Yes, but only because I wear very good shoes."

Bronwyn sent him a flat look. "You were warned."

Lady Malvinea gave a too-loud laugh. "You were indeed warned, Your Highness. Bronwyn, I believe Mairi is speaking with an acquaintance of yours sitting with the other chaperones. She said something about a recipe you were promised, but I didn't catch it all."

"Of course." Bronwyn sketched a curtsy. "Your Highness, thank you for the dance."

"It was my pleasure," he said gravely, hoping she could hear the deeper meaning in his tone. He started to add that he hoped to see her again, but she was gone before he could form the words, heading toward the chaperones like a compass needle finding north.

Lady Malvinea pulled Miss Sorcha forward. "I believe Your Highness has bespoken this dance with my daughter?"

Alexsey stifled his irritation. If his Roza believed he was finished pursuing her, she was wrong. *We will be alone again soon. I will make certain of it. And I will find a way to keep the world's eyes from us, a way that will soothe that overcareful side of you.*

He would have to be very, very cautious, but she was worth it.

In the meantime, it was to his advantage to keep himself in her family's good graces. Aware of Lady Malvinea's approving gaze, Alexsey took Sorcha's hand and bowed over it, smiling. "Shall we?"

"I would be honored, Your Highness."

He led Miss Sorcha into the swirl of dancers, Lady Malvinea's beaming smile following.

Chapter 8

There are times, gentle reader, when even love needs a little nudge....

—The Black Duke *by Miss Mary Edgeworth*

Alexsey swung out of the saddle of his black gelding and handed the reins to a waiting groomsman.

"Welcome back, Yer Highness. Oy trust ye found yer ride to yer likin'?"

"It was invigorating." Alexsey rubbed his horse's neck. "Viktor and I enjoyed the path around the loch very much. This land of yours is beautiful at all hours, but especially in the morning mist."

The groom beamed. "Och, 'tis an auld land, Yer Highness. God took his time makin' her, and did it proper."

Alexsey patted Viktor's damp neck. "That He did. Viktor was especially impressed with the waterfalls. We have many such in Oxenburg and they reminded us of home."

The gelding wickered, cold puffs blowing from his nose as he nudged Alexsey's pocket.

"You look for your reward, do you?" Alexsey pulled

an apple from his pocket and fed it to the horse, before turning to the groom. "I walked him the last length home, so he has cooled down."

"Aye, Yer Highness. Oy'll see to it tha' he's watered, bathed, brushed, and combed."

"Thank you." Alexsey slipped a coin into the groom's waiting hand and watched as Viktor was led away.

Normally, after a late night at a ball, Alexsey would have still been abed. But somehow, he'd awakened with the dawn from a dream where he'd been dancing with a brown-eyed vixen with tumbled hair, sparkling eyes, and a wit as sweetly sharp as lemon candy. *So Bronwyn, you are invading my dreams now, are you?*

He shouldn't be surprised. After their dance last night, he'd thought of nothing but her, the feel of her in his arms, the flash of humor in her eyes, the way her lips pursed when she was considering something he'd said—her expressions were as changing as the sea, and he was thirsty to understand each and every one.

She tantalized him. Even this morning, while riding around the blue loch, the water kissing the gray stone shores, he'd imagined her riding with him, her eyes the same rich brown as the patches of peat nestled between the mountain ridges. It had been a long time since any woman had teased him so.

Alexsey walked toward the gate leading from the stable yard to the castle path, the gravel crunching under his boots. The sun was just now burning off the edges of the mist and slowly climbing the sides of the mountains that surrounded Tulloch. As the day brightened, the white morning revealed the green, brown, and purple glory of the Scottish countryside. *Such beauty, and yet it carries such strength, too.*

The sound of a horse approaching made him pause as he reached the gate. Out of the low roiling mist, Strathmoor appeared, riding a large bay. He waved to Alexsey before pulling up and dismounting. The viscount handed his reins to a waiting groom, speaking briefly to the man before striding down the path to join Alexsey.

Strathmoor looked Alexsey up and down. "Must you dress like a groom?"

"I wear what is comfortable. It is one of the few benefits of being a prince; I can be as out of fashion as I wish and yet society will not shun me."

"It would shun me if I wore such clothes." Strath shook his head. "I'm surprised to see you this early."

"This morning, I surprised myself."

Strath unlatched the gate and held it open. "Couldn't sleep?"

"*Nyet.* A dream." *A very good dream.*

"Too much lamb." The viscount closed the gate and then fell into step beside Alexsey. "I told my uncle he shouldn't serve it every meal, for it is bad for the digestion, but he never listens to me."

"Was it your digestion that awoke you this morning?"

Strath smiled. "No, a whim awoke me. A very vivid whim."

"Is this whim blond? Or brunette?"

"She's . . ." He trailed off, his smile fading as he

squinted toward the path that curled around the back of the castle.

Alexsey followed Strath's gaze just in time to see a cloaked woman disappear through the gate in a high stone wall. "Who was that?"

"For a moment, I thought . . ." Strathmoor shook his head. "It couldn't have been."

"Couldn't have been who?"

"Oddly enough, I thought it was Miss Murdoch."

Alexsey halted. "*Da?*"

"I'm sure I was mistaken. It's far too early for a visitor, and why would she enter the castle through the kitchens? That makes no sense."

I'm not so sure about that. "I think I must see this mysterious lady for myself."

Strath shrugged, though his eyes twinkled. "Off with you, then. I'm to breakfast, for I'm famished. Just don't forget to tell me the outcome of this tryst, whoever the lady is."

"Do not eat all of the bacon." With a wink, Alexsey set off across the lawn. He quickly reached the gate, unlatching it and passing through.

The kitchen garden rested against the back of Tulloch Castle, enclosed by three tall stone walls. Neat rows stretched before him, left fallow for the fall, although a few straggly greens near the castle door proved the stubbornness of the cook.

It was a pretty garden even without the benefits of full bloom, with neat paths of white rock and a wooden bench set under a tree. And there, walking quickly to a door leading into the castle, was the woman Strath had

seen. She was cloaked head to foot in a familiar cape,
and she held a large basket. He caught up to her just as
she reached the door. "Roza."

Bronwyn, her fingers already on the iron door handle, jumped, her heart thundering. *Surely not.* She'd
done nothing but think about him since their dance
last night, but she'd never expected to run into him this
morning.

Strong hands closed over her basket and lifted it
from her grasp. "I will carry this."

As usual, he didn't ask. *He rarely does. That must
be fixed.* There were many things about this man that
needed fixing, now that she thought about it.

"You are not going to wish me a good morning? I
think that is the required courtesy, *nyet*?"

She straightened her shoulders and pushed off her
hood as she faced him.

The second she did so, she realized she'd made a
grave error. It wasn't that she was underdressed—
for though she wore her oldest gown, her hair carelessly knotted in a bun at the nape of her neck, he was
equally attired. Once again, he wore the loose-fitting,
far-from-fashionable clothing she'd first met him in,
his brown jacket slightly worn at the elbows, his neckcloth tied with just a simple knot at the base of his
throat.

No, her error was in thinking for an entire night that
if she tried hard enough, she could stop responding to
the breathtaking handsomeness of this man. That, apparently, was an impossibility, and it would be in her
best interests to stop pretending she had control over a

purely human reaction—to appreciate beauty in whatever form one happened to find it. *I'm sure I'd be just as
breathless if I were facing a gorgeous statue, or a—*

Her eyes met his. Heat raced through her, a jolt so
strong that she wondered if it could be seen like a flash
of lightning. She'd never react this way to a statue.

His grin was as wolfish as the gleam in his eyes.
"Happy to see me?"

"I thought you'd be sleeping," she blurted.

"I was. I dreamed of you."

She opened her mouth, then closed it. Oh, the things
she longed to ask! But did she really wish to know? If
he'd had a good dream, that wouldn't help quell her
body's reaction every time he was near. And if he'd had
a ridiculous dream, where she'd fallen down stairs and
turned into a sea monster, or something equally as silly,
she'd feel a disappointment she didn't want to have to
explain to herself.

"Come. We will sit on the bench." He turned toward
the bench, but she grabbed the basket with both hands.

"I need to take these eggs and jams to Mrs. Durnoch."
When he didn't look enlightened, she stifled a sigh.
"She's the housekeeper here at Tulloch."

"Why would the housekeeper here ask you for sup-
plies?"

"She sent word to Mrs. Pitcairn, who serves as our
cook and housekeeper at Ackinnoull, that the castle
larder was woefully short of various items. Sir Henry
didn't give poor Mrs. Durnoch enough notice that he
was coming, and with such a large party, she's been
scrambling to keep the tables filled."

"There doesn't seem to be a lack of food. It's been quite abundant."

"Lamb is available locally, and Selvach and his huntsmen had quite a bit of meat already dried and salted. They've been bringing in fresh catch every day, too. They were out this morning hunting duck, for I saw them heading toward the loch."

"I will have to say my thanks to both Mrs. Durnoch and Selvach."

"I'm sure they would appreciate it. We have over twenty hens at Ackinnoull, and Mrs. Pitcairn's jams are famous locally, so we keep them supplied. In return, whenever Selvach has extra game, he sends it to Ackinnoull."

"That is very kind of him. I have seen this Mrs. Durnoch, I think. She wears a ring of keys at her waist the way men at war wear armor."

"She is at war. A war against disorganization and dirt."

"She is winning; the castle is very well run. Even my grandmother has been pleased, and it is not often she is so." He turned toward the kitchen door. "Come. We will deliver your basket."

"You can't go into the kitchens!"

But it was too late. He was already stepping through the door.

Bronwyn hurried to catch up to him, arriving just in time to see the shocked expression on the cook's face when she realized who was carrying the expected basket.

"Gor, 'tis the prince!"

Instantly every maid, cook, undercook, and kitchen boy stopped what they were doing and stared, the noise dying from a clamor to silence in one second.

Cook began bobbing curtsies as if she were made of them, while one of the kitchen maids toppled to the floor in a swoon, drawing another maid to her side, who fanned the woozy girl with an apron. A kitchen boy who'd been turning a roast on a spit fell into a fit of the giggles, while another maid turned so red, Bronwyn feared the girl would die of an apoplexy.

She couldn't blame them. A prince like Alexsey, so handsome and dashing, his black hair falling over his brow, his green eyes agleam in a ballroom, was potent. A prince like Alexsey, standing six feet two in a smoky, crowded kitchen looking totally devastasting, was the stuff of fairy tales.

"Welcome, Yer Highness!" Cook stopped curtsying long enough to wipe her hands on a cloth and take the heavy basket from the prince. "I . . . we . . . that is, I . . ." She cast a desperate glance at Bronwyn.

"His Highness saw me struggling with the basket in the garden, and he kindly offered to carry it inside."

Cook placed the basket on a nearby table and dipped another curtsy, this one much longer and far more dramatic. "Thank ye kindly fer bringin' the basket, Yer Highness."

Alexsey inclined his head. "It is Miss Murdoch who deserves your thanks. She carried the basket from her home. I merely brought it inside from the garden."

"Aye, but ye carried it inside wit' yer own hands. Tha' is no' somethin' to ignore!"

As Alexsey started to disagree, Bronwyn grabbed him by the elbow and propelled him to the door. "Thank you, Cook! Please tell Mrs. Durnoch we should be able to send even more eggs tomorrow."

As soon as the door shut, Bronwyn released his arm. "Next time, just say 'thank you.'"

"But I did nothing."

"You visited the kitchen. That was enough. They were honored you graced them with your presence."

He snorted.

"If it helps, I wasn't impressed with your efforts at all." She walked past him toward the gate. "I must bid you good-bye; I've many things to do today."

He lengthened his stride and stayed at her side. It was annoying how easily he kept up.

When she reached for the gate handle he caught her hand, lifting it to his warm lips for a kiss. "Surely you have ten minutes to spare."

She did, she supposed. But talking to him, as innocent as it was, felt illicit, as if she were doing something she shouldn't be. After all, there was no one here to act as chaperone. *But what could be wrong with talking?*

Not a single, blasted thing, she told herself. "I suppose I can spare a few minutes."

Before she knew it, she was being led to the small bench, his hand warm over hers.

The hovering fog still hung low and thick inside the garden walls, and since it was the morning after a ball, the lords and ladies of Sir Henry's house party would be abed until well after noon. And while there were servants about, most of them were busy with their morning chores—lighting fires in bedchambers, buffing boots, preparing food for the midday breakfast trays, ironing gowns, polishing silver, and completing any of the dozens of things that had to be finished before the lords and ladies of the house awoke. So she and Alexsey wouldn't be seen here in the garden. *No harm can come of a calm, polite chat.*

They reached the small bench and Alexsey pulled out a kerchief to brush the dead leaves from the seat. "After you."

Bronwyn sat, neatly tucking her cloak about her.

The prince joined her, his knee brushing hers and sending a quiver of awareness through her. His shoulders were broad and they couldn't both sit comfortably without him turning slightly to one side, his arm resting along the back of the bench.

Already breathless, and achingly aware of his arm resting so close to her shoulders, Bronwyn glanced at the gate. The garden wall was high, with green vines clinging to the rough cut stone. But the gate was only as tall as her waist and anyone could see over it. She wondered if they'd believe their eyes, seeing the prince sitting in the garden with her. But perhaps it wasn't such an odd match, after all.

Somehow when she was with Alexsey, she felt finer—taller, even. She wasn't sure if it was his admiring gaze, or the fact that she just felt so alive when he was nearby, but she couldn't help but feel . . . well, prettier. She rather liked that. *It's good for me to spend time with him. And good for me to remember our kiss. No matter what happens, I'll have memories of our dance, of sitting in this garden, and of our kiss. Especially our kiss—*

"I know what you are thinking about," he announced, as if no one in the world might question him.

She lifted her brows. "I doubt it."

He merely smiled. "You are thinking about our kiss, *nyet*?"

"Why would you think that?" She tried to keep the belligerent tone from her voice, but wasn't certain she succeeded. *How does he know?* "I don't often think about it," she lied.

"Yet I think of nothing else." His eyes gleamed with warmth. "I will kiss you again, little one, but I won't tell you when."

"What? That is ridiculous. Why would you threaten to kiss me, and then not tell me when you plan on doing it?"

"Because it will add an element of surprise."

"I don't like surprises."

"You'll like this one." He smiled in a way that made her want to slip into his lap and loop her arms about his neck. "You should be prepared."

"I'm prepared to refuse you. You don't get to decide when I am to be kissed."

"*Nyet*, we will decide together." He captured her hand and brushed his lips over her fingers, sending her a look from under his lashes. "Perhaps soon. If the mood strikes, of course."

The touch of his lips on her bare skin instantly sent her heart pounding, and Bronwyn found herself in the mood for a kiss much more quickly than she expected.

Irritated with herself for reacting so quickly to him, she pulled her hand free and tucked it beneath her cloak. "What brought you into the garden this morning?"

"You. I was with Viscount Strathmoor and he noticed you entering the gate. Naturally, I had to see why you were indeed sneaking into the castle through the kitchens."

"I wasn't sneaking."

"It looked like it to me. And knowing your questionable nature—"

"What?"

"I thought you might be bent upon some nefarious caper, but instead, I find you saving us all from hunger with a delivery of eggs and jams."

Her lips quirked. "I'm glad you appreciate my efforts, although you really should thank Mrs. Pitcairn instead. She is quite talented at coaxing our chickens to produce eggs, or we'd have none to share."

"I shall make it my duty to do so." He traced his fingers along the line of her cloak where it covered her leg. "Tell me about Ackinnoull. It is your home, *nyet*?"

"I was born there, and my father before me, and his father before him, and—oh, it goes on and on. It has been in our family for a very long time. But to me, it is just home."

"That is a good feeling, to be home."

She thought about this, trying to ignore the tantalizing sensations his wandering finger on her knee was causing. "Sometimes I feel more at home at my reading place."

"Where I first met you in the woods?"

She nodded. The morning breeze puffed through the tree overhead and rained browned leaves upon their heads. She brushed some from her cloak.

"I like the woods, too." He plucked a leaf from her hair and tossed it over his shoulder, turning toward her even more. "Did you meet my grandmother at the ball last night?"

"The Grand Duchess Nikolaevna? No. I saw her from across the room, though. Mama pointed her out."

"She is Romany. A Gypsy."

Ah! That explained the prince's dark hair and exotic looks. "Mama had heard that rumor, but didn't believe it."

"It's true. My father was riding along the river in the fall, and he came upon my mother near the Romany camp. As soon as he saw her, he knew she was for him. So he married her."

"Our royalty have far stricter rules about whom they can marry."

"So did my country—but my father overcame every barrier so that my mother remained by his side. When I grew to be six or seven, I would stay with my grandmother and grandfather every winter, sharing their caravan at the Romany camp. My grandfather, Dyet Nikki, was the *voivode*, their king. Those were days filled with adventures. I would follow Dyet as he went about his duties, visiting the families, checking on the weak and the young, settling disputes, presiding over weddings, overseeing trades with local farmers. . . . When I was a child, I thought he was the wisest man in all the world."

"Your father is a king. Doesn't he do the same things?"

"Some. But the kingdom is much larger, so he must administer through his council. He cannot meet all of his subjects face-to-face. He does not know their names. Does not know their troubles. Dyet Nikki knew the name of everyone in our *kumpania,* whom they were related to, what troubles they'd faced in the past—everything."

"What's a *kumpania?*"

"Our Gypsy band. There are many bands but only one law, the *Romano Zakono.* It is not written down, but is passed from generation to generation. Dyet Nikki knew the law and he taught it to me."

"Because he wished you to assume leadership of the Romany?"

"It was his wish, I think so—but it was not his decision to make. There is a council and they select the *voivode* for life."

"Surely you can go to them, tell them how much you'd like to assume your grandfather's position?"

"Now that my grandfather is no longer alive, and no new *voivode* has been named, the council listens to one person and one person only: the *phuri dai.* Every *kumpania* has one. She is an old woman, usually the oldest in the band. In this case, it is my Tata Natasha."

"Your grandmother?" When he nodded, she noted a line of tightness about his mouth. "I take it she doesn't wish you to become the *viovode?*"

"She withholds it from me, hoping to bend me to her will. Sadly for her, I am not made of soft lead, but steel. I do not bend."

The sparkle of rebellion in his green eyes made Bronwyn feel braver, too. "How can you become the leader of the Romany if you're a prince of Oxenburg?"

"I have three brothers. And as Tata Natasha is fond of telling us, there is not room on the throne for four asses. My oldest brother, Nikki, will sit on that throne. My youngest brother, Wulf, is already doing what he does best, bringing wealth to our country. My brother Grisha is a soldier, one of the fiercest fighters in the history of the world. He will lead our armies."

"And that leaves you free to help the Romany."

"Not so free, perhaps, but *da*, it is what I will do when the time comes." He reached over to brush a leaf from her shoulder, trailing his fingers back to her neck and then up to her cheek. "And you? What do you dream of, Roza? What far shores beckon? What mountains do you wish to climb?"

His voice was seductive and silky, and she had to fight the urge to turn her cheek into his hand. "I'm quite content where I am."

Puzzlement turned his eyes a darker green. "Content with the place, that I can understand. It is lovely here. But surely there are things you wish to accomplish yet."

"I'd like to see both of my sisters well married and happy."

Alexsey frowned. "That is a dream for them, not for you. What do *you* want to do?"

She tilted her head to one side, a thoughtful expression on her face. "I don't really know. I've been so busy helping with Sorcha and Mairi, and helping my father with his patents—he's an inventor and must file the paperwork or lose any profits. I haven't really thought of doing anything else."

"You must have dreams of some sort," Alexsey insisted. "I already know you possess an adventuresome spirit, one that allowed you to share a most delightful kiss with a huntsman you'd just met in the woods." He cupped her cheek and brushed his thumb over the fine line of her cheekbone. She had delicate features, deliciously at odds with the errant sprinkle of freckles that dusted her nose.

Her cheeks pinkened, but she didn't move away. Indeed, he thought she might have leaned into his hand just the slightest bit.

She cleared her throat, her voice still husky. "People are usually adventuresome in some aspects of their lives, while not as much in others."

"We should rise to all challenges. Fortunately, the things that frighten us can also tempt us." Alexsey brushed a curl from her cheek, tucking it behind one of her shell-pink ears. He couldn't seem to stop touching her. Just having her so close, her hip against his on the small bench, made his body ache with yearning. "What frightens you, Roza? What do you both want, but fear?"

Her gaze met his, and he knew his answer. She desired him, yet feared the consequences of that desire. His body leapt in answer, and he found himself leaning forward, his lips brushing hers with the lightest of touches.

It was a teasing kiss, one meant to tempt her into wanting more, but he never had the chance to place the second kiss, nor the third. For the moment his mouth brushed hers, she moaned softly, fisted her hands in his coat and yanked him toward her, pressing her mouth to his and opening beneath him with demanding insistence.

Alexsey was lost in a flood of desire. He pulled her into his lap, never breaking the kiss, running his hands over her, molding her to him. She gasped against his mouth and he deepened the embrace, running a hand along her side to cup her breast. It was as deliciously full as he'd expected. Moaning softly, he found her nipple and flicked it with his thumb.

She arched against him, moaning desperately as he—

The gate creaked, and instantly Alexsey moved her back to his side.

They sat for a long moment, their breathing harsh as the gravel crunched down the pathway. From the swirling mist a maid appeared, carrying a basket of linens. She walked past them, turned toward the kitchen, and disappeared through the door, never seeing them.

As soon as the door closed, Bronwyn leapt to her feet, her hands on her hot cheeks. "That's not what I expected to . . . I mean, it's . . . Oh dear. I should really . . . No, don't get up! I'll—" She dipped a quick curtsy and then disappeared into the mist. A second later, the gate slammed shut.

Still sitting on the bench, Alexsey wondered if he should walk to the loch for a cold swim, or call for an ice bath. Either way, he feared it would not be enough.

The afternoon sun shining overhead, Sir Henry Davidson stood on the terrace overlooking the south lawn, wishing he could spend more time here. It was a beautiful castle, one that deserved far more attention than he had time to give.

Though solidly built, the castle needed improvements in a dozen ways. If he made Tulloch one of his permanent residences he'd have to update the kitchens, add more water closets, install lighting, fix the roof over the west wing, repair the long drive—all expensive items for a castle he rarely visited. No amount of money could move the castle closer to Edinburgh, and Sir Henry couldn't imagine living so far away from civilization.

He'd come to Tulloch for one reason alone: because the woman standing at the end of the terrace had asked him. Or perhaps *ordered* was more correct.

At one time in his life, he would have given his right arm just for a glance from the fine eyes of the slender woman who was glaring across the lawn at his guests. But now he was forty years wiser, and time had changed things.

Given the choice now between the lady's still fine eyes and, say, a well-basted leg of mutton, he'd take the mutton.

Of course, that might be because it was far past his normal dinnertime, and the lady had called him away from the buffet just as he'd been ready to partake of an especially lovely lemon cake, which hadn't concerned his guest in the least.

His stomach grumbled in protest.

Not noticing, Tasha waved a dramatic hand at the guests enjoying the unusually warm afternoon. "Just *look* at him!" she ordered. "He's *impossible*!"

Henry joined Natasha, reluctantly tearing his gaze from the wide doors that led to his library, located a few steps away. Inside, a waiting scotch decanter called him. He could also ring a bell and have a footman bring him some tea cakes, and perhaps a roasted—

"Are you listening?" Her eyes narrowed on him. "We are talking about my grandson."

He swallowed a sigh. "Och, of course." He searched the pastel gowns and dark coats strolling about the leaf-strewn lawn. It took him but a second to locate the tall young man who stood to one side of the lawn, surrounded by a bevy of young ladies. "Your grandson cuts quite an impressive figure. How many grandsons do you have?"

"Four. One married and the other three stubborn."

That made him laugh. "Stubborn he may be, but Prince Menshivkov is a fine mon. And he appears to be enjoying the company, too."

"He likes women well enough," she said darkly. "*Too* well."

"Then surely 'tis only a matter of time before he's wed."

Natasha fixed a fiery stare upon him. As she was as tiny as a fairy, her gesture merely brought the top of her head a mite closer to his shoulder. "Not this one. Look at him smiling at them, talking to them, giving them hope. But all he really wishes is to bed them and then leave."

Which, as plans went, had its own merits. But Sir Henry knew better than to say so aloud.

He nodded as if in full agreement and stared at the prince with what Henry hoped was a look of disapproval. As he watched, Prince Alexsey reached down and scooped up Natasha's dog—a small white fluff of an animal—and, patting it soothingly, said something that made the women about him laugh. The breeze ruffled the prince's black hair and flattened his coat across his broad shoulders, which made the women stare hungrily as if he were a giant sweet ice.

Henry rubbed his chin thoughtfully. "Tasha, if you dinna mind a man's thoughts on this . . ." He waited.

She cut him a curious glance. "*Da?*"

"It's possible—just possible, mind you—that you're being a wee bit overconcerned. Give the mon time. He'll find the right lass and settle. You'll see."

"I won't see, for he has no intentions of doing any such thing. He's made it very plain to us all—all he wants is a flirtation, flirtation, and nothing but a flirtation."

"That's all most men want, until we meet the right one. Your grandson's educated, sophisticated, intelligent, a fine shot and a better hunter, and he plays a damned good hand at whist. He's a fine mon and the lasses love him. Added to that, he's wealthy and a prince, to boot. That is a recipe for marriage if I ever heard one."

Tasha absently fingered the thick gold chain that hung about her neck. "Despite my complaints, I have hopes he will soon change his ways."

Encouraged, he added, "At least he made some attempt to meet the local beauties at the ball last night."

"He danced with two women only. Miss Bronwyn Murdoch, and her sister, Miss Sorcha."

"Miss Sorcha is very lovely—a blonde with vivid blue eyes and a delicate, graceful nature. Everyone is in raptures over her."

"She was lovely," Natasha agreed. "Do you think he was interested in her?"

"Very," Henry said boldly, though to be honest, he hadn't paid much heed to the prince's expression. "She's from a good family, she is. Her mother is Lady Malvinea, the youngest daughter of Earl Spencer."

"I don't remember a Lady Malvinea, but there were many people at your ball."

"Had you met the Murdochs, you would have remembered them. Lady Malvinea is a woman of forceful character, and her daughter Sorcha is quite beautiful, as I've said. There are two daughters other than Sorcha; one is younger, while the other—an older stepdaughter—serves as chaperone. The father, Mr. Murdoch, is a genteel man of a good and ancient name—'tis a charming family."

"Good. Very good." A thoughtful expression entered Natasha's eyes. "You believe this Sorcha would make a good wife to a restless man like Alexsey?"

"Och, o' course. I wouldna mind having her in my family, had I any sons to share. Lady Malvinea has spared no expense regarding her daughters. They are fluent in several languages, possess refined accents and manners, and are accomplished in musical arts. Whatever you might wish a wife to know, the daughters know. At least the two younger ones."

"But not the stepdaughter?"

"Nay. The vicar's wife told me Miss Murdoch was sixteen when Lady Malvinea came to Dingwall, much too old to benefit from her stepmother's guidance."

"But this Sorcha, she sounds well suited." Natasha's gaze fixed on her grandson. "I wonder . . ."

Sir Henry's stomach rumbled and he winced, wondering if he dared suggest tea at such an early hour. He was just about to mention it when Natasha said, "Perhaps I should meet Lady Malvinea and Miss Sorcha."

"That would be easy to arrange. But . . . a word of warning. Though her heart is good, Lady Malvinea can be a bit abrasive."

Natasha flicked him an unconcerned glance. "I do not fault a woman for having ambition for her children. This Sorcha has potential. Potential is a beginning. And since Alexsey took the time to dance with her, he must be attracted to her."

"He also danced with the eldest, less attractive daughter," Sir Henry reminded her, "perhaps for politeness' sake."

A faint look of approval crossed her face. "That was well done, and quite unlike him. Perhaps you are right, and he is interested in this Miss Sorcha." Natasha pursed her lips. "I will invite the Murdochs to the castle for tea. I wish to meet this girl myself, and Lady Malvinea, as well."

"Of course."

"That is done, then." She smiled, a flash of humor in her black eyes. "Come, let us find you some sustenance. Your stomach has been grumbling nonstop. I fear if we do not answer it, and soon, it will decide to go to dinner without you."

He laughed and proffered his elbow. "I'm a sad case, Tasha." He wagged his brows suggestively. "Always hungry, especially where you were concerned."

"I'm hungry, too." She tucked her hand inside his elbow. "But only for tea cakes."

He patted her hand. "Then cakes it will be."

Chapter 9

Lady Catulino gave Lucinda a handkerchief. "My dear, you are such an innocent. Men were made to drive women to madness, either with what they will do, or what they won't. It is simply the nature of the beast."
        —The Black Duke *by Miss Mary Edgeworth*

Sir Henry's liveried footman opened the door and then stood to one side as Mama, Sorcha, and Mairi entered the sitting room. Bronwyn trailed behind, taking in the luxurious, if rather out-of-date, appointments of Tulloch Castle's sitting room with deep appreciation.

Since talking to—or rather, kissing—Alexsey in the garden, Bronwyn had been a tangle of thoughts, trying to put everything that had happened into some kind of order. But all she'd managed to do was realize two difficult and sadly conflicting things.

First, prince or no, Alexsey possessed a highly sensual nature. A nature that, most likely encouraged by his upbringing in an exotic land, and the fact that princes rarely faced correction by societal rules, had obviously gone unchecked. Sadly, she reacted strongly to that sensual nature; his mere presence made her heart flutter and her knees quake.

She wasn't pleased with this realization, but it was better to admit the truth of things rather than hide them.

Her second realization was about herself. When faced with Alexsey's unfiltered sensuality, her imagination was thrown into an instant war with her common sense. She *knew* a dalliance of any kind with Alexsey was dangerous, and would likely go further than it should. Yet despite knowing how disastrous that could be for her future, she still found herself imagining what might happen if they *were* ever alone again. It was as if the moment he touched her, she became someone else, someone far more adventuresome than she'd ever thought herself to be.

Faced with these contradictions, all she could do was to make certain she and Alexsey were never alone, so she'd never have to make a choice between her imagination and her common sense. She feared she already knew which one was stronger.

"Bronwyn?"

Her mother and sisters had taken their seats and were looking at her expectantly.

Flushing, she hurried to join them. "Sorry, I was admiring the rug. It's beautiful."

Mama's lips thinned, but she turned to the waiting footman. "Please inform Her Grace we have arrived."

"Yes, my lady. She will be down shortly."

Mama inclined her head in what she obviously thought was a regal manner, but only succeeded in looking awkward. "Thank you."

He bowed again and then left. The second the door closed behind him, Mairi hopped to her feet. "Have you ever *seen* such elegant furnishings? These chairs! The settee! The rugs! Even the footstools are elegant; they all have golden feet!"

"It's beautiful," Bronwyn agreed. The long room had glittering golden candelabras upon a large marble mantel, rich oriental rugs covering almost every inch of floor, and gorgeous silk-covered furniture arranged throughout.

Sorcha looked about her in wonder. "It was so kind of the grand duchess to invite us to tea."

"It wasn't mere kindness." Mama couldn't seem to keep her smile to herself. She had been in a particularly sunny mood since the ball, and now she beamed at them all. "It's my belief it wasn't the grand duchess who issued the invitation. In fact, I'd wager my best shoes on it."

Mairi turned from admiring a particularly lovely ormolu clock. "If the duchess didn't, then who? Surely not Sir Henry, for the invitation didn't bear his name, only hers."

An impatient look crossed Mama's face. "*Think*, Mairi. We didn't even meet the grand duchess, so why would she invite us to tea? Someone *else* manipulated this little meeting. Someone who spent time with us at the ball."

Good God, she thinks Alexsey is behind our invitation! Bronwyn couldn't have disagreed more.

The prince's intentions were far from pure, but she couldn't imagine he was so lost to propriety as to induce his grandmother to assist him with a seduction.

Had he been a weaselly sort, she supposed it might be true, but he wasn't a bit weaselly.

Frankly, she thought him boldly honest, even when the truth made him seem a libertine. She found his honesty appealing. She bit back a wistful sigh. "Mama, I don't believe the prince was behind the grand duchess's invitation."

Mama's smile faded. "Of course he was. I think he wanted to see Sorcha, and it is a great honor that he wishes her to be introduced to his family."

Sorcha, pink-cheeked, shook her head. "No, Mama. I think you're reading far too much into this."

"I'm not! My dear, just think. The prince paid particular attention to you the night of the ball. You are the only woman he danced with."

"He also danced with Bronwyn."

"She's not an eligible parti. Besides, he left the ball right after he danced with *you*. In fact, he barely spoke to anyone else." Mama looked as if she might explode with happiness. "The entire neighborhood has been roaring with speculation. Many people have commented upon his behavior."

Probably spurred on by Mama's own hints. Bronwyn wisely kept her thoughts to herself.

Sorcha shook her head, her knuckles white about her new reticule. "Mama, you exaggerate. He barely spoke when we were on the floor. Meanwhile, he talked to Bronwyn the entire time they danced. I know, for I saw them."

And he'd had far too much to say to her, Bronwyn thought.

Mama's smile faltered, but only for a moment. "He was probably lost in thought. You know how some men are at large functions—they dislike dancing and the noise makes conversing difficult. That's most likely why he had the grand duchess invite us today, so he could speak with you in a quieter setting."

"I have nothing to say to him."

"Of course you do! And if he should ask, it would be perfectly acceptable if he drew you to one side of the room while I speak with his grandmother. So long as you stayed within sight, you two could have the most comfortable of cozes." Mama cast a sharp look at Bronwyn and Mairi. "When you see the prince take Sorcha to one side, pray do not jump up and follow them."

Mairi sniffed. "What if the prince invites us?"

"I daresay politeness will make him do so, but you're both to refuse. After a nice visit, we'll invite the grand duchess and the prince for a visit, although"— Mama ran her hand over a silk-tasseled pillow, a dissatisfied shadow darkening her eyes—"I don't know how I'd ever welcome them into our poor sitting room. Obviously Her Grace is used to the finest of everything and there we'll be, our house barely fit to view."

Bronwyn bit back a sigh. "Mama, this is Sir Henry's home, not Her Grace's. Who knows what she is used to?"

"I'm sure *her* home is even grander. Oxenburg is one of the wealthiest nations in the world. I know, for I read about it."

Sorcha turned to her mama in surprise. "Where did you read about Oxenburg? I'd never heard of the country before this week."

"I found a book in your stepfather's library that contained a remarkable amount of information." Mama glanced toward the closed door and then said in a low voice, "The country is known for its wealth, which comes from vast dairy lands, the quality of its lace and fabrics, and—and—" She frowned. "I can't remember the third thing, but it was something rather boring, like timber or barley."

"What else was in this book?" Bronwyn asked, curious despite herself.

"The king has a rather large family—four sons, in fact. Which means our prince has three brothers."

"He's 'our prince' now, is he?" Bronwyn said drily.

Mama didn't hesitate. "He will be once he spends more time with your sister."

Sorcha looked miserable. "Mama, please don't say such things. It's entirely possible he may not like me at all."

Mama's beaming smile faded. "Don't be ridiculous. You were raised to be a princess."

Mairi snorted. "Do princesses steal pastries from the kitchen when they think no one is looking? Sorcha took the last pastry from the kitchen last night, even though Mrs. Pitcairn had saved it for me."

"I didn't know that," Sorcha said hotly just as the door opened and a footman appeared.

He bowed. "Her Grace will see you now. Tea has been set up on the terrace."

"Lovely!" Mama leapt to her feet and smoothed her hair. "Come, girls."

The footman held the door wide and waited as they left the room. When they were all gathered in the hall, he closed the door and then led them down the wide hall.

They were near the terrace door when Sorcha came to such an abrupt halt that Bronwyn almost ran into her.

"Oh dear! I left my reticule in the sitting room."

The footman stepped forward. "I'll fetch the reticule, my lady."

"And leave Her Grace waiting?" Mama huffed. "I think not. We'll find the reticule *after* tea."

Sorcha said, "But Mama—"

"I'll fetch it now," Bronwyn offered, "and then I'll join you. You can make my excuses to Her Grace, if you need to." Perhaps she would take her time fetching the reticule, too. She had no wish to watch Mama fawn over the grand duchess.

"Thank you, Bronwyn." Mama nodded to the footman to proceed.

Brownyn made her way back down the hall. Going into the sitting room, she found the reticule. She'd just left and was getting ready to walk past the grand staircase in the huge foyer when she heard male voices.

"What a waste of time," Alexsey said. "Why do you Scots have tea so often?"

He was coming down the stairway, his footsteps muffled by the thick runner that cascaded down the marble steps.

Viscount Strathmoor answered, "Have you felt our weather? If we didn't warm ourselves each afternoon with a spot of tea, we'd all be frozen stiff by dinner."

They were almost upon her. Her heart thudding, she looked for a place to hide. She wasn't ready to see him again. Not yet. And not without the protection of one of her sisters.

With a feeling akin to panic, she slipped into the small alcove carved into the sidewall of the staircase and squeezed behind a pillar holding a bronze Cupid statue. One of the bronze arrows captured a lock of her hair, and she hurried to untangle it.

"It is colder in Oxenburg," the prince continued. "I do not even like tea."

Viscount Strathmoor chuckled as they descended the stairs. "Teatime is socially important. It's where, over delicate cups of bohea, women critique one another via heavily phrased compliments."

"Tata Natasha is using teatime for another purpose—matchmaking. She has invited someone she wishes me to meet. I can tell."

"She is single-minded, is she not? Which beauty do you think your grandmother is wishing you to peruse this afternoon? Miss Carmichael? Lady Muiren?"

"I did not ask and she does not tell. She only sends a note to my room saying it is my responsibility to attend. Pah! A treaty negotiation is a responsibility, but this—Papillon, leave my boot tassel alone or I'll throw you in the pond."

"That is the worst-behaved mongrel I've ever seen."

Their footsteps sounded as the two men stepped off

the last covered step onto the marble foyer floor. They took a few desultory steps, the dog prancing along with them, before they stopped.

"Papillon's ill behavior is due to my grandmother spoiling her, but she hunts with the heart of a lion. I can forgive much for that."

"So could I, if she didn't growl at me every time I reached down to pet her."

"She doesn't like your cravat. I've been holding back a growl myself all morning."

Strathmoor made an outraged noise while Bronwyn smothered a laugh.

"There's nothing wrong with this cravat."

"It's so high you cannot lower your chin."

"I could if I didn't mind marring the lines. This is all the fashion."

Bronwyn could imagine Alexsey's unconcerned expression. "After we join my grandmother on the terrace for tea, we will ride out to Ackinnoull Manor and visit the Murdochs."

Bronwyn's eyes widened.

Strathmoor murmured, "Ah, so Miss Sorcha made an impression."

"Sorcha? *Nyet*, I go to see Bronwyn."

Me? Despite herself, Bronwyn couldn't help a flutter of happiness.

"Really? Even after you've met Sorcha?"

Her smile faded. Well. That was certainly harsh.

"Sorcha is too young." Bronwyn could almost hear the prince shrug. "And boring. She had nothing to say for herself the entire time we danced."

Bronwyn's good humor was gone. Sorcha was never boring! Had Alexsey made the slightest effort to speak, Bronwyn was certain Sorcha would have, too.

"Perhaps Miss Sorcha is shy." The viscount's voice was studiously disinterested. "She seemed pleasant enough to me when I danced with her."

Ha! Bronwyn could have kissed the viscount. Curiosity burning, she sidled around the statue and tried to catch a glimpse of them, but they were out of sight.

"Perhaps." The prince couldn't have sounded more bored. "If you like that sort of woman."

"Yes," Strathmoor drawled. "Men find ivory skin, petal-pink lips, and beautiful blue eyes far too mundane, and much prefer plumpness, freckles, and spectacles."

Bronwyn hadn't considered herself vain until this moment, but hearing herself dismissed so summarily hurt more than she'd have imagined. She peeked around the statue into the mirror on the opposite wall. She wasn't plain. Her features were good, her skin well enough even if it lacked Sorcha's creamy paleness, and her eyes were lively. Or so she'd thought until now.

Maybe she could see the men and judge their expressions better if she leaned out a bit. Moving carefully, she held on to the pillar and leaned forward. She could just see the prince's broad shoulder.

Frowning, she slipped an arm around Cupid and leaned out farther still. Now she could see both men in clear profile at the bottom of the steps.

The prince was shaking his head. "It is not about prettiness, which is as cheap as cheap wine, but about spirit, verve, passion. *That* is hard to find."

"I prefer a woman who saves her spirited responses for when we are alone."

The prince laughed and smacked Strath's shoulder. "This is why you and I never fight—we like different types of women. Like you, my grandmother favors Miss Sorcha."

There was a moment of silence. "Does she?"

"*Da*. Yesterday Tata Natasha asked many questions about my dance with the girl. If the Murdoch family meets Tata's approval, she'll sanction the match."

"And by sanction you mean—"

"Attempt to shove it down my throat."

"Ah. That kind of sanction. I wonder if that is not who awaits us at tea now. What does your grandmother say about the elder Miss Murdoch?"

"She's heard that Bronwyn is—how do you say—on the shelf? And that she has few social graces, which my grandmother holds very dear. Tata Natasha would never approve of Miss Murdoch, which is fine with me."

Strathmoor lifted a brow. "So you're still of a mind to pursue Miss Murdoch?"

"I will have her."

The words brushed over Bronwyn like a heated wind. He said it without hesitation, as if he already knew she would capitulate. And looking at him, his black hair falling over his brow, so tall and broad shouldered—

A shiver went through her, making her grip on the statue slip. Before she could fall, she pulled back into Cupid's shadows.

Papillon, who'd been sitting at Alexsey's feet, suddenly turned in her direction.

She held perfectly still. *No, don't come here. Please don't come here.*

But it was too late. The dog arose and trotted down the hallway, sniffing this way and then that, her bright eyes returning again and again to where Bronwyn was hidden.

She held her breath, willing the dog to stop, but to no avail: the dog came within a few paces and, tail wagging, looked directly at her.

"Go!" she whispered, glancing uneasily at the two men at the end of the hall.

The dog wagged her tail harder.

"Papillon, where are you?"

Bronwyn froze.

Alexsey sighed. "You silly mutt, what are you doing?"

The dog backed up two steps and barked, her tail wagging frantically. She looked from Bronwyn, down the hall, and then back at Bronwyn, as if wishing she could share the news of her find.

Bronwyn heard Alexsey's footsteps as he moved to look down the narrow hallway toward Papillon.

"What is it?" Strathmoor asked.

"I don't know. She probably smells a mouse."

Alexsey returned to the bottom of the stairs where Strathmoor waited, and Bronwyn sagged in relief.

Papillon, her plumed tail still wagging, sat down, her hopeful gaze fixed on Bronwyn.

She shook her head at the dog and then, as silently as she could, slipped an arm around the statue for balance and leaned forward to see both men.

"My grandmother will be the death of me," Alexsey said. "She wishes me to woo a woman in earnest, to find a wife. I've refused, but she still nags and nags. Worse, she's started threatening me with the loss of my birthright."

"Is she still dangling that ring before you?"

"Every chance she gets. She thinks to control me with it." The prince blew out his breath in an aggravated puff. "She is wrong."

"I wouldn't tell her that. I've never met a more decisive woman. Frankly, she scares me a bit."

"She can be overbearing." There was a moment of silence, and then Alexsey chuckled. "You know, there may be a way to silence her."

"You cannot kill your grandmother."

Alexsey laughed. "No, no. But I can perhaps stop her constant nagging, and prove that while I seek the *kaltso*, I will not sacrifice my principles."

"And how will you perform that miracle?"

"I will woo Miss Murdoch openly, court her for the world—and my grandmother—to see."

Bronwyn started, and her head banged against Cupid's quiver. She winced and gritted her teeth to keep from crying out.

Strathmoor sounded puzzled. "You wish to court Miss Murdoch in earnest?"

"It will *look* in earnest to everyone, including my grandmother. Which will make her worry that perhaps I am in love. She will then stop her infernal matchmaking and will instead attempt to convince me that perhaps she was hasty and I shouldn't court anyone at all. I already know she finds Miss Murdoch unqualified to be a princess."

Bronwyn found that, with the right encouragement, her hands could curl into claws.

"What's wrong with Miss Murdoch?"

"According to my grandmother, Miss Murdoch is too old for babies, too outspoken for a lady of quality, and has a decided lack of polish."

Oh! Bronwyn rubbed her pained head harder, scowling fiercely.

"I didn't know they'd met," Strathmoor said.

"They haven't. Tata Natasha has heard nothing but rumors from a vicar's wife. Sadly, Tata is quick to judge and slow to open her heart. She will never warm to Miss Murdoch now. Fortunately for me, all of the things Tata dislikes about Miss Murdoch, I find charming."

"Hmm. An interesting plan. But what about Miss Murdoch? She might believe your behavior, and think you are serious in courting her."

Bronwyn listened intently.

"I will never let it progress that far. Miss Murdoch doesn't desire marriage for herself. She told me so."

It stung like a betrayal to hear her opinions used in such a way, and casually thrown before Lord Strathmoor, whom she barely knew.

The prince's deep voice traveled through the foyer easily. "I will seduce Miss Murdoch in private but court her in public. I will kill the boredom of this visit, and keep my grandmother at bay, as well."

"And then?"

"And then, as we both desire, we will go our separate ways. It will be a charming several weeks, and we will both be the happier for it."

"I don't know, Alexsey." Strathmoor's voice held a note of concern. "It seems like a tenuous plan. Much could go wrong with it."

"Not as much as you might think."

"But Miss Murdoch—"

"Is the one thing I'm certain of. She will come to no harm, I promise. She is refreshingly honest and has already displayed a great aptitude for passion. I will tease her until she desires me beyond thought, and then I will satisfy that desire. I will be happy, my boredom dispelled. She will be happy and will have many good memories. And my grandmother will be silenced. It is perfection, *nyet*?"

"I suppose. So long as no one is injured, why not?"

"Exactly. Now come—let's get this tea over with so we may go for a ride. I've no wish to spend such a gloriously beautiful day indoors." He whistled. "Papillon!"

The dog bounded away to his master.

The prince's and viscount's booted feet echoed as they left the foyer.

"You'll have me, will you?" she muttered. "And then leave, eh? Ha! Just *try* to seduce me now!" She stepped out from behind the statue, her mind working furiously. How dare he so casually plan to amuse himself at her expense!

What an insufferable plan! What an insufferable *man*! She could imagine the reactions of her stepmother and sisters when she told them what she'd overheard. Mama would be upset to know he wasn't interested in Sorcha (or anyone, for that matter). Sorcha and Mairi would be as furious with the prince as she was, and would refuse to attend any events where he might be present. Which would be wonderfully loyal and . . .

Disastrous.

Bronwyn's London Season had been miserable because she'd known no one and didn't understand the rules of society. She couldn't allow the same fate to befall Sorcha. Even though her sister was naturally more sociable, every moment Sorcha spent at this castle, meeting the men and women who made up the guest lists of the season, growing accustomed to the complex rules of society, brought her closer to a happy future.

Which means I can't tell anyone about the prince's arrogant plan.

So how would she handle this problem? What would shake the prince's façade?

Perhaps . . . perhaps I shouldn't reject his courting. If I seem to capitulate, perhaps I can turn the tables on him; maybe I can make him want me. And then, when he is mad for me, I will laugh in his face and send him on his way, a humiliated but hopefully better man.

Yes. Why not? Imagining his expression, she bubbled with laughter. The day wasn't lost after all. Perhaps she—

The sound of a prancing dog echoed through the huge foyer.

"Blast it!" Bronwyn slipped behind the statue again, hoping against hope that Papillon would continue on her way. But the paw steps came closer . . . and closer. The second Papillon reached the statue she stopped, wagged her tail, and barked.

And then a deep, rich, deliciously accented voice said, "Roza? What are you doing?"

Chapter 10

Sir Mordred rubbed his hands together, his evil breath as foul as his soul. "I will never rest until she is mine!" Hearing him, Roland laughed. "Even evil cannot withstand the steel of a good heart."

—The Black Duke *by Miss Mary Edgeworth*

Bronwyn didn't know what to say as Alexsey, his arms crossed over his broad chest, regarded her with a questioning grin.

He was dressed in riding clothes, his boots sporting tassels, a neckcloth carelessly knotted about his strong neck. With his hair falling into his eyes, his firm mouth curved in a knowing smile, he looked mischievous and devastatingly handsome.

Her mind flying, she quickly slipped out from behind the statue. "I was admiring this statue." Nothing unusual at all. People admired statues all of the time, didn't they?

"Indeed?"

"It's extraordinary. I left the sitting room just now, where I'd been fetching my sister's reticule, and this astonishingly well-rendered Cupid caught my eye." She patted the statue while meeting Alexsey's gaze. "I find it enormously appealing."

Alexsey nodded to where her hand touched the statue. "You seem to have quite a *grip* on this particular subject matter."

She followed his gaze. "Oh!" Cheeks burning, she jerked her hand away from Cupid's private area, which was framed by fig leaves. "That was—I never meant to touch—" She closed her mouth, unable to say another word.

He chuckled. "Were you admiring the whole statue, or just . . ."

"All of it," she said firmly. "It's very lifelike."

"Roza, I promise you, *that* is not lifelike."

She regarded the statue again, this time with a critical eye. "It is for a Cupid. Or so I'd imagine." That didn't sound right. "I mean, so I would imagine *if* I had ever thought about it. Which I haven't. Until now, of course."

He laughed softly, the sound warming her like a fireplace on a chilly night. "Oh, Roza, Roza. I never need to wonder what you think." He captured her hand, tugging her closer.

She tried to resist, but her body tingled with instant awareness of him, her skin burning where he touched her. She instantly yearned for more . . . but this was exactly his plan. To seduce her into unwise decisions as a double convenience to himself—a way to satisfy those same desires in him, and to manipulate his grandmother.

Oh, how fun it was going to be to turn the tables on him. He wanted to seduce her, with no thought of her feelings or future? Well, she wanted to make him fall wildly, passionately, crazily in lust with her before she boldly dashed his hopes into dust.

She couldn't keep a pleased smile from her lips. Meeting in the woods, talking and kissing, then finding one another at a ball and dancing—those moments had been right out of one of her novels. And she had plenty of just such books that could show her how to achieve her plan—he wouldn't even know he was being led down the primrose path until he was deeply tangled in thorns.

Feeling giddy at her temerity, she gazed up at him, lowered her lashes, and said in a breathless voice, "Your Highness, we shouldn't be alone." *Not yet, anyway.*

After a surprised second, his eyes warmed and he moved closer. "Such is the burden we bear for society's sake." He captured her hand and kissed her fingers. "At some point, we must find our way back to your reading tree."

She ignored the tremors the brush of his lips sent through her and concentrated on his words. *Getting him to flirt with me is ridiculously easy, but I should go slowly or he'll suspect something.* She freed her hand. "That would be too risky, I fear."

"We are safer here, you think?" At her nod, he shrugged. "We are in plain view of the world. Besides, we have Papillon. She can be our chaperone."

"I'm not sure that will still wagging tongues."

"Perhaps. I—" He hesitated, as if a thought had just occurred to him. "Roza, I hope you do not mind my asking, but how long have you been in the hallway?"

She tried to keep her face expressionless. "A minute or two. Why?"

"So you didn't hear Lord Strathmoor and me come down the stairs earlier?"

She blinked. "Lord Strathmoor?" She glanced down the hall as if expecting to see the viscount. "Is he here, too?"

Alexsey regarded her with narrowed eyes. He wasn't certain if he believed her. On the one hand, it was suspicious as hell to find her standing behind the statue, but on the other, she returned his gaze so forthrightly that he couldn't help but feel she was telling the truth.

He hoped to the heavens she hadn't heard him talking to Strath. Not that his little plan was anything other than an excuse to be close to her, and what woman wouldn't see that for the compliment it was? Besides, she didn't appear angry or upset. Not even a little. So if she had heard, she didn't seem to hold it against him.

From what little he knew of her, he was certain she'd show her feelings. "Your family is with my grandmother, taking tea on the terrace."

"Yes, I was on my way there when Sorcha realized she'd left her reticule in the sitting room. And after I found it"—she smiled into his eyes—"I met you."

She didn't move closer. In fact, she didn't move at all. Yet Alexsey was aware of the warmth of her gaze, framed by her spectacles, and of the air of intimacy in her smile. They added a touch of come-hither that hadn't been there before.

Well. Perhaps it wouldn't take as much effort to seduce her as he'd thought. *She wishes for this as much as I.* The thought thrilled him. And the beauty of it was that, in courting her, he would have all the time in the world to answer her, to kiss her in new ways, to teach her— *Stop. Now is not the time to think of that.* He was becoming so impassioned, he wouldn't be able to think.

She smiled now, the sunlight from the side windows rippling over her hair and touching the brown with auburn. "I must join my mother and sisters; they will be wondering what has become of me."

"I shall escort you. I am having tea, as well."

"How fortunate for us both." She smiled and slipped her hand inside his elbow. "I thought you might have better things to do with your afternoon than take tea upon the terrace."

He covered her hand with his and smiled into her eyes. "No, little one. You are my only duty today."

Her lips, so ripe and full, returned his smile. "Then let us go."

He took a step forward, but then stopped. "Before we are back with the others and cannot speak, there is one thing I wish to know. . . ."

"Yes?"

"It is silly of me, but at the ball, you mentioned marriage."

Her smile faded, but only for a second. "Yes?"

"You said you did not desire it for yourself. May I ask why? We didn't have time to truly discuss that, and it has fascinated me."

"I am quite satisfied with my life as it is. Happy, even. I am an important part of my father's business;

he could not run it without me. Helping him allows me plenty of time for my books, and for my sisters." She shrugged. "What more could I wish for?"

That made sense. He nodded slowly as they began walking through the foyer, the dappled light flickering over them. "You seem to have a very rewarding life. I never met a woman who so boldly proclaimed she did not wish to marry. Most seem to wish for it very much. Perhaps too much."

"I'm not a mere girl right out of the schoolroom. I like my freedom as an unmarried lady. In fact, there's only one thing that would change my mind about marriage."

"Yes?"

"If I were to fall deeply in love."

He almost missed a step. "So there is a caveat."

"Yes, but I doubt it would ever happen. I've never been in love, and I doubt I ever shall be. I'm simply not the romantic sort."

"But the book you were reading in the woods—"

"—is fiction. I enjoy reading about pure hearts and fairy-tale love, but those don't often exist in real life. For that reason and others, it is highly unlikely I'll ever find love, and I'm perfectly content with that."

Alexsey nodded and took the first opportunity to change the subject. The conversation had reassured him, but it had also let him know that Strath had been right—as he and Bronwyn progressed with their flirtation, Alexsey would have to watch her carefully. If she seemed to be getting too attached to him, he'd end it. He had no desire to hurt her.

Meanwhile, he looked forward to the next few weeks, when he would court this woman in public and seduce her in private. She would enjoy both, he decided, though he rather thought she would find the seduction far more to her liking.

His gaze flickered over her as they walked, and he rejoiced in the lush curves of her body and the intelligent twinkle in her eyes. His body ached for hers, and he longed to sweep her into one of the many sitting rooms and show her the pleasure life had to offer those brave enough to enjoy them.

Soon, he promised himself. *Very soon. When she is ready and welcomes me.* From the way she was smiling at him now, that time wouldn't be long in arriving.

And with a returning smile, he opened the door to the terrace and led her out into the sunshine.

Chapter 11

Roland sat beside his little sister. "You are too young to know this, but love cannot grow in rocky soil. It must be planted in a tender heart, cared for with the gentlest of touches, warmed with happiness, and protected from all that might wish to harm it."

"That sounds like a lot of work," Melisandre said.

"It is a lot of work. But if it's true love, then it will be the lightest burden you'll ever carry."

—The Black Duke *by Miss Mary Edgeworth*

The next day, Alexsey walked down the grand stairs, his hat in one hand, his riding gloves in the other. A swift glance at the clock standing by the dining room doors told him he was late, and he hurried his steps.

Reaching the foyer, he told the butler, "I'm looking for Lord Strathmoor. Have you seen him?"

Davies replied, "He went toward the stables not ten minutes ago, on an errand for Sir Henry."

"I shall catch him there, if I can. We were to ride out together, but it seems he's forgotten."

"Shall I send a footman to see if he's left?"

"No. I'll go myself. It'll be quicker."

"Very good. Before you go, Your Highness, I should mention that—"

A hand closed over Alexsey's arm. Heavily wrinkled, the fingers were stained as if the owner stirred her tea with her bare fingers.

Davies offered an apologetic smile. "Her Grace has been looking for you since breakfast."

"And now she has found me." Alexsey covered the hand with his own and turned to his grandmother. "How are you this morning, Tata?"

"My back aches, my ankles are swollen, and I've a need for a good purge." She put a hand on her stomach and grimaced. "That turtle soup last night was too rich."

Alexsey exchanged an amused look with the butler. "Thank you, Davies. I believe I have it from here."

"Yes, Your Highness."

"Tata, though you may feel unwell, you look radiant."

"Pah!" she said. "Do not try to cozen me. I caught you trying to sneak away; do not deny it." She pointed to his riding boots.

He laughed. "Sneak? Through the front door in broad daylight? If I truly wished to slip away, you would not catch me."

"Ha!" She turned away, gesturing for him to follow her. "Come. Sir Henry has given over his Green Salon for my use while I am here. We will speak there."

This would be a good time to begin hinting to his grandmother that he was willing to change his ways and look for a wife. Then, of course, he'd admit to his intended target. He'd have to tread carefully and not give in too suddenly, though, or she'd know something was up. Tata Natasha was well versed in treachery. She would recognize it in another without even trying.

As they approached the salon, a footman hurried to hold open the door.

She paused beside the young man. "Papillon?"

"She has had a bath, as you requested, and is now being dried by one of the maids, Your Grace."

"Excellent. Once she's dry, put a blue riband on her neck and bring her here."

The footman bowed and the duchess swept into the parlor, Alexsey following behind.

As soon as the door closed, he said, "Poor Papillon, to be forced into a bath and then made to wear a riband."

"She would not have needed a bath at all if you and Strathmoor would stop taking her out to visit every mud puddle in Scotland," she sniffed, settling onto an overstuffed settee.

He came to stand beside the fireplace, looking with approval around the small, elegant salon. "It was very thoughtful of Sir Henry to set aside a room for you." Decorated in gold and green, it was both cozy and imposing. *Sir Henry knows my grandmother well. Very well.*

She glanced about her with indifference. "I prefer red, but this will do." She gestured to the chair across from her. "Sit. We will talk."

She spoke in Romany, her eyes locked on him as if she wished to pin him in place. "Where were you yesterday after tea? You were there, speaking with the Murdochs, and then poof! You disappeared like a ghost."

Alexsey made himself comfortable in the chair. "After tea, I went riding with Viscount Strathmoor. We returned while dinner was being served, so we ate in the breakfast room." *And drank a good bit of Sir Henry's best scotch, too.*

All in all, yesterday had been a very satisfying day. In addition to developing a most brilliant plan to gain some freedom from Tata Natasha's incessant complaints, he'd also found a way to spend time with his Roza. After tea, he and Strathmoor had ridden to Ackinnoull Manor, scouting the least-used roads around the house. They had ridden near the house, close enough to see the rambling manor through the trees, but they hadn't visited. Not yet.

Alexsey wanted to give Bronwyn some time to think about their conversation and, hopefully, of him. He'd found himself thinking about her, too. Wondering what she was doing, what she was thinking. He almost laughed at himself. He rarely bothered with such idle speculation, and yet this time he was awash in it. *Such is the price of being so bored—I am overly excited by every amusement.*

"You should not have been late for dinner." Tata shot him an impatient look. "That was rude."

"Sir Henry didn't even notice. I know, for I spoke to him this morning and he asked what I thought of the lamb at dinner."

"*I* noticed." She shook her head, her black eyes dour. "You should find a good wife and have some children. That will cool this hot blood of yours."

"It would chill my soul, that's for certain."

"Pah! You do not know what it would do. But"—she eyed him narrowly—"what did you think of our tea yesterday?"

"I wasn't fond of the small sandwiches, but the tarts were excel—"

"*Khvah tet!* If you cannot be serious, then be silent." She waited for a second, her fingers tapping a rapid beat upon the arm of the settee. "You know exactly what I mean; what did you think of the Murdochs?"

"They seem like a fine family."

"They are more than fine. Though not wealthy, they are of exemplary birth. Lady Malvinea is the daughter of an earl, and Mr. Murdoch's family line can be traced back to William the Conqueror."

"You found out all of that at tea?"

She frowned. "No. Sir Henry explained their lineage to me. And you have not answered my question. What did you think of the Murdochs?"

"The mother seems frightening. She didn't stop smiling the entire time she was here. I began to wonder if she was frozen that way."

"She is a bit high-strung," Tata said grudgingly. "But a woman of sense where her daughters are concerned. What about the daughters?"

"The youngest told a very funny story about a ride she went on. She fell in the mud, and a pig—"

"*Da, da.* I heard it. What about the other?"

"The oldest daughter? She has a lovely laugh." He would bet his best dueling pistols that she had lovely breasts, too. "She was charming." And he was charmed.

"Yes, yes, but—" Tata leaned forward. "What about Miss Sorcha?"

He returned her look.

Tata raised her brows.

He lifted one shoulder. "She's very pretty, of course."

"Pretty? She's *krysivyj*." Tata Natasha glared at him as if daring him to say otherwise.

"Fine. She's beautiful. But she also seemed . . . rather predictable."

Tata Natasha muttered a Gypsy curse. "Oh! I would that you had given the poor girl a chance. Talked to her. Gotten to know her, at least, before you damned her with your words."

That was almost humorous, when he thought of how she'd done the same to Bronwyn. "Tata, I'm afraid Miss Sorcha's not—" He spread his hands wide. "She's not the one."

"How do you know?"

"I've met this woman. I've observed her. I've spoken to her. I even danced with her. And now I've had tea with her. And she's not for me."

Tata's frown deepened. "She's beautiful, young, well-born, intelligent—everything a prince would wish for in a bride and more."

"Except interesting."

"I can't believe you do not find her appealing."

"I find very few women appealing." He leaned back in his chair. "Father said it was the same for him until he met Mother. Then, he said, it was like a lightning bolt." Alexsey thought about how they looked at one another, how he often caught them holding hands or kissing as if they were newly married. *And after so many years. That is passion.* "I don't believe I'll ever have that."

Her expression softened. "Oh, Lexsey. Who has hurt you so badly that you believe that?"

Surprised, he laughed. "No one has hurt me."

She regarded him closely. "Never? Not even once?"

"Not even a little. Am I not blessed?"

"That is not a blessing, but a curse."

"Nonsense." He winked at her. "You worry too much. Have no fear that I'll be hurt. I'm always in control of my emotions."

"And the women you have been with before this? Did you feel nothing for them?"

"Nothing that didn't disappear after I had to face them over breakfast twice in a row."

Tata Natasha threw up her hands, the sleeves of her gown fluttering. "Pah! I do not know why I even talk to you."

"Because I am your favorite grandson, and you love me more than all of my brothers."

"*Nyet.* You are the most *frustrating* of my grandsons. Find a good woman, marry her, have children—then you will be my favorite."

"Perhaps I shall settle for second favorite. What would that take?"

"Cease your infernal teasing. I am serious." She folded her hands together, her eyes shimmering with emotion. "Alexsey, it is fate that you are here. You will meet someone here who can make you happy and help you fulfill your destiny as prince, if you'll just open your eyes and heart. I know this. Do not ask me how, but I do."

"Are you a fortune-teller now, oh queen of the Gypsies?"

She didn't laugh. "I have the blood of a seer, *da*. But I have the soul of a grandmother and as the *phuri dai* of our *kumpania*, I know things that can and will be."

"So you think love might strike me like lightning, as it did Father."

"The person struck by lightning doesn't always know it has happened, not at first. The only question is who the fortunate woman will be. If you won't have Miss Sorcha, we will keep looking. During breakfast this morning, Sir Henry mentioned a family that's related to the king. The MacDougals or MacDonalds— Pah, I can't remember, what with the MacThises and the MacThoses. They have two daughters of marriageable age—*young* daughters, well brought up, and quite beautiful. Those qualities are important to consider in regard to your official duties."

"Tata, I am one of *four* princes. Nikki will take the throne as the oldest. Grisha will oversee the army. And Wulf has the good sense to make certain the royal coffers are overflowing with gold."

"So?"

"So there is no need for me to marry."

"If you wish to wear the *kaltso*, you will marry."

"Grandfather already had the ring when you met him; he was not married."

"Your grandfather was different; he was responsible for his family from the age of seventeen. You had no such weight upon your shoulders."

His jaw tightened. "You must admit that it is not a

requirement of the position that I wed. It is only you who think it necessary."

She shrugged. "I will admit that."

"That's scarcely fair."

"You will be better for it. Trust me. It is the one thing your father and I agree on—that you should marry before taking on the *kaltso*."

"*Bozhy moj,* you and Father never agree on anything."

"We agree on this."

He slid her a look under his lashes and then pretended to frown thoughtfully. "That is too much, even for me. I can fight you, or I can fight Father, but I cannot fight the both of you."

Her gaze narrowed, an arrested expression on her face. "What do you mean?"

"Perhaps you are right. I wish it were otherwise, but . . . Fine. I will start taking this endeavor of yours more seriously. As much as it pains me, I will start thinking about taking a wife. But just thinking about it. No more."

She couldn't have looked more pleased. "You mean that?"

He sighed. "I do."

"Very good. Very, very good!" She rubbed her hands together. "We must find a good candidate. It's a pity you won't give Miss Sorcha the time of day. Of all the women at the ball, she seemed to— It does not matter." Tata waved her hand generously. "If she is not for you, then we shall find another."

He rubbed his chin. "Actually . . . there *was* a woman I found intriguing. . . ."

She leaned forward, all eagerness. "Oh?"

"The oldest Murdoch daughter."

She sat back in her chair. "What?"

"She has a way about her. . . . I do not know what it is, but there was something. I like that she is no innocent miss, too. An older woman would please me."

"You are serious?"

"Of course. She is the only woman I've found interesting."

Tata made a noise that sounded like a cat choking on a piece of string. "*Nyet!* She is too old! She'll never have children."

"She's only twenty-four."

"Soon to be twenty-five, and would be even older by the time you courted and married her. Add another year to conceive a child, she could be twenty-seven or twenty-eight, much too old." Tata shook her head. "There must be someone else."

He pretended to think, his grandmother's eyes upon him. Finally he said, "*Nyet.*"

She scowled. "Of all the women at the ball, you like only this one, a woman too old to have children, dowdy and plain and plump and—"

"Miss Murdoch is neither plain nor plump." To his surprise, a faint flare of irritation invaded his good humor. "She's attractive and lively. And for once, I have met a respectable woman I wish to know better." That was true, at least.

"She isn't—"

"Do you or do you not wish me to take my responsibilities more seriously?"

"I do," Tata said in a sour voice.

"Then stand back and let me. I will spend some time with Miss Murdoch, get to know her, see if this lightning strikes or not. And if, at the end of a few weeks, she still intrigues me, perhaps I'll ask for her hand in m—"

"Don't be so hasty! Courting is not something one rushes into."

Alexsey hid a grin. Ten minutes ago, Tata Natasha would have said the opposite. He shrugged. "I am intrigued by Miss Murdoch, and I'm rarely even that. Perhaps that is enough."

"She is too old, she wears spectacles, and her hair is never as it should be. Yesterday she came to tea with a *cobweb* in her hair."

Sir Henry's maids should dust the statuary more often. "She may not possess the sort of beauty the poets write of, but it is there. It is quieter, softer." *It shines in her eyes and bubbles with laughter from her lips.* Alexsey caught himself and nearly laughed. *I'm being almost poetic.*

He continued, "And fortunately for my new directive to spend time with Miss Murdoch, I'm to accompany Lord Strathmoor to visit some of the local families. I'm sure we'll stop to visit Ackinnoull, where I'll sit over a cup of tepid tea and admire the length of Miss Murdoch's astonishing eyelashes." *If fate smiles, I may even win another kiss from the plump lips of the most intriguing Scottish lass I've met yet.*

Strath's voice drifted from the foyer.

"Ah, there he is now." Alexsey bent and kissed his Tata's forehead. "I will find you when I return. Meanwhile, enjoy your visit with Sir Henry."

"Forget Sir Henry." She caught Alexsey's hand and held it between her own, her eyes narrowed. "Do you really like this Miss Murdoch?"

"I am truly interested in her." That much was true.

Finally, with a short nod, she released him. "Go. Have your fun. But do not think you can hide from love. The right woman will find you—and when she does, you will never be the same."

Alexsey laughed. "I'm not sure if I should hide or arm myself, but I promise you this, Tata: when I am done, you will happily hand me the *kaltso*." And with that, he left to meet Strath.

Chapter 12

*At the dinner party, no fewer than fourteen important in-
troductions had been made, three couples had flirted outra-
geously over the beef, and during dessert, one eager young
gentleman had made so bold as to ask a certain young lady's parents for an audience to "beg a favor." Lucinda's
aunt declared the affair a most happy one.*

*Yet Lucinda could not be so excited. The couples who
had flirted were all married to others, the introductions
had been orchestrated by grimly determined mamas wishing their sons and daughters to marry for wealth rather
than happiness, and the young lady who'd been forced
to endure the unwanted advances of the drunken gentleman who'd asked her parents for an audience had burst
into tears when her father had joyously agreed to hear the
young man's request. All in all, Lucinda thought the evening a sad waste of time.*

—The Black Duke *by Miss Mary Edgeworth*

In her sitting room on the top floor of Ackinnoull
Manor, Bronwyn dropped another book onto a pile at
her feet. Slips of paper stuck out from the book covers
in the stack, all marking crucial passages. Somewhere

within the pages of her favorite novels was the answer she sought. Ever since she'd overheard the prince at Tulloch the day before, she'd been consumed with one question: *how does one make an arrogant prince fall in love?*

She stretched her feet toward the fire, causing the sleeping Walter to stir on the rug before the snapping flame. Of course, it wouldn't be true love. But a strong infatuation would do, the sort that hinted at exciting things to come and left one breathless with potential. Just enough so that when she finally revealed that she'd known of his caddish intentions all along, he felt a powerful sense of loss. It was the only fair punishment.

She picked up *The Lady of Beaumont* and began to page through it. Within these books were some well-kept secrets of womanhood that she needed. That was the beauty of novels: in the middle of the fantasy were golden kernels of truth. Like when Miss Edgeworth described the pernicious social appetite of society mamas, or when Lady V wrote about the frustrations of a young woman who'd lost her mother. Bronwyn knew those moments well. To her, they'd been very real and, sweetened by the sweeping romance of the rest of the pages, all the more poignant.

She picked up the list she'd been making. So far she had three items that held some promise. In *Castle Graystone* by the divinely talented Lady V (who was supposedly a true member of the peerage, although Bronwyn suspected that rumor to be a ploy to sell more books), she'd found a passage that described how the hero's reason had been swept away by the faintest hint of the heroine's perfume. At one point, he'd even found himself stealing her kerchief to carry her scent with him.

She tapped a finger on the page. Where did one find a scent that no other woman might have? That could prove tricky, but she'd think of something.

The next hidden gem was from one of her favorite tomes by the ever-popular Miss Henrietta Opal, *My Lady Lost*. Bronwyn had discovered three pages devoted to how the hero admired the heroine's dulcet tones as she sang while playing the pianoforte. Bronwyn didn't play the pianoforte, nor did she often sing in public, but her voice was quite acceptable. At least, it was no better or worse than anyone else's. She pursed her lips. It might be worth a try.

The last hint in seduction came from one of her favorite books of all time, *Dark Castle*, written by the prolific Mary Edgeworth. In this book, the heroine—a lady of great resources who spent the better part of two chapters precariously balanced on the windswept ledge of a rain-lashed castle as she orchestrated an escape from her evil cousin's clutches—had captivated the hero with her deep knowledge of his family home and estate, both of which were real locations that carried historical significance, which made the book all the more enjoyable. Bronwyn would have to find the book on Oxenburg that Mama had read.

Feeling more hopeful, she yawned and stretched her arms before her, peering out the window to where the sun spilled onto the rooftop. Her rooms consisted of a sitting room, a dressing room, and a small, cozy bedchamber. Back when Ackinnoull Manor had housed a wealthy miller and his large, growing family, these rooms had made up the nursery suite.

Lady Malvinea hadn't been happy when Bronwyn had asked to move to this floor, but to everyone's surprise, Papa had agreed. Bronwyn thought he knew the real reasons she'd wished for the upper floor to herself—so that she'd have some peace and quiet so she could read and, most importantly, sneak her dogs in and out of the house without Lady Malvinea knowing.

She bent down and patted Scott's head, which lay in her lap. "I expected Alexsey to visit yesterday, but he never came. The duchess must be keeping him busy. But that is good; it'll give me time to prepare."

Scott rested his chin on her knee, his large brown eyes so soulful, she was forced to kiss his forehead. "Prince or no, Alexsey will never be as adorable as you."

Scott wagged his tail.

Despite the sting of being used, she couldn't stop thinking about the first time she'd met Alexsey, when he'd merely been a handsome huntsman. *Those kisses.* She shivered at the memory. Kisses were far more exciting than she'd realized.

But that was all in the past. Now she was dealing with a smug prince who deserved a setdown, and planning how to do that was unexpectedly exciting.

Yet the whole thing had her topsy-turvy. Though she was prepared to give as good as she got, she couldn't stop her well-fed imagination from whispering, *Is that all? Don't you really want more?*

She might want more—but the real question was, should she?

It had been disconcerting to discover that some princes really *were* make-your-knees-weak handsome. It seemed unfair of fate to put such handsome men on earth and then give them flaws like arrogance and— Well, that was really the only flaw she knew he had, but there were sure to be more. And they would all help her resist his seduction attempts.

Which would be difficult: they had already kissed, and the memory of those alone tempted her. And oh, what delicious kisses those had been. They still made her skin tingle, her heart pound, her nipples harden—

Argh! She moved Scott's chin from her knee and stood. "Princes and kisses. Both should be avoided by people with large imaginations who—"

Someone came running up the steps; then the door popped open and Mairi stumbled in. Her hair was a mess, a comb sticking out over one ear, her gown wrinkled where she'd grasped it with both hands as she'd galloped up the stairs.

She placed a hand on her chest and leaned against the doorframe, panting.

"Goodness! What's gotten into you?" Bronwyn asked.

"Mama—says—you—all of us—must come—now! The prince—Strathmoor—sent a note!"

A swell of excitement warmed her. *Finally!* "When will they be here?"

"Mama says—we are to be—in the sitting room— ready—by noon!"

"Excellent." Bronwyn glanced at the clock. "That's a half hour, just enough time to get ready. Thank you,

Mairi. And walk back to your room. You won't be fit to speak to anyone if you run up and down the stairs like a terrier looking for a rat."

With a grin, Mairi left, her footsteps only slightly slower as she went downstairs.

Meanwhile, Bronwyn hurried toward her wardrobe, then stopped short. If she dressed in something bonnier than usual, it would make the prince think she wasn't the woman he'd met in the woods. And he'd been attracted to that woman. To plain old her, without the frills and furbelows her mother thought so necessary to secure a man's attention.

Well. Perhaps I just learned one lesson in seduction—use what works. Smiling to herself, she turned to the dogs. "I won't change, then. Let him see me as I am. Meanwhile, it's time I let you two out to play."

At the word "out," both dogs rose to their feet, stretching and yawning.

Humming to herself (she really did have a nice voice), she took the dogs downstairs and let them out the back door to roam the fields. "Don't chase Mr. MacGregor's sheep. He'll come a'yelling if you do."

With nearly fifteen minutes still left on the clock, she stopped long enough to collect a cup of tea and a biscuit from Cook before making her way to the sitting room. As the frantic sounds from the upstairs bedchambers were audible, she wasn't surprised to find herself alone.

She finished the small biscuit and put her tea on a side table as she walked to the shelves that lined one side of the room. There, she looked up and down until she found the tome on Oxenburg that Mama had mentioned.

Within moments, she was pages deep into the book.

Later she heard the door open and Papa wandered in, a messy stack of papers in his hand, a harassed look on his face. He was a slight man of slender build, with brown eyes and a mass of thick white hair that never seemed to have been combed, though her stepmother made certain it was done at least once a day. Ink stains marred his left hand, while a large inkblot colored the center of his crooked cravat where a pin should have rested.

He brightened on seeing Bronwyn. "I've been a-lookin' all over for you, wee 'un."

"How odd to see you abovestairs," she teased, setting her book aside. "It's not even dinnertime."

He looked at the clock, mild confusion flickering over his face. "Is it time for dinner already?"

"Not quite yet. And you'd be sorry to miss it, for Cook has made apple tarts especially for you."

Papa brightened. "Well! Tha' is something to look forward to, then." He squinted at the book she'd left beside her chair. "Oxenburg, eh? Interesting country, tha'."

"Why do we have a book about it?"

"Two of the researchers I correspond with are from there. I wanted to know a little aboot their country."

"It's very interesting. What are you doing out of your workshop at this time of the day? Mama must have mentioned our visitors."

He grimaced and, with a harried look at the open

door, said in a greatly lowered voice, "Is tha' what she came blithering aboot down in me workshop? I was runnin' the new gas machine and couldna hear a word she said, but dinna wish to hurt her feelin's, so I just nodded and went on with my business."

Bronwyn patted his shoulder. "That's all right. I'm sure Mama didn't wish you to join us, or she'd have asked you to change your clothes."

His brows knit. "She might ha' said somethin' aboot tha', but I dinna know. 'Twas too noisy in the shop. But now tha' I have ye here, perhaps ye can help me with some correspondence while we're waiting. I canno' find me spectacles to save me life."

Chuckling, she rose on her tiptoes and slipped his spectacles from the top of his head back to his nose. "They were hiding on your head, as they always do."

Papa grimaced. "I should ha' looked there first, bu' I was distracted by this letter fra' Lord Watt."

"About the rotative gear?"

"Aye, aye. He questions all of the reports I've sent, and wonders if the gear is truly as efficacious as the tests show, the bloody arse!"

She frowned. "Lord Watt thinks you're forging the results?"

"He hints at just tha', though he's no' mon enou' to come right out and say so." Papa scowled. "I hate such mealymouthed methods."

"Oh dear. That doesn't sound like Lord Watt at all. He's usually so direct. Perhaps I should read the letter?"

He dutifully handed it to her.

She read it quickly, her brow clearing as she turned the page. "Papa, Lord Watt doesn't question your results. He just says he can't read your handwriting, and asks you to use a chart to display your findings. That's all."

"Oh!" Papa squinted at the letter she'd returned. "Hmm." He sent her a hesitant look over the rim of his spectacles. "Perhaps I should look up Lord Watt's last paper on propulsion and see wha' format he used for testing? If I matched tha', he might better understand my results."

She arched a brow at him. "I take it you'd like me to find that paper for you?"

He brightened instantly. "Och, me wee, sweet bairn, tha' would be jus' the thing."

"It should be in the bound works from the Royal Society. The newest version is in your study. I'll look after dinner."

"Tha' would be lovely." He adjusted his spectacles and then returned to the messy stack of papers and began shuffling through them. "Also, I received a letter fra' Knightley and he says the patent description you wrote was perfect, and the drawing quite thorough, too." He beamed, pressing a kiss to her forehead. "You are a treasure, Bronwyn. I dinna know wha' I'd do without you."

Normally, when Papa said such things, Bronwyn would hug him or tell him not to worry, for she had no plans to be elsewhere than at Ackinnoull with him. But for some reason, the words stuck in her throat. In that instant, in a wild, unfettered moment, she had an image of herself and Alexsey, kissing under her favorite reading tree.

It was a ludicrous vision and she instantly banished it, but the memory lingered. *Do I really wish to be here for the rest of my life? Will I still feel useful, filing Papa's patents when I'm thirty? Forty? Fifty? Will there come a day when I'll wish I'd lived a more adventuresome life?*

It was funny, but before she'd met the prince, she'd never thought about such things. Now she was aware of—not a lacking in her life, for that implied she'd been dissatisfied, which wasn't true—but a lack of ambition on her part when considering her future. Perhaps that was because Sorcha and Mairi had come into Bronwyn's life when normally, she would have been dreaming of her own happy ever after. Whatever it was, somewhere along the way she'd stopped thinking of her future as being any different from her present, which was a great injustice. Things would change; *she* would change. Sorcha and Mairi would marry and have families of their own, while she—

She frowned. What would she do?

She captured her ridiculous imagination and forced it back into its box. *Of course I'll still be happy. Papa and I make a good team, and his work is so important.*

Footsteps sounded on the stairs and then Lady Malvinea swept into the room, followed by Sorcha and Mairi. "Perfect!" she said, smiling brightly. The smile faltered when she saw Papa's ink-stained cravat. "You didn't change your clothes."

He blinked, clearly surprised at the idea. "Why would I do tha'? 'Tis no' time for bed."

"You are hopeless." But she smiled again as she shook her head and placed a peck on her husband's cheek.

He turned pink and shuffled from foot to foot, looking for all the world like a schoolboy. "Och, Malvinea. No' in front of the girls."

Mama laughed. "It cannot hurt our daughters to know that a restrained show of affection between a husband and wife is perfectly acceptable in the privacy of one's own parlor."

Bronwyn eyed her stepsisters' brightly hued gowns. "Dressed like princesses for the prince. Very pretty!"

Papa's brows knit. "The prince? What prince?"

Lady Malvinea sighed. "Murdoch, I expressly visited your workshop not thirty minutes ago to tell you we were expecting guests—important guests!"

"Ah yes, so you did. I ah, I forgot in the excitement of—" He waved the papers. "I had letters and Bronwyn needed to help and—"

"And you didn't hear a word I said," Mama said impatiently. "You *do* remember that you agreed to go with me to Tulloch Castle to see Sir Henry, to return the honor of the prince's and Strathmoor's visit today?"

Papa instantly looked contrite, even as he shifted toward the door. "I promised to visit Sir Henry?"

"Yes. And soon. He's in residence at Tulloch now, but heaven knows how long he'll stay."

Bronwyn's happier thoughts instantly dimmed. *How soon will the prince leave?*

"Tulloch Castle, eh?" Papa eyed the door now, looking as if he'd like to disappear out of it.

"In fact," Lady Malvinea said, warming to the topic, "it would be appropriate for us to call on Sir Henry tomorrow, even though it *is* pushing things a small bit. Were these normal circumstances we should wait another day or two before we returned the courtesies."

"But Malvinea, I'm quite busy right now, wha' with my new gear system and—"

"William," Lady Malvinea said firmly. "Just one visit. For your daughters."

"Of course. Of course." Papa backed toward the door with more certain steps. "Seein' as how I'm not dressed for the visit today, per'aps I should go and leave the prettier ones in the household to do the pleasantries."

"No. You must at least greet the prince. You don't have to stay for the whole visit, though." She sighed, but waved him on. "Go. I'll send one of the girls to fetch you once the prince arrives."

He agreed with a sigh. "I will be in my workshop."

"And tomorrow you'll escort us to Tulloch?" Mama asked.

"Aye, as soon as my model is finished and I've answered a few letters and tried to make a chart t' show the . . ." His voice trailed off as he vanished out the door.

Bronwyn saw the flash of hurt in her stepmother's eyes. "Papa always hides from humanity when he's in the grip of a new invention," she said soothingly.

"He's never comfortable with people." Mairi hopped up to fetch a pillow from the chair by the window.

Mama forced a smile. "He's the shyest man I've ever met. It's a wonder he gathered up the nerve to propose to me."

"He loves you," Bronwyn said softly. "There's no other reason he'd have done so."

Mama's smile quavered a moment, and she quickly bent to stir the coals, her face now hidden from view. "I do wish the maid would learn to make a proper fire."

Bronwyn wondered if she should say something else or perhaps even hug her stepmother, but the older woman wasn't comfortable with displays of affection. It was one of the many ways she differed from Bronwyn's mother, and perhaps one reason Papa had chosen her.

Mother had been bubbly light, the house filled with laughter, muddy shoes, and stories by the fireplace. When Mother was alive, the curtains and tabletops had never been free from dust, but the walls had been warmed by laughter. Lady Malvinea, meanwhile, kept Ackinnoull perfectly clean, the draperies ironed, the bed linens always fresh. No hint of dust was ever allowed to gather. The house was perfect, but colder.

Bronwyn thought her father felt that loss keenly. Once Lady Malvinea and her daughters had been installed in their home, he'd seemed to find more and more reasons to stay in his workshop, away from the family, leaving them to their own devices.

It's not fair. No matter Lady Malvinea's faults, she was capable of great love. Though Bronwyn had very little interest in the things that stirred her stepmother, she was deeply grateful for the older woman's efforts to include her.

Mama replaced the poker and came to join them. "Well, my dears! We must discuss the prince's visit." She sank into a chair, collecting herself enough to send a teasing look at Bronwyn. "We sadly missed you at breakfast. Reading another book, were you?"

"Yes, I was rereading some of my favorite scenes." *Plotting the punishment of a certain prince.*

"I would like to read *The Black Duke* when you finish." Mairi plopped down on the settee, her skirts billowing.

"Mairi, your manners!"

"No one is looking, Mama."

"As I've told you time and again, a lady never forgets her manners, even in private."

Mairi sighed. "I'll try, but I can't imagine everyone actually acts in private the way they do in public, never putting their feet up or talking about anything other than the weather and the latest gossip in London. Well, except old Mr. Grisham from MacCuen Hall." She grinned. "I'll wager he does exactly the same in private as he does in public, which is to fondle maids, belch loudly, and drink ale."

"Mairi, Mairi!" Mama pinched the bridge of her nose between two fingers as if she had a sudden headache.

Sorcha and Bronwyn barely held their laughter.

Schooling her expression, Sorcha patted Mairi's arm. "Mama is right; please show some comportment."

"I'm showing comportment. Besides, I'm not the one wearing muddy boots."

All eyes turned to Bronwyn.

"I'm sorry. I went for a walk early this morning, and completely forgot about my boots."

Mama glanced at the clock. "Sadly, there's not enough time for you to change them. You'll just have to wear them as they are. Tuck them back under your skirts, please. That will have to do."

Mairi turned a pouting face toward Mama. "How come you never worry about Bronwyn's clothes?"

"Bronwyn is twenty-four, my dear, past the age to be wishful of a suitor."

Though she'd thought the exact same thing herself many times, the words hit Bronwyn with a new force, her stepmother's tone damning in its casual finality. Good God, *was* she too old to ever have a suitor? Why did that stark sentence pinch so much?

Mama caught her surprised look and, with a concerned frown, added, "Not that you couldn't do so if you tried, but you seem content with the way things are."

"I am—I mean, I have been. I've never met a man I wished to marry." *Just one I enjoy kissing.*

That was a beginning, wasn't it?

Mama's expression softened. "Perhaps one day you'll meet someone who will change your mind."

And perhaps someone was well on his way to doing so. Or had been, until she'd seen his true colors.

Sorcha smiled at Bronwyn. "The truth is that you are too in love with the men in your novels to spare your time on mere mortals. How can one compete with Miss Edgeworth's Roland?"

Mairi clasped her hands together beneath her chin and stared dreamily into the air. "Oh, Roland!"

Bronwyn couldn't keep back a chuckle. "Fortunately, I am well aware of the vast difference between fact and fiction. And speaking of facts, Sorcha, it dawned on me last night that you've barely mentioned your dance with the prince when we were at the ball."

Mairi turned her attention to her sister. "Did the prince dance as well as Lord Strathmoor? It seemed to me the viscount was lighter on his feet."

"The viscount was the better dancer." She didn't seem at all happy about it. "Although his manners left much to be desired. I was glad when our dance was over."

"Viscount Strathmoor is not a concern," Mama said. "I asked about him, thinking he might do well for Mairi, but he has almost no income and, despite his close relationship to Sir Henry, does not stand to inherit in that direction, either."

"A pity," Mairi agreed. "I thought he had kind eyes, but—" She dusted her hands. "I shall focus my attentions elsewhere, for I'm determined to wed a wealthy man. I've books to buy and gowns to purchase, jewels to wear, and—oh, a thousand very *expensive* things."

Bronwyn had to laugh.

Sorcha smiled but said in her soft tone, "Mairi, a wealthy man will never consider you if you behave like a hoyden in public."

Mairi sniffed. "At tea, the prince laughed no fewer than four times when he spoke with me. I didn't see him so much as smile when he was with you. He even yawned. I saw him!"

"Now Mairi, that's not true," Mama chided. "The prince smiled quite pleasantly both at tea and the ball when he took Sorcha into the set. They made quite a pretty pair, too, if I say so myself. Several ladies in attendance said something to me about Sorcha's gracefulness later, and they were all very complimentary about her comportment, too, which is very telling. In general, women are much harsher critics than men."

Bronwyn had never seen her stepmother quite so happy.

Sorcha adjusted her shawl over her shoulders. "I'm cold."

"It's always cold in here," Mairi said. "The sun never warms this side of the house. We should add some more coal to the fire—"

"Here." Bronwyn picked up a lap blanket from where it hung over the back of the settee and handed it to Mairi. "This will keep you warm."

As she handed the blanket to Mairi, a sudden breeze burst down the chimney, puffing smoke into the room. Sorcha and Mairi cried out, coughing and covering their faces, while Bronwyn hurried to throw open the window.

Her arm pressed over her face, Lady Malvinea waved at the smoky air with her skirt. "I wish Murdoch would have that flue fixed."

The smoke slowly seeped out, replaced by colder air.

"Close the window!" Sorcha cried once the smoke had mostly cleared.

"Yes, yes," Mairi agreed. "It's even colder now!"

Bronwyn closed and latched the window and returned to their settee.

Sorcha shivered and looked longingly at the coal bin. "Mama, surely we can add more coal, with guests coming soon. Then the room will be the perfect temperature for a nice visit."

As if on cue, a horse neighed outside, the noise followed by the unmistakable sounds of male voices.

The women exchanged startled looks, and then Mairi and Sorcha leapt to their feet and raced to the window, peering through the curtains.

"It's the prince," Mairi exclaimed, "with Viscount Strathmoor!"

Mama was on her feet in a trice. "And the room is still smoky!"

She added coal to the fire and then began snapping out orders like a general in the heat of battle. "Sorcha, run and tell your papa we have guests and he must come immediately. And don't take no for an answer. Mairi, pull the shades a bit; a shaded room will hide the threadbare carpet, not to mention we will all look the better for it.

"Bronwyn, run to the kitchen and tell Mrs. Pitcairn we'll need tea immediately, and not to even think of using those hard scones she tried to serve yesterday. Tell her to fix a nice pot of the bohea, and not to be shy about the leaves, and to serve the apple tarts she was saving for dinner tonight. There are only four of them, so have her cut them in half. That will make eight, although none of us should ask for any, in case His Highness or Lord Strathmoor might wish for two."

Lady Malvinea waved her hands. "Off with you! It will take His Highness only a few moments to secure his horse and ring the bell, and everything must be perfect!"

Sorcha scurried off to do her mother's bidding while Mairi hurried to the curtains and started arranging them as she'd been instructed.

Bronwyn lingered by the doorway. "Must we sacrifice our dessert for mere visitors? I doubt they'll stay long enough to eat them, anyway."

"Bronwyn, these things—balls and morning visits and even apple tarts—are all sacrifices we must make if we wish Sorcha and Mairi to succeed." Mama fluffed pillows and folded up the discarded blankets and shawls, leaving the faint scent of rosewater in her wake. "If we do things right and make His Highness feel welcome here, then we will see much more of him."

"And you think an apple tart would bring the prince back for more visits?"

"La, child, I've seen men climb cliffs for a side of beef, so yes. Just think what your papa would do for black pudding! Men have their favorite dishes, and they often hear better when you speak to them through their stomachs. Oh dear—do hurry, for I think I hear footsteps upon the portico! Have Mrs. Pitcairn answer the door, too, would you?"

Bronwyn hurried to the kitchen. Today she would smile, seem interested in whatever the prince had to say, and laugh at his jokes. *I know a few things about Oxenburg, too, which should charm him. He'll believe I think it the most lovely of all countries and that by dint of being its prince, I think the same of him. In his weak mind, that will affirm what he's already decided: that I can easily be wooed with soft words.*

She just couldn't allow herself to think about those dratted kisses. *Talk about Oxenburg, let him think I find him fascinating, pretend to be interested,* she repeated over and over as she headed down into the kitchen.

Chapter 13

Gentle reader, never ask a woman for her thoughts. Some things are best left to the imagination.
—The Black Duke *by Miss Mary Edgeworth*

Ackinnoull Manor was situated on a lovely knoll, the long green lawn reaching to a stand of trees that encircled it. Alexsey placed his hand upon one of the columns that supported the portico. "This is a lovely old house. Tudor, I should think, though not in the traditional style, since it's built of stone."

Strath, who stood in the drive, glanced at the house indifferently. "You think it's that old?"

"I know it is. Look at the windows. But these"—Alexsey patted the impressive column—"are newer. This portico was added in the eighteenth century, I would think, less than a hundred years ago." He shrugged at Strath's questioning look. "A good prince is a master of many useless trivial arts. That, and I read."

"You read far more than is healthy. You could go blind squinting at pages so much, you know." Strath tied up his horse, climbed the steps to the portico, and reached for the bellpull.

A deep, long gong sounded, echoing with a somber timbre. "Good God, that's a frightening sound. Exactly what one might expect to hear in a crypt." He glanced right and then left and then said in a much lower voice, "Which is not at all surprising, considering Lady Malvinea lives here. Gives me the shivers, that woman does. And her daughters . . ." He shook his head.

"I thought you found Miss Sorcha a beauty."

Strath shrugged. "She is, if one likes the insipid blond sort. By the way, I did some research for you about Miss Murdoch, and I have some very bad news. Horrible news, in fact. She's a demmed bluestocking."

"What is this bluestocking?"

"A woman who fancies herself a member of the intelligentsia." He lowered his voice. "It's against the laws of nature."

Alexsey lifted his brows. "Why are you whispering? Afraid of bluestockings, are you?"

"All smart men are. They like to argue. A lot. And often."

"Ah. Then yes, I think Bronwyn is indeed a member of this black-stocking group."

"Bluestocking. They're horrid. A man can't have a day's worth of peace with them about."

"Perhaps I do not want peace, but excitement. Perhaps I wish to play with the fire of her mind and stir the heat of her heart."

Strath blinked. "Good God, Alexsey, you make her sound attractive."

"She is."

"Hmmm." He sent his friend a sly side-glance. "Perhaps I should give her another look-see."

Alexsey's smile crashed into a frown. "That would *not* be wise—"

The door creaked open and a short, rotund woman with a mobcap smashed upon her iron-gray curls looked out onto the portico. She offered no greeting, but stared at them.

An awkward silence ensued until Strath cleared his throat. "Pardon me, but is this Ackinnoull Manor, home of the Murdoch family?"

"Aye." The woman opened the door a fraction of an inch more, her chins quivering as she looked head to toe at one of them, then the other, her brow knit in a frown.

Alexsey hid a grin. "I beg your pardon, but you are . . ." He lifted his brows and waited.

"Och, oy'm Mrs. Pitcairn, both cook and housekeeper." She released the door long enough to smooth her black gown. Now that the door was slightly more opened, Alexsey could see the flour scattered over one of her cuffs. As if in explanation, she added, "I dinna normally answer the door."

"Ah," Strath said, offering a charming smile as he whipped off his hat. "You are doing a fine job thus far. Well done, Mrs. Pitcairn."

She eyed Strath the way a cat might eye a snake. "It dinna take much in the way o' talent."

His lips twitched, but he managed to say with suitable gravity, "Very true. Still, it is not your usual duty and yet here you are, performing it as if you'd done it hundreds of times before."

The housekeeper looked at Strath from head to toe again. "Humph."

Alexsey hid a smile. "I do hope we've not come at an inopportune time?"

The housekeeper considered this. "Nay, I suppose no'."

Strath threw himself into the breach once again. "Excellent! I believe introductions are in order. Gentle lady, I'm Viscount Strathmoor and this is Prince Menshivkov. We've come to visit Mr. and Mrs. Murdoch and their lovely daughters."

"Prince?" The cook's eyes widened and she looked at Alexsey with renewed interest. "Ye're a prince? A real 'un?"

Alexsey bowed.

Mrs. Pitcairn opened the door a bit wider and said in a voice tinged with awe, "Lor' love ye, oy've ne'er met a prince a'fore. But guidness, ye do look th' part. All tall an' handsome and quite a set of shoulders upon ye. Ye look good enou' to eat, ye do."

Strath made a choking sound while Alexsey asked with caution, "I take it we may enter?"

"Och, o' course ye can enter." She stepped out of the way, swinging the door wide. "Come on in, and mind ye wipe yer feet, fer Miss Bronwyn mopped the foyer yesterday mornin' and oy'll no' ha' it marred, e'en by a pr—"

"Mrs. Pitcairn!" Lady Malvinea's frozen tones cut through the servant's prattle.

The housekeeper whipped about, her back suddenly stiff. "Aye?"

"You were asked to escort Lord Strathmoor and his guest into the sitting room. *Not* inform them about mopping and such!"

"Och, weel, they ha' mud upon their boots, an' I thought 'twas a guid idea fer them to—"

"That is enough. I'll take it from here. You may return to the kitchen."

The servant huffed, "Dinna start yer sharp tone wit' me! I dinna wish to even come up fro' the kitchen to begin wit', but Miss Bronwyn said I had to—"

"Mrs. Pitcairn, that is *enough*." The icy tone made even Strath stand a bit straighter.

The housekeeper stiffened, and after a few grumbled words, she stomped down a side hallway and disappeared.

Lady Malvinea faced Strath and Alexsey with her fixed smile. "Lord Strathmoor, Your Highness! How kind of you to visit." She gestured to the open door behind her. "Won't you join us for a small repast? We were just waiting on tea."

"Of course." They followed Lady Malvinea into a small sitting room. One swift glance told Alexsey that while Lady Malvinea's other two daughters were present, Bronwyn wasn't. He had to stifle a surprisingly strong urge to turn on his heel and go find her.

Lady Murdoch paused by the fire and said in a triumphant voice, "Your Highness. Lord Strathmoor. I believe you've met my daughters, Sorcha and Mairi."

The two girls had hopped to their feet as Alexsey and Strath had entered the room, and now bobbed simultaneous curtsies. Alexsey and Strath answered with bows of their own.

Strath said in his usual tone, "How could anyone forget the lovely Misses Murdochs?"

"I believe there were three of you last night." Alexsey paused expectantly.

Lady Malvinea, who'd been beaming, blinked. "Oh yes, Bronwyn. I wonder why she's not here? She went on an errand."

The youngest daughter, Mairi, chuckled. "I daresay she found a book. She does that, you know, goes on an errand, but then finds a book and never returns."

Sorcha nodded. "Sometimes she is gone for hours."

"I'm sure she hasn't done any such thing this time," Lady Malvinea said. Her fixed smile returned. "Won't you stay for some tea?" She waved a hand at two available chairs strategically placed directly across from her daughters. "We have apple tarts."

Strath took the seat across from Sorcha. "I live for apple tarts."

Mairi giggled, winning an approving look from Strath, but Sorcha barely smiled.

Bronwyn's sisters looked like dolls, dressed in expensive gowns, their hair styled just so. They seemed as opposite to Alexsey's imperfect and passionate Bronwyn as possible.

Strath made a casual comment about the good riding paths, and Lady Malvinea spoke of the other delights to be had in the surrounding countryside. His gaze wandering over the small room, Alexsey caught sight of a book left open on a table. Did Bronwyn read in this room, her feet tucked under a shawl, her lips moving silently as she read? He could picture her doing just that, and the image made him smile.

He noticed Miss Mairi rubbing her arms as if chilly, and he glanced at the fire, which was burning merrily, a bucket of coal at the ready. It was a bit cold in the room. Perhaps they had only lit the fire recently. *Or perhaps they cannot afford to be so generous with coal and have just stirred this one up for their company?*

The thought disturbed him, and he looked more closely about him, noting the faded rugs, and the mended hems of both curtains. *Ah, little Roza, you come from modest circumstances. I can help you with that.* Yet even as he had the thought, he realized she'd never allow anyone to "help." From the set of her jaw, he suspected she had more pride than any ten men he knew.

He'd spent many summers among the Romany camps, living simply with his mother's people. He enjoyed that life and found it a welcome change from the constrictive opulence of court, but he also knew the cost of struggling to find food and shelter. The weight it could put upon narrow shoulders, too delicate to bear—

He caught Strath's amused gaze. "I beg your pardon?"

"Miss Sorcha just asked you something, but you were busy staring into the distance."

"I'm sorry. I was lost in my thoughts." Ignoring Strath's barely stifled snicker, Alexsey said, "Miss Sorcha, if you don't mind repeating your comment?"

Sorcha frowned but said in a soft voice, "I didn't have the chance at tea to ask if Your Highness enjoyed the ball."

"It was the best ball I've attended in Scotland."

"Oh my!" Lady Malvinea looked absurdly pleased. "That's quite the compliment."

Mairi pursed her lips. "Maybe it is, and maybe it isn't."

Lady Malvinea's smile faltered for a moment. "Mairi, don't—"

"It depends on how many balls His Highness has attended in Scotland." The younger girl raised a brow, suddenly reminding him of Bronwyn. "How many have there been?"

Lady Malvinea sputtered. "Mairi, you can't— That is, there's no reason to—"

"It is fine," Alexsey said with a grin. "I have been to two balls in Scotland, and one of them was wretched indeed. It was given by Lord Dalhousie. His lordship wouldn't allow the fires to be lit and the castle was freezing. There was nothing to eat other than stale cake so hard you could use it to build furniture, the musicians were drunk, and there were no spirits to be had."

"Why would anyone have such a ball as that?" Sorcha asked.

"I believe his daughter asked him to host one. And while he wished to please her, he wished even more to keep his coins in his coffers."

Strath snorted. "Never met a man cheaper than Dalhousie. He once—"

A noise sounded in the hallway and Alexsey turned toward the door as Bronwyn entered, a cheerful whirl of rumpled skirts and breezy friendliness.

"I'm sorry I'm late, Mama. Mrs. Pitcairn needed some assistance in the kitchen." She curtsied toward Strath and Alexsey, then took the empty seat beside Mairi. "I apologize for not being here to greet you, but I was attending to a few matters belowstairs."

Alexsey and Strath, who'd stood upon her entering the room, now returned to their seats. To Alexsey, it seemed as if the clouds had parted and the sun shone. The room was brighter now, the faded carpet no longer obvious, blessed by the sunshine. Beside Bronwyn with her dark hair and lightly golden skin, her sisters seemed like pallid hothouse orchids next to a vibrant wild rose.

Bronwyn smiled at Strath. "Viscount Strathmoor, how kind of you and the prince to call. I'm sure my mother and sisters have told you how much we are enjoying your uncle's hospitality. We rarely have such affairs here in the country, and these few weeks of events will be discussed for months."

"Indeed, they have," Lord Strathmoor said. "We've had a most pleasant conversation."

"So we have," the prince said, his gaze locked on Bronwyn. "Most pleasant."

Bronwyn's face heated. She'd decided not to look his way until she had a good grip upon her emotions, but now she found herself gazing directly into his eyes.

The man had the longest lashes. They gave him a sleepy, sensual appearance even when he was only innocently looking at her. Except "innocent" wasn't a likely word to describe him.

Even the way he sat bespoke a casual sensuality.

Lord Strathmoor sat with the unconscious dignity one expected of a viscount, while the prince was sprawled, his arms crossed over his broad chest, his legs before him as if he were in a hunting lodge in the Highlands. *He looks far more like a dangerous, dashing huntsman than a prince.*

She now noted his clothing. His cravat was a mere knotted kerchief, his boots dull from lack of polish, his coat far too loose for common fashion. His hair curled over his collar, while his handsome face was graced with a scruff of a beard. It was difficult to believe this man would be lavishly welcomed into every drawing room on the continent. *Yet even though he's dressed in such a way, he still looks twice the man of any I've ever met.*

"Prince Menshivkov, pray tell us about Oxenburg," Mama said. "Is it cold there this time of the year?"

Bronwyn smiled. This was her chance. "Oxenburg experiences mild temperatures in the fall, but it's not unusual for them to experience sudden snowfalls come September."

Everyone looked at her.

Encouraged, she added, "Though the temperatures in the mountain ranges can be extreme, those on the plains are pleasant most of the year."

Mama blinked. "I—I had no idea, Bronwyn."

"Yes. Part of Oxenburg has heavy snows in the winter, and the mountain roads are often impassable except by horse and sled."

Sorcha looked from her to Alexsey and then back again. "Really?"

Bronwyn nodded. "There are two major mountain ranges in Oxenburg, with four major peaks."

She slipped a glance at Alexsey and caught him watching her with an odd smile.

What else? Ah yes. "There are seventeen rivers, and a number of flood plains, as well as"—she frowned, trying to remember—"was it seven major cities?"

"Six," Alexsey offered.

"Six." She gave him a grateful smile. "Oxenburg has no coastline, as it is entirely surrounded by other countries, but lakes are plentiful. There are more than a hundred and"—she squinted and bit her lip—"fourteen lakes, all of them surrounded by lush farmlands and—"

The prince stood, startling everyone. "Lady Malvinea, Strathmoor and I *must* take your daughters for a walk in your gardens."

Bronwyn blinked at the urgent note in the prince's voice.

Mama nodded. "Of course! Sorcha and Mairi would be glad to—"

"And Miss Murdoch," Alexsey said.

Her gaze flew to his. He inclined his head, a faint smile curving his hard mouth. "Such a recitation. I am impressed."

Her face flushed at the warmth in his voice, her entire body softening. *And I only read the first chapter. How will he react when I read more? Will he—*

A noise sounded in the foyer and Mama, who was looking none too pleased, brightened. "Ah! There's tea now. The walk can wait."

A scrambling sound came in the hallway, followed by a muffled thump.

Bronwyn frowned at the door. "What on earth is that?"

The door burst open and Scott galloped in, a red kerchief in his mouth. Hot on his trail was Mrs. Pitcairn, her mobcap askew, a broom in one hand as she swung unsuccessfully at the dog's rump. "Bring tha' back, ye bloody hellhound!" she snapped, her face as red as the kerchief.

Lady Malvinea rose, grasping one arm of her chair. "Bronwyn, get your animals under control!"

Bronwyn was already on her feet, stepping into Scott's path.

Walter appeared in the doorway, his tail wagging as he watched the fray. With a loud bark, he ran in to join the fun.

"Scott, stop!" She grabbed at him as he raced by, but, spurred forward by the housekeeper's chase, he was out of reach before she could grab his collar.

"Bring back them tarts, ye hellhound!" Mrs. Pitcairn screeched, swinging the broom.

Scott leapt over a small table with ease and Mrs. Pitcairn, perhaps thinking she could swat his rump while he was in the air, accidentally brought her broom down on a large vase of fall flowers, which flipped spectacularly in the air, scattering water and flowers all over poor Sorcha.

Wet stems clung to her head and face as she gasped in shock. Water dampened her gown and plastered one of her curls to her forehead.

Mairi and Lord Strathmoor both let out a whoop of laughter while, red-faced and furious, Lady Malvinea dug a kerchief from her pocket and rushed to Sorcha's aid.

Bronwyn ran after Scott, who was trying to scramble under a chair to evade the whapping broom. But the chair was too small for such a large dog, and he only succeeded in moving it forward, his rump still in plain view and an easy target for Mrs. Pitcairn.

Bronwyn caught the broom just before it landed and tugged it away from the angry housekeeper. "Mrs. Pitcairn, *please*!"

Mrs. Pitcairn shoved her askew mobcap back onto her head. "Tha' dog stole our tarts!"

"He shouldn't have done that, but chasing him about the house isn't going to help." Bronwyn moved in front of Scott, who was now trying to wiggle free of the chair.

The cook's hands curled into fists. "Miss, I jus' want to gi' him one good smack fer stealin' my tarts! One smack, an' no more."

"No smacks, and no—" Bronwyn caught sight of Walter where he was licking spilled water from the floor. "Walter, *out*!"

The dog wagged his tail and gave the floor one last lick.

She scowled at him.

Seeing the steel in her eye, he lowered his head and trotted out the door.

Scott, finally free, scrambled to join him, and soon Bronwyn saw the two dogs racing past one of the windows. "You left the door open!"

"I was tryin' to herd them oot the door when they stole me tarts." Mrs. Pitcairn plopped a fist on her hip and leaned against her broom. "And now we dinna ha' naught fer his lordship and the prince fer tea."

Bronwyn glanced at their guests. Alexsey now sat in his chair, rubbing his chin as if to wipe his grin from his face, looking for all the world as if he were at a show of some sort. Lord Strathmoor was offering his hand-kerchief to a sputtering Sorcha, his eyes alight with laughter.

Bronwyn's heart ached as she caught Sorcha's mor-tified look as she wiped water from her face, one flower sticking out from her hair like a broken antler.

Mama pinned Bronwyn with a furious look. "Those animals are your responsibility!"

"I'm sorry they ate the tarts."

"They're hellhounds," Mrs. Pitcairn cried, stomping out the door. "Hellhounds, I tell ye!"

Lord Strathmoor cleared his throat. "I, ah, think the prince and I should be going. We'll return for that walk some other time."

Alexsey stood, towering over everyone in the room. He bowed, his gaze locked upon hers. "I've enjoyed my visit very, *very* much."

I'll wager you did, Bronwyn thought with irritation. She'd worked so hard to make an impression, and for a wild moment, she'd thought she'd succeeded. He'd had eyes for no one but her. But now the moment was lost.

"Thank you, Your Highness," Mama said. "I'm so sorry for the mess and—and everything. I assure you we are usually far more boring than this!"

Strathmoor laughed. "If anyone understands the demands of a dog, it is the prince. His dog is a monster."

"Papillon is the worst dog in all of Oxenburg," the prince agreed without malice. "Everyone says so."

"Especially your grandmother."

Alexsey nodded. "She would like Papillon to be a lapdog, but she is not accommodating."

"I haven't met this dog, though I've heard about it." Mama cut a sharp glance at Bronwyn.

Alexsey offered, "Papillon is small, bred for hunting rats."

"Rats?" Mairi looked fascinated.

"And the—what is the word?" His gaze flickered to Bronwyn. "Ah yes, 'hares.'"

Mairi brightened. "I love small dogs."

"But she is much trouble," Alexsey said. "Like a woman."

Strathmoor burst out laughing. "Now we really *must* go; we've other visits to make. But first, my uncle wished me to invite all of you to our house for a turtle dinner the day after tomorrow."

Mama beamed. "A turtle dinner, you say? How elegant! We'd be delighted."

"Excellent. At eight." The viscount bowed. "We look forward to your visit."

Bronwyn felt the prince's gaze upon her as she made her obligatory curtsy, but she refused to give him the satisfaction of a single look. It was only when he was walking out the door, Lady Malvinea fluttering behind, that she allowed herself a long look at his broad shoulders as he disappeared from sight.

Chapter 14

"Men." Lucinda sighed. "Their wants are so simple, but their feelings are like a river, ever moving and oft deep."
—The Black Duke *by Miss Mary Edgeworth*

As they untied their horses from the iron rings mounted on the posts by the portico, Strath grinned. "Well, that was entertaining."

"Miss Sorcha would not agree."

Strathmoor's grin broadened. "To see her all wet and covered in stems—" He laughed.

Alexsey lifted a brow. "You are not usually so unkind toward women."

Strath shrugged. "She's been told her entire life how beautiful she is. It's good for her to realize she's a human once in a while."

"She does not strike me as being overly focused on her own beauty."

"Then why was she so upset at having water dumped upon her?"

"Because it was cold and uncomfortable. I daresay you'd have felt the same." Alexsey swung up into the saddle.

Strath remained beside his horse, a questioning look in his eyes. "You really think that was all it was?"

"*Da.*"

"Hmmm. I think you're giving her far too much credit." Strath climbed into the saddle, and they turned their horses down the drive.

At the end of the drive, Alexsey caught Strath's curious glance. "What? And don't tell me it's nothing, for I would not believe you."

"Very well. You don't have to answer, as it's just idle curiosity. But what was Miss Murdoch about, spouting off nonsense about Oxenburg?"

Alexsey chuckled. "I think she was trying her hand at flirting."

Strath gaped. "That was *flirting*?"

"Her version, I think so, yes."

"Well, I'll be damned. I never would have thought that." For a moment they rode in silence. "And your demand to take the ladies for a walk?"

"I had the most unusual reaction to her flirting, bad as it was."

"Oh?"

"I wished to kiss her. I was going to get her away from her sisters in the garden."

"Ah, so I was to help you."

"Wouldn't you have?"

Strath grinned. "Of course."

"You are a good friend, Strath." Thinking about Bronwyn, Alexsey chuckled. "I like seeing her flustered. I get the feeling very little flusters her."

"She seems very self-possessed."

"Aye—but I can make her flush with one look." It was odd, how much that amused him. Women often became flustered around him, trying far too hard to attract his attention. And today so had Bronwyn, but she'd done it in such an unusual, *earnest* way, he was charmed. More than charmed.

Strath said thoughtfully, "She was quite talkative today; she is usually very quiet."

"Very true." *Because she wished to let me know she was . . . interested. That is good, because I am, too. Even eager. But I dare not progress too quickly. It is obvious she is new to this and if I startle her, she will retreat, as she did in the garden.*

Aware of Strath's questioning gaze, he said, "She is very capable. There she was, chasing that dog about the room, facing a furious housekeeper armed with a broom, and a nearly hysterical stepmother, yet Bronwyn was calm and collected. Not a whit out of breath. I find that intriguing."

Strath shook his head. "You're a strange one. Well, whatever your intentions are with her, have a care. In Scotland, even a prince can't ruin a woman of good reputation and just walk away."

"I have no intention of ruining anyone."

Strath gave him a flat look.

Alexsey laughed. "Fine. I may have *some* ruination in mind, but only a very, very private one."

"Good." Strath sighed. "Scotland is stuck in ancient morality, while Europe gambols ahead. Why, just look at your grandmother. A Gypsy could never marry into the royal family in this country."

"Things are different in Oxenburg."

"Well, here things are run by an invisible court of public opinion, undeterred by common sense and fueled by the cruelest of gossip. Have a care you don't end up prosecuted under their unwritten laws."

Alexsey sent Strath a puzzled look. "You are full of heavy, unhappy advice today, my friend. Do not fear for me, or Miss Murdoch. We play a game, but I will make certain it stays within safe boundaries. I've no wish to harm her."

"I'm sorry. I'm cross today, and I've no idea why."

"You need a woman."

"Most likely."

"Find one, then. One who will offer you a challenge. Someone with enough fire in her soul to provoke, and enough brain in her head to win an argument. Beauty is easy to find. But interesting . . . ah, that is something to be treasured."

Strath shook his head. "You know, for all you like to pretend that you're a frivolous sort, you're a deep one."

Alexsey raised his brows. "Let's see how 'deep' you think me once I beat your sorry nag back to Tulloch."

Strath opened his mouth to protest, but the prince was already galloping away. "Bloody hell!" He kicked his heels and was off, chasing Alexsey's dust.

Chapter 15

Lucinda pulled her shawl tighter as the winds frenziedly whipped the moors. Swirling gray clouds filled the sky; there was power in the coming storm. She could feel it prickling along her skin, making her hair rise. Lightning snaked across the sky; thunder rumbled so loudly that it sucked all other sounds from the air. And with a great whooshing sigh, the skies opened and the rain poured down. . . .

—The Black Duke *by Miss Mary Edgeworth*

The next evening, Mairi turned away from the sitting room window, letting the heavy curtain cover the glass. "I hate rain. It's so gloomy."

Bronwyn, curled up on the settee with a blanket over her lap, looked up from her book. The steady thrum of the rain against the side of the house made her smile. "I rather like it."

Sorcha held her stitching closer to the lamp. "It's so cozy, being indoors while the weather rages outside."

Mama, who'd been darning Papa's socks, tied off the last stitch. "We're lucky to have three candles this evening. We're running short and will need to fetch some from Dingwall soon." The clock chimed a soft melody, and she sighed and closed her sewing basket. "It's late and we should go to bed." Seeing Bronwyn rubbing her eyes, she asked, "Bronwyn, are you well?"

"I've just a headache. I'm sure it will be gone in the morning."

Sorcha's delicate brows knit. "Oh dear! I hope so. You won't want to miss the turtle dinner at the castle."

Mama came to touch Bronwyn's forehead, her hand cool against Bronwyn's skin. "You don't feel as if you've a fever."

"Of course I don't; I'm not sick."

"Don't challenge fate, Bronwyn," Sorcha warned with a smile.

"Indeed," Mama agreed. "I'm quite excited about tomorrow's dinner, though we've much to do to get ready for it. Sorcha, how's that hem?"

"Almost finished." Sorcha shook out the gown, showing her mother the neat stitches.

At her mother's approving nod, Sorcha put her needle and thread back into her sewing box. "I will finish the hem in the morning, which will give us plenty of time to prepare for dinner at the castle."

Lightning flashed through the window, and made a portrait of their lawn for a startling second before dropping a curtain of darkness. A loud crack of thunder rolled across the sky, sending vibrations through the floor.

Mairi rubbed her arms. "I hate thunder."

"You can sleep with me tonight, if you'd like," Sorcha offered.

"Yes, please!" She cast a cautious glance out the window.

"I rather like storms," Bronwyn said. "It's a good night to read in bed."

Sorcha sent her an amused look as she closed her sewing box. "What night isn't a good one to read in bed?"

Bronwyn smiled. "Very true."

Sorcha carefully laid her new gown over a chair, then turned to collect one of the precious candles. "Coming, Mairi?"

"Good night, dears," Mama called.

"Good night!"

Once they were gone, Mama picked up one of the two remaining candles. "Be sure you go to bed soon; you don't wish to have circles under your eyes at the dinner party."

"Yes, Mama." Bronwyn turned the page, the history of Oxenburg dancing through her imagination. Though small, the country had a colorful history. And the fact that she knew one of its princes made the read all the more engrossing. She could almost hear his rich honey-silk voice reading the words to her, telling her about his land and ancestors, sharing the vast—

"Bronwyn?"

She looked up.

Mama stood in the doorway. Her gaze flickered to the small tome in Bronwyn's hands. "Still reading about Oxenburg, I see. Are you finished with Miss Edgeworth's book, then?"

"Not yet. I am reading it slowly so it will last."

Mama smiled. "I sometimes wonder . . ." She paused. "Bronwyn, you're not interested in the prince, are you?"

Bronwyn's face heated. "No! He's far too frivolous for me."

"So I would think, too. I've never seen you display the least interest in a gentleman before, but there are times I've seen you look at him. . . . And when he visited yesterday, you began to spout facts about Oxenburg, so I wondered if you were attempting to gain his interest."

Should she mention the conversation she'd overheard between the prince and Strathmoor? No. It would anger Mama, and the rest of the visit would be socially awkward. Mama was horrible at hiding things. "It didn't mean anything; I was just trying to make conversation. Besides, he's not for me."

The words sounded hollow to her ears, but Mama seemed reassured.

She nodded, the candlelight softening the lines on her face. "He would make Sorcha happy, I think. We are very fortunate to have this opportunity for her."

Bronwyn bit her lip. "Perhaps, although . . . the prince doesn't seem to have the slightest interest in finding a wife."

"No man thinks he wants a wife, but they all do."

"I'm not sure that's true about this man. And . . . he and Sorcha are so very different."

Mama looked surprised. "Do you think so? I thought they made a stunning couple. He so dark and broad shouldered, and she so fair and delicate—"

"They would make a beautiful couple, but they have very little in common. She is somewhat shy, while he always ends up being the center of attention. She takes no pleasure in arguing, yet he thrives on it. She cares for fashion and politeness, and he has the barest amount of both. His morals are questionable, hers are not."

"How do you know so much about him?"

She knew because he'd told her, and she'd seen it for herself, but she only said, "I've heard things."

"Idle gossip, then. I'm a good judge of character, and I think he's sincere. The prince may have lived wildy, but now he has settled down."

"You know best, of course, but . . . I would want Sorcha to be part of a happy couple, not just a handsome one."

"So would I." Mama was silent, her face inscrutable in the flickering candlelight. "Let's watch them and we'll discuss this again later. Meanwhile, if you don't mind, pray don't mention your thoughts to Sorcha. Whether she responds to the prince or not, it needs to be her decision and not ours."

Bronwyn nodded. "I won't say a word."

"Thank you. As usual, you take good care of your sister." She smiled at Bronwyn. "Go to bed, child. It's late. I . . ." Her smile faded. "Are you well? You keep rubbing your ear."

"It tickles, that's all."

"Well, we'll keep an eye on it. Good night."

Hours later, tucked snugly into her bed, Bronwyn put away the small book on Oxenburg. After snuffing out the candle she closed her eyes, wondering about the prince.

One part of her—the part that lingered over the adventurous scenes in her books, had started longing for a larger life and whispered that here, at least, was a real adventure she could embark upon. But the other part of her—the part that treasured the constancy and comfort of her life here, warned that she was playing with fire, one that could potentially destroy her comfortable life.

What if I fall in love? she wondered, absently rubbing her ear. She found the prince intriguing, but that wasn't love. *And he won't be here long enough for my feelings to be at risk, anyway.*

She rolled toward the window so she could watch the lightning. The rain thrummed loudly on the roof, while one of the dogs snored softly. Her bed was clean and cozy, the quilt and pillows cocooning her in softness. She thought about her sisters, and all of the laughter they'd shared. She thought of Papa and his inventions, and Mama and her ambitions. She thought of their neighbors, and all the people who brought life to Dingwall. She loved it all, and hoped with all of her heart that none of it would ever change.

But it *was* changing. Sorcha and Mairi were growing up, and would marry and move away. Once they were gone, it would just be her and her parents. She'd stay busy, helping Papa with his patents and Mama with the household chores . . . Suddenly Bronwyn wasn't sure how she felt about that. Would she just remain here for the rest of her life, never experiencing any adventures? Or would she find a way to live in a larger fashion?

Perhaps getting to know the prince was an opportunity to live a larger life. . . .

And since he'd only be here a brief time, flirting with him was the safest adventure she could have. The fact that he wanted only a brief dalliance, that he'd never fall in love with her and demand that she leave with him, made it safe. A flirtation would give her a dose of confidence, and who couldn't use more of that?

Perhaps once Sorcha and Mairi are gone and Papa and Mama are settled, I will leave Ackinnoull for a month each year. I will travel and visit the places I've read about, and explore foreign lands.

She smiled. That would be something, indeed. And perhaps the first country she'd visit would be a green jewel of a place nestled in the blue and white mountains of Europe.

A few minutes later she fell into a deep sleep where, in a tiny hamlet under the shadow of a mountain, a handsome huntsman with green eyes chased her around a tree and tried to steal kisses.

Ϯhe next evening, Mairi stood in the front foyer and adjusted her pale-green silk shawl so that it draped over her shoulders just so. "I can't believe you're not coming to Sir Henry's dinner with us."

From the settee, her head wrapped in a shawl to cover her aching ear, Bronwyn fought the desire to pout like a child. "Me, too—I so wished to go. I love turtle soup." *And then there's Alexsey. . . .* She sighed.

Sorcha, looking concerned, placed her cool hand on Bronwyn's forehead. "You're still hot. But you don't seem to be in as much pain as you were this morning."

"The ache is almost gone now." Bronwyn shifted restlessly, kicking at her blanket. "I've been on this settee all day. While you're gone, I might take a walk and—"

"No," Mama said. "Dr. Leith said you were to keep your ear wrapped at least until tomorrow. He said to use those drops every few hours, and to avoid noise, bright light, and all forms of excitement."

"Taking a walk is hardly exciting."

"It will be if it rains again," Mairi said. "It was still gray outside when night fell."

Bronwyn sighed again.

Sorcha tucked the blanket about her. "We'll tell you everything that happened when we return."

Mairi nodded. "I'll pay especially close attention to everyone's gowns so I can give you descriptions of them. I'm so glad Sir Henry sent a coach. It's so luxurious, compared to our musty old one."

"It is quite an honor," Mama said, looking pleased. "We're very fortunate."

Sorcha turned to Bronwyn and held her arms out to either side. "What do you think?" Her round Circassian robe of pink crepe over a white satin slip accentuated her delicate figure. The gown was fringed at the hem and had a bodice of pink satin laced with silver, and ornamental Spanish slashed sleeves from which white crepe peeked whenever she moved.

"You look lovely," Bronwyn said.

Sorcha beamed. "Thank you."

Mairi grinned. "Sorcha's determined to look especially good since the prince and Viscount Strathmoor saw her wearing flower horns two days ago."

"I am not!" Sorcha frowned. "I don't care what either of them thinks."

The clock chimed and Mama said, "We must go. Come, girls. No more dallying." As they left, she turned back to Bronwyn. "Your father is visiting Colonel Washburn this evening, hoping to borrow his wagon for something or another, but Mrs. Pitcairn will be here until nine. Don't forget to take your medicine." She pointed to a small brown bottle sitting on the table at Bronwyn's elbow.

Bronwyn wrinkled her nose. "It makes me dizzy."

"Then take it right before bed. You'll feel better in the morning."

She left, and Bronwyn soon heard the coach pull away.

Throwing off the blanket, she arose and found the tome on Oxenburg that she'd hidden under an almanac. After Mama's conversation last night, she'd thought it might be better to keep the book out of sight. She returned to the settee and began to read.

That occupied her for the next hour, though she kept finding her gaze on the mantel clock. Slowly, the time passed. Finally, after a particularly dry chapter on the various treaties negotiated by a seemingly very active Oxenburg parliament, she closed the book and tossed it aside. Aside from the crackle of the fire and the tick of the clock, the room was silent.

"Well. Here I am." Her words echoed in the empty room, and she longingly thought of the laughter she'd have shared at Sir Henry's dinner. *Stop that. Thinking about the fun you're missing just makes you feel worse.*

She shoved the thoughts aside and, realizing it was time for her medicine, uncorked the small bottle and poured a dose into the spoon her stepmother had left lying next to it. Shuddering at the bitter taste, she recorked it and pulled the blanket closer. And within a few minutes, she was fast asleep.

Chapter 16

There was but one woman who lit his soul afire, one woman who—with but a glance—could either melt his bones into liquid or rend him limb from limb.

And every day, he blessed the day he'd met her.

—The Black Duke *by Miss Mary Edgeworth*

Some time later, Bronwyn slowly awoke, like a person surfacing in a pond. Her ears felt muffled, her body faintly numb, her senses dulled. She sent a sour glance at the little brown medicine bottle, feeling as drunk as if she'd emptied a wine bottle by herself.

With a huge yawn, she sat upright and stretched. Her ear didn't hurt a bit, so that was good—well worth the fuzzy brain.

A jingle in the drive outside made her look toward the door.

"They're home!" She arose, staggering a little as she pulled the blanket about her like a cape. Slowly, she weaved her way to the window to look out of the curtains.

No carriage stood in the drive.

She rubbed her eyes. Had she dreamed it? "That's

the last time I take that medicine." She was starting to return to the settee when a knock sounded on the front door. *Had Papa forgotten his key again?*

She made her way unsteadily to the door and swung it open.

Instead of Papa, her eyes locked upon a gold button.

It was real gold, too, and not brass. The surface had been pressed to resemble a lion, which gleamed menacingly at her.

Slowly, she slid her gaze up over a blue waistcoat, past a carelessly knotted cravat pinned with a large emerald, to a tanned throat. And up to Alexsey's amused face.

His black hair was mussed by the wind, his green eyes agleam, and he wore a mischievous expression that made her heart leap as if in recognition.

"Ohhhhh . . ." *So pretty*, her bemused mind sighed. *So very pretty.*

His brows rose, and she noted again how they flared the tiniest bit at the corners, giving him an exotic look. "Oh?" he repeated.

She tried to kick her fuzzy brain into action, but nothing happened, so she just nodded.

Amusement and curiosity showed in his eyes. "And here I have ridden like a madman to see you. While I didn't expect a hug or a kiss, I did expect a 'Hello, how nice to see you.'"

A yawn that would not be repressed began to torment her. She covered her mouth and hoped he wouldn't notice.

The prince's gaze narrowed, his smile now gone as

his eyes raked over her hair and took in the blanket. "*Ya ni panilah*, have you been ill?"

"Yes. Earache." She saw his lack of comprehension, so she patted her ear. "I'm better now, but the medicine—whew!" She leaned her head against the door, hanging on to the knob to keep her balance as she tried to make her eyes focus on him. "So . . . what are you doing here? The dinner cannot be over yet."

"I am visiting you." He removed his gloves and stuffed them in his coat pocket before he placed a hand under her elbow, his fingers warm.

She really liked his hands. They were large, but always so gentle.

"Roza, forgive me, but you look as if at any moment you might fall."

"No, no. I'm holding on to the knob." She nodded down at her hands, which were completely hidden by the blanket. "See?"

He looked at the blanket. "*Da.*" Then one of his arms slipped behind her while the other found her knees. With the smallest of efforts he straightened, and suddenly she was in his arms.

It was heavenly. So very, very heavenly. She dropped her head against his broad shoulder.

Alexsey kicked the front door closed behind him. "Where do I take you, little one?"

She pointed a languid finger toward the sitting room. As he carried her there, she admired the strength of his arms and the width of his chest. If she wished to touch him, all she had to do was lift her hand.

It was so tempting.

So very, very tempting. And it was the last thing she should do.

Her heart thudded in an oddly happy way and she watched him through her lashes. "You know what I think, oh great prince?"

He stopped by the settee and smiled into her eyes. "No, but I know you will tell me."

"Yes. You shouldn't be here."

"I know." He placed her on the settee, then set his hat on the small table beside it. "Yet here I am, unable to stay away."

She tried to sit up, only halfway managing it. "I'm unchaperoned. That's not allowed. You must go." She pointed toward the door.

"Do you wish me to go?"

She blinked. Of course she did. Or did she? Somehow her gaze found his mouth. Never had she met a man with such a sensual bottom lip. Just seeing it made her breath catch, her knees grow weak, her—

"Then I stay for a while." Satisfaction curved his mouth, breaking the spell. He unbuttoned his coat and shrugged out of it, displaying his elegant dinner coat and blue embroidered waistcoat. His simple cravat was held by a gold and emerald pin, the fire of which matched his gaze.

Though his cravat pin sparkled, she couldn't seem to look away from his eyes. They were so pretty. So very pretty.

Bronwyn knew she should insist he leave, but her fuzzy mind just hummed along happily.

He came to sit beside her on the settee, which suddenly seemed very small. "You are a very big man."

"And you are a very small woman. Like a bird."

She considered this, pretending not to notice when his hand found hers. "What kind of bird?"

He chuckled. "A sparrow, perhaps."

"How about a hawk? I would like to be a hawk."

He kissed her fingers. "With me, Roza, you may be anything you wish."

With him. She liked that. A lot. Her common sense whispered an urgent warning, one she couldn't quite hear through her haze. "The dinner cannot be over." Surely she'd said that before, but he hadn't answered.

"No. It continues. I told them I had a headache; then I came here." He continued kissing her fingers, looking at her as he did so. "I couldn't stay away."

He looked so delicious, every touch of his lips sending tremors of sensation through her. She wondered how much stronger they'd be if not for the medicine, and the answer almost frightened her. She pulled her hand free and crossed her arms. "No. This is most improper." The words stuck on her lips, as if disliking to be said. "If we're caught—"

"I know: there would be a scandal." He grinned. "So we will not get caught."

"How can you be so cer—" His gaze had dropped down to her chest and she looked down. In crossing her arms she'd unwittingly pressed her breasts upward, causing them to round softly above the neckline of her gown.

She hastily dropped her arms, her face afire as she

rewrapped the blanket around herself, which was impossible to do as she was sitting on most of it. "That's quite enough of that." She tried to sound stern, but she ruined it with a giggle.

Goodness, what a situation. But perhaps it would serve her well. *I'm to make him fall wildly, madly in love with me—or at least deeply in lust, and now is the time to woo him, subdue him, make him desire me as no other—* She caught sight of herself in the side mirror and gasped. "My *hair*!"

He chuckled as she frantically tried to pat the unruly curls into place.

"It's not funny. I look like a—a—a—I don't know what, but it's not— This won't work at all!"

He tugged her to his chest, tucking her head under his chin. "There. Now I cannot see your hair, just feel its softness." He ran his fingers over her curls. "I like your hair. It is silken."

"You like it uncombed?" she asked dubiously.

"I like it however you wear it."

She suddenly wondered who was trying to make who fall in lust—and then she remembered they were both doing the exact same thing. Somehow, she hadn't seen it in that particular way before, and she laughed a little at her surprise.

"What is it?" he asked, his heartbeat warm against her cheek.

"I'm just laughing at us. At you. You are trying to seduce me."

A dark smile flickered over his face. "Trying? I do not try anything. I do."

"I do, too. A lot." *Ha—take* that.

He ran his fingers over her cheek and down to her gray-blue gown, which was wrinkled from her having lain on the settee all day.

He *tsk*ed. "I do not like that color on you. You should wear reds, Roza. Like the flower you resemble. I will buy you many gowns, all red. You will wear those."

She lifted her head so she could see him. "Stop princing."

"Princing? What is that?"

"You may be a prince in Oxenburg, but this isn't your country." Her voice grew louder, and she poked him in the chest with her finger. "I'm not a subject, and I won't take orders from you like a serf."

He chuckled as if richly amused, and stretched an arm across the back of the settee. "My beautiful Roza, we don't have serfs in Oxenburg. But if we did, you would be a very bad one. Always you argue. Never you do as asked."

She opened her mouth to retort that she would make a very *good* serf, but the absurdity of the idea made her choke on a short laugh. "I'm rather proud of being a bad serf."

His gaze swept over her. "Fortunately, I like a woman with pride."

And she liked that he enjoyed her, unfettered and uncensored. That he didn't mind if she poked him in the chest while making a point, or that her hair was uncombed and her gown wrinkled. . . . She liked a lot about this man. Too much.

She snuggled her head back on his shoulder and

sighed against his neck. "Ah, Alexsey, what are we to do?"

His arms tightened about her and for a moment, she thought he wasn't going to answer. Then he tipped up her face to his. "Has anyone ever told you that you think too much?"

She nodded. "Everyone who knows me."

He kissed her nose. "They are right."

Feeling surrounded by him, protected, she looked up at him through her lashes. "My stepmother and sisters might return soon. I don't wish you to get caught."

"*Nyet.* They won't be home for another hour, at least. The dinner was very elaborate and there was talk of whist being played afterward."

"You're certain?"

"Positive. People were quite animated."

She eyed him up and down. "I can't believe you pleaded a headache and anyone believed it."

"To assuage any suspicion, I hinted to my host that I had an assignation with a willing housemaid."

"So you came to visit me . . . and nothing more?"

His gaze raked over her. "I will not pretend I don't wish to touch you, Bronwyn. I will not pretend you haven't been tormenting my thoughts."

She, the most nonthreatening woman on the face of the earth, had been tormenting the thoughts of a handsome prince? She fought the desire to smile. "There are far more beautiful women out there than me. Sorcha, for instance."

"You are beautiful in the way I like. Sorcha is not."

"You can't deny her beauty."

"Why not? You are denying yours."

She stared at him, surprised. "I . . . I suppose I was."

"Roza, every time I look at you, I see your shining hair, your warm eyes, the light of your smile, your full breasts, your—"

"Yes, yes." Her face felt as if it were afire, for his eyes had followed the progression of his speech. "That's very flattering. But my stepmother has hopes you'll notice Sorcha."

He couldn't have looked more uninterested. "Roza, do you not understand? This attraction we have is rare. This spark we have, it does not happen often."

"Spark?"

His eyes darkened. "When I do this . . ." He traced a finger along her collarbone, lingering in the hollows, his skin warm against hers.

She shivered, her breasts peaking, a sigh escaping from her lips.

His arm tightened about her. "*That* is what happens between us. I have met your sister several times, and there is nothing between us. You cannot make a spark where none exists."

He rested his hand on her knee, his voice warm. "Enough about your sister. We have too little time, my sweet. Far too little."

Though there were layers of skirt and petticoats between his hand and her skin, the warmth and weight of his hand set off a reaction so strong, she nearly gasped. Her body had tightened, her skin prickled awake, and her breasts tingled as if aching for his touch. *Good God, I'm lost.*

He cupped her chin, turning her face toward his, then removed her spectacles and placed them on the side table. "I would see you without these."

Humor, passion, and intelligence shone in his eyes. His jaw bespoke a strong character, while the gentleness of his hands left her aching for more. There was so much about this man that she liked. He'd called the way her body reacted to his a spark; she'd call it an out-and-out fire.

She yearned for him like a woman starved. And suddenly, looking into his eyes, she didn't care about doing the right thing. She didn't care about the future.

She grasped his coat, leaned up, and kissed him.

Chapter 17

Roland, hidden in the shrubs, looked toward the noise. Lucinda was walking through the roses, her fingertips brushing the petals of the flowers. He watched as she came closer, ever closer to him and farther away from the dangers of the dark castle, her gown tugged by the playful wind, her long blond hair tossed about her face. Soon he would reveal himself to her, and watch her eyes light with love and— A crunch on the pathway made him crouch lower.

Someone else was coming. And just like that, the moment was lost.

—The Black Duke *by Miss Mary Edgeworth*

Alexsey's large hands grasped her waist as he slid her into his lap without breaking the kiss, and she shivered and pressed against him.

This is it. This *is what I want!* Everywhere he touched, everywhere she wished him to touch, was aflame with longing and desire, answered need and unanswered yearning. She wound her arms about his neck, pressing her chest to his, trying to get closer.

His lips covered and offered, gave and took. Bronwyn shivered against him and offered herself without reservation.

Each kiss tantalized and teased, and washed away more and more of the haze the medicine held over her. His caresses grew bolder, stronger, his hands moving over her back, her hips, to her breasts—

She gasped as his thumb found her nipple even through her gown and chemise, and she pressed her breast into his hand, wanting, needing—

His kiss turned fierce, letting her know that he, too, was aflame with need. She moaned against his mouth.

He broke the kiss to nuzzle her neck, his breath harsh. "Roza, Roza," he murmured, punctuating the words with kisses. "You feel so good. You belong in my arms."

She opened her eyes. She belonged in *his* arms? No, no, no. He was supposed to feel as if *he* belonged in *her* arms. Blast it, she'd forgotten her purpose once again.

How could she switch this, turn this into her win and not his? What had she learned in her books . . . ? Oh yes.

But would that really work? There was only one way to find out. "Alexsey?"

Aching with desire, he captured her hand and kissed the palm. "Yes, my sweet?"

With her hair mussed about her face, her cheeks flushed from their kisses, and her eyes half closed, she looked like a woman who'd just been thoroughly loved. *One day she will look this way because of me.* Pleasure raced through him at the thought. God, he loved the feel of this woman, of her full curves, and the—

He frowned. What was she . . . was she *humming*?

He pulled back and looked at her.

She smiled and, with an archness at odds with her usual expression, her humming changed into a song.

She was singing to him.

He managed a smile, though it took some effort. Was this a Scottish tradition? A way to woo that he'd somehow missed? Or was she just being . . . Roza?

She must have taken his silence for approval, for she sang louder. Her voice alternated between husky sweet and painfully flat, and yet somehow it didn't matter. She was here, in his arms, singing to him. Only to him.

He didn't know why that mattered, but it did.

He tightened his arms about her, a fierce surge of passion thrumming in his veins. Her lips pouted over a vowel, and then pressed together to make a *p*, and with each movement of her soft lips, he was newly enthralled, newly charmed, more deeply stirred.

When she took a breath to begin a new stanza, he kissed her with all of the pent-up passion she'd roused. He kissed her to let her know he wanted her. To let her know he'd been thinking of her, and dreaming of her, and that this—holding her in his arms and tasting her, sent his senses reeling—

A door opened and then closed somewhere in the house and she started, breaking the kiss and staring out at the foyer.

He had to curl one of his hands into a fist to fight back the passion she'd left hanging in his soul. After a second, he could speak. "Roza?"

"I thought—" There was the sound of the door opening and closing again, followed by footsteps disappearing. She relaxed in his arms. "It is just Mrs. Pitcairn leaving for her cottage."

Bronwyn ran a finger over his lips, her eyes bright with passion. "You . . . you liked my singing?"

"It stirred me." With a wink, he gently bit her finger. "Too much."

She chuckled, the sound warm against his chest. "I am glad you left the dinner early, but this is a crazed idea, Alexsey."

"I know. But I will not go until fate forces me, or you ask me."

She lifted her lips to his ear and whispered, "I don't want you to go. Not yet." With that, she slid her lips to his jaw, kissing a path to his eager mouth.

Bozhy moj, she was so succulent and sweet. He held her to him, taking and giving, awash in waves of passion unlike any he'd ever experienced.

Bronwyn reveled in the urgency of his kisses, of his hands. *Ah, this. This is what I wanted.*

His hands were splayed over her back. As he kissed her, he slid one of them down to her waist and along the curve of her hip. It was such an intimate touch, shivery shards of longing danced through her. He slid his hand down her leg over her gown to her knee, then below; she could feel each of his fingers as they slid over her ankle and held it.

Through the haze caused by his kisses, she felt his hand slip up under her skirt to cup her calf. She gripped fistfuls of his coat, pressing against him.

His tongue brushed hers and she opened for him. He thrust his tongue against hers as his hand slid up over her knee, above her stocking. His palm lay flat against her naked thigh. She gasped eagerly against his mouth, opening her legs, moving restlessly, yearning for all she'd never known. Never wished for. Until now.

He held still, breaking the kiss, his breathing as ragged as hers. He rested his forehead against hers. "Bronwyn, do you—"

She grasped his wrist and tugged his hand higher, sliding his hand up her thigh, his fingers dangerously close to her core.

Breathless at her own daring, she waited, her heart pounding furiously. All of her life, she'd read about passion. Because of Alexsey, she was at this very instant living the moments that before now had only been pale, vague words upon a page.

She was really living now, tasting life, feeling the wind and the joy and the passion. She closed her eyes, her body quivering on the brink. The freedom of this moment was almost unbearable. With hands that shook with desire, she guided his hand higher, until it rested there, tucked under her gown and chemise, warm against her womanhood.

As he felt her thighs part, Alexsey clenched his teeth against a crashing wave of his own desire. She was so sweet, so passionate, so *his*. She was everything he'd thought she was—wildly passionate, vibrantly alive, sharing herself with him in a way that made his wild Romany blood sing with joy.

She moved restlessly against him, pressing herself

into his hand. He massaged her gently, smoothing the slick folds with his palm. She moaned against his neck, writhing against his fingers, moist and swollen, ready for him.

Alexsey's breath caught, his cock swelling in instant response. God, he wanted her with an insistence he'd never before felt. Wanted her under him, in his bed, and no one else's.

He stroked her slowly, trailing his fingers over her, stroking her lightly at first, then with increasing pressure. She gasped, grabbing his coat, his shirt, twisting in heated need, her sweet, hot breath trailing over his jaw and sending shivers through him. He trailed his fingers again, and again, feeling the center of her desire harden against his fingers, her arousal increasing with each movement, each touch—

With a startled cry she arched against him, calling out his name as she clenched her thighs on his hand, wave after wave of passion washing through her. He crushed her to him, holding her close until her movements ceased, fighting his own desire. This moment was for her.

As her breathing stilled, he was shocked to see a single tear roll from the corner of her eye, a diamond drop against the dewy softness of her skin.

"Roza?" he asked softly.

She rested her forehead against his. "That was—" She gulped back a sob. "That was—"

He kissed her gently, his heart tight with an unnamed emotion.

Bronwyn's mind was too abuzz to think. Her eyes

wet with happiness, and her body humming. She'd never felt more alive, more complete, more *herself*. She snuggled closer to him.

He gave a muffled laugh that ended with a moan. "Please do not move, my Roza. This embrace has stirred me, too, and I cannot continue without—"

She waited, looking at him.

He moaned, his voice husky with desire. "I will explain it later. Ah, Roza, what you do to me. No one has ever tied me in such knots."

"Never?"

"Never," he declared, his breathing slowing slightly.

Deeply happy, wrapped in his arms, she felt . . . treasured. And yet, she couldn't keep a small thought from creeping into her cocoon. *Where does this end? And how?* Desperate to think about something else, she asked, "Do you enjoy being a prince, Alexsey?"

He looked surprised. "No one has ever asked me that. I suppose I do, as much as I can."

"What do you mean?"

He shrugged. "Do you enjoy being a daughter? A sister? We are what we are; we do what must be done. And if it is what we've known since we were children, then we do not imagine other ways or lives."

She eyed him curiously. "But you do imagine other things. I know it."

He gave a reluctant smile. "Sometimes I do. But never for long."

She sighed, thinking of her own life, of how they all worked to reach their goals—Papa's patents and Sorcha's season. "All we can do is the best we can do."

"Now you sound like a Gypsy. My grandmother would be proud."

"I wish I really *were* a Gypsy, and you really a huntsman." It was such a lovely fantasy, better than any book. But it was just that—a fantasy. She sighed.

His eyes were half closed as he watched her, a pleased smile on his lips. Who had won that round? He'd certainly taken her much farther down the path of seduction; her body still trembled with aftershocks.

But she also saw a warmth in his gaze that was more . . . intimate. *Then I made some inroads, too.* "Alexsey, do you think—"

The sound of a carriage arose outside, the jangle of a bridle and the crunch of wheels.

Bronwyn sat upright. "Oh no! My stepmother and sisters!" She was on her feet in a trice. "You said they wouldn't be back for hours!"

"So I thought." With a great sigh, Alexsey stood. "I must go."

"But they will see your horse and know you've been here!"

"Do not worry; I tied the horse to the side of the drive. They will not see it in the dark." He bent and kissed her soundly. "I will go out the window." He swiftly pulled on his coat.

Outside, Bronwyn heard the coachman's voice and the opening of the carriage door. "Hurry!" she whispered.

He collected his hat and then bent to kiss her one last time, sweetly and insistently.

Despite the danger, she clung to him.

The sound of the carriage door closing made her release him. "Go!"

"I will see you soon, little one."

As he went to the window, she headed to the sitting room door, shutting it behind her and reaching the foyer just as her family entered.

"How are you feeling?" her mama asked.

"Much better, thank you. How was the dinner?"

Sorcha, rosy-cheeked from the wind, untied her bonnet. "Oh, Bronwyn, I've never seen such wondrous food!"

"There were courses and courses and courses," Mairi said. "And the desserts—" She kissed her fingers to the air the way their French tutor did whenever he was pleased with something.

Bronwyn laughed and helped them remove their pelisses. "Tell me all about it, for I couldn't help but think of your wonderful dinner when I wasn't napping."

"It was *lovely*," Sorcha said, her eyes sparkling. "The dining hall was decorated with pine boughs and it smelled heavenly."

"But Sorcha was forced to sit next to Viscount Strathmoor at dinner," Mairi said.

"That was unfortunate," Mama agreed, hanging her pelisse on a coat hook.

Bronwyn led the way into the sitting room, glancing at the windows, which were all closed. "Was Strathmoor rude?"

Sorcha made a face as she sank onto the settee. "He only spoke to me twice all through dinner, leaving me completely to the gentleman to my left, horrid Mr. MacInnis."

"Who is a thousand years old and can't hear." Mairi snickered. "Sorcha had to yell for him to hear her."

"He says the most inappropriate things, too," Sorcha said in a huffy tone. "He told me he liked 'younger women' like me, and he spent the entire dinner leering at me in a very disgraceful way."

Bronwyn shook her head. "A pity. I hope the two things Lord Strathmoor said to you during dinner were pleasant?"

"No. First he asked for the salt dish. Then, before the men retired for port, he told me he'd had the pleasantest dinner conversation of his life." Sorcha's lips thinned.

Mama sniffed. "He's not worth your time and he knows it."

"The prince spoke to Sorcha," Mairi added.

"He was most kind," Sorcha said. "He asked about you, Bronwyn, and said he hoped you would feel better soon. Then he told me which of the dishes he'd enjoyed most and asked me the same." She absently smoothed out a pillow on the settee.

He is kind. And passionate, too. The thought made her face warm.

"It's a pity he didn't stay after dinner," Mama said, a dissatisfied look in her eyes.

"Oh. Where did he go?" A flutter of happiness arose despite her attempts to quell it.

"His grandmother said he had a headache," Sorcha said. "She seemed quite unhappy with him about it, although how he could avoid a headache, I don't know."

"Her Grace talked to Sorcha, too," Mairi said from

the fireplace, turning so her back now benefited from the warmth. "For nigh on a half hour."

With obvious satisfaction, Mama said, "Her Grace was quite kind to Sorcha."

"Yes, but I felt like a horse at auction. She kept *looking* at me, as if she wished to pinch me and see if I were healthy enough."

Mairi chortled. "I thought the same thing! I expected her to ask to see your teeth."

"I believe Her Grace is a Romany," Bronwyn said. "Perhaps that explains her behavior."

Mairi said, "She makes me shiver! When I laughed aloud, the look she sent me—I wouldn't be surprised to wake up and find myself turned into a toad!"

Sorcha laughed. "If you turn into a toad, I shall claim all of your bonnets as my own."

Mairi stuck her tongue out.

"Girls, please!" Mama did not look amused. "You're talking about a grand duchess of Oxenburg."

Sorcha obediently lost her smile. "I'm sorry, Mama, but Her Grace *is* an oddity."

"She is still a very well-respected lady."

"Yes, Mama." Sorcha turned to Bronwyn, the twinkle in her eyes letting her sister know she wasn't entirely subdued.

Lady Malvinea hid a yawn. "I suppose your father hasn't yet come home?"

"I haven't seen him since dinner," Bronwyn said truthfully.

The clock chimed and Lady Malvinea stood. "It's late and we should all be getting to bed."

"I don't know why," Mairi said in a grumpy tone. "Sir Henry has planned three whole days of hunting, so there's nothing to get up early for."

"We won't see anyone until Friday." Sorcha looked as put out as Mairi.

Bronwyn's heart slid a bit, and she realized how much she was looking forward to seeing Alexsey again.

"Friday will be here before you know it," Mama said calmly.

"What happens on Friday?" Bronwyn asked.

Sorcha brightened. "Sir Henry's having a dinner, and he's promised games to liven up the evening."

"That will be fun." Bronwyn rose to her feet, Sorcha following suit. Mairi opened the sitting room door and they headed toward the stairs.

Mama stopped at the bottom of the steps. "I shall wait for Papa to return. He shouldn't be long. Good night, girls."

As Sorcha and Mairi chattered on about who'd worn what and who had said what, Bronwyn followed. When she reached the landing she glanced back, just as Mama bent to pick something up from the floor.

Bronwyn's heart stuttered. It was a man's glove. *Alexsey's glove.*

Mama looked up, her gaze meeting Bronwyn's.

Without thinking, Bronwyn turned and hurried back downstairs. "You found it!"

Not giving her stepmother more time to think, Bronwyn snatched the glove from her hands and tucked it into her own pocket. "I bought a pair of gloves for Papa's birthday and lost one of them."

"How did it come to be here?"

"The— My dogs must have carried it here. I shouldn't have allowed them in the house."

"You had them indoors again? You promised not to."

"I know, but I was feeling poorly, and they're such good company."

"Your Papa's birthday isn't for another two months. You are planning well in advance."

"Yes, I happened to see these in a window and knew they'd be perfect for Papa, so . . . I got them."

Mama's gaze never left Bronwyn's face. "It seems rather large for him. Perhaps I should look at it again."

"Oh, he won't care. He's not exactly a fashion plate, is he?" With a forced smile, Bronwyn turned toward the steps.

"Bronwyn?"

Oh God, does she suspect? Please don't let her think anything, please! Bronwyn pasted a smile on her face and turned back to her stepmother. "Yes?"

"I'm glad you're feeling better."

"Much better, thank you. My ear doesn't hurt at all now."

"Good. Sleep well, my dear."

"Good night." Her heart thudding, Bronwyn hurried up the stairs, aware of her stepmother's gaze following her.

Chapter 18

Lady MacClinton looked at Lucinda, pity in her old eyes.
"My dear, society was not developed to protect the heart,
but to prevent your heart from engaging on its own."
—The Black Duke *by Miss Mary Edgeworth*

"If you are determined to be in a foul mood, pray take yourself elsewhere."

Alexsey, who'd been scowling into the fireplace, sent a black look at Strath. "If you dislike my mood, feel free to leave."

"This is *my* uncle's study." He eyed the glass of scotch in Alexsey's hand, went to the sideboard and poured himself a glass, and then came to stand near Alexsey.

They were dressed in formal dinner wear, although Strath's fingers itched to do something about Alexsey's casually knotted cravat. "What's wrong, my friend? You've been like a bear with a sore paw for the last few days."

"Roza is avoiding me. I've been to visit three days in a row now, and she won't see me alone. I fear I've frightened her away."

Strath frowned. "What did you do? She seems rather fearless."

Alexsey shrugged. "She is fearless for herself, but not for her sisters. If there were a scandal, she would feel responsible."

"Ah. Then you need to be more discreet."

Right now, he was willing to do anything but give up on her. For the last three days, he'd been unable to think of anything but Bronwyn. Of her sighs. Of her kisses. Of her soft skin. Of her passion as she writhed against him. Of her breasts, so lushly plump that his hands couldn't contain them.

The memories made him burn with the desperation of a man dying of thirst in a desert. "I must meet her without her sisters and mother."

"Ah yes. The chaperone problem. In France you'd have no problem seeing a single lady alone, providing her chaperone was in an adjoining room. And if you slipped a few coins into that hand, sometimes you could sweep your lady away for hours on end, with no one the wiser."

"In Oxenburg, we do not treat women as glass vases in a case, or expect them to perform tricks. Yesterday, I sat for two hours in the bloody sitting room while Lady Malvinea tried to talk Miss Mairi into playing the pianoforte."

Strath shuddered.

"Indeed. Thank God she refused."

"Does Miss Bronwyn play?"

"She sings, but only when drunk."

Strath's mouth dropped open.

"From laudanum. She had an earache."

"Ah. I couldn't imagine otherwise."

Alexsey sighed. "This morning, I briefly saw her

and her mother in town." Bronwyn had been wearing a straw bonnet that framed her face adorably. He'd itched to take it off and let her thick hair down, one pin at a time. He'd imagined doing so all day. "Bronwyn's mother watches me."

"If Lady Malvinea is giving you the eye, she's likely mentally measuring you for a groom's coat for Miss Sorcha." A bitter note chilled Strath's voice. "My uncle says Lady Malvinea has been hinting that she believes her ripest, juiciest plum is worth nothing less than a royal tiara."

Alexsey sipped his scotch. "She'll never receive one from me."

Curiosity was bright in the other man's gaze. "You've no interest at all in that diamond of the first water?"

"None."

Strath regarded his glass with a thoughtful air, then sent a cautious glance at Alexsey. "I have to wonder . . . I've never seen you pursue a woman with such intensity. Don't lose sight of your original intent, a harmless flirtation with a pretty woman and thwarting your meddling grandmother."

Alexsey thought of Bronwyn's large brown eyes, velvety dark, the lashes so long they tangled at the corners, and of her full mouth, so tender and ready to open for him. Of the way her eyes sparkled when he won a smile from her—

He tossed back some scotch. "I know exactly what I am about, and so far, she's been worth the pursuit. She's more beautiful each time I see her."

Strath whistled. "She has truly captured your attention. She seems rather . . . unapproachable to me."

"She is not an easy woman to conquer, but I will prevail. *If* I can get past the dragon guarding her."

"Her mother?"

"Her own fears."

"And then?"

"Then I will light her passion."

"And then leave her, just like that."

"Once our passion has burned itself out, she will be glad to see me go. I have been very plain with her about my expectations, as she has been plain about hers."

Strath looked impressed. "You've had that conversation, and she didn't eat you alive?"

Alexsey shrugged. "She knows how things stand. I hope to spend some time with her this evening after dinner. Although it will be in front of everyone, it will be something."

"We should rearrange the cards on the table so that you may sit with her. I've used that little trick on occasion."

"I looked earlier, but Sir Henry and my grandmother were already there, moving cards about as if they were playing some sort of game. And now that the silver is set, staff have been assigned to watch the tables." He set his glass down. "I may need to do something rash."

"I'm happy to help you. Just let me know what you need." Strath turned toward the window. "Ah, that's the first of the carriages." He crossed to the door and held it wide. "Let the rashness begin!"

As he'd glumly expected, Alexsey wasn't seated anywhere close to Bronwyn at dinner. She and her sisters were all near Strath, who'd ended up with Miss Sorcha at his side. The viscount didn't appear to be fond of the arrangement, for he barely said a word to her, or she to him, during the entire three hours it took to suffer through dinner. He spent most of his time talking animatedly to the beauty seated at his other side, while Sorcha sent him furious glances whenever she wasn't speaking to her other dinner partner, an elderly man who dozed at his plate, waking only in time for dessert.

Tata's heavy hand could be discerned in the guests seated at Alexsey's sides. On his left was a viscount's daughter who had a tendency to use the word "I" to excess, while on the other was a duke's daughter who was too tongue-tied to address more than two words to him throughout the entire dinner.

Alexsey ignored them and watched Bronwyn instead. She spoke to the people to either side of her, but didn't look especially comfortable doing so. At one point she must have said something bold and Bronwyn-like to the man seated at her left, for he flushed and then turned, refusing to look at her for the rest of the evening.

Bronwyn didn't seem to notice, but every once in a while, she glanced Alexsey's way and their eyes would meet. Each and every time, he found himself fighting off a flicker of pure heat. To other people, she looked shyly sweet, the type of woman who didn't raise her voice unless pressed, but he knew better. Behind those liquid brown eyes was a brain sharper than most, and a streak of powerful passion.

Sir Henry finally signaled the end of dinner and

stood. "Normally, I would suggest the men join me for a glass of port, but tonight the ladies wish to play charades and whist, and will need partners. Therefore, I suggest we join them immediately, lest they find other men to do so."

This was met with a gentle round of laughter and everyone rose.

"Port, sherry, and refreshments will be served in both salons where the games will be played," Sir Henry announced.

The crowd began to move toward the doors at the end of the dining room, and Alexsey lost sight of Bronwyn in the crowd. "Damn it. Where did she go?" he asked Strath.

"She and her sisters decided to play charades. It's being played in the Green Salon."

"Is that a card game?"

"No, it's a silly children's game."

"And adults play it?"

"Silly adults play it at silly house parties like this, where the silly host thinks nothing of torturing the rest of us by withholding port."

Alexsey glanced around. "Where is this Green Salon? We are joining the game."

"What? No. I don't play charades."

"You do now."

"But—it's quite the lamest entertainment ever. Men never play it, only women."

"Men will play this one."

Muttering to himself about being misused, Strath led the way to the Green Salon.

As soon as they went through the wide doors, Alexsey instantly found Bronwyn. Her back was to him, and she and Sorcha were speaking with a young lady with red hair.

Strath squinted at the redhead. "That's Miss MacInvers. Wealthy family, the MacInvers, and only one daughter. She's considered quite a catch, but that laugh—" He shook his head. "I'd put a rope about my own neck before the first week ended."

"I will avoid her. Who is the man pretending to sleep in the back row of chairs?"

"Oh, that's Mr. MacPherson. His wife must be playing." Strath glanced around the room. "She's by the refreshment table along the back wall, speaking with Lady Malvinea and Miss Mairi."

Alexsey saw Lady Malvinea at the same time she saw him, and there was no mistaking the way her jaw firmed with determination.

He'd often gotten just such a look from his grandmother, so he knew exactly what it meant. She would soon send Sorcha his way. He turned back to Strath. "Everyone seems to be holding slips of paper."

"Yes. Everyone is assigned a number so they know which order to participate."

"Indeed." Alexsey looked about the room. "You said men do not play this game, and yet Lord Perth appears to be playing, for he has a slip of paper. And there is a gentleman by the fireplace, although he doesn't have a— Ah. Someone just gave him one, so he is also playing, as is—"

"Yes, yes. Mr. MacKennit. I see them all, but seriously, Alexsey"—Strath leaned closer—"they're not men. They're lapdogs, every one."

Alexsey lifted a brow. "You lied."

"Me?" Strath tried to look shocked, then sighed. "Fine. I hate this game. I'd rather be shot point-blank with bird shot and have it all removed with fireplace tongs than play."

"I will be unhappy if we do not play this game, which is a pity. I was going to take you out tomorrow morning to shoot my new dueling pistols, but now I will not feel like doing so."

Strath straightened. "You have a new set?"

"I purchased them from Felligrino himself."

"That—I've tried to buy some from him, but he won't sell them to me."

"He only sells them to those who can shoot."

"I can shoot!" At Alexsey's raised brows, Strath sighed and added, "Somewhat."

"You would like these pistols. They are balanced like a feather on a pinhead, silky smooth to shoot, the action—"

"Demme you, Menshivkov. My one weakness!"

"And did I mention the handles have silver engraving? Not too much, as it might offset the balance. But delicately, like a butterfly's kiss—"

"Fine, I'll play your demmed game of charades! But I warn you, I'm horrible at this game and suspect you won't be any better."

Alexsey shrugged, his gaze finding Bronwyn once more. *We will be together soon, Roza. I will see to it.* "Do not count me out, Strath. I am very competitive and do not take failure lightly. Explain how this game is played."

"The person organizing this game is Miss MacInvers, as she's by the front of the room where the play table has been placed. First, everyone is assigned a number. When your number is drawn, it is your turn to play. You go to the front of the room, pull a slip of paper—"

"A different one?"

"Yes. You pull this one from a hat or a bowl or some such holder, and then you act out what it says."

"Act? As if on a stage?"

"Yes, but you can't say a word. While you're act-ing out the object or person or thing that is written on the slip of paper, people in the audience call out their guesses. If someone guesses correctly, you give him the slip of paper. At the end of the game, whoever has the most slips of paper wins."

"That's ridiculous."

Strath brightened.

"But we will play anyway. Tell me more."

"Bloody hell. Let's see . . . what more is there to tell? Ah yes—though you can't speak, there are some gen-erally accepted signals. People use this gesture"—he tugged his ear—"to mean 'sounds like.'"

"I will remember. What else?"

"This"—he tapped his nose—"means 'spot-on.'"

"Very well. And what do I win if I get the most slips of paper?"

"Something ridiculous, like a paper crown or a small cake."

"A pity. Games are more fun if there is money in-volved."

"That would make it tolerable. Or scotch."

Alexsey nodded.

"Then I'll go give our names to Miss MacInvers." Strath sighed and left.

Alexsey continued to watch Bronwyn, who'd been joined by her stepmother and stepsister. She glanced around the room and when her gaze met his he bowed, smiling.

She flushed, a pleased look flashing over her face as she took an involuntary step in his direction. But before she could take a second step, her stepmother took her elbow and whispered something urgently in her ear, her posture stiff. She and Bronwyn spoke briefly; then Lady Malvinea turned and said something to Miss Sorcha.

Sorcha sent him a quick glance and turned as red as the cushions on the settee.

Lady Malvinea said something else, her tone obviously more strident, for Alexsey caught it from across the room. Sorcha, with what looked like a brave nod, left her mother's side and slowly made her way to Alexsey.

The sacrificial lamb. He bowed when she curtsied her greeting. "Good evening, Miss Sorcha. I see you and your family will be playing charades."

"Yes, we love charades."

"Who doesn't?"

She nodded and started to say something but bit her lip, obviously ill at ease. Finally, she said, "Your Highness, it's . . . it's lovely to see you here." Her voice carried an arch breathlessness. "Most men don't enjoy charades."

"My grandmother's family loves drama. Every evening, after the sun went down and the campfires were lit, they would sing and dance and perform silly comedies, and sometimes bits of Shakespeare."

"It sounds wonderful."

"Sadly, most of the plays they knew weren't fit for mixed company."

"Oh."

He hid a grin as he watched her realize that of all the lessons she'd had about making conversation with a prince, none addressed how to discuss inappropriate Gypsy plays.

She managed a thin smile as she stammered, "That's— But of course no one would ever think— I mean— It's very—"

Fortunately for the tongue-tied Sorcha, Strath returned. He cast a dismissive glance at her and favored her with the briefest of bows, which she reluctantly returned, her own mouth tight with displeasure.

Strath handed a slip of paper to Alexsey. "Miss MacInvers informed me there was room for only one more player, so I've designated myself your interpreter, should you draw a word or phrase you aren't familiar with."

Alexsey took the paper, which had an elegant #20 written in script.

Miss Sorcha dipped a curtsy. "I should rejoin my mother, if you'll excuse me—"

"Please stay with us. The game is about to begin, and I see three seats that are together." Alexsey proffered his elbow.

She hesitated, but only for a second, and he escorted her to the seats. Once they arrived, Miss Sorcha took a seat, Strath following suit.

Alexsey said, "I will be back shortly. I wish to speak with Miss MacInvers before the game begins."

"What for?" Strath asked.

"Rule clarification. You may keep Miss Sorcha company while I do so."

"But—" Strath and Sorcha said at one and the same time.

Alexsey slipped away, making his way to where Bronwyn and her mother and younger sister stood with a small group of ladies.

Chapter 19

Lucinda watched the flower as it was washed down the path and into a great puddle. There, it floated. Though the rain pelted it cruelly and the wind shoved it hither and yon, the little flower remained afloat. Though delicate in design, it was flawlessly strong in heart.
—The Black Duke *by Miss Mary Edgeworth*

Bronwyn wished for the tenth time that she were anywhere else. Her stepmother was on one side, Mairi on her other, as Lady Alexandra, the daughter of Earl Mercer, complained again about the temperature of the room, which she found too warm for her complexion. As the lady's complexion was ruddy due to the whiskey she constantly sipped out of a silver flask when she thought no one was looking, it was difficult to maintain an air of genuine concern.

It was with relief that Bronwyn felt someone at her elbow. Thinking it was Sorcha, she turned with a smile and found herself staring straight at the green emerald embedded in the prince's knotted cravat.

Her heart leapt in satisfaction, her stomach aflutter.

She braced herself and tilted back her head, only to find herself drowning in Alexsey's eyes.

No man should have such beautiful eyes.

"Ah, Your Highness!" Mama clutched Bronwyn's elbow and tugged her gently away from the prince. "How pleasant to see you this evening."

Mairi sank into an immediate curtsy. "How good to see you again!"

Bronwyn followed suit, catching her spectacles as they slipped on her nose, her heart beating an odd rhythm. She cast a cautious glance at Mama, only to find that lady eyeing the prince with a closed expression. A sense of unease filtered through her. For the last three days, she'd caught Mama watching her, an odd look upon her face. Yet when Bronwyn had asked if anything was amiss, Mama had just changed the subject.

She can't know anything. At least, I hope not. Bronwyn wasn't certain how she'd explain the relationship between herself and the prince. It broke all rules, smashed through all boundaries, and left her feeling breathless and deliciously alive. Who knew such feelings could be so freeing?

But perhaps "feelings" was the wrong word. "Desires" would be more appropriate, and she had plenty of those. Delicious, potent desires that invaded every waking thought, slipped into every dream, threaded through every book she read.

It was difficult hiding those thoughts from her sisters and stepmother, especially as Mama seemed unable to give up her dreams of Sorcha becoming a princess. What would Mama say if Bronwyn admitted that she wanted the prince herself? Though that wasn't strictly true. She wanted more kisses, more embraces, more passion . . . but the marriage Mama was dreaming of was out of the question. Neither she nor Alexsey wanted it. He because he valued his freedom, and she because the match was unthinkable.

His warm voice enveloped her. "Lady Malvinea. Miss Murdoch. Miss Mairi. How do you do?"

"We are quite well, but"—Mama pretended to peek over his shoulder—"where is Sorcha? You were speaking with her just a moment ago."

"She is speaking with Viscount Strathmoor."

Bronwyn glanced past him to see Sorcha sitting stiffly by Strathmoor's side, neither speaking.

"They don't look very happy," Mairi observed.

Alexsey shrugged. "Perhaps they have had a falling-out."

"Your Highness!" Lady Alexandra turned so that she was thrust into their small circle. A thin and rather birdlike woman, she eyed Alexsey the way a blue jay might look at a particularly plump worm. "How lovely of you to join our game."

Bronwyn blinked. *Surely not.*

As if he'd heard her thoughts, the prince sent her a quick side look. She'd read the phrase "a laughing gaze" in many of her books, and now she knew what that meant.

His eyes mirrored his every thought—which was good, for she never had to wonder what he was thinking. She could only hope her eyes weren't so easy to read, or everyone would know she was thinking of a way to climb back into his lap and—

She hoped her face wasn't as warm as it felt, but Bronwyn caught her stepmother's gaze upon her, a knowing, almost disappointed look in the older woman's eyes.

She knows.

Bronwyn's heart sank and she again wondered at its direction. When they were sharing heady kisses and more, the sun shone brightly, her heart was happy, and she was secure in her direction. But the second she was alone doubts crept in, and fears for her future. Even more disturbingly painful, the desire to *have* a future beyond taking care of her family began to creep into her mind. She found herself wondering if she'd been too hasty in thinking she belonged at Ackinnoull forever. She wondered if perhaps there was a better place for her somewhere else. *With someone I love.*

Love—the one thing she didn't share with the prince, nor would she ever. They were involved in this game of his doing, each trying to win over the other. While it added a piquancy to their relationship, it also held them at bay, hiding bits of themselves from each other.

It was unfortunate, but that's how things were. She had to remember her original purpose in flirting with him: the awakening of her sensuality was merely a bonus. But oh, what a deliciously surprising bonus it was.

She watched him from under her lashes as he spoke to Lady Alexandra, his gaze meeting hers now and again. *This is progress.*

There were other signs his interest in her was increasing. He'd visited Ackinnoull several times these past few days, but Mama had been too present. And tonight, his gaze had been on her all throughout dinner. He clearly wanted to spend time with her; she needed to find a way to get him alone and—

"Bronwyn!" Mama's voice held a touch of exasperation.

She realized that both Lady Alexandra and Alexsey were looking at her, one with a questioning look, the other with one that was far too knowing.

"Lady Alexandra asked you a question." Mama forced a smile. "Pray pay attention."

Lady Alexandra chuckled. "Lost in your own mind, were you? I know a thing or two about that."

"I'm sorry. I should have been listening."

"Nonsense. I never listen myself, unless I have to. I asked if you thought His Highness would lose the game due to his lack of experience?"

Alexsey lose? Somehow, she didn't think such a thing possible. Fearing to risk a glance in his direction while Lady Malvinea hovered so close, Bronwyn forced a smile. "I'm sure he'll surprise us all."

Lady Alexandra laughed. "An excellent answer, my child."

Miss MacInvers clapped her hands. "We are ready to begin, if everyone will take a seat."

Bronwyn sat with Mairi and Mama, while Alexsey and Lady Alexandra sat behind them. Alexsey's long legs rested to one side of Bronwyn's chair, his boots casually crossed at the ankle, resting against her skirts.

Miss MacInvers explained, "On the table is a silver bowl containing the slips of paper bearing the words

that must be acted out. Remember, no speaking, no
letters, and no spelling out. And the first participant
is"—she reached into her pocket and pulled out a
number—"number four!"

"That's me!" Lady Alexandra jumped to her feet.
She hurried to the front of the room and drew her challenge from the silver bowl.

She squinted at it, muttered something to herself,
and slipped the paper into her pocket. Then, facing the
audience, she began hopping on one foot.

Predictably loud and merry, the game progressed.
Bronwyn found it difficult to pay attention, though.
Every time Alexsey moved, she felt his foot come into
contact with her chair, and she could hear the rustle of
his clothes as he shifted in his seat, and smell the faint
scent of his cologne.

She only half listened to the clues being given by the
participants, and even as she and Mairi talked about
the marvelous refreshments, even as she kept an eye on
Sorcha, who had gotten caught up in the game and was
yelling out answers much to the amusement of Lord
Strathmoor—even with all of the distraction around
her, Brownyn was aware of every breath Alexsey took.

Laughter erupted and Bronwyn watched as dig-
nified Mr. MacPherson walked about the front of the
room, his thumbs tucked under his arms, his elbows
flapping like a chicken.

Lady Alexandra leaned forward and yelled, "You're
a chicken! Goose! A duck! A partridge! A—"

MacPherson pointed at her and touched his nose.

"A partridge it is!" she said, looking pleased.

He frowned and shook his head.

Her smile disappeared. "A duck?"

He scowled and jerked his thumb over his shoulder.

"You're a chicken, then!" Lady Alexandra clutched her reticule in excitement. "One with a-a-a thumb!"

He stomped his foot, his face red.

Lady Alexandra burst out, "Bloody hell, just *tell* us!"

Mairi sank into a gale of laughter, while Lady Malvinea's lips thinned. From behind her, Bronwyn heard the deep rumble of Alexsey's laughter all of the way down to the soles of her feet.

"He's not to speak or he'll be disqualified," Miss MacInvers warned.

"I know what it is," Mrs. MacPherson called out. "You're a *goose!*"

Mr. MacPherson tapped his nose happily, then grabbed a doily off a nearby table and set it on his head. He tied an imaginary bow under his chin, then held out his hand to two imaginary children.

Miss MacInvers called out, "A nanny?"

He shook his head. He pretended to pick up one of the children and fondly kissed it, then pointed to it and then himself.

Sorcha guessed, "You're a female goose! Not a gander, but a—a— Oh, why can't I remember what that's called?"

"He's *Mother Goose!*" called Lord MacDavid.

"Yes, thank God!" Mr. MacPherson snatched off the doily and mopped his brow. "Bless you for putting me out of my misery, MacDavid."

Amid much laughter, Miss MacInvers drew another name from her pocket and Sorcha's number was called.

She read the slip, bit her lip, and then looked about the room. Finding an empty chair, she stood on it and acted as if she were making a great speech.

"*Romeo and Juliet,*" Strathmoor said.

He said it so quietly that everyone was still a moment.

Turning red, Sorcha gave a jerky nod and climbed off her chair. She brought him the paper and then took her seat again, not looking at him.

"How on earth did he guess that so quickly?" Mairi whispered.

"I have no idea," Bronwyn replied.

Miss MacInvers was reaching into her pocket to draw another name when Alexsey said in a deep voice, "There is no need. It is my turn."

Everyone looked at him.

Miss MacInvers tittered. "Your Highness, you're not supposed to call out a turn—but it's your first time, and no one can fault you for being excited to play. Will anyone mind if the prince goes next?"

A chorus of voices instantly arose in agreement.

Bronwyn frowned. *He must be accustomed to that— perhaps that's why he always expects to get his way. And why he finds it so easy to live in the moment, without thought of any consequences.*

He reached into the silver bowl and drew a slip of paper. He read the word, his face inscrutable.

"Do you need an interpretation?" Lord Strathmoor asked.

"*Nyet*. This is a word I know very well." He placed the paper on the table, his gaze locking with Bronwyn's.

Oh dear. Why is he looking at me?

He stood very straight. The room fell silent. With a slow, almost caressing movement, he made a very curvaceous female outline in the air.

Silence met this.

"Oh my," Lady Perth said in a faint voice.

Her face red, Miss MacInvers cleared her throat. "Your Highness, I don't believe common decency will allow—"

"A woman!" Strathmoor called out.

Alexsey nodded and then, as an afterthought, touched his nose. He looked at Miss MacInvers. "This means yes?"

She nodded, but whispered, "You're not supposed to speak."

"I will be silent now." He made the outline again, only this time, he paused at the knee area and drew a fish tail.

"A mermaid!" Mairi called out.

He touched his nose.

Mairi gave an excited hop in her seat and clapped.

Alexsey now touched his throat and pantomimed singing.

"A mermaid and singing?" Mr. MacPherson mused. "What could that be?"

Mairi leapt to her feet. "A-a-a—" She turned to Bronwyn. "What were those called? They were in that epic you read to us when we were children, about an old witch and a mermaid, and— Oh! A siren!"

Alexsey looked directly at Bronwyn and she knew exactly what he was thinking. She'd sung to him, and he'd responded with a passion she was now remembering in agonizingly vivid detail. Her body heated, her nipples peaked, and for an instant, she wondered if she could speak.

Seeing her flush, a pleased look warmed his face. "*Da*. It is indeed a siren." His voice caressed, and only she knew it.

The assemblage clapped appreciatively.

Lady Malvinea cleared her throat. "Your Highness, I'm surprised you know that word."

"It is almost the same in my language—*sirenya*," he said. "I love to hear the *sirenya* song. It makes a man's blood pump."

"Oh!" Miss MacInvers said, looking faint.

Bronwyn couldn't look away. What was it about this man that made her want things she'd never wanted, dream of things she'd never allowed herself to dream of? Things she'd only thought about when presented between the protecting covers of a book?

Alexsey resumed his seat, his hand brushing Bronwyn's shoulder ever so lightly, his legs once more stretching out until his booted feet rested against her skirts. Instantly, her body warmed and her heart trembled.

As the game continued Bronwyn drew the phrase "fox hunt," which was quickly guessed, as so many of the guests had recently participated in a hunt. The entire time she was in the front of the room, Alexsey seemed to devour her with his dark green eyes and lazy smile. She was relieved when the time came to take her seat.

Finally, the last participant acted out her scene and the slips were counted. Lady Alexandra received a lovely Dresden teapot. Mairi, who'd come in second, received a shawl embroidered with rosettes, while Mrs. MacPherson won a potted rose for third place.

"That was quite lively," Mama said as they stood.

"I don't know when I've laughed more." Mairi hugged her new shawl. "We must play this at home. If we were to practice, and knew one another's signals, we could win every game. Think of all the prizes! We'd have to use one of the guest rooms to hold them all."

Bronwyn had to laugh. "If we were to win all of the time, other people would tire of playing and no one would invite us anymore."

Mairi's face fell. "I suppose so. We'd have to lose a few games on purpose. Oh, look! There's the prince's grandmother by the door, speaking with Sir Henry and the prince. She's tiny, isn't she?"

"We should stop by to pay our respects before we leave. Where's Sorcha?" Mama looked about. "There she is. Oh dear."

Sorcha was marching away from Lord Strathmoor as he watched, his mouth twisted as if he'd tasted a lemon.

When Sorcha reached them she pressed her fingers to her temples. "I've such a headache. May we go soon, Mama?"

"Of course, my dear. Mairi, could you ask one of the footmen to send for the carriage? The rest of us will make our good-byes."

Alexsey hid a pleased smile when he saw Bronwyn and her mother and sister navigating their way toward him. Now was his opportunity to speak to her. He would pull her a little out of the way and offer to meet her somewhere close by.

"Your Highness?" Miss MacInvers stood looking up at him, a question plain in her eyes.

He bowed. "Yes?"

"That was an amazing performance, but . . . I wrote all of the words to be guessed, and I don't remember the word 'siren.'"

He raised his brows coolly. "I do not know what to tell you. That was my word."

She blinked. "Of course. I don't know what I was thinking. My wretched memory—"

"It is no problem. I played your game and enjoyed myself very much. You did a very good job."

She flushed, looking inanely pleased. "Thank you, Your Highness!"

He bowed and she left.

His grandmother looked at him, her eyes narrowed. "What word did you draw from the bowl?"

"It is unimportant."

She held out her hand. "I would see the word, please."

He shrugged, dug into his pocket, and pulled out a strip of paper.

She looked at it. "'Pall-mall.' What is this?"

"I don't know. I don't care, either. I knew what word I wished to enact."

Tata started to say something, but Lady Malvinea arrived at that moment to say her good-byes.

Alexsey bowed over Bronwyn's hand. "I have waited for this all evening," he murmured.

Her smile froze, her gaze flickering to her step-mother and his grandmother.

"Stop looking like a hare before the chase. You will only draw more attention. Tell me, Roza, have you been avoiding me?"

She plastered a faint smile on her face, but her eyes shot cautiously toward her mother before she said, "You left your glove at my house. My stepmother suspects something."

"Ah. That explains it, then. I thought you were angry with me."

She looked surprised. "No, no. I just—" Her hand tightened over his. "We must be more cautious."

Relief flooded him. Had they been alone, he would have swept her into his arms and covered her with kisses. As it was, he merely covered her hand with his. "I will. But I must see you again. Alone."

For a moment he thought she'd refuse, but something flickered in her eyes and she said in a husky voice, "I would like that, too. Very much."

Bozhy moj, she had such sensual eyes. They looked right through him and made him yearn for her anew.

She lowered her voice. "Tomorrow, come to—"

"Bronwyn." Lady Malvinea linked her arm with her stepdaughter's, a bright smile on her face. "Poor Sorcha has a headache. We really must go."

"Yes, of course." But as she was hustled off by Lady Malvinea, Bronwyn sent him a quick, regretful glance, leaving Alexsey certain he'd see her again soon.

Chapter 20

*Roland ran the smooth stone along the edge of his sword.
With each steady stroke, a fine glittering of metal dust
floated through the air, leaving the blade sharpened in its
wake. It took the strike of a hard stone to sharpen a blade.
And a strong blade to withstand a stone's strike.*

—The Black Duke *by Miss Mary Edgeworth*

The Black Duke in one hand, her cloak thrown over her arm, Bronwyn ran down the stairs to the kitchen. Scott and Walter trotted behind her, hard on her heels. "Good morning!" she called to Mrs. Pitcairn.

"Good morning, miss." As the older woman set a lid on a fragrant pot, she saw the dogs. "Och, dinna bring them in here!" She lunged for a leg of mutton that was resting on the table just before Walter reached it. "This is no' fer the likes o' ye, ye wild beastie!"

Walter managed to look both hopeful and apologetic, but Mrs. Pitcairn was having none of it. "Oot wit' ye, ye mangy mutt, and take that sneak-thief brither of yers wit' ye!"

She wrapped the leg of mutton in waxed paper and placed it on a high shelf, while Bronwyn opened the kitchen door and watched the dogs race into the early-morning sunshine. It was a beautiful day, unusually warm for this time of year, the sun spilling golden rays across the brown and green hills.

If not for the dogs waking her, she'd still have been in bed. She'd fallen asleep very late, unable to stop thinking about Alexsey.

She was sure he would visit today, and she needed to be ready—more ready than she had been at their last encounter, when she'd been seduced in the midst of her own seduction. She couldn't succumb to him every time he was near or she'd never gain the upper hand, which she was more than ever determined to do.

She'd underestimated her opponent. He knew far more about the ways of seduction than she did. From now on, she had to think in a more complex fashion, tempt him in more sophisticated ways, give him just enough hope—but not too much—to make him mad with lust. And then, just when he thought he'd won her over, she'd laugh and inform him how mistaken he was.

What a glorious day that would be! But first she had to find a way to maintain control over her reactions to his overtures. While that sounded simple right now, when Alexsey was nowhere to be seen, it was much harder to remember when he was kissing her senseless.

But today she would turn the tables and show Alexsey Romanovin that he wasn't the only one capable of overwhelming another person's wits and calm sensibilities.

Sadly, all she had left in her arsenal of seduction techniques gleaned from her novels was the power of scent. She had to find a scent that would make him think of her every time he smelled it, one that would torment him with memories after she'd gone. One that would make him regret being so callous as to plan to seduce a woman for no better reason than he'd been told not to. Of all the valid reasons there were to seduce someone—love, admiration, passion—stubbornness of character was the least attractive.

Such an insult must be answered and all she needed was a perfume so seductive that he would grow passionate just upon smelling it. But there was one problem. Yesterday, while Mama and Sorcha had been out visiting the vicar and his wife, Bronwyn had gone to Mama's bedchamber to sample perfumes, but she found they were all too cloying or heavy. She wanted to drive Alexsey mad with lust, not make him think of funeral flowers. So next, Bronwyn had sampled Sorcha's perfume, which was much lighter and nicer. Bronwyn had almost borrowed it, when a thought occurred: if she wanted the scent to remind Alexsey of her whenever he smelled it, then the last thing she should do was borrow another woman's perfume.

Frustrated, Bronwyn had reluctantly put the idea behind her. She didn't have the time to find a scent for Alexsey to identify with her. Besides, if she did find one, in order to drive the prince mad with desire (if it even worked), she'd have to pay a servant to spritz some about Tulloch Castle, which would never do.

She sighed, wondering how she could seduce someone who was so good at seduction. As she did so, she caught the delicious aromas rising in the fragrant kitchen—cinnamon, nutmeg, basil, dill—was that thyme? Perhaps she'd been thinking about scents in too narrow of a fashion. What if she instead smelled like something he came into contact with every day, something that would make him remember their time together, their kisses, their embraces?

Mrs. Pitcairn dried her hands on her apron. "Off to read, are ye?"

"Yes, but I've only an hour. Mairi and I are to polish the silver this morning."

"Ye work hard; ye deserve some time to play." Cook lifted the damp cloth covering a large bowl and removed a ball of risen bread dough. "Yer sisters willna' be here forever, miss. Once't they're married, 'twill jus' be ye and yer ma' and yer da'. Wha' will ye do then?"

"I'm not really sure." Bronwyn hesitated. "At one time, I thought Ackinnoull was my future. It was all I wanted. But now . . ." She leaned against the table. "I'm not certain what the future holds. Perhaps once Sorcha and Mairi are settled, I'll travel."

"Where would ye go?" Mrs. Pitcairn pulled out a stone pestle and mortar, placed some rosemary in the bowl, and began to grind it.

The clean, fresh scent tickled Bronwyn's nose. *Hmm— rosemary. Sir Henry's cook serves herbed bread frequently, and almost always uses rosemary. That has potential.*

She caught Mrs. Pitcairn's questioning gaze. "I'm sorry—where would I travel. I would love to visit Greece and Italy, but that would be much too expensive. Perhaps instead, I'll take a trip to the Hebrides and the northern lochs."

"The lochs are breathtakingly lovely, miss. Me brother lives in the north, so I've seen them. And they're no' so far away." Mrs. Pitcairn finished grinding the rosemary and set it aside, then turned to fetch some butter melting in a small pot by the stone.

Bronwyn leaned over the table and took a pinch of rosemary. With a quick look at Mrs. Pitcairn's turned back, she rubbed some of it on her neck.

Goodness, it was quite potent when freshly ground— almost eye-watering, up close. She looked about for a cloth to rub it off, but Mrs. Pitcairn returned before Bronwyn could do anything.

The cook brushed the dough with the melted butter, then sprinkled it with the rosemary. "If ye travel, ye'll need a companion. Women canno' travel alone."

"Of course they can," Bronwyn said. *Surely the smell will fade before the hour is out.* "We don't live in medieval times; women travel alone to many places." Older women, to be sure, many of them forced by their circumstances to do so, but it was accepted.

Still, the thought of traveling alone wasn't as appealing as that of traveling with someone with the same sense of humor. Someone who would enjoy a line or two from a poem by Walter Scott while admiring a beautiful loch. Someone who disliked formality and could kiss away the storm clouds—

Stop that! She shook her head, hoping to dislodge her plaguey thoughts.

Mrs. Pitcairn chuckled. "Ha' ye a bug in yer ear, miss?"

"No, just a troublesome thought."

Mrs. Pitcairn placed the bread loaf onto a large wooden paddle and slipped it into the oven. "Ye'll ha' to shake harder than tha' to lose a thought."

"I'll just go read. You can't read and worry—it's not possible."

"I worry aboot ye, all alone outside. Someat' could happen to ye and no one could hear yer screams."

"The dogs are with me; they are protection enough."

Mrs. Pitcairn wiped her hands on her apron. "Hmph. Ye think more o' th' beasties than I do, but there's no turnin' ye. Go on wit' ye. There're apples in tha' cask; take one in case ye get hungry."

"Thank you." Bronwyn tucked the shiny apple into her pocket, then put her cloak on. As she closed the door behind her, she whistled for the dogs. They came running from a nearby field and fell in behind her as she set off down the trail, her book a pleasant weight in her pocket.

The sky was bright blue and the sun warm as her boots crunched along the path; she didn't really need her cloak until she reached the shade of the woods. The dogs roamed here and there, sniffing the grass and rocks, an occasional leaf floating down to land before them. The growing sound of the stream announced their arrival at their favorite clearing.

Scott and Walter each picked a place in the sun to stretch out, and soon their eyes closed.

The ground was too damp sit on, so she untied her cloak and threw it over her shoulder, tucked her skirts into her waistband, and then climbed to a thick, low branch of her reading tree. There, she settled into the crook, resting her back against the trunk as she stretched her legs along the wide branch. Satisfied she was in no danger of falling off, she threw the cloak over her legs, making sure it didn't brush the damp grass.

With a happy sigh, she pulled the apple and her book from her pocket. The quiet was lovely and calming, a respite from the tensions that now filled Ackinnoull. Mama hadn't been the same since she'd discovered Alexsey's glove in the foyer, although she had been oddly reluctant to mention it. Bronwyn thought to re-open the subject, but feared it would only add to Mama's already sharp suspicions, and so they'd settled into an uneasy silence. The rest of the family was in just as much turmoil: Papa's head was buried deeper in his workshop than usual, and they rarely saw him; Mairi was constantly bubbling with excitement over events at the castle; while Sorcha had been quiet of late from the strain of their new social life.

Bronwyn herself had been on edge, her mind never at peace. No matter where she was—at home, at the milliner's, at church—the moment she heard a door open, her heart lurched in anticipation of it being Alexsey. When it was him, she was thrown into a state of physical arousal and emotional turmoil, neither of which was given any relief. And when it wasn't him, she was bitten by deep disappointment that lingered for hours.

She supposed the disappointment was only natural; she was eager to teach Alexsey a very needed lesson and her time was running short. All too soon, Sir

Henry and his guests would leave Tulloch Castle, and life would return to its previous boredom.

She frowned. *I wasn't bored at Ackinnoull before Alexsey arrived, and I won't be bored after he leaves.* And yet . . . she had to admit things would be less lively.

She stifled a sigh and took a vigorous bite of her apple, appreciating the sweetness as the skin gave way to the flesh. When she finished, she threw the core into the clearing, where Walter and Scott leapt upon it, playing with it before they settled down and ate what was left. She wiped her fingers on the bottom of her cloak and then picked up her book, taking a deep breath of the chilled forest, the musty scent of dropped leaves and damp ground tickling her senses. She opened her book and within a few paragraphs was lost in the words.

She wasn't certain how long she'd been reading when Walter and Scott woofed and stared into the woods. Startled, she lowered her book.

As if he'd risen from the pages, there was Alexsey, dressed much as he'd been that first day.

Bronwyn's breath caught. *How could a man look so good in such common clothes?* She tapped a finger on her book. Miss Edgeworth had obviously never seen a fine male figure adorned in the clothing of a working man, or she'd have shown Roland in just such clothing, still looking as handsome and noble as if he were in formal dress.

With a bark, Papillon burst into sight, her feet muddied and her tail wagging so fast it was a blur. Walter and Scott ran to greet the small dog.

Alexsey walked toward Bronwyn, his gaze hot and

possessive. "You look like a wood nymph, perched in your tree."

"I sat here because the grass is damp."

"Ah. That, I can fix." He took off his coat and spread it over the grass at the bottom of the huge trunk. He looked more approachable now, wearing a loose white shirt that clung to his broad shoulders and then fell in graceful folds about his waist.

"I didn't expect to see you here so early."

His lips twitched. "You think I'm a slug-a-bed who doesn't arise until late, complaining about having to meet the day? I am not so paltry a man."

"Paltry" was not a word she'd have used to describe anything about this man.

"And do not worry that I will interfere with your reading time." He reached into his pocket and pulled out a small book. "I have a book, too."

How many men would join her in reading? None she'd ever met before. She really wished she could stop finding things she liked about him; it made it more difficult to maintain her distance, which she desperately needed to.

But . . . maybe this was just a ploy to win her favor, to advance his attempts at seduction. "How did you know I'd be here?"

"I stopped at Ackinnoull and spoke to Mrs. Pitcairn who was on her way to fetch eggs. She told me you'd be in your special glen, so I knew you'd be reading."

"And you just happened to have a book in your pocket?" She couldn't keep the dubious tone from her voice.

He waved a hand. "It is a gift for you, *mayah dara-*

*gahya. S*ince you are already reading, I will read with you. Afterward, it is yours."

To her chagrin, more of the knots she'd tied around her heart eased. Not only was he willing to sit and read with her, but he'd brought her the one gift she loved over all others—a book. *Blast it, must he be so kind?* She realized he was looking at her, a question in his eyes, and she managed to say without seeming ungrateful, "Thank you. You know me almost too well."

His smile glinted with heat. "What I know about you, my little Roza, I like very much. And I know I will like the rest, too."

The purr in his words made her body warm in reaction.

He lifted a brow. "May I join you?"

Of course, her heart whispered. *More touching, more kisses, more embraces. I want them all.*

That's not wise, her brain whispered back.

Be quiet, Bronwyn told them both as she swung her feet over the edge of the limb and dropped to the ground.

"What were you just thinking?" Somberness darkened his eyes. "Doubts have found you, *nyet*?"

"Doubts? No. Nothing like that."

"You were thinking about us. About our kisses. What to do. Is it too much? Is it too little? I see your face, Roza, and I know."

Good God, he can read my mind.

"You think too much." He reached out to capture the edges of her cloak, pulling her toward him. "I see it in your eyes all of the time—doubt this, doubt that, question this, question that."

Did she do that? Should she stop? Was it bad that she didn't wish to live an unexamined life? Perhaps—

He laughed softly. "See? You are doing it now."

"I suppose I do worry about things. Don't you?"

"At times. But never with you." He looked surprised he'd admitted such a thing, but he quickly recovered. "Under normal circumstances, I would let time settle the questions in your mind, but we do not have time, we two."

Bronwyn found it hard to swallow. "You . . . you will be leaving soon."

"A week maybe, but not much longer. Too soon, Roza. So when I see that frown in your eyes, I know I must say something."

"You don't need to say a thing; this was never meant to last. It's merely a flirtation." *That's all it is, a very potent, very heady flirtation. One I will miss dearly.* The realization caught her by surprise, and her heart ached with it.

"Do not look so, Roza." He tugged her closer. "You must fight those voices."

"Which voices?"

"The little ones that whisper in the night that you should not trust me, should not be with me—do not let them claim you. We will vanquish them with kisses and laughter, living in the moment like the Romany. No one is happier than they."

She shook her head. "But we Scots are the opposite. While your Romany can pack up and move on if things are not as they like, the Scots dig into rocky hillsides and build stone castles so they may stay for centuries. Living in the moment feels wrong. It is against my blood."

His lashes obscured his expression as he ran his finger down her cheek. "You Scots do love your castles."

She shivered at his touch. "We plan for winters, because we must. And since meeting you, I've realized that I must plan for mine."

He slipped his arms around her as he smiled into her eyes. "You are far from your winter years, Roza. Today, we have sunshine, soft grass to cushion us, books to read, and . . . other pleasurable things."

She fought the lure of his words. *He's supposed to desire me unto madness—not the other way around. I cannot forget that.*

Yet when he bent to kiss her, she instantly lifted on her toes to meet him, her eyes closed as his mouth descended on her and—

He pulled back.

She opened her eyes.

He sniffed.

Ah! The rosemary! Holding her breath, she waited.

He sniffed again. "Is it an herb, *nyet*?"

She nodded, smiling shyly. "Rosemary."

"The cook at Tulloch puts it in turtle soup."

Her smile faltered. She smelled like a turtle? Not a fragrant loaf of bread, but a turtle? "Surely you've smelled it in some other dishes, too. Bread, perhaps?"

He shook his head.

"In a delicious stew, then? Something savory and warm?"

He released her cloak. "In my country, we throw rosemary onto graves."

She just looked at him, appalled.

"That seems odd to you, *nyet*? Rosemary keeps fresh the . . . How do you say—?" He tapped his forehead. "Thoughts about times no longer here."

"Memories?"

"*Da!* Rosemary keeps fresh the memories of the dead."

Lovely. She smelled like a turtle and the grave.

"Why do you smell of rosemary?" he asked.

"Oh. I was helping Mrs. Pitcairn in the kitchen. She was grinding rosemary to brush on a loaf of bread and, ah, I must have spilled some on my gown." She stepped away from him, hoping he couldn't see her heated cheeks. "Perhaps we should read for a while." Bronwyn gathered her cloak and sat, scooting to one side to make room for him.

He joined her, sitting too close, his thigh pressed against hers, which felt far too good. "Alexsey, the rosemary . . . it won't bother you?"

"I like the rosemary. You smell like the forest."

She brightened. That was much better. Now, whenever he walked in the woods, he would think of her. Of course, he'd also think about her whenever he ate turtle soup or attended a funeral, which wasn't ideal, but it was better than nothing. Not bad for a pinch of herb.

He shifted, his broad shoulder against her arm.

"I'm sorry. Do you need more room?"

A wicked light warmed his gaze. "With you, I always want more—especially kisses."

She found herself looking at his mouth, wishing— *No. Not yet.* She shifted away. "Perhaps after we've read a bit."

"When you decide you wish for a kiss, just tell me. I will wait." He leaned against the tree and looked around. The leaves played in the breeze as the stream bubbled by. The three dogs slept in the sun, leaves tumbling by. "I like this. I cannot read at Tulloch. It has grown much too noisy."

"I'm surprised you couldn't find an empty room somewhere. The castle is huge."

"Empty, I could find. Quiet, *nyet*. Someone suggested a talent show for those who do not hunt. Many of the guests must secretly believe they are professional quality singers, and they have been practicing all week. Loudly."

She couldn't help laughing. "I take it none of them are good."

"Their caterwauling has given me a headache."

Her smile slipped. "I thought you liked singing."

"Good singing, *da*, but this—" He slid her a look before shrugging. "This is such a peaceful place, we should sit quietly and let nature sing for us."

"That sounds lovely." She decided not to read too much into his comment, and settled back against the tree to read.

A breeze stirred through the clearing and she caught the faint scent of his cologne. She instantly remembered their first kiss here—and then later, the way he'd touched her so very intimately, leaving her panting and yearning for more.

Her body tingled with awareness. Just being near him made her feel off balance and faintly dizzy. *Which is not what I wish at all. This is how* he *is to feel. Not me.*

"What do you read, Roza?" He leaned over to see her book, his cologne teasing her even more. She watched as his gaze traveled over the page. He hadn't shaved this morning, and the shadow of a beard framed his mouth, making her yearn to trace her lips along his jaw.

His lashes were lowered, so he was almost done reading the page. Such thick, long lashes. She wondered what he must have looked like as a child. *What would a child of ours look like?* The thought was so unexpected that her cheeks heated.

At that exact moment, he straightened, his gaze meeting hers.

For one breathless moment, she thought he could read her thoughts as he'd done before, but he merely nodded thoughtfully. "Miss Edgeworth's pen is sharper when she's not writing about kisses."

"Yes. She quite missed the mark with those."

Alexsey glinted her a smile and then returned to his own book.

She dragged her gaze away from him, pushed her spectacles back into place, and stared at her book. How could one read when a handsome man sat literally right beside one? A real man. One who smelled so good, too.

She caught herself leaning a little his way as she tried to catch his cologne once more. It was masculine and spicy, and very faint. She peeked at him from under her lashes and was relieved that he seemed to be immersed in his book.

He turned a page, seemingly oblivious to her, his eyes moving over the words without pause. There was something about him—perhaps it was his size and his lazy smile—that made him appear sleepy, like a lion sunning itself. One knew the lion could outrun anything it wished to; the question was only how long its prey could withstand it.

She realized she hadn't turned a page in a while, so she quickly did so, dragging her gaze away from him. It was difficult, though. A man who loved to read. A man who could make her laugh. A man who was everything he should be, except— She remembered him at the foot of the stairs, casually informing Strath of the way he would pass a few weeks at her expense.

How could such an arrogant man also be so intriguing? In a week or so, Sir Henry's house party would be over, and the guests would disperse back to their usual lives. In her case, days filled with nothing more exciting than the occasional new book. At one time that would have seemed more than enough. Now, she wasn't so sure.

She stifled a sigh and wondered how he could stay so focused on his book when she couldn't read a single word of hers. What book had he brought her, anyway? A novel? A book of poems?

Under the pretext of tucking a loose curl behind her ear, she turned her head to look. A description of an Egyptian tomb met her interested gaze and she scanned the page, leaning closer to examine a delicately drawn picture of a particularly beautiful sarcophagus.

"Do you wish to read this book instead of your own?"

Startled, she looked up to find his amused gaze on her.

She flushed. "I'm sorry. I caught a glimpse of the picture and forgot it was your book."

"I'll trade you if you'd like."

"No, no. This is fine." She returned to her book and was grateful when he did the same. She didn't dare look at his face or book again—he was far too quick to notice. But his legs were another thing. If she lowered her book just a bit she could see the long, muscular length of his legs, stretched before him and crossed at the ankles.

There was nothing more dashing than a man with strong thighs in breeches and riding boots. As she stared at his thighs he recrossed his legs, his muscles flexing in the most distracting way. *Oh my. I wonder what they feel like, bare skin to bare sk—*

"You are not reading."

No, she wasn't. Not a single word. She snapped her book closed. "I'm sorry, but I can't read with you here."

He closed his book. "To be honest, I have not been reading, either. I have been looking at your boots."

She looked at them. "My muddy walking boots?"

"I can't look at them without wanting to unlace them."

There was a purr to his voice that stirred her. "Unlace them," she repeated breathlessly, instantly caught in the image.

"I want to make you want what you shouldn't, make you do what you said you wouldn't. Do you remember when I touched you, Roza?"

Good God, how did one forget such a thing? It took her a moment to regain control of her voice. "I . . . vaguely remember." She tried to sound airy but must have failed, for he laughed softly.

"My little Bronwyn, always denying yourself."

She wasn't denying herself anything; she was merely attempting to maintain her control. If she wished to tease him the way his mere presence was teasing her, then she had to be the one who led the dance.

She lifted her chin and met his gaze, and said in a suggestive tone, "So what are we going to do, since reading is apparently out of the question?"

His gaze darkened. "If you want more kisses, you've but to ask. . . ."

Just ask, she told herself. But no—that wasn't what she really wanted. She smiled teasingly. "No. *You* ask."

Something flashed in his eyes; his jaw tightened. "You don't wish for kisses? Then you won't have them."

My prideful prince needs such a setdown! His stubbornness bolstered her resolve not to be just another kiss under a tree, but to be the one kiss he'd remember on his deathbed. The kiss that no other kiss ever measured up to. *That* was what she wanted. And if it meant denying the heat that was simmering in her blood now, then she'd find the strength to do it. "Fine, we'll just talk, then."

Disappointment darkened his gaze and he tossed his book to one side with a bit more force than necessary. "What do you wish to speak about?"

"Books, politics, art, religion—"

"You." He caught one of her curls where it lay against her shoulder and twined it about his finger. "Your hair is so soft, like spun silk."

She had to swallow before she could answer. "Touching is not talking."

"Hmm," he said in an abstracted tone, his gaze on her curl.

She moved her head, tugging her hair free. "Tell me about Oxenburg and your brothers. Are you close to them?"

He stifled a sigh, but answered her. "We do not argue, if that is what you mean, but we have lives of our own. My brothers Nikki and Wulf are in court more than I. Nikki is to be the king, so he must stay there."

"He enjoys it?"

"I think so, *da*, although he dislikes the—how you say—foot kissing?"

"And your other brother?"

"Wulf has a head for keeping our coffers filled. Right now, he and his wife are developing our lace industry, which was already thriving. But with their help, we've begun making enough to double our exports to various cities, and for a higher price. It is much in demand."

"I would like to see this lace."

"It is beautiful. My third brother, Grisha, the soldier of the family, is rarely home. He prefers to stay with the army and run drills when they are not assisting our neighboring countries to fulfill treaty obligations."

"And you, when you are not living with your grandmother's people?"

"Until recently, I was the ambassador."

She looked at his clothing, and he laughed. "I am not one to like ceremony, so there is some irony, *nyet*? But when I must dress, I do. I mainly attend parties, pretend to remember people I do not, and carry messages from other kings and parliaments."

"It sounds rather boring."

"I do not enjoy it." He leaned forward. "What I *do* enjoy are pert Scottish misses who dance as if they have three left feet, sing with great enthusiasm, smell like the forest, and would rather bury their heads in a book than wear silks."

She'd never seen anyone with such deep eyes, the color endless. "Some of the women you've met must have been beautiful."

He shrugged, his shoulder warm against hers. "You are beautiful, but that is not enough. Beautiful is only for looking. You cannot hold it." He gave her a lopsided smile. "I will have a favor from you."

Finally, he'll ask for that kiss! She nodded, her breath increasing.

He lifted her spectacles from her nose and folded them. "I wish to see your eyes." Setting them aside, he cupped her face with his large, warm hand. "Your eyes make me think of the fields near my summer home in Oxenburg.

"Every year, the soil is turned, and it is rich and dark and brown like your eyes. Those fields grow the most golden wheat the world has ever seen. Gold like the flecks in your eyes, like the lights in your hair." He brushed a curl from her face, his fingers trailing over her cheek to her bottom lip. "I drown in your eyes."

Her mouth suddenly dry, she wetted her lips. His gaze followed the delicate swipe of her tongue.

He drew in his breath. "Damn it, Roza, ask me to kiss you."

He wanted to kiss her! And she wanted him to. Wanted it so badly that her heart stuttered, her skin tingled in anticipation.

She turned her face into his palm and kissed his warm skin. "You must ask me," she whispered, begged.

His mouth tightened, and she saw the war he was fighting—he wanted the kiss as badly as she, but his pride demanded her capitulation.

"Ask," she whispered, grasping his wrist and trailing her lips over his fingers. "One word, Alexsey."

He caught his breath when she nipped at his fingertips, her gaze now locked with his. "Ask," she whispered again.

A flicker of naked desire flashed across his face, and he winced as if in pain. "*Nyet.* You must be the one."

Bronwyn thought she'd burst into a fireball if he did not touch her soon. Her entire body craved his touch with a longing that left her squirming with need.

What could one kiss hurt? her passionate side asked.

But the future—her Scottish side urgently whispered.

Forget the future. I want this right now.

"To hell with asking." She pulled his head down and kissed him.

Chapter 21

Lucinda melted into his arms, and Roland's heart warmed.
—The Black Duke *by Miss Mary Edgeworth*

With a pained moan Alexsey scooped her into his lap, his mouth possessing hers. She twined her arms more tightly about his neck and opened to his seeking tongue, answering him kiss for kiss. She fought to both breathe and devour, writhing to get closer, to taste him more. He broke the kiss to nip passionately at her bottom lip and she gasped with need, her body aflame with a yearning that was almost painful.

Alexsey's breath shortened at the sound of Bronwyn's small gasp. She clutched at his shirt and strained against him as he slid his hands over her ripe curves, deepening the kiss as he did so. God, she was a delicious conundrum, prickly and soft, defying him with one sentence and then the next, kissing him as if she never wished him to stop.

He ran his hands over her body, exploring her generous curves, loving that she felt like a woman and not a sack of bones. He could hold her without being afraid of breaking her. Her full breasts and hips were made for holding and tasting.

One hand traveled down the swell of her hip to her thigh, while his other smoothed up her back. Her heart beat wildly, sending a prideful thrill through him. *Ah, Bronwyn, this is what happens when you stop thinking. You feel.*

He teased her lips and stroked her tongue with his own. Panting and flushed, she returned his embraces, mimicking everything he did with even more passion.

She was a creative lover, and every time he got her alone, she surprised him. On the outside, she was a neat brown paper package primly tied with a string, but inside was an explosion of the richest spices, the most expensive wines, the most delicious morsels. The desire to unwrap her and lay open her secrets was irresistible.

He untied her cape and pushed it off. Then he found the tie to her gown and tugged it free, pushing her gown open and sliding his hands over her thin chemise to her full, round breasts with a groan. They filled his hands and more, making his cock ache with need. God, he loved her fullness, her wholeness. He gently cupped her breasts, watching as her lashes fluttered at his touch, her sharp gasp urging him on.

He pushed her gown down so he could see the generous circles of her rosy areolas through her thin chemise, his eyes feasting on the sight. Then he bent to take her nipple in his mouth through the material, rolling his tongue over and over the hardened nub, encouraged by her heated gasps. From one breast to the other, he ministered slavishly, denying himself as he urged her passion higher and higher.

She clutched at him with greedy hands, her legs

opening to his searching fingers, her hips moving rest-lessly. His body ached with the need to bury himself in her, but he fought for control. She was too delicious, too precious to gulp. This was a woman made to be savored, over and over, long and leisurely.

Slowly, he slid his hand up her leg to her warm thigh, her soft skin sliding under his fingertips. He paused just short of her womanhood, trailing kisses from her breasts to her neck. He slowly, ever so gently, slid his fingertips over her, barely grazing the wet, swollen folds.

She jerked in his arms. He held her tight and contin-ued to stroke her, speeding his movements.

Wet and wanting, she clutched his shoulders in her need, her legs parting yet more. He stroked her more firmly now, enjoying the expressions that crossed her face. She was so wild, so wanton, sprawled in his lap, as he stroked her once, twice— She convulsed, her cries soft and desperate as passion rolled through her.

The sound left him with a deep ache that made him grit his teeth. He rested his forehead on hers, their breath-ing loud. "You are so beautiful," he managed to gasp.

Seconds passed and then she moved against him, her voice husky and low. "Alexsey." Her gaze locked with his. "I want more."

"But—"

Her fingers curled about his shirt and she jerked him close. "You said I had but to ask. I am not asking, but telling."

He laughed and kissed her swollen lips. "I cannot say no to you. I have never been able to say no to you." He hadn't had that power since the moment he'd met her, and the realization was staggering. Before he could wonder about it, she slipped her hand into his lap and cupped him.

He sucked in his breath as his erection throbbed anew. What seemed like a scant second later they were both undressed; then he was lowering her—naked and flushed with need—to his coat.

He kissed her everywhere he could see, worshiping the softness of her skin, the rose of her areolas, the flush of passion on her cheeks. And then gently, ever so gently, he moved between her legs and pressed his rigid cock to her.

She was wet and waiting, and he slid in until he rested against her maidenhead, surrounded by her heated warmth. She was so deliciously tight, her movements innocently wanton. He gritted his teeth to hold off his reaction and slowly pressed forward.

She grimaced and arched against him.

"Bronwyn," he managed to gasp out. "This may—"

"Stop talking. Just—" She pressed against him, gorgeously abandoned.

He steeled his jaw and thrust through her maidenhead, capturing her cry with a rain of kisses, silently begging her forgiveness even as his body moved within hers.

A deep ache that was both pleasure and pain filled Bronwyn. She clutched his shoulders, gasping as, through the ache, a powerful need grew to pull him to her, to get closer, to *feel* him. She slid her hands to his waist, and then his hips. With a sudden effort, she pushed against him, engulfing him completely.

He moaned her name.

Encouraged, she wrapped her legs about his hips and, lifting her own, buried him deep inside her. She did it again and again, the dull ache receding with each stroke. And each time she pulled him inside, a gasp of pleasure was ripped from Alexsey's lips.

He joined her, thrusting in the rhythm she'd set, their bodies damp as they fiercely pleasured one another. Moments later a wave of pleasure ripped through her, making her cry his name. And this time she took Alexsey with her as they rode wave after wave of passion, finally collapsing together, clinging to one another under the sky.

A long time later, she sighed with happiness. She felt wildly powerful and rather naughty, almost drunk on the sensations coursing through her body. "So that's what all the fuss is about."

He chuckled and lifted up on his elbow to smile down at her, his hair falling rakishly into his eyes. "*Da,* that is what all the fuss is about."

"It's—" "Wonderful" was too pallid. "Amazing" was too technical. "Blissful," she said.

"Yes, it is." He kissed the corner of her mouth. "Are you glad you stopped thinking?"

"Oh yes. A million yeses." She smiled sleepily. "In fact, I may decide to never think again." Which would be blissful: to never have to consider what-ifs and what-fors, but just *be.* Suddenly she understood why that held such appeal to so many people.

"I am spent, my love. You have drained me." He kissed her bare shoulder, then rolled to his back and tucked her against him, her head against his shoulder.

She fit perfectly, and he smiled when she snuggled against his neck, the scent of rosemary and lily tickling his nose.

Not only did he feel replete, but he also felt proud, as if he'd accomplished something uniquely special. He supposed he had; he'd won his way into the arms of the most fascinating woman he'd ever met, and now, he was loath to let the moment pass.

Holding her to him, he brushed her silken hair from her cheek. "We are good together, we two."

She raised her head to look at him. "May we do it again?"

He laughed. "Of course, though I must recover first. And you will need time, too. You may be sore for a day or two and might not feel like—"

She rolled on top of him, her eyes laughing. "*Nyet*." She ran her hands over his chest, his stomach, down to his half-sleeping cock. "I feel like it right *now*, Alexsey."

"Sadly, men need time to replenish. Women, not so much."

She regarded him through half-closed eyes, a wistful expression crossing her face. "How long will it take, for I must return to Ackinnoull soon or someone may come looking for me."

He wrapped his arms more tightly about her, holding her warm body to his. "It is early still, so you will be safe here, with me. Besides, it is good manners to linger after a romp." He rubbed his cheek to her hair, tugging her cloak over them like a blanket.

"A romp, eh? That's what it was?"

"A romp, a tryst, lovemaking . . . call it what you will."

"Whatever you call it, it was very nice." She curled against him like a cat warming itself on a rock.

Her chest was pressed to the side of his and he could feel her heart, the beat as steady as she, her skin warm against his. *A man could get used to this.*

For several minutes they remained thus, both enjoying the closeness of the moment, but all too soon, Bronwyn sighed and then rolled away. "It grows late. I must dress."

He reached for her but she eluded him, climbing to her feet and gathering her clothes. "Stay here," she instructed. "I'll be back."

She was gone before he could protest, and he heard her washing in the stream. He gave her some privacy, rising to gather his own clothing. Soon she returned, looking flushed but presentable. With a quick kiss on her swollen lips, he went to the stream, as well.

When he returned, he saw a faintly troubled look on her face.

"*Nyet.*" He sat on his coat and patted the seat beside him.

"No, what?"

"You may not start thinking yet." He captured her hand and tugged her down to his side.

"Yes, but—" She turned to look up at him. "Alexsey, what are we doing?"

"Enjoying one another. It seems right, doesn't it?"

"Yes." But there was doubt in her voice.

Because she wishes for this to mean more? Or because she fears it means too much? He looked into her face, but now, when he most needed to, he couldn't tell what she was thinking. Her eyes were dark, her brow knit, but no clue rested in her expression. "Perhaps our purpose is simply pleasure," he said cautiously.

"Perhaps."

She didn't look happy, but neither did she look disappointed.

He sighed. "We are making memories, Roza. Memories to enjoy long after this moment is gone."

Her smile seemed tight. "And you can remember it whenever you smell rosemary."

He would, too. He would remember this day until the last breath left his body. That was good, wasn't it?

From far in the woods arose a call.

"Mairi!" Bronwyn grabbed her book from where it sat on the ground, while trying to pat her hair back into some semblance of order, and looked adorably flustered. "I was to help my sister polish the silver. She mustn't find us here."

An odd pang went through his heart. "I don't wish you to leave."

"I don't wish to leave, but I must."

Reluctantly, he found her spectacles and handed them to her. "I must see you again."

She slid the spectacles onto her nose. "We will. We're to come to the castle soon. I will see you there."

"That's not enough!" He slipped an arm about her waist and tugged her closer. "There is so little time left, and I want to see you alone—not with dozens of people."

Her lips turned downward. "It's all we have."

"I want more. Bronwyn, let me come to you tonight."

Her eyes widened. "You mean . . . to my bedchamber?"

"Let me spend the night with you, and show you—"
How I feel. The words froze his tongue. *How* do *I feel?*

She pulled away, shaking her head. "No. That's—Alexsey, we can't. We can't risk getting caught. Besides, my rooms are in the attic. There's a tree there, but it's not safe to climb."

"Bronwyn!" Mairi called, her voice closer. "Where are you?"

Bronwyn tugged her arm free. "I *must* go."

He took a step after her. "Send me a note. Tell me where to meet you and I will be there."

But she was already gone, running down the path, her dogs loping after her. Only once did she look back, and Alexsey thought he saw the shadow of a smile before she disappeared.

Papillon whined.

"Me, too." Alexsey stood for a long while, staring down the path. Finally, with nothing left to see, and filled with feelings that warred with one another until he could make no sense of any of them, he started to leave. As he did so, he caught sight of the book he'd brought Bronwyn.

He rescued it from the ground and tucked it into his pocket, then looked around the small, idyllic clearing. No other reminder of the magic that had just occurred remained.

Oddly bereft, he made his way back to his horse, Papillon at his heels.

Chapter 22

Lady MacClinton sighed woefully. "Who knows what lies in the hearts of men?"

"Or women," Lord MacLynd answered. "Their hearts are just as complicated and black as ours."

—The Black Duke *by Miss Mary Edgeworth*

Two days later, Alexsey stood in the foyer with Strath, Papillon panting at their feet. As they put on their coats, a footman approached. "Pardon me, Yer Highness, bu' Her Grace, the grand duchess, is askin' fer ye."

Alexsey closed his eyes, his jaw tightening. *How does she know when I'm on my way to Ackinnoull?* He wasn't sure who was spying for her, but they were remarkably accurate and he was getting damned tired of it. "Tell Her Grace I'm on my way out for a ride with the viscount. I'll see her when I return."

The footman was pale, his hands shaking. "I'm sorry, Yer Highness, bu' Her Grace ordered me na' to take no fer an answer, an' if'n I did—" He gulped and then whispered the words as if it might make them less powerful, "She said if I returned wit'oot ye, she'd turn me into a goat."

Alexsey's jaw tightened. "Did she?"

The footman nodded, his gaze wide and pleading. "Oy've no wish t' be a goat."

"I would imagine not."

"Bloody hell!" Strath made a frustrated noise. "Your grandmother . . . I'm glad she's not mine."

"Most people are." He turned to the footman. "Tell her you searched high and low and I wasn't to be found. She won't turn you into anything if she thinks you simply couldn't find me."

The footman cleared his throat. "One more thin', Yer Highness. It seemed Her Grace was havin' a difficult time tryin' to breathe. She was almost panting, sort of catchin' her breath, as it were. She looked pale, too."

Strath instantly frowned. "That is different. Alexsey, you must go to her."

Alexsey gave a short laugh. "Nonsense." He looked at the footman. "Her Grace told you to say that if I balked, didn't she?"

The footman shifted from foot to foot, his expression one of sheer misery.

"And she paid you a few pounds, too, I'll wager."

The footman couldn't have looked more miserable. "Five, Yer Highness."

"I thought so. She can wait, then. I've an errand to run." *And a woman to see, one I've been thinking about for two days and nights now.*

Strath shook his head. "Alexsey, as much as it pains me to say this, you should go to your grandmother. She's old. What if this once she really is ill? You would never forgive yourself."

Bloody hell. *Is everyone trying to keep me from Bronwyn?* But one look at the genuine concern on the viscount's face made Alexsey sigh. "Damn it." He swallowed the impulse to kick at the stairs to vent his frustration. "Fine. You go on ahead; I'll catch up soon."

Strath nodded unhappily. "That's the second time in two days this has happened. I wonder what she is up to?"

"I wonder, indeed." But Alexsey knew. He waved off the footman, who offered to take his coat. "I'll keep the damn thing on, for I'm not staying long." He snapped a look at Papillon and gestured to the viscount. "Go with Strath."

Papillon sat.

Strath shook his head. "Even the dog spurns me. I feel the need for a strong glass of spirits and it's early morning yet."

Alexsey snapped his fingers again. "Go!"

Head hanging, Papillon went to stand with Strath.

"I'm always a second choice." Strath tugged on his gloves. "You'd think I'd be used to it by now. I would wait for you, but if my uncle sees me loitering about with nothing to do, I'll never leave the castle. He's taken to talking about the improvements he'd like made to this wretched castle, and I can't bear another four-hour conversation about the drainage issues caused by the slope of the roof on the south side."

Alexsey nodded. "My apologies, Strath. I will see you shortly." With that, he stalked off.

Since his tryst with Bronwyn in the woods two days ago, he'd been trying his damnedest to see her again, but fate and, he suspected, his grandmother were against him.

He reached the landing and followed the footman down the wing toward his grandmother's suite. Tata Natasha had been in rare form these last two days. The first day, while he'd still been muddled from his tryst with Bronwyn, his grandmother had pressed him into service for what was supposed to be a quick trip to a nearby village to purchase some lace.

What Tata Natasha had failed to tell him was that she'd invited Miss Carolina Acheson to join them. A wealthy debutante used to being made much of, Miss Acheson was none too pleased when Alexsey—recognizing Tata Natasha's heavy-handed attempts at matchmaking—summarily ignored her. The young lady wasn't shy about letting her feelings be known, and the entire trip quickly became a pain in the ass.

Worse, they found neither the lace nor the village his grandmother had described, and the snooty Miss Acheson made certain they were all aware that she was tired, hungry, and cold. Her temper didn't fare any better when a heavy rain struck on the way home and the carriage ended up bogged down on a narrow lane, two of their four wheels sunk axle deep in mud.

After two solid hours of pushing and pulling, Alexsey and the groom had managed to get the carriage free, but it had been well after dark when they'd pulled into the lane that led to Tulloch Castle, far too late to visit Bronwyn. Adding to his already foul mood, Miss Acheson had succumbed to tears long before they reached the castle, and Tata had spoken quite sharply to her in lieu of a good-bye, leaving him to placate the nearly hysterical woman while a footman ran to fetch her doting mama.

By the time all was said and done, all Alexsey had wanted was a hot bath and to never see his grandmother—or Miss Acheson—again.

The next day had dawned, and with it his growing desire to see Bronwyn. He'd decided to join the hunting party with Strath and break off from the rest and ride to Ackinnoull.

He never made it. He'd barely sat down for breakfast when the first summons from his grandmother had come. A giggly miss named Lady Jane, who Alexsey had already decided had the intelligence of a dead squirrel, had informed him that his grandmother was ill and needed him immediately.

He'd thought it might be a ploy, but he was honorbound to go see the old woman. He'd made his excuses to the others in the breakfast room and left for his grandmother's, only to discover Lady Jane at his elbow, having been ordered to escort him like some sort of frill-bedecked guard with an annoying tendency to hang upon his arm as they walked.

When he'd arrived in Tata Natasha's suite, he'd discovered her sitting up in bed looking regal and well, and it quickly became apparent that she was only sick of his independence. He'd politely made his inquiries after her health, had pretended sympathy when she'd complained of vague aches and pains that were keeping her in bed. To free himself from her for the rest of the day, he'd agreed to fetch her a bottle of "Olympian Dew" and something called "Gorland's Lotion," both of which she'd vowed she must have or she couldn't rise from her bed.

Alexsey had intended on handing her task off to a footman, only to be circumvented when his grandmother had insisted that Lady Jane accompany him. Never one to mince words, Tata Natasha let Alexsey know that the giggly girl was the daughter of a wealthy earl, and that any insult could be cause for an international incident.

It was a ridiculous assertion, but Tata had said it in front of the blasted wench, who hadn't had the sense to be insulted when she should have. Instead, the woman had looked so thrilled at the prospect of merely riding in the carriage with him that Alexsey, his sympathy stirred, had agreed to the trip, vowing to make it as short as possible.

Thus, instead of visiting Ackinnoull as he'd wished, he'd found himself dashing off a note to be delivered to Bronwyn before driving to the nearest town to fetch Tata's potions, a prattling Lady Jane at his side. He'd discovered in short succession that Lady Jane loved fashion, the color blue, French braids; pink lemonade, small dogs, and bonnets almost as much as she hated politics, books, opera music, and museums. He'd never been so bored in all his life.

Though he'd done his best to discourage Lady Jane's bubbly belief that she was a witty conversationalist, it had been to no avail. She'd talked from the second they'd climbed into the carriage to the second he took his leave of her in the foyer. She'd even talked as he'd walked away, noting her love of clocks.

Even more frustrating than Lady Jane's prattle was the massive storm that had gathered while he'd been on his mission. It broke a few moments after his return, with thunder so strong that the guests were agog to note how they could feel it even when deep inside the castle walls. Risking a horse in such weather was pure folly, so his visit to Ackinnoull had to be postponed yet again. Thus, another opportunity to visit Bronwyn was lost. As the storm crashed over the castle, he wondered what Bronwyn was thinking. He could only hope she didn't believe his absence was in any way connected to the consummation of their relationship.

So this morning, in a supreme effort, he'd decided to leave the castle before Tata Natasha was awake. He and Strath had arisen at an ungodly hour before the sun was even up. Sadly, it appeared he'd underestimated her conniving.

He stalked grimly through the hallways. He would not be put off another day. *She knows I wish to see Bronwyn, though I don't know how. That's the only explanation for these ceaseless tasks.*

When he reached her suite, he dismissed the footman and knocked on the great oaken door. A faint call to enter followed.

Tata was sitting up in her bed, dressed in an elaborate bed coat trimmed with bows and frills, a lacy cap perched atop her perfectly coiffed curls. On the bed before her sat a tray; her maid was just pouring the tea.

"Humph. There you are." Tata flashed a look at the maid. "Leave. I will speak with my grandson now."

The maid curtsied and, taking the covers from the plates, left.

As soon as the door closed, Tata said, "It took you long enough to come."

"I came the second I was informed you wished to see me."

Tata's brows rose.

"Correction, I came the second I heard you might be dying, even though I didn't believe it in the least."

A smug expression rested on her face. "I thought that might do it."

"You'll cry wolf one time too many and—"

"You won't come? Please. You have your father's quixotic propensities. All of his sons do. You can't help yourself."

He gritted his teeth. "What do you want, Tata?"

"Where were you when the footman delivered my message?"

"In the foyer. In another two minutes, I'd have made good my escape."

Her brows rose. "Escape? It's come to that, has it?"

"*Da*. Again, what do you want, Tata?"

She took a sip of tea. "First, I seem to have lost my dog. Again."

"Papillon is with Strath, who should be riding the south trail by now."

"She gets filthy when you take her to the fields."

He shrugged. "She needs exercise."

Tata didn't look happy. "Bring her back when you return, but have her washed first."

"I shall. Now, what hugely important duties do you

have for me today? Not more Olympian Dew or Gorland's Lotion, I hope? I purchased all they had at the
village apothecary's yesterday."

"No, no. I have plenty now." She pressed a hand
to her heart and sighed. "It has been a great help already."

"Indeed. Last night at dinner I sat beside Miss Mac-
Invers, who has some experience with medicines as her
mother is quite elderly. I asked her what she thought of
your two potions."

Tata Natasha dropped her hand from her chest, her
gaze suddenly evasive.

"She said she preferred Olympian Dew, as it made
her skin the softest, while Gorland's was better for
those with freckles."

Tata took a hurried bite of ham.

"You told me you needed those. *Needed* them, Tata."
She swallowed. "I do need them."

"You led me to believe your health was involved,
that they were medicinal. They are not."

"At my age, beauty lotion *is* medicinal," she replied
crossly.

He sighed. "Tata, for the last two days, you've kept
me busy running errands. I've allowed it, but not today.
Today, I will do as *I* wish to."

"And what is it that you wish to do that's so important?"

And there it is. "As I said, I'll return Papillon to you
this evening."

"Pah! Keep the dog. She prefers you, anyway." She
poured herself some tea and then regarded him over

the rim of her cup, her dark eyes narrowed. "You are making a mistake, you know."

He'd turned toward the door, but at this, he sighed and turned back.

She clacked her cup down on the saucer. "I am old, not stupid. I know what you're doing, and I worry. Of all your brothers, you are the most restless."

"Me? What of Grisha? He hasn't been in Oxenburg more than three days in a row for the last four years."

"He's a soldier-prince. He must train the army."

"Even when the army is home, he finds reasons to stay gone. Don't tell me Papa and Mama have not mentioned it; I know they have."

Her thin lips twitched. "He's a problem for another time. This minute, you are the problem." There was a sulky tone to her voice. "Nikolai and Wulf never cause such worry as you."

"Nikki is the heir, so he cannot afford to cause problems. And Wulf is now married, which means he's no longer your concern. That leaves you far too free to bother me."

"I have concerned myself with you because you refuse to pay court to a woman who would make your family proud! Always, you find the ones who are unsuitable—singers and dancers and actresses, and now this little mouse— Pah!"

"Leave it, Tata. You don't know what you're talking about."

She gave him a grim look. "I know more than you give me credit for."

Because she wasn't above bribing footmen, no doubt.

Footmen always seemed to know which way the wind blew. "You wished me to court a woman of quality."

"Not one like this. Bronwyn Murdoch has no manners, no grace—nothing a princess will need. She would not know how to welcome a foreign dignitary and make him feel at ease, or how to speak to fellow guests at a royal dinner. She dances like a performing bear and says the most outrageous things—Sir Henry tried to make genteel conversation with her at the last dinner, and she blurted out that she didn't like talking to people she didn't know. What sort of princess is that?"

Alexsey had to hide a smile. "I dislike talking to most people, myself."

"But you do not announce it. You can make polite conversation when you need to; she cannot."

"That's your only objection?"

"That and she is too old to have children."

"You had a child at her age."

Natasha paused. She'd hoped he wouldn't remember that. "I have the strength of the Romany. She would be useless as a princess."

"You are exaggerating. And I've said nothing about making her, or anyone else, a princess."

Not yet, she thought. "I doubt any man has ever paid her the slightest attention before. She will be desperate to win you, and will trick you if she must."

"Enough." His voice was pure ice, and he turned for the door.

"For your family's sake, and if you wish to ever hold the *kaltso*, you will not pursue her. You will shame us all."

"I shame no one by sharing my time with a woman of intelligence."

"Intelligence?" Natasha favored him with a narrow look. "You love her, then?"

Surprise crossed his face. "I don't know what I feel, but today I wish to be with her. That is enough."

She scowled. "If you must have a Murdoch, then marry her sister. I've spoken to Sorcha, and her manners are beautiful and charming. She speaks three languages fluently and her mother assures me she can play the pianoforte with talent. She converses with knowledge and grace. Court Sorcha instead, and keep the older sister for a mistress."

Alexsey's mouth was white with anger. "I've no interest in Sorcha, or anyone else but Bronwyn."

She hid a faint flash of hope behind a shrug. "For now. It will pass. It always does. You told me so yourself."

"Perhaps. Tata, if you knew Bronwyn, you would not feel as you do. She is honest and cares for her family and her sisters. She is thoughtful and imaginative and . . ." He paused and drew in his breath. "She is more royal in nature than I will ever be."

"So you say. But we both know what you want of this girl. Don't deny you've set out to seduce her. I know you, Alexsey. But it is dangerous to play with a virtuous woman of genteel birth. Things are not the same here as they are in Oxenburg. If there is a scandal, there is no paying your way out of it. You will pay with your freedom."

He turned and stalked to the door.

"Wait! I'm not finished speaking. Where are you going?"

He offered her a black smile as he opened the door. "According to you, I'm going to ruin my life and destroy my future."

"*Nyet!*" She threw back the covers. "Alexsey, if you'd wished to prove that you're no longer the irresponsible rakehell you once were, this is not the way to do it." She reached for the *kaltso*, pulling it from under her robes, and held it aloft. "This is not for a man who would throw away his inheritance for a mere dalliance with a nobody."

His eyes narrowed, his back so straight, he looked more like his soldier-brother than she'd ever seen him. "I wish to be the *voivode*, yes. But not at the cost of my pride. I will choose my own way, Tata. With you, without you. With the *kaltso*, without it."

"So you would give up your hopes for this woman."

"I give up nothing. Not to you, not to fate, not to her."

She scooted to the edge of the bed. "Alexsey, you must think! You cannot—"

But she spoke to an empty room, the door slamming ominously. *This will not do.* She tugged the bellpull, and then hurried to the gilt desk and scribbled a note. A footman arrived seconds later, just as she was folding the note. She handed it to him. "Take this to Lady Malvinea at Ackinnoull and wait for a reply."

"Yes, Yer Grace."

"Take it now and ride like the wind." She pulled a gold coin from a silk bag on the desk. "Do you see this?"

His eyes were as wide as saucers. "Aye, Yer Grace."

"You shall have it if you return with the reply in less than a half hour. But if you are a second longer than that, you'll get nothing. Now go!"

He practically ran from the room.

Chapter 23

Lady Bartram sighed deeply. "Lucinda is to be pitied as much as she is to be admired. There is something about a girl who's lost her mother—a tragic set of her lips, a tender expression in her eyes, a softness of spirit . . ."
—The Black Duke *by Miss Mary Edgeworth*

Later that afternoon, Bronwyn held up the fashion plate from *La Belle Assemblée* ladies' magazine beside the mirror, looking from it to her hair. The print featured a lady in a lovely pale-blue pelisse, her gloved hands warmed by a large white fur muff. The lady's hair was dressed in a style known as à la Sappho, which Bronwyn had tried to re-create.

She turned to Walter and Scott, who were stretched before the fire. "What do you two think?" She held up the magazine. "Is it close enough?"

Both dogs wagged their tails, although neither with enthusiasm.

She sighed and tossed the magazine to her dressing table. "I was afraid of that. I thought to do something different, but this wasn't a wise choice."

She looked back at the mirror and tugged on some

of the curls, trying to rearrange them. The trouble was that her hair was too thick to hold a proper curl. Instead of the delicate circlets from the picture, her curls looked more like thick sausages.

She sighed and adjusted a pin, hoping for a miracle. She'd been trying to stay busy since her last meeting with Alexsey. Their time had been so sweetly passionate, so . . . exciting. *Better than any novel.*

But she hadn't seen him since that day, a fact that was causing her greater and greater unease. She'd expected a visit, or at least a note. *But there was that horrible storm.* That would have kept him away; only a fool would risk his horse in such. Still, there was no reason why he couldn't have written a note. A few words would have calmed her fears to no end.

But so far, no note had arrived. She swallowed a lump in her throat. *Did it mean so little to you, Alexsey?*

She didn't know, and wouldn't until she spoke with him again.

Scott lifted his head and glared at the door. Walter followed suit.

A firm knock sounded upon the wooden panel.

Bronwyn opened it, blinking in astonishment when Mama smiled back at her, though her gaze widened when she saw Bronwyn's hair.

"Mama—what a surprise." Suddenly remembering the dogs, she threw herself into the doorway.

Mama brushed her aside. "Bronwyn, please. I've known since the day you moved into these rooms that the dogs would be coming with you."

"Oh." Bronwyn closed the door behind her mother.

Mama sent her a flat look. "A good mother knows everything about her children."

Good God, I hope not. Bronwyn gestured to the chairs before the small fireplace. "Won't you have a seat? This is the first time you've visited me here."

Mama sat in the nearest chair, eyeing Bronwyn's hair and gown. "You are dressed. I wasn't aware we'd anywhere to go until tomorrow's dinner and talent performance at Tulloch."

Bronwyn sat opposite Mama. "I was thinking of wearing this tomorrow." It was a gown from her long-ago season. She'd found it in the back of her wardrobe, forgotten and sadly wrinkled. At the time, the pale-blue silk with white netting had been all the rage, but no more. Still, it was better than her usual gowns.

Once Mrs. Pitcairn had done some magic with her iron and had removed several rows of faded silk flowers, Bronwyn thought the gown suited her well. Though not fashionable, it was at least pretty. And if, perchance, a certain handsome prince happened to see one wearing it . . . well, it couldn't hurt to be properly gowned for once.

Ever since her meeting with Alexsey, she'd felt bolder somehow. The world seemed brighter, the sun shinier, noises softer—and she was ready for more adventures. More caresses. More Alexsey.

But why, then, hasn't he visited? Her pleasure dimmed. Perhaps he was waiting to invite her to a secret tryst, somewhere they could be alone once again. It was breathtaking to think of sneaking out to meet Alexsey. Breathtaking and bold and perhaps wrong. He'd said they were making memories. When he was gone, she'd need a lot of memories to keep her company in the years ahead. The thought didn't cheer her as it ought to have. Indeed, it made her eyes water in a most annoying way.

Mama pursed her lips. "The style suits you, but it's dreadfully out of fashion. The waistline is too low and those sleeves—" She shook her head.

Bronwyn managed a smile. "Such praise! I hardly know how to respond."

Mama instantly looked contrite. "I'm sorry. I said that quite poorly."

"You said what you think, which I value. By the way, your gown is quite lovely."

"Thank you. It's one of those we ordered from the *modiste* in Edinburgh for Sorcha's season. The ones ordered for me fit perfectly, but the two we ordered for Sorcha don't fit at all."

"Oh dear. How did they get them wrong? They measured Sorcha in the shop."

"I'm sure I don't know." Mama folded her hands on her lap. "Your father was livid, thinking we'd have to pay for the alterations, but I assured him that the *modiste* will fix them and at no extra charge. But that means I must take Sorcha back to Edinburgh to have new measurements taken."

"What a coil!"

"It's a pity, for I especially wished Sorcha to wear the pale-blue crepe gown tomorrow evening. It's the perfect thing for a young lady just coming out." She sighed. "Now we'll have to settle for one of her older gowns."

"Fortunately, she's been out so little that no one will realize they're her older gowns."

"I hope so." Mama leaned back in her chair, her gaze flickering over Bronwyn in a searching manner. "It's been a mad, crazed few weeks, hasn't it?"

"It's been a very mad few weeks—though I know that's not why you are here."

Mama flushed. "Yes." She paused a long moment and then took a deep breath. "You know I love you as if you were one of my own daughters. I hope you realize I would only say something critical if I thought it in your best interest."

Bronwyn waited, a flash of dread making her nod rather than reply.

"I want to ask . . . Oh dear, I don't know how to say this, but . . . have you been meeting with Prince Menshivkov in secret?"

Bronwyn blinked. Of all the things she'd expected her stepmother to ask, that was the last one. Feeling the older woman's gaze upon her, she wet her lips, hoping her face wasn't as red as it felt. "I wouldn't say we've met in secret." That was true, for anyone could have walked in on them.

"I thought as much." Mama folded her hands in her lap. "He paid a visit not an hour ago."

Bronwyn started. "What! Did he ask for me?" She couldn't keep the breathlessness from her voice.

Mama's eyes darkened. "He asked for you, but I told him you were on an errand in Dingwall."

"Why did you tell him that? I wish to see him." She *needed* to see him.

"Which is exactly why I told him you weren't here." Mama sighed. "Bronwyn, please . . . this must stop before someone gets hurt."

"No one is going to get hurt." Bronwyn couldn't keep the stubborn note from her voice.

Mama's eyes suddenly seemed very wise. "My dear, I fear you already have."

Tears unexpectedly burned Bronwyn's eyes. "No."

"Really?" Mama's voice was unexpectedly gentle. "I must tell you that when I told him you weren't available, he spent a good twenty minutes talking to Sorcha. And he was *very* attentive."

Bronwyn's heart panged. "I'm sure he was just being pleasant. He . . . he's very polite and . . ." But was he really? He didn't mind leaving a ball in the middle of it merely because he was bored, and he thought nothing of ordering people about without so much as a by-your-leave. And Sorcha was so very lovely.

Not that Alexsey had promised Bronwyn anything. In fact, neither of them had placed boundaries on what had started as a flirtation, turned into a challenge, and then became . . . what was it now? She didn't even know.

It was suddenly hard to swallow. Had she been mistaken in him?

No. It wasn't possible. If he was speaking to Sorcha, it was because it was the only thing to do in the situation.

Mama patted her hand. "Oh, Bronwyn. I wish I'd realized what was happening. I've been remiss and I'm so, so sorry."

"You did nothing wrong."

"I'm not sure. Earlier today, I had tea with the grand duchess. She believes you might be developing certain feelings for Prince Menshivkov." Mama paused, her color high. "Feelings that are not returned in the way you might wish."

Bronwyn's heart thudded sickly. "How would she know?"

"She's spoken to her grandson about you."

Bronwyn stiffened. "Whatever feelings do or do not exist between the prince and me are no one else's business."

"My dear, an innocent like you, sheltered and with little experience of men, is easily deceived. I explained that to Her Grace, and assured her you had no intentions regarding her grandson—that you're not attempting to trap him into marriage or—or anything else."

"Of course not! Marriage was never mentioned." And yet . . . she had to admit that somewhere along the way, she'd been dreaming about something more. Not marriage, perhaps. Not yet. But her heart had been headed in that direction and the realization sent hot and cold shivers through her.

As if sensing her turmoil, Walter arose and came to stand against Bronwyn's knee. She patted him automatically and he sank to her feet, leaning against her leg.

Mama sighed. "Please, don't look so tragic."

"I'm not. There's nothing between us. We both like to read, and talk." *And kiss. And make love.* Her hands were clenched so tightly together, her fingers were white.

"Yes, but . . . do you love him?" Mama asked gently.

She had to swallow twice before she could answer. "No." So far, she only liked him very much. Love included passion and kindness, caring and—

She closed her eyes as the truth burst before her. *Oh dear, I do love him. When did that happen?* She couldn't breathe, couldn't think.

"Oh, Bronwyn," Mama said softly. "I'm so sorry."

Bronwyn could only nod.

"However it came to happen, I must agree with Her Grace: falling in love with the prince would be disastrous. She said he has always vowed he will not wed. He's told her numerous times that he's never been in love, and plans to never be so."

Every word was like an arrow into her heart.

Mama sighed. "For your sake, for everyone's sake, you—we—must stop this right now."

Bronwyn's throat was so tight, she couldn't even swallow. *Why would he have said such a thing to his grandmother unless he wished it to be repeated to me? I didn't teach him a lesson at all—but he certainly taught me one. Love is as painful as it is pleasurable.*

Scott came to join Walter at her knee, both dogs leaning against her. Her heart like a lead weight, Bronwyn wrapped her arms about them both. "Thank you for coming to speak with me. I know it can't have been easy."

"What's not easy is seeing you hurt. I wish—" Mama sighed.

Hot tears stung Bronwyn's eyes, but she held them at bay. "If you don't mind, I'd like some time to think about this."

"Of course." Mama stood, uncertainty on her face. "I'll tell your sisters you won't be attending tomorrow's dinner at Tulloch. Shall we just say you don't feel well?"

Bronwyn didn't look up. "For now, that will be fine."

Mama started to say something more, but on seeing Bronwyn's bent head, she instead turned and quietly let herself out, leaving Bronwyn alone with her dogs and her thoughts.

"*Y*ou won't find any answers in there, I fear."

Alexsey looked up from the golden depths of his scotch to find Strathmoor in the doorway of his bedchamber, clad in a red velvet dressing coat. "You never know. I've found answers in stranger places."

Strath sauntered in and closed the door behind him. "You left your door open. I will take that as an invitation."

He shrugged. "We're practically alone in this wing."

"My uncle's none-too-subtle way of letting us know he thinks us hellions." Strath paused to pour himself a glass of scotch before he came to take the seat across from Alexsey. "Let me know if you find answers, questions, or anything other than good smoky scotch in there. For if you do, then the footmen have not been washing the glasses as they ought." He stretched his legs before the fire and took an appreciative sip.

Alexsey eyed his friend. "You are up late. Did the brightness of your dressing coat prevent you from sleeping? It is keeping me awake right now."

Strath waved his glass. "Mock all you wish. I bought

it in France and paid a fortune for it, and have heard nothing but praise for it."

"Whoever praised it was merely being polite."

Strath grinned. "Probably, but for what I paid, I'll accept any compliment I receive. I was so foxed when I bought it, I could barely count out the coins." He ran a hand over the velvet. "At least it's warm."

"That's a good thing here."

"Ah, 'tis a chilly old castle."

The two men sat in silence for a while, the crackling fire the only sound in the room. Finally, Strath said, "Look at us, two boisterous, happy chaps. I barely know how to bear our overwhelming cheerfulness."

"I'll admit it; I'm gloomy this evening."

"Because of the Murdoch chit?"

"Aye. I went to visit her today. Twice. Her stepmother received me both times and seemed rather odd. She lied to me and told me Bronwyn wasn't home either time."

"Perhaps Miss Murdoch was reluctant to see you and sent her stepmother to speak with you instead."

"I thought of that, but when I last saw Bronwyn—" He frowned into his glass. "No. It's her stepmother. But I can't help thinking that perhaps I'm at fault. If perhaps I've pushed things too far, too fast with Miss Murdoch, expected too much. . . ." He shook his head. "I don't know."

He shouldn't have been surprised; he'd asked her to act far outside her normal area of comfort.

"I can't believe this. You, the man who's never refused by any girl, downright gloomy over a woman?"

Hell yes. A very stubborn, uncooperating, infuriating, and totally adorable woman. Realizing Strath's eyes were upon him, Alexsey shrugged. "I'm being gloomy, yes. It is nothing, probably caused by the gray weather that's moved in. When it clears tomorrow, I'm sure we'll all be in better fettle."

"Clears?" Strath snorted. "You obviously don't know Scotland. Our weather is rainy, misty, foggy, hazy, icy, and—for two weeks every year, whether we deserve it or not—sunny."

"Yet there is a certain mystical charm to your weather. Much as there is to your women."

"'Mystical charm.' That's a good way to put it." Strath nodded and swirled his scotch slowly. "I've been thinking about someone myself."

"Anyone I know?"

Strath took a swallow of the scotch. "It doesn't matter, for she won't have me."

Alexsey looked at his friend in surprise. "You're in love?"

"Lud, no. I'm in deep lust. I don't believe in love."

"Oh?" Alexsey lifted a brow.

"No," Strath said in much too stubborn a voice. "But this woman . . . she is the devil's own to decipher. One moment she's hot, then she's cold, much like our weather."

"Ah. She is reluctant, then?"

"Very. But then, so am I."

Despite his low spirits, Alexsey had to laugh. "Both of you reluctant, so how did the two of you even come to be?"

"I don't know. That's the devil of it. There we were, denying one another one moment, and kissing the next. Now we tear between those two extremes until we're both dizzy with it."

"She likes you, then, or there would be no kisses."

"For now. Sadly, women change their minds as frequently as they do their gowns."

Alexsey nodded. His spirits would be dragging even lower if he didn't hold on to the fact that he had not yet spoken to Bronwyn. Until he did, he would not accept this version her stepmother kept putting forth, that she had experienced a change of heart and wanted nothing more to do with him.

Of course, he wasn't in love like poor Strath. What Alexsey felt was deep, agonizing lust combined with a strong dose of like. He liked Bronwyn. And somehow that made everything more difficult. He couldn't seem to stop thinking about her. Everything reminded him of some moment they'd shared.

"You're staring into your glass again, only now you're scowling."

"I wish your uncle would tell his cook to stop using so much rosemary."

Strath blinked. "What's wrong with rosemary?"

Every meal now served as a reminder of Bronwyn. "Every bloody dish has rosemary in it. Every one."

"I don't even know what rosemary smells like."

"I do. If you knew, it would annoy you, too. And there is too much singing in this house, too."

Strath looked even more confused. "Singing. That's bothering you, as well?"

"*Da*. The housemaid who sets my fires in the morning hums. Then, when she is in the hallway, she sings. I don't wish to hear singing."

"I take it her voice is wretched."

"It is pleasant enough. It isn't that which bothers me."

Strath shook his head. "Sometimes I don't understand a word you're saying."

"It is nothing. I am like a bear with a sore paw. Everything bothers me. I'm trying to figure something—and someone—out. That's all."

"Good luck with that." Strath held up his glass. "Here's to women who are too smart for their own good."

Alexsey lifted his glass.

"What are you going to do about seeing Miss Murdoch?"

"I will keep visiting; if she wishes to see me, she will." And if she didn't . . . he would think about that when he had to.

"You would let her decide everything?"

"I would let her make all of the choices. It must be her decision."

"Hm. Doesn't seem fair to me, but what do I know? I can't even bag the easy ones."

"If you want this changeable woman, you'll win her over. I have confidence in you. But . . . are you sure it's mere lust? I've never seen you so determined to win a woman before."

Strath waved his glass. "Trust me, I know the difference."

"Oh?"

"Aye. You can slake desire, but love is forever hungry. The more you feed it, the more it wants. I intend on slaking this desire at the earliest opportunity and being done with it." He put down his empty glass, yawned, and stood. "It is late; I should go."

"Aye, we should both get some sleep." Not that Alexsey would, for he'd be thinking about Bronwyn, remembering how it felt to sink into her soft—

Clink.

He turned toward the window. *That sounded like a pebble on the glass.*

The noise came again. *Clink. Clink, clink, CLINK!*

Could it be . . . ? *Surely not*—

"What *is* that?" Strath took a step in that direction.

Alexsey almost leapt to his feet, blocking Strath's path. "It's the wind."

"The wind goes 'clink'?"

"Yes. It, ah, blows through the cracks in the window and makes the shutter creak. That's a creak you hear, not a clink."

"I know what I heard. It sounded like something hitting the glass."

"*Nyet,*" Alexsey said in a firm tone.

Strath's brows rose. "You're so certain?"

"The footman checked it last night when I mentioned it. It's made that noise every night since I arrived." Alexsey took Strath by the elbow and directed him to the door. "But I've grown used to the noise and now find it soothing."

"Soothing?" Strath said dubiously.

"*Da.* It reminds me of our country house in Oxenburg. The shutters there make the same noise. Clink, clink, clink—all night long."

"Bloody hell. Remind me to never accept your invitation to visit."

"I shall." Alexsey opened the door and guided Strath to the hallway. "Good night." He closed the door and, for good measure, turned the key in the lock.

After Strath's reluctant footsteps faded, he strode across the room, flung the curtains aside, and threw open the window.

The pale moonlight rested upon Bronwyn's upturned face and glinted off her spectacles.

Alexsey could have kissed her from head to toe. "Roza!"

"Shhh!" Her furious whisper barely reached his window. "Do you wish us to be caught?"

"*Nyet*, of course not," he whispered in return, though there was no one on this side of the castle who could hear them. "If you'd sent me a note, I would have come to you."

A grim look flickered over her face. "Too many people have been talking already."

"Is that so?" He would have to ask what that meant, but now, he just wanted her in his arms. "Wait there. I'll come down and—"

"No need."

To his astonishment, she tossed her skirts over one arm and began to climb the trellis.

Fear gripped him. One misstep and— *Nyet, I cannot think of it.* He fumed, unable to so much as utter a word for fear of startling her.

She climbed higher, moving slowly, carefully.

Alexsey muttered a string of curses under his breath. "You little fool!" he whispered.

She continued to climb, steadily growing closer.

As much as he hated that she was taking such a chance, he had to give her credit. She might not be able to dance, but she knew how to climb. She did it well and swiftly. *Only Bronwyn*, he thought with pride.

Soon she was at his window, and he lifted her into the room. The feel of her softness against him made him ache anew, but he set her on her feet and turned to close the window.

Bronwyn was breathless, not only with the effort of her climb, but at her own boldness. She couldn't believe that she was doing this. Yet here she stood, alone with the prince, as deliciously light-headed as if she'd had champagne.

Alexsey pulled the curtains over the windows and turned to face her, his eyes dark. "You came to me." His voice vibrated happiness.

"Yes." *Explain that, Mama. Explain why he's so obviously happy to see me, if he doesn't care.* After Mama's visit, Bronwyn had known she had to see Alexsey. She'd taken stock of all she knew about him, and it didn't fit with what Mama had said.

"I came to talk to you. I have been thinking a lot lately, about my life, and yours. You were right about one thing."

"Only one? I am disappointed."

She smiled. "You once said I should live in the moment, and not so much in my books. Over the years, books have become my companions. I could travel without traveling, meet people without leaving Dingwall, become someone else when my life seemed too much. Feel without really feeling."

"A waste of a good life."

"Yes. I want to live as well as read. So"—she spread her hands—"I am doing just that. But I have a question for you, and you must answer it now, before this continues."

"*Da?*"

"Am I a passing fancy, to be forgotten the second you leave?"

"No, Roza." His voice deepened. "If I were to live a thousand years, I could never, ever forget you."

The words soothed her, and his sexy smile told her he desired her as much as ever. It wasn't love, of course. But he'd never promised her that, and she'd never asked. It was what it was, and that was enough for this moment. *Isn't it? Can it be?*

She turned away from Alexsey's watchful gaze under the pretense of examining the room. It was twice as big as the sitting room at Ackinnoull Manor. At one end stood a large bed, hung with red velvet curtains and piled high with snow-white pillows and sheets. A deep-blue coverlet was neatly folded at the foot of the bed. Just looking at the bed made her chest feel odd.

She'd come here to talk to him, to look into his eyes and know for certain that he wasn't less than the man she'd come to know. But she'd also come for something else: *more memories. More of him. Before he leaves.*

Her gaze returned to him, and she realized all he wore was a loose white shirt tucked into black breeches.

The shirt was untied at his neck and revealed his strong throat. His black hair was mussed as if he'd run his hand through it several times, and his eyes were bright with curiosity.

Funny, but she hadn't thought past climbing into his room. Now here she was, punch-drunk on her own bravado, and with nothing to say. She knew what she wanted, though.

The deepening of his gaze told her that he knew, too.

Lifting her chin, she untied her cloak and tossed it over a nearby chair. "I won't be needing this."

"No you won't." He chuckled and walked toward her. Never had he looked more lionlike than now, his muscled thighs rippling as he approached her, his broad shoulders outlined against the fire. She remembered how easily he'd plucked her from the trellis and her skin warmed, as if she were already in his arms.

He stopped in front of her and ran the back of his hand down her cheek. "I am so glad you came to me."

"So am I."

"You look cold." He picked her up as if it were the most natural thing, and carried her to the fire. He hooked his foot about a chair leg and turned the chair closer to the flames, and then sat, cradling her to him.

He grinned, his teeth white in the dim room. "There. You like, *nyet*?"

She rested her head against his shoulder. "I like, yes."

"Good." He paused to slip her spectacles from her face and place them on the small table at their side. "There. More comfortable?"

"Much more comfortable."

It was quite warm wrapped in his arms, toastier than any fireplace. Since they'd sat down, his hands had never been still, one stroking her back, the other her knee.

She looked at his hand, noting the signet ring with the gleaming emerald. He had such beautiful hands. If she closed her eyes, she could imagine them touching her, stroking her, making her writhe against him. The memory made her squirm.

Alexsey's hands stilled, then clasped her to him. "Please do not move like that, Roza."

Startled by the husky tension in his voice, she turned to look at him.

His jaw was tight, his mouth pressed into a white line.

"I'm sorry. Did I hurt you? I'll get up—"

As she moved, his arms tightened. "Just . . . stay still a moment so I can compose myself."

She clamped her lips over the rest of her sentence and sat quietly until his breathing slowed. "I'm sorry, but I don't know what happened."

His smile was tight, but less pained. "A man's excitement can only be repressed for so long. I have been thinking and dreaming about you all day, and I am a powder keg. And now you are here, the match to my powder."

She smiled. "Perhaps we should explore this powder keg of yours more closely."

His eyes darkened, and he whispered, "Where have you been all my life?"

She felt her smile quaver as she whispered back, "Waiting for you."

His arms tightened about her. "You have taken a great chance this evening. I am honored."

"I surprised myself. I never imagined I'd do anything like this—visiting a man in his bedchamber."

"The Romany would say your spirit is as strong as it is beautiful. There is no higher compliment among them."

"One day I would like to meet them."

"We will visit them in the fall, when they return after their summer travels."

And just like that, he enfolded her into his future. It was imaginary, of course, but lovely all the same. "I would like that."

"It is beautiful, Roza—tents and caravans as far as the eye can see, all lit with gay lights." As he spoke, he slowly ran his hand up and down her back. "There are a thousand campfires, and songs aplenty. The music pulls at the heart."

"And one day, you will lead them."

His smile disappeared, a sudden darkness resting on his face. "I will," he said grimly. "There is more than one way to find your destiny."

She tilted her head to one side. "What do you mean?"

"Nothing, little one. A small obstacle I must overcome, that is all."

He looked so serious that she impulsively caught his face between her hands and nuzzled his neck. "You may overcome it tomorrow. Tonight there is us, and nothing else."

His breath quickened as she trailed her lips to his ear.

"Please," she whispered, trying unsuccessfully to keep the quiver from her voice.

"Of course, Roza. Just us." Without another word, he stood and carried her to his bed.

Chapter 24

Roland looked at Lucinda's small hand, tucked into his. There were times in a man's life when a decision had to be made. Now was that time, and his heart warmed at the thought.

—The Black Duke *by Miss Mary Edgeworth*

Bronwyn slowly came awake, aware of a comforting weight about her waist. She opened her eyes and, in the flickering light of the candle, saw Alexsey's arm wrapped about her, his chest pressed to her back as he cuddled her to him, their legs entwined.

Memories of the night before teased her further awake. What a glorious night. She smiled and settled against him, the soft sheets tangled about them both. She felt warm, and safe, and loved.

Yet there was a deep chasm between them, one made from their desires and their positions in life. It was as if they were in the same book, but on far different pages.

She trailed her fingers over his muscular arm, and was overcome by the desire to bask in his warmth.

Despite all the love stories she'd read, she hadn't understood the power of passion or the pain of one's own pride. Just thinking about never seeing Alexsey again caused an almost physical pang in her chest. *When the time comes, I will have to let him go and I will have to do it with a smile.*

She swallowed to keep the tears at bay. She wouldn't—couldn't—make this difficult for him, pleading her love, wishing he could care for her the way she cared for him. So she would leave before he awoke, before he could read the truth in her eyes. Steeling herself, she slowly slipped out of bed. As silently as she could, she washed and dressed, finally collecting her cloak.

Tiptoeing, she made her way to the window. Rather than risk being caught by a footman inside, she'd climb down the trellis. The full moon would light her way well enough.

She reached for the sash—and then froze. Along the bottom of the curtain was a thin line of light. *Sunlight.*

Her heart pounding, she turned and looked at the clock on the mantel.

It wasn't the middle of the night, but morning.

Trying not to panic, she opened the curtain a crack and saw several guests walking below, dressed for a hunt. Bronwyn closed her eyes. *Dear God, what do I do now? I'll be missed at Ackinnoull soon, if I haven't already been.*

She turned toward the door. If she walked confidently enough, she could simply go down the stairs and out through the garden. Once she was free of Tulloch, she could say she'd just gone out for a morning walk. No one would suspect a thing, then.

Crossing the room, she paused by the bed and looked at Alexsey. As she'd guessed, he slept boldly naked, his body rivaling every Greek statue she'd ever seen. Her fingers itched to run along the muscles of his thigh, to encircle his powerful arms and trace the lines of his broad chest. But more than that, she wished to feel the steady thrum of his heart under her cheek once more.

She curled her fingers into her palms and turned away. Moving quietly, she crossed to the door and carefully unlocked it. She opened it a crack and peeked into the hallway.

It was thankfully empty.

Relieved, she slipped out into the hall, softly closing the door behind her.

Then she walked confidently forward—

"Miss Murdoch?"

Bronwyn froze, then turned around to see Lord and Lady Duncan standing by the top of the steps with Mrs. MacPherson. They were all blinking with surprise.

Oh no!

Mrs. MacPherson gave a breathless giggle. "I didn't know you'd decided to join the house party! I wonder why Sir Henry assigned you to this wing?"

Bronwyn forced a smile. "I'm sure I don't know."

Lord Duncan said in a confidential tone, "The east wing is much better. There's gas lighting in every room."

Lady Duncan nodded in agreement. "We're here to collect Lord Strathmoor. He's to hunt with us this morning and—" Her eyes widened as they suddenly looked over Bronwyn's shoulder. Lady Duncan's mouth dropped open.

Mrs. MacPherson turned bright red and stared as well, while Lord Duncan harrumphed and said, "I *never!*"

Slowly, afraid of what she'd see, Bronwyn turned around.

Standing in the doorway of the room she'd just been seen leaving was Alexsey. Her spectacles hung from one of his hands, while the other covered a critical part of his spectacularly naked body.

$\mathcal{T}$ata stomped up and down the room, again stopping where Alexsey sprawled in a chair by the fire, his hooded gaze locked on the flames.

She clenched her fists. "You fool! You— She— I never— *Pah!* How could you be so *stupid*?"

He still seemed lost in thought, not acknowledging her now any more than he had when she'd first entered the room over a half hour ago.

"You aren't listening to me! You never have! If you had, you wouldn't be in this predicament!" She whirled on her heel and stomped up and down the room again. "How did I come to have such fools for grandsons? None of you will marry to suit your father's honor. Look at Wulf, who married a nobody! A nobody—"

"Whom the people love."

His sudden reply made her turn. "Finally, you speak."

"Wulf married well, and you know it. She's made him very happy."

"She's naught but a dressmaker."

"Who, with her dress designs, has made Oxenburg lace worth ten times what it was before. Because of her, there are widows who can now afford to put meat upon their tables, girls who will marry with full dowers, children who will have shoes and clothes, and—"

"Pah!"

His gaze narrowed. "You took credit for that marriage."

She planted herself before his chair. "Only because I had no choice. He was wildly in love with her. And while she was not of the bloodlines I'd have liked, she is a strong woman. They will have strong children."

"You are not so generous in your estimation of Bronwyn."

"She is a mouse who quakes at the thought of speaking to her partner at a dinner party!"

She'd expected to infuriate him, but a faint smile touched his mouth. "And yet I have never met such a stubborn, strong woman." Faint amusement warmed his eyes. "Even you and my mother pale in contrast."

Tata frowned. "You sound as if you admire her."

"I do. Very much."

"And yet you ruined her!"

"I did, didn't I?" A wondering smile touched his mouth. "And with all of the pleasure in the world."

"*Nyet, nyet!* You don't understand what that means in this country! In ours, it would mean you owe her family a bride gift to be passed on to her chosen husband. There is no shame in that; it is the way of the world. But here, it means you are expected to marry her yourself!"

He met her gaze steadily. "I knew that before I 'ruined' her."

"And yet you took the risk?"

That odd smile returned, a look of wonder in his eyes. "It wasn't a risk."

"Pah! As the lord of the land, Sir Henry must demand you offer for her. But you've told me a hundred times that you never wished to marry, so you must leave."

"What?" Alexsey looked startled.

"Now, before Sir Henry can act. Find a ship and go home."

"I will not run like a coward."

"You *must*. This woman is no good for us. She—"

"Enough!" Alexsey stood, his eyes ablaze. "I will hear no more of your bitter words. Bronwyn is to be respected. I *demand* that."

His anger was so hot that Natasha took a step back. But only for a moment. She pulled out the chain holding the *kaltso* and shook it. "This will *never* be yours if you marry that woman."

"Then it will not be mine. But no one can stop me from helping the Romany. Just as no one can stop me from marrying Bronwyn Murdoch." He turned and walked away.

"Don't be foolish! What are you going to do?"

"I'm going to send a letter to Bronwyn. Tonight, at Sir Henry's dinner, I will ask her if I may announce our marriage."

"She won't have you. She is proud, that one. It is her one good trait."

"I will win her over." He hesitated. "But you're right; she is very proud. But if I'm very lucky, and the fates are kind, then she'll realize we have no choice and must marry."

"You are being noble and wish to save the girl from embarrassment. That is good. But there are other ways. If you will give me time, I will find a way out of this—"

"It is my mistake. I must fix it." He went to the small writing desk beside the window. He pulled out some paper and ink and sat down, writing furiously. He re-read what he'd written twice, making small changes, then he sanded the missive, folded it, and tucked it into his pocket.

Then he headed for the door. "Until dinner."

"Where you will destroy your life—I cannot wait to witness that debacle."

He left, the door slamming behind him.

Tata's scowl disappeared, and for a long time she merely stood and stared. Then she gave a sharp nod and hurried to the bellpull by the fire. She tugged it once, then went to the desk and scribbled a hasty note. She'd just sealed it when the footman appeared.

He brightened when he saw the letter. "Another missive fer Lady Malvinea?"

Natasha nodded. "This time, bring her back with you. I have invited her to tea, so tell the butler on your way out to have a tray sent here to my room."

"Yes, Yer Grace. And if I bring her within thirty minutes, will I get another gold coin?"

"Two, if she arrives in less than that time. But if she arrives later, then you will become a goat."

"Och, Yer Grace, I'll ha' her here in under twenty minutes, see if I dinna." He snatched the letter, made a half bow, and bolted from the room.

Shortly afterward, she heard a carriage racing down the drive. Nodding to herself, she settled by the fire and waited.

Chapter 25

*Lucinda stared at the stars twinkling in the sky above.
There were so many. Was Roland looking at them, too? In
the loneliness of the moment, a star twinkled and she felt
his soul touch hers.*

—The Black Duke *by Miss Mary Edgeworth*

Bronwyn read the note for the fourteenth time, even
though she was fairly sure she had it memorized.

My dear Roza,

*We must speak. I will meet you at Sir Henry's
tonight, and we will resolve our difficulties without
the interference of others.*

*Sincerely,
Alexsey Romanovin*

Bronwyn refolded the note, feeling the same
flicker of disappointment. What did he mean, "resolve our difficulties"? The words were so cold . . .
so unfeeling.

But perhaps she was expecting too much from a

mere note. Or perhaps that was all he had to offer—an uncaring offer made only to appease society.

For that is what they were doing—appeasing society. Blast it, why oh why had he appeared in the hallway without proper covering? Not that it mattered, she supposed, for she'd have been ruined either way. Still, it wouldn't have made such a sensational story.

She thought of his demeanor when he'd brought her the letter earlier today. Of course Mama had been present, determined not to let things get "further out of hand."

But Alexsey had been all that was polite. He'd been so unlike himself, so stiff and formal, that she'd felt awkward and had barely said two words to him.

There'd only been one moment when he'd seemed more himself. It had been when he'd said his good-byes, and he'd held her hand longer than was necessary, and stared into her eyes as if searching for something.

The whole thing had been odd and she was at a loss to know what anything meant.

As soon as he'd left, Bronwyn had read the letter, aware of Mama's gaze over her shoulder. Naturally, Mama had asked to read the letter. Oddly, it had seemed to incense her. She'd declared that Bronwyn would not attend the dinner, and at the time Bronwyn had agreed.

She wouldn't—couldn't—be tied to a man who would never look at her without wishing for his freedom. She wanted to be a wonderful memory, not a dark one.

Perhaps Mama was right—the best thing Bronwyn could do was write him back and refuse to listen to his offer, release him from this painful situation. She would never marry for anything less than love, and all Alexsey had to offer was duty. She would free him from that duty. It was the least she could do.

Rubbing her chest where it had tightened, she turned to hear voices outside her bedchamber door, breathless and giggling. What on earth? She opened the door to find Mrs. Pitcairn, Sorcha, and Mairi, their arms overflowing with petticoats, ribbons, and shoes.

They pushed past a gaping Bronwyn.

"I thought I'd never make it up the stairs," Mairi exclaimed, puffing.

"Where shall we pu' these?" Mrs. Pitcairn asked, peering over a stack of petticoats.

"On the bed," Sorcha directed. "Scott, off!"

The big dog went to join Walter by the fire.

"I don't understand," Bronwyn said. "What are you doing here? I'm not going to dinner this evening. Mama said—"

"Forget what Mama said," Sorcha replied. "You *are* going to dinner tonight, and that's that."

"I don't know. Alexsey doesn't seem very . . . warm, and everyone will be talking." She pressed her hands to her hot cheeks. "I don't want to face them. Or him."

"You must, and you'll do it dressed properly."

"But Mama said—"

"Mama isn't always right." Sorcha's mouth thinned. "In fact, there are times when she's simply wrong." She dusted the coverlet fastidiously, then placed a long, sheet-wrapped bundle on it. The stack of petticoats joined it.

Sorcha turned to Bronwyn. "We've come to make

certain you go to dinner dressed like someone expecting a very proper and romantic proposal."

"Which you should get, if the prince is half the man we think he is," Mairi added.

Bronwyn shook her head. "I'm not going to accept. Mama says—"

"Mama. Isn't. Always. Right." Sorcha repeated the phrase with a staccato punctuation that made Bronwyn's brows rise.

"She means well."

Sorcha flushed. "True, but she doesn't understand that love doesn't always happen on a schedule."

Bronwyn shook her head. "I never said anything about love."

"You didn't have to."

Mairi nodded. "We've known for a while now."

"*Quite* a while," Mrs. Pitcarin added.

Bronwyn couldn't deny anything with three pairs of expectant gazes pinned on her. She sank onto her dressing room seat. "But how? I only realized it myself in the last few days."

Sorcha smiled. "We know you. And tonight, whether you decide he's worthy of you or not, you're going to go there looking ravishing. Because if you don't, you'll spend the rest of your life wondering 'what if.' And there's nothing more painful than that."

Bronwyn looked curious. "You sound as if you know all about love."

"Not enough." Sorcha busied herself sorting the items on the bed. "I wonder if we can replicate the braiding Mairi did for my hair, for yours?"

"No, we can't, although the idea is lovely. My hair is much too thick." Bronwyn took Sorcha's hand and turned her sister to face her. "This is very kind of all of you. I don't know how to thank you." She smiled at them all.

"I wish we could stay and help you dress," Mairi said, "but Mama will come to see our gowns, so we must be in our rooms and ready. We don't want her to know you're coming until the last possible moment."

"Then it will be too late for her to do anything about it," Sorcha said.

"Which is why I'm here," Mrs. Pitcairn said, smiling cheerily. "Ta' help ye get dressed."

Bronwyn looked at the letter in her hand. They were right. She and Alexsey deserved a final face-to-face meeting.

"Come see what we've brought you." Sorcha went to the bed. There were two pairs of slippers, some stockings, evening gloves, and a spangled shawl dotted with blue silk roses. "We weren't sure what would fit you best, so we brought everything we weren't using."

Mairi picked up the pair of slippers. "You have smaller feet, but you can put paper in the toes. I wasn't certain which would look best with the gown. Wait until you see it!" She unwrapped the sheet bundle.

Gleaming softly in the candlelight was a gown of pale-blue crepe over white sarcenet. Two folds down the front of the gown were lined with pearls, while a double row of pearls and tiny white flowers decorated the sweeping hem.

Bronwyn touched the gown reverently. "Where did you get this?"

Sorcha smiled. "It's mine, but it doesn't fit me. Mama was going to send it back to Edinburgh to have the skirt lengthened and the bodice taken in, but I think it will fit you. And I want you to wear it tonight."

Bronwyn looked at the beautiful gown, tears clouding her eyes. She engulfed Sorcha in a huge hug.

Mairi laughed and wrapped her arms around them both. As they hugged, Mairi said, "When you two are married, you must find me a husband just as nice as yours. *But* he must be at least an earl, devastatingly attractive, and have enough money to keep me in books forever."

Bronwyn laughed as she untangled herself from her sisters. "You have my word on it."

A shrill call rang out in French, and Mrs. Pitcairn sniffed. "Tha' be yer mum's Frenchie maid. She'll be wantin' t' help ye get ready."

Sorcha grimaced. "We must go. Come downstairs at exactly eight. That's when we're leaving, and Mama will change her mind about allowing you to attend once she sees that you are ready. We'll make *certain* she does." She whisked out the door, Mairi on her heels.

Bronwyn realized her sisters were right. She had to face her fate tonight, not hide from it. And what better way to do it than in a new gown? Her spirits buoyed, she began to go through the stacks of clothes.

An hour later Bronwyn stood before the mirror, the soft glow of a lantern shimmering over the gown and making the pearls glow. Mrs. Pitcairn had pinned her hair up in a simple yet elegant style. She looked better than she'd ever looked before. *It's a pity I'm dressing to refuse an offer—one that, if it had been made under different circumstances, would make me the happiest woman on earth.*

She gulped back a rush of emotion, hurriedly wiping her eyes. As she pushed her spectacles back into place, she glanced at the clock. Five till eight—time to go downstairs. She picked up her cloak and tied it about her neck.

Click!

Bronwyn whirled to the door. *That sounded like . . . the lock?*

She hurried over and tried to turn the handle. Nothing. It was locked from the outside. "What is this? Who's out there?"

Mama's voice floated in. "Your sisters told me of their plan. This is for your own good, Bronwyn. I promise."

"No! You can't do this!"

"I must." Mama's voice was thick with tears. "Just wait there. I truly have your best interests at heart—you'll see. I can't say more, but just wait."

"Mama, *please* don't—" Her voice broke and she had to gulp to steady herself. If she didn't go, then Mama would be free to deliver the coldest of answers to anything Alexsey might have to say. Her heart thudded sickly. "Mama, let's talk about this. Come inside and—"

"Good night, Bronwyn. I'll unlock the door when we return."

Her footsteps receded, and soon Bronwyn heard the distant sound of the carriage as it left. Her heart pounding in her throat, she sank to the floor, her mind working furiously.

Chapter 26

She'd stolen his heart with just one kiss, a kiss as chaste as an angel's wing, light and filled with innocent promise.
—The Black Duke *by Miss Mary Edgeworth*

From a window in the upper hall, Alexsey watched the carriages stream into Tulloch's courtyard. All day, his body had hummed and he'd felt light on his feet, like a snow leopard on the hunt, simmering with excitement and a sense of purpose. Today, he would claim Bronwyn for his own. *It's about damn time.*

He didn't regret the passionate night he'd spent with Roza—come a hundred scandals, he'd never regret that. That night had made him all the more determined to have her in his life. But he did regret the necessity of this proposal. The whole thing—the scandal, the gossip, the fact that other people were now involved in his and Bronwyn's relationship—that was the untenable part and it had greatly complicated things.

Bronwyn would never accept a marriage offer made for society's sake. She was far too stubborn and too independent for that, and he relished that about her. But now, because of their situation, she would think that was all he had to offer. Because of his carelessness, things had become complicated. *She will refuse me. I know it.*

He tugged at his neckcloth, his palms damp. He would not accept her refusal. He'd need a plan, though. Yes, a plan. He'd have to win over her pragmatic side first. Their circumstances dictated that they marry, and he was more than willing, so that was that. But her romantic side would present a bigger challenge. He'd have to prove that more than necessity had brought him to her, and that there was a very good reason to wed. The best one of all. Because he loved her.

If only I'd admitted it to her earlier. But his heart had been stubborn in yielding its secrets. *Damn it, I should have wooed her properly from the start, but I was a fool and had planned on just a flirtation.* He cringed to think of that now. But all of that could be overcome, he was certain of it. Because he could not accept the alternative. Not this time.

Fortunately, he was not a novice. He patted his coat pocket, where a bundle rested. There was more than one way to woo a woman who loved a good book. *It must work. Our happiness depends on it.*

Below in the courtyard, Sir Henry's coach pulled up. Alexsey leaned forward as the coach dislodged its guests, but the portico blocked his sight. Cursing, he left the window and headed downstairs to the ballroom. *Finally!*

Once inside the ballroom, he bowed to those nearest the doorway and made his way into the crowd, aware of the whispers and looks that followed him. The rumors were thick, but he couldn't have cared less.

Strath left a small group of men and joined Alexsey. "Ah, the happy groomsman!"

Alexsey looked around, frowning. "I don't see her. Do you?"

"No." Strath's gaze narrowed. "Tell me something: was it worth it?"

"A thousand times yes."

Strath didn't look convinced. "She'll not have you, you know. I've heard she's only coming to refuse you."

"Then I will change her mind."

"Good luck. The Murdoch women are a stubborn lot."

"They are Scottish. I expect no less."

Strath laughed. "I suppose so. Just . . . don't do anything rash. You could make this offer, let her refuse you, then go on your merry way, free and unfettered."

"Free and unfettered do not have the benefits I once thought."

"Amen," Strath muttered under his breath. "I must say, you are the most willing of unwilling grooms I've ever encountered. You are positively aglow with—"

"Your Highness!"

They turned to find Lady Malvinea. Though always stiff in bearing, she was even more so tonight, her hands clasped tightly before her.

Alexsey looked past her but there was no one there. Pushing his impatience aside, he bowed. "Lady Malvinea, where are your lovely daughters this evening?"

"Sorcha and Mairi were both dancing when I last saw them."

"And Bronwyn?"

"That's what I came to tell you. She—" Lady Malvinea looked at Strath, who was pretending not to listen but obviously was. She frowned. "Lord Strathmoor, I would like to speak to His Highness in private."

Strath flushed. "Since I was standing with him when you addressed him, I could hardly leave without being rude."

"You may leave now."

Strath's mouth grew white, but without a word, he turned on his heel and left.

Alexsey frowned. "Strathmoor is a good man, my lady."

"If you knew how many times he's—" She closed her lips. "It doesn't matter. If we may walk and converse, there will be fewer interruptions."

He escorted her away. "Well?" he said as soon as they were distant from the crowd. "Where is Miss Bronwyn?"

"She refused to come."

He'd never considered that a possibility. He'd been certain that she would at least attend the dinner. He'd imagined it all—she'd arrive, they'd talk, even argue, she'd perhaps even leave with things unresolved. But he'd never imagined that she might not even speak to him. *What if she refuses to ever speak to me?* His heart grew cold.

Lady Malvinea watched him closely. "That upsets you, I can see."

"I must speak to your daughter, Lady Malvinea."

The older woman sighed. "If only it were that easy.

Your Highness, she will not marry you. She's determined to free you from this situation and move on with her life."

His chest tightened with each word. "She has told you this?"

She nodded. "Bronwyn does not wish to correspond in any way. She asks only that you respect her wishes and leave as soon as possible, so that she may continue her life as it was before."

His heart sank and he fought for breath. He realized Lady Malvinea was waiting for him to speak. "I am sorry, but this news . . . I cannot accept it."

Her expression softened. "Perhaps . . . perhaps we can ask for some assistance. Bronwyn has a fondness for Sir Henry. We could ask him to speak to her on your behalf. She might be willing to see you then."

Why not? "Yes. That would be good."

"Here's the library. Why don't you wait there, and I'll fetch Sir Henry. I just saw him by the stairs, and it would be better if I asked for his attendance. He's not happy that the incident happened under his roof. He's a bit irritated with you now, but once he knows you wish to make things right, I'm sure he'll come around."

Alexsey didn't have anything to lose. "I will wait here." Hopefully there would be some scotch in the library.

As she left he went inside the room, only to find it quite dark, lit by only one candle.

Frowning, he took a step toward a lamp beside the candle.

"Hello?"

He turned at the sound of a woman's voice. Squinting into the gloom, he saw someone rise from the settee beside the fire, the high back having obscured her from view. He frowned. "I'm sorry. I thought this room unoccupied."

"Oh! Your Highness, I didn't realize it was you." She dropped a curtsy.

"Sorcha?" Alexsey frowned, walking closer. "What are you doing here?"

"Mama has a headache, and she told me to wait here while she fetched some hartshorn."

He froze in place. "Your *mother*?"

"Yes. She said she'd . . . return . . ." Her words diminished to a whisper, her eyes widening.

"Damn it!"

He turned toward the door, but before he could take more than two strides, Tata Natasha and Lady Malvinea entered, Sir Henry behind them. Sir Henry was in the middle of telling the ladies a story about a fish he'd once caught, but he came to an abrupt standstill when he saw Alexsey and Sorcha.

It looked damning—the empty room, him and Sorcha in the near dark—

"Well!" Tata Natasha said, satisfaction on her face. "What have we here?"

Lady Malvinea's eyes gleamed, though she shook her head in condemnation.

"Damn you, sir!" Sir Henry stomped forward, his face obviously flushed. "How many Murdochs are you trying to ruin?"

Chapter 27

Lord Thomas leaned closer. "Roland, I will tell you an ancient secret. There are two ways to woo a woman. The first is to use all the weapons at your disposal. The second is to never run out of weapons."

—The Black Duke *by Miss Mary Edgeworth*

Alexsey seethed. Was *nothing* to go right today?

Lady Malvinea turned to Sir Henry. "The prince has ruined Sorcha. I demand an accounting."

The words sounded as contrived as they were.

Alexsey made his way to the nearest lamp, flooding the room with a brighter glow.

"Mama, no!" Sorcha hurried to her mother's side. "Nothing happened, and you know it. You were the one who—"

"Quiet, child. Let Sir Henry handle this."

Sorcha's chin rose. "No, I won't let it be! *You* caused this. You—"

Tata *tsk*ed. "Sir Henry, forgive the girl. She's obviously distraught."

Alexsey narrowed his gaze on his grandmother.

She didn't seem the least upset. In fact, he detected the faintest glimmer of a smile in her eyes.

"With good reason!" Sir Henry glared at Alexsey. "Your Highness, you have much to answer for!"

"I did not attempt to seduce Miss Sorcha."

"You were here, so was she, the lamp turned down, and nearly all of the candles were out. Who did that, if not you?" Sir Henry blustered. "How dare you abuse my hospitality in such a way!"

"I did not know Miss Sorcha was in the library when I entered. Lady Malvinea did not mention that she'd left her daughter here."

"He never touched me," Sorcha added.

"Ha!" Tata Natasha said.

Alexsey caught the quick, meaningful glance she shared with Lady Malvinea. His gaze narrowed. "Tata, you and Lady Malvinea have been plotting. But what? I wonder."

Tata sniffed. "Don't ask for help from me; this matter is in Sir Henry's hands." She turned to him. "Sir Henry, you know what you must do."

Sir Henry's glower faded a bit. "Aye?"

"Tell my grandson he must make a choice. He has to pick which he will marry."

Sir Henry blinked. "I do?"

"Of course. What else can you do?"

"I don't know. I suppose that answer serves as well as any other." He turned to Lady Malvinea. "Is that what you would have me do? If it were me, I'd rather toss the blackguard into gaol for the rest of his life."

"You cannot," Tata Natasha said serenely. "He's a prince of Oxenburg."

"I don't give a damn if he's a prince of England," Sir Henry huffed. "As far as I'm concerned, that rakehell lost his immunity when he seduced *two* women under *my* roof."

"My lord." Lady Malvinea cleared her throat. "Her Grace's idea has merit; let's allow His Highness the choice."

Tata nodded. "It is an easy choice. Bronwyn is not of a marriageable age. Sorcha is perfect. It is decided." She inclined her head to Sir Henry. "Marry them as soon as possible."

"I'll fetch a vicar now and—"

"*No.*"

Everyone turned to see Lord Strathmoor standing in the open doorway, his face white.

Sir Henry frowned. "This is none of your affair."

"Like hell." Strath held out his hand to Sorcha.

With a muffled sob she hurried to his side, slipping into the circle of his arm as if she belonged there. "I'm so glad you came! Mama asked me to wait for her here—I didn't know she was tricking the prince into joining me here, or—"

Tata stomped her foot. "*Bozhy moj!* Is everyone in this castle hiding their loves?"

Lady Malvinea's mouth hung open. "Sorcha? What is this?"

Strathmoor pressed a kiss to Sorcha's cheek, then bowed to Lady Malvinea. "Sorcha and I owe you an apology. I have come to you many times requesting your permission to court your daughter."

"Too many times," she said curtly. "You have nothing to offer her."

"I have love, my lady. And for us, it is enough." He took Sorcha's hand and kissed it. "We married two days ago."

Silence met this.

Alexsey choked on a laugh. "You lucky bastard."

Strath sent him a pleased look. "I wished to tell you, but you were in the middle of your own storm."

"I am glad to see we're to be brothers, once I convince Bronwyn to have me, that is."

"Pah!" Tata Natasha threw up her hands. "This ruins *everything*."

Lady Malvinea nodded, tears in her eyes. "Our plan . . . all of our scheming . . ."

"*Da*," Tata said with a regretful shrug. "It was a beautiful idea, but it did not work so well, eh?"

"I don't understand." Sir Henry rubbed his eyes as if he hoped to see through the confusion more clearly. "Strath . . . married to Miss Sorcha? I thought you couldn't stand one another."

"Trust me, there were times I positively hated her, and she me." Strath sent an amused glance at his wife, who blushed. "She said no many, *many* times."

Sorcha smiled shyly. "But he kept asking, each time in a better way."

"Sorcha, how could you?" Lady Malvinea's face folded in tears. "How could you not tell me? I'm your mother!"

"I wanted to, but every time I mentioned Strathmoor, you dismissed him and started talking about the prince."

"But . . . he's only a viscount, and has so few prospects. How will you live?"

Sorcha slipped her arm through Strathmoor's. "I love him, and we will make our own prospects."

Lady Malvinea turned to Sir Henry. "You must do something about this!"

"I'm afraid I can't. If they're married, that's all there is to be said about it." Sir Henry sighed. "I suppose I can do one thing, though. I was already thinking about this, so I'll make it official." He quirked a brow at Strath. "What do you think of a bride gift in the form of this castle?"

Strath's eyes widened. "Tulloch? For us?"

"Aye." Sir Henry looked fondly about the library. "I love the place, but it needs someone who'll live here and invest the rents back into the lands. I've no time for that, but you could do it, lad. You're young and have the intelligence."

Strath looked down at Sorcha. "Well? Would you like to be the lady of Tulloch?"

Sorcha beamed. "I'd happily be the lady of a crofting hut, as long as you were there."

He hugged her and turned to his uncle, gratitude in his voice. "I can't thank you enough, Uncle. You won't be sorry. I'll implement every change you've suggested."

Sir Henry looked pleased. "You're a good one, Strath. I've always thought so. And I'm ashamed I haven't kept Tulloch up as well as she deserves. Now I can visit every year and you can show me the improvements you've made."

He cocked his brow at Lady Malvinea. "There, my lady. I've sweetened the pot with a castle and all of its rents, which are considerable. Your lass will be well cared for. Not hugely wealthy, but she'll be comfortable and safe, and will have a grand home for herself and her bairns."

"I'll live close by, too," Sorcha added, beaming. "You can visit all of the time."

Alexsey caught Strath's wince, but Lady Malvinea glowed.

She turned to Sir Henry. "I can't thank you enough."

"Och, 'tis nothing. It's settled, then, and we're all quite happy for it." Sir Henry straightened, his gaze turning to Alexsey as his expression turned grim once more. "But that dinna fix our other problem."

Tata waved a hand. "He's not a problem. Bronwyn is the problem." She turned to Lady Malvinea. "Our plan would have worked, if not for this complication."

Alexsey asked, "What was this plan, Tata?"

"Ha! You would have liked it. It was for your own good."

"And Bronwyn's," Lady Malvinea added.

"So you both knew I would never choose Sorcha."

"Of course we knew that!" Tata scowled.

"Unlike other people"—Lady Malvinea sent a meaningful glance at Sorcha and Strath—"everyone knew how you felt about Bronwyn, and she about you."

"Everyone?"

Sir Henry cleared his throat. "Actually, I had no idea."

"Neither did I," Strath said.

Sorcha looked up at her husband. "Really? It was so obvious."

Alexsey threw up his hands. "Tata, just tell me what mischief you've been up to! I've no patience for this."

Tata smirked. "It has been obvious to me for some time that you meant to have Miss Bronwyn, will she, nill she. She is a very independent miss. Very strong-willed."

"Which you did not like. You threatened to withhold the *kaltso*."

"I didn't like it at first, perhaps. But Lady Malvinea came to see me. She told me things about Bronwyn that I did not know. About her strength and her caring. I decided the girl would do very well."

"You said she was too uncomfortable in public to be a princess."

"Easily overcome with practice."

"You also said she was too old to marry and have children."

"Pah. At twenty-four, she is a mere child. I was twenty-seven when I had your mother."

"So you just *pretended* not to like Bronwyn?"

"I wanted to see how hard you were willing to work to be with her."

"So that's why you had me do all of those useless errands."

"And protested, and demanded you stop seeing her. But no matter what I did, no matter what Lady Malvinea did, you did not let it stop you. You didn't let anything stop you. But *then* you botched it royally when you let her get caught leaving your room. What a foolish move!"

"I did not mean for that to happen. But it is nothing.

I will have Bronwyn for a wife. Tonight I was going to ask her to marry me."

Tata threw up her hand, a pained expression on her face. "And she would have thought it was only because you were forced to."

"I would tell her that is not so."

"She would think you were merely being kind," Lady Malvinea said softly. "She would have refused you. That's why, at Her Grace's suggestion, I made certain Bronwyn would not be here tonight, so that this would happen."

Alexsley slowly nodded in understanding. "And I would have to make a choice."

Lady Malvinea smiled. "And you would have chosen Bronwyn."

"You think that would have softened her to my cause?"

Tata blew out her breath. "Did you not listen to a word we have said? Her pride would not let her accept a forced marriage. If you had a clear way to get out of it and didn't take it, then her pride would no longer be an obstacle. Of *course* then she would say yes."

Strath moved impatiently. "I'm surprised you would play with Sorcha's reputation in such a way."

Tata waved her hand. "No one would have known what happened here except us."

Lady Malvinea added, "And if anyone did come upon us, Her Grace would claim she was in the room the entire time. No one would dare challenge her. We thought of everything. Or thought we had."

Alexsey walked toward the door.

"Wait!" Tata took a step after him. "Where do you go?"

"To see Bronwyn, wherever she is."

Tata said, "Take her flowers."

"Or a gift," Lady Malvinea said. "That would be nice."

"A ring is always welcome." Sorcha glanced at Strath, who chuckled.

"Soon, my love," he murmured as he tucked her hand in the crook of his arm. "We will go to London this week and you can select one."

At the door, Alexsey looked back at Lady Malvinea. "She is at Ackinnoull?"

She nodded.

Sorcha added, "She was to come with us but she never came down, and we couldn't keep Sir Henry's coach waiting."

Lady Malvinea winced. "Actually, I locked the door to her room."

"Mama!" Sorcha's eyes widened. "Why would you do that?"

"Because if she'd been here, we'd have never gotten the prince away from her long enough to enact our plan."

At Alexsey's dark look, Tata said defensively, "We couldn't just tell her to stay away from you. You can't tell a strong woman not to do something. That's the same as—"

But Alexsey was already gone.

Chapter 28

Gentle readers, love is elusive, but worthwhile. So, so, so worthwhile.

—The Black Duke *by Miss Mary Edgeworth*

Alexsey galloped up the drive to Ackinnoull and was halfway out of the saddle before the horse had even stopped. He threw the reins over an iron ring and then slammed his hand against the door.

No one answered.

He banged louder.

Still no answer.

He was debating kicking in the door when he heard Mrs. Pitcairn's frantic voice behind the house.

Bronwyn. He ran to the rear of the house and found the cook standing under a large oak tree, one hand covering her mouth.

"Mrs. Pitcairn! What's wr—"

She let out a wailing cry and threw herself upon him. "Ye have to save her! Ye must!"

His heart thudded sickly as he looked around. "Where is she?"

Mrs. Pitcairn burst into tears and pointed up.

Confused, Alexsey looked up . . . and saw Bronwyn high in the oak. She stood on one limb, her skirts hooked on another branch, a great tear in her sleeve, and her hair falling down about her face. As he looked, the branch on which she stood gave a crack and dropped down an inch, bouncing Bronwyn madly.

"Her skirts are caught," Mrs. Pitcairn said, wiping tears from her eyes. "She was climbin' oot the window to escape, and her skirts got caught upon a branch and now she canno' move."

"Are you injured?" he called to Bronwyn.

She cast a startled glance down. "Lovely," she muttered. "The one time I want to look composed, and what does the ass do but show up as if he's some knight in—"

"I can hear you."

There was silence, and then, "Oh."

"Are you injured?"

"Only my pride, but that is quite bruised."

The humor in her voice should have calmed him, but didn't. "Stay where you are."

"As if I had a choice," she returned. "My spectacles fell. Could you—"

"They are not important. Mrs. Pitcairn, there's no way to climb this tree; the bottom branches are well over my head. How do I reach the window nearest Miss Murdoch?"

"Follow me." She stopped to yell, "Hang on, miss! His Highness is comin' fer ye!"

Bronwyn muttered something that Alexsey was fairly certain was inappropriate for a woman of good birth, but he couldn't blame her.

He followed the cook up stairs upon stairs until they reached the top floor.

"Oh, look!" Mrs. Pitcairn pointed to the key in the lock. "Tha' is why she climbed oot. Someone locked her in."

Alexsey opened the door, and Walter and Scott bounded upon him. "Down, you pestilent pups!" he growled, pushing past them to the open window.

Bronwyn was several branches below him, and he could see where her skirt had twisted around a knot well over her head. She was short a shoe, too.

"Don't move," he ordered. It took him a few minutes, but with care, he climbed out the window and into the tree, and slowly worked his way to her side, careful not to disturb the branch upon which she stood.

She let out her breath. "I can't believe this. I never slip, but I was in a hurry."

To see him. "You shouldn't have been in a hurry, *lyubovnitsa*; I would have waited. And now, you've torn your gown and lost your spectacles and your shoe."

"I can do without the crticisms. I'm well aware of my precarious situation."

"Good. Hopefully, you are done with climbing." He placed his foot securely on a thick branch and wrapped an arm about another. Finally, he could reach her.

"You didn't complain when I climbed the trellis to your room," she pointed out in a fair voice.

"That was different." With his free hand, he bent down, slipped an arm about Bronwyn's waist, and lifted her up.

She clung as he lifted her level with him. As her feet found purchase, she loosened her ferocious grip from his neck. "Whew! I was quite frightened. Thank you so much for your help. Mama locked me in my room and— Do you already know about that?"

"I will help you back into your window, and then we'll discuss all of the evening's events. Unless you wish to do it here. This is quite comfortable, but I cannot kiss you properly without endangering our lives."

She turned a pleased shade of pink but almost immediately shook her head, regret clouding her eyes. "We will wait."

He bent down to carefully untangle her skirt from the broken branch. "This reads like one of your novels."

"Except in my novels, the hero never engages in wasted small talk when a rescue is necessary."

He chuckled and continued to try to free her skirts.

She watched him. "It doesn't look as if it's coming free."

"I can't tug any harder, or I might accidentally knock you from your perch." He released her skirt. "You'll have to take it off."

"Take it off—" She blinked. "Here?"

"*Da.* I will help with the tie. I'm very good at ties."

She sighed. "I begin to wonder if you're rescuing me, or if I'm merely entertaining you."

"I'm fairly sure we can accomplish both goals at the same time, but not in a tree."

Her lips quirked. "Fine." With a few swift movements, she untied her gown and, with a careful step, climbed out of it.

She wore nothing but her chemise, stockings, and one shoe; her cheek smudged, and her hair a mass of tangles. Alexsey had never seen a more beautiful woman.

"There." She reached for a nearby branch. "I can get back to the window myself." Without giving him another look, she began the climb.

He kept an eye on her, but she kept her balance quite well. His Roza was a woman of many talents.

She finally climbed back through the window, Alexsey following. They were greeted by cries of happiness from Mrs. Pitcairn and large licks from the dogs.

Mrs. Pitcairn clasped her hands under her chin. "Och, 'twas so romantic, miss!"

Bronwyn found a robe and hurried to slip it on. "I wouldn't call it romantic at all."

"It might no' ha' felt as if it were, but it seemed like it fro' the window."

Alexsey turned to Mrs. Pitcairn. "I believe your mistress could use some of this tea you Scots seem to drink all the time."

"Och, tha' will be jus' the thing." Mrs. Pitcairn scuttled to the door, then stopped and turned around. "Miss, 'tis no' proper fer ye to be alone oop here wit' a mon, miss. I couldna—"

"It's quite all right, Mrs. Pitcairn," Alexsey said. "Miss Murdoch and I are about to become engaged."

Bronwyn stiffened. "We are not."

"Aye, we are," he replied. "If not today, then very soon." He looked meaningfully at the servant. "It will be sooner if we are alone."

Mrs. Pitcairn beamed. "I'll go an' make the tea." Despite Bronwyn's murmured complaint, she disappeared down the stairs.

Alexsey sat on the edge of the bed, admiring the lace chemise his bride-to-be was wearing where it peeked from her robe.

Her face heated, Bronwyn dove back into her wardrobe and looked for a gown. "There's no need for you to stay here."

"I wish to speak to you. I've waited all evening to do so, and now is a good time."

She found a gown and hurried to pull it on, aware of his hot gaze.

Alexsey's eyes were dark and inscrutable. "Much has happened over the past few weeks since we met."

"Yes, and some of it has implications for our futures. Alexsey, I know what you are going to say, but I must be clear; I can't marry you."

His eyes warmed. "You don't know what I'm going to say. I wasn't going to talk about marriage yet. I have other, more important things to say. Like how much I love you."

She threw up a hand. "No! You don't have to say that."

"Have to?" He looked amused. "I don't have to do anything. I could leave this country right now and go home, and no one could stop me."

She stiffened. "You could, couldn't you?"

"*Da.* But I don't want to. Not unless I am able to take my prize with me."

"Prize?"

"You, Roza." He took her hand and pulled her toward him, standing her between his legs. "There are two facts I have failed to admit to either you or to myself. Bronwyn, I want you, and no one else. And I will have you, or I will have no one."

"Want? That's not enough—"

"It is. I want you in my life for one reason and one reason only. Because I love you."

Bronwyn's throat tightened. She so wanted to believe him. "Alexsey, I know why you started courting me. I overheard you talking to Strathmoor at Tulloch."

He winced. "That was wrong of me and I owe you a great apology. I was selfish and bored and . . . none of it is to my credit. But since it brought you to me and let me see what an amazing, beautiful woman you are— Bronwyn, I am not the same man who stood in that hallway, a man who did not believe in love. Whether you have me or not, I will never again be that man." His eyes glowed with truth.

"I have to admit something myself," she said. "After I heard you, I wished to punish you. I tried to seduce you, to make you mad with lust for me."

"You succeeded."

"And then I was going to reject you." She pursed her lips. "I never really got around to the second part."

He laughed and moaned at the same time. "It has been agony! I could not tell you no, even when I wished to. You drove me mad with lust, and then with desire, and then with love. I am yours, Bronwyn. I will never belong to anyone else." He cupped her cheek. "I was going to ask you to marry me tonight, but not because I had to. I was going to ask you to marry me because I can't imagine not having you in my life. My future without you is a desert, a lone tree in a windy plain, a rock perched on a mountain with nothing but echoes to keep it company."

Her eyes had grown wide at his words, the faintest quiver of a smile on her lips.

Alexsey raised his brows. "Well?"

"That was beautiful. I especially like the desert/plain/mountain part."

He was silent a moment. "To be honest, I stole that part."

"From Sir Gordan Bradford."

He sighed. "I can see I'm going to have hell to pay for marrying a well-read woman."

"I haven't said I'd marry you."

"Not yet. But you will." He stood. "I have something to show you. But first, you must sit."

She perched on the edge of the bed. "Why?"

"You will see." He knelt before her.

As she watched, he reached into his pocket and pulled out a thin, narrow package. He unwrapped it and held it up.

"That's . . . that's my shoe!"

"You left it in the woods the first time we met."

"And you kept it all this time?"

"I kept it in my drawer and wouldn't let the servants touch it." His warm hand clasped her stockinged ankle, and he lifted her foot. His gaze rose to hers. "May I?"

It was a moment like one of her books—only better, because it was real, and *he* was real, and he was here, with her. "Yes."

His lips quirked and he held the shoe in one hand, his other around her ankle. "You have very delicate ankles."

"Thank you. I suppose that is what made you love me?"

"How can I resist a woman with a leaf in her hair—"

"Oh no!" She patted her hand until she found it.

"—and who smells like turtle soup, and sings with such passion even though she cannot carry a tune?"

She stiffened. "You didn't like my singing?"

He slipped his hand up her calf. "I would have you sing to me every day and every night, just to see the happiness in your eyes."

She tried to ignore the warm hand on her knee. He *must* love her, to still wish her to sing. "I know quite a bit about Oxenburg, too," she added helpfully. "The highest mountain is thought to be over 12,520 feet tall."

"I am impressed." His thumb made a lazy circle on her knee as he held the shoe near her foot. "Before I do this, I must tell you it is my intention to court you."

She felt a flicker of disappointment. "I thought you wished to marry me?"

"I plan to court you, too."

"After we are married?"

"Before, during"—he slipped his hand to her thigh—"and after. I plan on courting you every day until the end of days. I will give you everything your heart desires. New gowns, a library full of books, a clerk to help your father file his patents—"

"Oh! How lovely! Can we afford an assistant who could help him with his experiments?"

"Of course. But now—" He slid his hand back down to her ankle and pulled her foot forward. "Bronwyn Murdoch, most troublesome of all women, would you do me the honor of marrying me? Will you promise to love, honor, and— Well, I will not ask for what you cannot give. Let us just say 'love, honor, and listen once in a while.'"

She chuckled, her eyes alight. "Yes, Alexsey Romanovin. I will."

He slipped the shoe onto her foot. "That will do." Happiness warmed him from head to toe and he joined her on the bed, pulling her against him. He nuzzled her neck, then nipped at her left earlobe.

"It's only fair to tell you, I'm not sure I'll enjoy being a princess."

He trailed a kiss to her neck. "I sometimes snore."

She clutched his shoulders tighter. "I don't like crowds."

He nipped at her chin. "I get seasick every time I am on a boat."

Her hand rested in his lap. "I'm not good at remembering people's names."

He placed a line of heated kisses along her collarbone. "I cannot stand chocolate."

She froze and lifted her head. "We may have problems with that."

"With you, Roza, problems do not scare me." His smile turned wicked, and he leaned her back on the bed. "Let me start this courtship with a kiss."

And she did, knowing she'd found the man she was supposed to be with. One who made her laugh and shared her love of reading, a man who would encourage her to take new chances—all while making beautiful, fulfilling, maddeningly wonderful love to her.

With a smile, she slipped her arms about his neck and showed him exactly what she thought of him.

Epilogue

"This is not how I thought to see my grandson married. They should have waited until we returned to Oxenburg and had the wedding in our grand chapel."

Sir Henry stood beside Natasha at the top of the steps and watched the happy couple climb into a carriage bedecked with red roses. He handed her a glass of scotch. "No, but you canna doubt he is happy."

Natasha watched as Alexsey bent to kiss his bride's nose, knocking her spectacles askew. The two laughed, and Alexsey readjusted the spectacles with the greatest of care. "They love one another," she said in a satisfied tone.

"She dinna marry him for his money."

Natasha nodded. "True."

"Nor his position."

"Which she hates."

Sir Henry took a thoughtful sip of his scotch. "He dinna seem very fond of it, either."

Natasha paused. "I used to think he would grow into it, but he has not. Fortunately, he now has the *kaltso.*" They'd used the ring during the wedding, which would make it mean all the more. "Because of that, she is married to both Alexsey and the Romany cause. They will do well helping my people."

From where he stood, Sir Henry noticed how the ring caught the afternoon sun. "I saw that ring before the wedding. The ruby . . . 'twas interestin', it was."

She didn't answer, but took another sip of whiskey.

"It's fake," Sir Henry said baldly.

"My husband Nikki was known to gamble at times."

Sir Henry gaped. "He dinna!"

"He was a Romany." She shrugged. "No one knows. It is too big for the bride's finger. She will wear it about her neck as I did, and no one will see it."

Sir Henry had to laugh, turning his gaze back to the couple, who were even now saying their good-byes to the Murdoch family. "Will the Romany accept an outsider?"

"They will do what their *phuri dai* tells them, or I will turn them all into goats."

He chuckled. "I pity the council."

"They need a strong hand; Alexsey will be quite busy, I think. As for his princess, it may be time for someone to take charge of the Great Library."

"I dinna know Oxenburg had a great library."

"It is frivolous. My son-in-law purchases thousands of books. He re-created the great library lost at Alexandria, but once the building was finished, he could find no one able to organize the collection." Natasha took a sip of the scotch, letting it warm her. She couldn't hold back a smile of satisfaction. "There are many benefits to be had with the woman my grandson has selected. She is very good at organizing. We need that in Oxenburg."

Sir Henry grinned over his glass. "My dear, you are brilliant."

"I have many talents. Many, many talents." She held out her glass to Sir Henry with a smile. "I shall have more of your fine scotch. I've much planning to do. I've two more grandsons, you know."

"Och, and no doubt both are as stubborn as you." Sir Henry grinned. "At least, they think they are."

She smiled, but said nothing. There was much left to do before she was ready to step aside and let her family rule itself. Much. But for now, she could enjoy a few peaceful, happy moments.

With a satisfied sigh, she accepted the glass of scotch from Sir Henry and watched the rose-bedecked coach that carried her grandson and his new bride disappear down the road.

Don't miss the first delightful novel about
the Oxenburg Princes from *New York Times*
bestselling author Karen Hawkins

HOW TO PURSUE A PRINCESS

On sale now!

Lily slowly awoke, her mind creeping back to consciousness. She shifted and then moaned as every bone in her body groaned in protest.

A warm hand cupped her face. "Easy," came a deep, heavily accented voice.

Lily opened her eyes to find herself staring into the deep green eyes of the most handsome man she'd ever seen.

The man was huge, with broad shoulders that blocked the light and hands so large that the one cupping her face practically covered one side of it. His face was perfectly formed, his cheekbones high above a scruff of a beard that her fingers itched to touch.

"The brush broke your fall, but you will still be bruised."

He looked almost too perfect to be real. She placed her hand on his where it rested on her cheek, his warmth stealing into her cold fingers. *He's not a dream.*

She gulped a bit and tried to sit up, but was instantly pressed back to the ground.

"Nyet," the giant said, his voice rumbling over her like waves over a rocky beach. "You will not rise."

She blinked. *"Nyet?"*

He grimaced. "I should not say *'nyet'* but 'no.'"

"I understood you perfectly. I am just astonished that you are telling me what to do." His expression darkened and she had the distinct impression that he wasn't used to being told no. "Who are you?"

"It matters not. What matters is that you are injured and wish to stand. That is foolish."

She pushed herself up on one elbow. As she did so, her hat, which had been pinned upon her neatly braided hair, came loose and fell to the ground.

The man's gaze locked on her hair, his eyes widening as he muttered something under his breath in a foreign tongue.

"What's wrong?"

"Your hair. It is red and gold."

"My hair's not red. It's blond and when the sun—" She frowned. "Why am I even talking to you about this? I don't even know your name."

"You haven't told me yours, either," he said in a reasonable tone.

She hadn't, and for some reason she was loath to do so. She reached for her hat, wincing as she moved.

Instantly he pressed her back to the ground. "Do not move. I shall call for my men and—"

"No, I don't need any help."

"You should have had a groom with you," he said, disapproval in his rich voice. "Beautiful women should not wander the woods alone."

Beautiful? Me? She flushed. It was odd, but the thought pleased her far more than it should have. Perhaps because she thought he was beautiful, as well.

"In my country you would not be riding about the woods without protection."

"A groom wouldn't have kept my horse from becoming startled."

"No, but it would have kept you from being importuned by a stranger."

She had to smile at the irony of his words. "A stranger like you?"

The stranger's brows rose. "Ah. You think I am being—what is the word? Forward?"

"Yes."

"But you are injured—"

"No, I'm not."

"You were thrown from a horse and are upon the ground. I call that 'injured.'" His brows locked together. "Am I using the word 'injured' correctly?"

"Yes, but—"

"Then do not argue. You are injured and I will help you."

Do not argue? Goodness, he was high-handed. She sat upright, even though it brought her closer to this huge boulder of a man. "I don't suppose you have a name?"

"I am Piotr Romanovin of Oxenburg. It is a small country beside Prussia."

The country's name seemed familiar. "There was a mention of Oxenburg in *The Morning Post* just a few days ago."

"My cousin Nikki, he is in London. Perhaps he is in the papers." The stranger rubbed a hand over his bearded chin, the golden light filtering from the trees dancing over his black hair. "You can sit up, but not stand. Not until we know you are not broken."

"I'm not broken," she said sharply. "I'm just embarrassed that I fell off my horse."

A glimmer of humor shone in the green eyes. "You fell asleep, eh?"

She fought the urge to return the smile. "No, I did not fall asleep. A fox frightened my horse, which caused it to rear. And then it ran off."

His gaze flickered to her boots and he frowned. "No wonder you fell. Those are not good riding boots."

"These? They're perfectly good boots."

"Not if a horse bolts. Then you need some like these." He slapped the side of his own boots, which had a thicker and taller heel.

"I've never seen boots like those."

"That is because you English do not really ride, you with your small boots. You just perch on top of the horse like a sack of grain and—"

"I'm not English; I'm a Scot," she said sharply. "Can't you tell from my accent?"

"English or Scot." He shrugged. "Is there so much difference?"

"Oh! Of course there's a difference! I—"

He threw up a hand. "I don't know if it's because you are a woman or because you are a Scot, but thus far, you've argued with everything I've said. This, I do not like."

She frowned. "As a Scot, I dislike being ordered about, and as a woman, I can't imagine that you know more about my state of well-being than I do."

His eyes lit with humor. "Fair enough. You cannot be much injured, to argue with such vigor." He stood and held out his hand. "Come. Let us see if you can stand."

She placed her hand in his. As her rescuer pulled her to her feet, one of her curls came free from her braid and fell to her shoulder.

She started to tuck it away, but his hand closed over the curl first. Slowly, he threaded her hair through his fingers, his gaze locking with hers. "Your hair is like the sunrise."

And his eyes were like the green found at the heart of the forest, among the tallest trees.

He brushed her curl behind her ear, his fingers grazing her cheek. Her heart thudded as if she'd just run up a flight of stairs.

Cheeks hot, she repinned her hair with hands that seemed oddly unwieldy. "That's— You shouldn't touch my hair."

"Why not?"

He looked so astounded that she explained. "I don't know the rules of your country, but here men do not touch a woman's hair merely because they can."

"It is not permitted?"

"No."

He sighed regretfully. "It should be."

She didn't know what to say. A part of her—obviously still shaken from her fall—wanted to tell him that he could touch her hair if he wished. Her hair, her cheek, or any other part of her that he wished to. *Good God, what's come over me?*

"Come. I will take you to your home."

She brushed the leaves from her skirts and then stepped forward. "Ow!" She jerked her foot up from the ground.

He grasped her elbow and steadied her. "Your ankle?"

"Yes." She gingerly wiggled it, grimacing a little. "I must have sprained it, though it's only a slight sprain, for I can move it fairly well."

"I shall carry you."

"*What?* Oh no, no, no. I'm sure walking will relieve the stiffness—"

He bent, slipped her arm about his neck, and scooped her up as if she were a blade of grass.

"Mr. Roma—Romi— Oh, whatever your name is, please don't—"

He turned and strode down the path.

"Put me down!"

"Nyet." He continued on his way, his long legs eating up the distance.

Lily had little choice but to hang on, uncomfortably aware of the deliciously spicy cologne that tickled her nose and made her wonder what it would be like to burrow her face against him. It was the oddest thing, to wish to be set free and—at the same time—enjoy the strength of his arms. To her surprise, she liked how he held her so securely, which was ridiculous. She didn't even know this man. "You can't just carry me off like this."

"But I have." His voice held no rancor, no sense of correcting her. Instead his tone was that of someone patiently trying to explain something. "I have carried you off, and carried off you will be."

She scowled up at him. "Look here, Mr. Romanoffski—"

"Call me Wulf. It is what I am called." He said the word with a faint "v" instead of a "w."

"Wulf is hardly a reassuring name."

He grinned, his teeth white in the black beard. "It is my name, reassuring or not." He shot her a glance. "What is your name, little one?"

"Lily Balfour." She hardly knew this man at all, yet she'd just blurted out her name and was allowing him to carry her through the woods. She should be screaming for help, but instead she found herself resting her head against his shoulder as, for the first time in two days, she felt something other than sheer loneliness.

"Lily. That's a beautiful name. It suits you."

Lily's face heated and she stole a look at him from under her lashes. He was exotic, overbearing, and strong, but somehow she knew that he wouldn't harm her. Her instincts and common sense both agreed on that. "Where are you taking me?"

"To safety."

"That's a rather vague location."

He chuckled, the sound reverberating in his chest where it pressed against her side. "If you must know, I'm taking you to my new home. From there, my men and my—how do you say *babushka*?" His brow furrowed a moment before it cleared. "Ah yes, grandmother."

"Your grandmother? She's here, in the woods?"

"I brought her to see the new house I just purchased. You and I will go there and meet with my men and my grandmother. I have a carriage, so we can ride the rest of the way to your home."

I was right to trust him. No man would involve his grandmother in a ravishment.

He slanted a look her way. "You will like my grandmother."

It sounded like an order. She managed a faint smile. "I'm sure we'll adore one another. However, you and your grandmother won't be escorting me home, but to Floors Castle. I am a guest of the Duchess of Roxburghe."

His amazing eyes locked on her, and she noted that his thick, black lashes gave him a faintly sleepy air. "I met the duchess last week and she invited us to her house party. I was not going to attend, but now I will go." His gaze flicked over her, leaving a heated path.

Her breath caught in her throat. *If the duchess has invited Wulf to the castle, then perhaps he is an eligible parti.* Suddenly, the day didn't seem so dreary. "I beg your pardon, Mr. Wulf—or whatever your name is—but who are you, exactly?"

He shrugged, his chest rubbing her side in a pleasant way. "Does it matter?"

"Yes. You mentioned your men. Are you a military leader of some sort?" That would explain his boldness and overassuredness.

"You could say that."

"Ah. Are you a corporal, then? A sergeant?"

"I am in charge." A faint note of surprise colored his voice, as if he couldn't believe that she would think anything else.

"You're in charge of what? A battalion?"

He definitely looked insulted now. "I am in charge of it all."

She blinked. "Of an entire army?"

"Yes." He hesitated, then said in a firm voice, "I shall tell you because you will know eventually since I plan on joining the duchess's party. I am not a general. I am a prince."

"A pr—" She couldn't even say the word.

"I am a prince," he repeated firmly, though he looked far from happy about it. "That is why Her Grace finds it acceptable that my grandmother and I attend her events. I had not thought to accept her invitation, for I do not like dances and such, and you English—"

She raised her brows.

"I'm sorry, you *Scots* are much too formal for me."

"Wait. I'm still trying to grasp that you're a prince. A real prince?"

He shrugged, his broad shoulders making his cape swing. "We have many princes in Oxenburg, for I have three brothers."

She couldn't wrap her mind around the thought of a roomful of princes who looked like the one carrying her: huge, broad shouldered, bulging with muscles and grinning lopsided smiles, their dark hair falling over their brows and into their green eyes. . . . *I fell off my horse and into a fairy tale.*

Hope washed over her and she found herself saying in a breathless tone, "If you're a prince, then you must be fabulously wealthy."

He looked down at her, a question in his eyes. "Not every prince has money."

"Some do."

"And some do not. Sadly, I am the poorest of all my brothers."

Her disappointment must have shown on her face, for he regarded her with a narrow gaze. "You do not like this, Miss Lily Balfour?"

She sighed. "No, no, I don't."

One dark brow arched. "Why not?"

"Sadly, some of us must marry for money." Whether it was because she was being held in his arms or because she was struggling to deal with a surprising flood of regret, it felt right to tell him the truth.

"I see." He continued to carry her, his brow lowered. "And this is you, then? You must marry for money?"

"Yes."

He was silent a moment more. "But what if you fall in love?"

"I have no choice." She heard the sadness in her voice and resolutely forced herself to say in a light tone, "It's the way of the world, isn't it? But to be honest, I wouldn't be looking for a wealthy husband except that I must. Our house is entailed, and my father hasn't been very good about— Oh, it's complicated."

He didn't reply, but she could tell from his grim expression that he disliked her answer. She didn't like it much herself, for it made her sound like the veriest moneygrubbing society miss, but that's what she'd become.

She sighed and rested her cheek against his shoulder.

He looked down at her, and to her surprise, his chin came to rest on her head.

They continued on thus for a few moments, comfort seeping through her, the first since she'd left her home.

"Moya, I must tell you—"

She looked up. "My name is not Moya, but Lily."

His eyes glinted with humor. "I like Moya better."

"What does it mean?"

His gaze flickered to her hair and she grimaced. "It means 'red,' doesn't it? I hate that!"

He chuckled, the sound warm in his chest. "You dislike being called Red? Why? It is what you are. Just as what I am is a prince with no fortune." His gaze met hers. "We must accept who we are."

She was silent a moment. "You're dreadfully poor? You said you'd just bought a house."

"A cottage. It has a thatched roof and one large room, but with a good fireplace. I will make stew for you. I make good stew."

It sounded delightful; far more fun than the rides, picnics, dinner parties, and other activities the duchess had promised. "I like stew, but I'm afraid that I can't visit your cottage. It would be improper." Furthermore, she didn't dare prolong her time with such a devastatingly handsome, but poor, prince. She had to save all of her feelings so that she could fall in love with the man who would save Papa.

Wulf's brows had lowered. "But you would come to my cottage if I had a fortune, *nyèt*?"

Regret flooded her and she tightened her hold about his neck. "I have no choice; I *must* marry for money. I don't know why I admitted that to you, but it is a sad fact of my life and I cannot pretend otherwise. My family is depending on me."

He seemed to consider this, some of the sternness leaving his gaze. After a moment he nodded. "It is noble that you are willing to sacrifice yourself for your family."

"Sacrifice? I was hoping it wouldn't feel so . . . oh, I don't know. It's possible that I might find someone I could care for."

"You wish to fall in love with a rich man. As my *babushka* likes to tell me, life is not always so accommodating."

"Yes, but it's possible. I've never been in love before, so I'm a blank slate. The duchess is helping me, too, and she's excellent at making just such matches. She's invited several gentlemen for me to meet—"

"All wealthy."

"Of course. She is especially hopeful of the Earl of Huntley, and so am I." Lily looked away, not wishing to see the disappointment in his gaze yet again.

Silence reigned and she savored the warmth of his arms about her. At one time, a wealthy gentleman had seemed enough. Now, she wished she could ask for a not-wealthy prince. One like this, who carried her so gently and whose eyes gleamed with humor beneath the fall of his black hair. But it was not to be.

She bit back a strong desire to explain things to him, to tell him exactly why she needed to marry a wealthy man, but she knew it wouldn't make any difference. As he'd said, he was who he was, and she was who she was. There was no way for either of them to change things, even if they wished to, so it would be better for them both if they accepted those facts and continued on.

For now, though, she had these few moments. With that thought in mind, she sighed and rested her head against his broad shoulder. *This will have to be enough.*

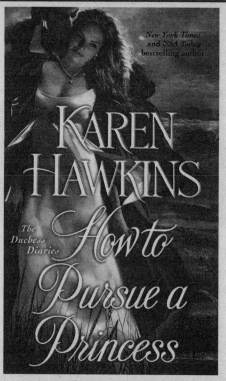